8/98

D1417829

The Undesirables

The Undesirables

Mary C. Smith

Black Heron Press
Post Office Box 95676
Seattle, Washington 98145

The Undesirables has been awarded the 1997 Black
Heron Press Award for Social Fiction.

ISBN: 0-930773-47-0

Cover art: Cami Lemke

Published by:
    Black Heron Press
    Post Office Box 95676
    Seattle, Washington

For my sister, Ellen Pepper Smith

ONE

I started to remake the world on March 13, 2120, a chilly Saturday afternoon in the Global Television Studios on Transition Avenue. I figured that changing the world would be easier under Mr. Brown than under either of the other two Chairmen—not that Mr. Brown trusted me; he didn't; but he was careless, the way high officials become when they let their staff do all their work for them.

That afternoon Mr. Brown sailed in under floodlights, on time for a change, but only barely. He liked to make these entrances, keep everybody on edge, waiting for him. Sometimes the other Chairmen became miffed when, at the last moment, they had to start reading my script, without knowing what was in it. Mallam Ahmed, all gentle smiles and as bland as over-cooked pasta, finally confided on the air that the People should excuse Mr. Brown because the latter was operating "on Northern time." This created a mini-crisis between the Northern and Southern regions and annoyed Brown so much that he started trying to be punctual.

That Saturday at precisely 5:25 p.m. he glided around the cameras, took the script from my hands, and seated himself at the apex of the triangular desk, flanked by stately Mallam Ahmed, last month's Chairman, and stocky Comrade Wong, next month's Chairman. The command of the World Federation of Democratic States rotated, so that the Northern, Southern, and Eastern regions of the world could all have equal time. Fortunately the Chairmen didn't actually *control* anything or it would have been chaos.

"What's the topic, Mark?"

"Review policy on the Undesirables."

"Again?"

"I know, sir, but Polyguide is worried about the housing riots in Stockholm."

"Ah, yes, Stockholm...." That was different; that was his area.

Mr. Brown's well-trimmed, brown goatee matched his suede lapels and epaulets. He didn't check to see if Polyguide had approved the text; he never checked anything.

Magda waved me out of camera range, and I stepped backward into the production control room, where Uche handed me a plastic cup of coffee that had been fermenting for decades in a steel urn. If you could drink the coffee, you were in with the production crew. I always drank the coffee.

The theme music swelled—drums and horns and temple bells— a sort of musical Esperanto that I heard in my sleep sometimes; and then "The Voice of the People" came on the air, broadcast live from the Federal Territory capital, most popular public service program of the week, not that it had much competition....

Mr. Brown said that he was happy to be able to come into the homes of the people of this great global community. He said he also spoke for Mallam Ahmed and Comrade Wong, who, courtesy of satellites orbiting above us, smiled and nodded at their supporters in the Southern and Eastern Regions.

Behind Mr. Brown loomed a photo of the world as seen from outer space, divided like a chicken breast: the raging seas, the towering peaks, the enormous sand dunes, the tiny specs of 9.5 billion people. A red circle ringed the Global Federal Territory on the U.S.-Canadian border, a dot at the capital of Alternative Four— the city of global harmony, "the alternative to war," now in its fourth location. We are here.

The Chairman began with the riots in Stockholm—eleven police-men killed, sixty-seven Undesirables terminated. While clearing the text by intercom, Cotterman had advised me against "advertis-ing" the riots by mentioning them. "Then knock the story off the evening news," I replied. "You know I can't do that," said Cotterman, who was against censorship, except of course internally. The De-partment of Policy Guidance believed that if the Administration officially ignored an event, time would rewind itself like a film until we reached the bloodbath scene, at which point we could stop and neatly excise the carnage.

I won that round, and so Mr. Brown began his speech with the riots. He called them a tragic event, but said we had to put them into perspective—perspective being the benign world, the Undesirables being the fungi nibbling at it.

It was time to review the People's policy on the Undesirables. Undesirables were those who undermined the healthy structure of the community. They were born genetically deformed. Not all were vicious; some were unfortunate, some sick, some even children, innocent victims who had inherited the bad genes of their parents. But who would want to live next door to a criminal, an anarchist, a believer in magic, an epileptic? To any whose minds were dark, different, abnormal?...

On the screen Mr. Brown disappeared, replaced by video footage in which a small boy ran before a six-foot bully with a knife, a woman was dragged into a stairwell, a man crumpled beneath blows at a bus stop, a mangy girl in a micro skirt blew cigarette rings at the camera, an auto-taxi burned amidst shattered buildings.... The clothes all looked dated. "Where did you get this stuff, George?"

The producer chuckled. "Footage from Transition era movies. Ancient history, right? We don't have any of that nowadays."

The sound engineer, Uche, said that, speaking of magic, her mother-in-law believed that you could predict someone's future by analyzing oil leaks underneath his car. "Do you think she's crazy enough to be an Undesirable? Could I have her sterilized?"

"Probably," I replied. "But not unless you want to get rid of your entire family."

On the screen a baby's gummy face drooled over a rattle clutched in a chubby fist. "George, you jerk the heart strings." George chuckled.

...To eradicate these problems, the People in their wisdom had found the humane solution: sterilization. Undesirables should live, but never to pass their diseased genes on to the next generation....

"Forget that joke about my mother-in-law," said Uche.

...However since Undesirables also corrupt carriers of dormant undesirable genes, UDs must be isolated in special districts and only allowed elsewhere if clearly identified as Undesirables....

The baby kicked back onto the screen, a fistful of mashed potatoes in its mouth.

"Would you live next to this baby?" asked George.

"Sick, sick, sick," I answered.

...True, UD districts were not ideal. Much of the housing was old, some dilapidated, in many cases insufficient. The Administration vowed to look into the Stockholm complaints. However, why hadn't the Undesirables themselves done something to clean up their districts? Why did they expect the People to take care of them?...

"Yeah," said Muamar, the lighting director. "Don't they want to make a better life for their children?"

Laughing at Global T.V. staff jokes was like drinking their chemical coffee.

On the screen now, energetic, UD-uniformed men were working on a scaffold high above a busy street. Maybe this was meant to show that UDs could build their own houses, or at least that they could learn how to work, particularly in dangerous jobs that nobody else wanted.

"What's that? The Global Trade Center in Singapore?"

"Close," said George. "Pan-World Data in Bangkok."

Mr. Brown was winding down now, declaring that thanks to the wisdom of the People, all the Undesirables would soon die off and the world would be populated with nothing but happy, normal, right-minded men....

Across the screen flickered smiling faces—grandparents, athletes, mothers and children in a playground, serious men around a conference table.

...In the meantime we must be kind to those less fortunate than ourselves. The People—and Mr. Brown and Mallam Ahmed and Comrade Wong—wished to decree next week "Be Kind to Undesirables Week." Mr. Brown said that he put forward this proposal in all humility, certain that the People would approve it since so many of them had written in requesting it.

Mr. Brown smiled into the camera.

The People had spoken.

By mark grimal, in small letters.

George whistled. Uche buried her giggles in the console. Muamar groaned. "Pat them or squeeze them or throw them a bone!"

George said: "That's not in my advance copy, Mark."

"No. Sorry. Brainstorm in the shower this morning."

"Stop bathing," recommended Muamar.

But I could tell George thought something was wrong—maybe not a big something, but a something. "We don't have to activate the People's TV Assembly to ratify this, do we? Because Polyguide's not here to open the box."

"No," I answered. "Admin decrees don't need ratification, especially not fluff like this. I checked. Don't worry."

"Good idea, Mark," said Mr. Brown, handing back the script in its red Admin folder. "Tell Polyguide the week's publicity should defuse some animosity. I hope the Program Department's planned spot ads, headers on the electronic mail, things like that."

"Right, Mr. Brown."

We hadn't, but we would, very quickly.

Via the underground subway that linked all the Global Administration offices in Alternative Four, I returned to the Speakers Division in the main Admin building. My intercom light was blinking.

"What the shit is going on?" shouted Kelly from Polyguide, shattering my office with her raunchy voice. "Where did you get that 'Be Kind to Undesirables Week' crap, Lover-Boy?" Kelly's metaphors were strong but predictable.

"Cleared by your office, Kelly.

"The shit we did!"

"Right here on the diskette, Kelly. Brown thinks it's a great idea."

"He does? So whose idea was it? Names, give me the fucking names!"

"My idea, Kelly."

"Yeah, so I guessed. Your head's getting as big as your prick, Lover-Boy."

I could have asked her how she knew, but I decided I hadn't better. I cleared my throat. "Brown wants a full campaign."

That stopped her. After a moment's silence, she said: "Fucking weird. Well, I was out last Tuesday. I'll check around."

She didn't even ask to see the diskette.

I walked over to Telecom where the cameras were repeating the Chairman's address in multi-lingual versions, duplicators were churning out radio-wave discs, news stories were being transmitted to the remotest areas by automatic punch key. "How's it going, Julio?" "Super, Mark. We knew we could count on you to give us a good Saturday lead." Reports were coming in: commentators in the Associated Territories already praised the initiative. In the official evening news sheet a telephone number was listed for the Office of UD Affairs. I picked up a phone and punched in the numbers. Nobody answered.

Nobody ever answered.

The "Be Kind to Undesirables" Week caper was just a practice run. Over the weekend I half expected an electronic message from the Program Department head, Eberhardt, but nothing happened. I spent the time writing snippets of text and strategy outlines for the Program Formation people, who were going to be annoyed at this unexpected addition to their calendar. Monday, early, I buzzed Eberhardt to break the bad news. During the conversation I never actually *said* that the commemoration had been Brown's idea; I just implied it; but Eberhardt had more important matters on his mind. All he replied was "Give it to Tom Ugaki to handle."

Tom chewed me out for not having called Eberhardt Saturday after the program. "I could have started work on this crap yesterday. Now I've got to cancel three appointments this morning to take care of it." I handed him my drafts, and he calmed down a bit. "Well...thanks, Mark. Good of you."

So that was that. By writing the proposal into the speech, I had cut out about two hundred hours of wasted time and nitpicking among a score of Admin officers; moreover, I had made policy.

Ordinarily speech writers don't make policy. Being a speech writer is a peculiar occupation; you second-guess what the other person wants to say and then say it better than he would but in his own style so that it sounds like him when he says it. In my job as Chief of the Speakers Division, I had to keep a lot of people happy— not just the Chairmen, but also high Admin officials who were always delivering policy addresses. I was good at keeping clients happy, although it helped when I had no strong feelings, one way or the other, about the topic. Up until last year I'd had no strong feelings.

Then last year one Friday Steve Maine asked me to ride home with him after work rather than take the underground. He said he wanted me to meet somebody who worked in his office.

We waited in Steve's vehicle outside the main Global Administration building. Steve's car was a discreet, solar-powered, energy efficient Haven, with a child's balloon seat in the rear and chewing gum on the upholstery. He sat next to me, jangling keys, scratching the side of his face. "I always drive her home," he said. "The UD buses only run on main roads...."

In a baggy, blue UD uniform, Christine Riccardi emerged from the revolving glass doors of the building and drifted toward us. Her black hair swirled around a pale face. She had chewed off most of her lipstick.

She got into the car and settled apart from us, in the back row, self-quarantined, next to the child's balloon chair.

"This is the man I told you about," said Steve. "Mark Grimal. The head of the Speakers Division."

Her voice was that of a polite child. "Writing speeches must keep you very busy."

"Yes," I replied. "People give a lot of speeches around here."

Steve pushed the starter button. The windows went up, the seats went down, the blinds rattled into shadow, the bubble opened above our heads, the solar panels expanded, the car skimmed the road under autopilot. Christine Riccardi stirred in her seat. The crinkly skirt on her uniform hiked above her knees. She pulled it back with strong hands that ended in short filed fingernails. She looked terrified. What had Steve told her?

"This is the UD district," said Steve, as we crossed the bridge and entered an area where tents ballooned among scarred wood and brick cornerstones, and clotheslines bound the roofs with rope knots. The canal rampway was lined with market stalls. Nobody lived like this anymore. Not real people. Not normal people.

"You've never been here, have you, Mark?"

"Not in this one."

As a child I'd visited the UD district in Fawkesburg—a small town, after all, where the contrasts hadn't been so great. Here in Alternative Four, capital of the Global Federal Territory, just across the canal from the soaring high rise structures where we Government officials lived, clustered these rickety buildings along open sewers.

Open sewers. That was interesting. Alternative Four had open sewers.

Steve stopped the car in front of a house with a missing front door. An African in an agbada leaned against the broken doorjamb, cleaning his fingernails with a knife. "Thank you," said Christie. I helped her from the car. One of the fortunate Undesirables: she had a job; she lived in a house. Why the hell didn't they at least put a door on the house?

Steve projected the vehicle into the outside lane of traffic.

"You...ah...have anything against working with Undesirables?"

Here it came. "Why should I? Work's work."

"Well, sometimes people have strange notions. I had a few myself until Christie came into the Human Rights Legal Division. But, you know, she's really a nice girl. Know why she's an Undesirable? Just because her father was. Does that make sense?"

"It's in the genes, Steve. That's the theory."

"Uh, well, of course. Still you can't help but feel sorry for her. The place she lives in—Did you see that? No door! Do you have any idea how cold that house must be in the winter? Why, I stopped in last month—April, mind you, and—"

"Steve."

"What?"

"Why did I have to meet that girl? Do you think my speeches about UDs might be better if I *met* some of them? I already know some of them."

Steve scowled at the road, glanced sideways, loosened his tie, bit a fingernail. When he argued a case before the cameras he acted just like this—head scratcher, nail chewer, sympathy pitch, honest indignation, the elimination of all shades of grey. My dear people, do you choose virtue or filth? Nobody chose filth.

"You, ah....you got any openings in the Speakers Division? You know, diskette file clerk, anything like that? You see, ...Rita's got this idea into her head that I'm having an affair with Christie. Now you know that's nonsense—I mean, who'd take advantage of one of Them?.... But Rita's upset and...if I just request Christie's transfer, then she might end up working for one of those guys—you know, like Dresmond. That would be a sweet thing, wouldn't it? Dresmond.... So that's why I'm asking you, because I know you're all right. Sure, you have your fun, who doesn't? But you always play it fair...."

"That's not what Lisa calls it, and Lisa has more reason than Rita for imagining things."

"I know," muttered Steve, "but, damn, who else can I trust? Vimalachandra in Records? That's such a small department...."

Steve had me pegged correctly: after seeing the girl and looking at the district, how could I say no?

That evening after dinner Lisa clinched the decision.

Curled up beside me in the viewing chair, she snuggled against my chest and asked: "Are you having an affair with Ingrid?"

"Ingrid?"

Lisa pointed to the wall screen. In front of us Ingrid Armfeldt was telereading the evening news. She had a new hairstyle, frosted ringlets, set off by a tailored suit with thick shoulder pads. The outfit worked, but just barely, like a stunt astronaut's trick in a space show.

"Oh, that Ingrid." I brushed Lisa's blonde hair from my mouth. "Not at the moment, Lisa, not at the moment."

"Well, it could be worse," said Lisa, her fingers, like little chains, wrapped around mine. "It could be an Undesirable, like Steve has. Look at the danger he's putting Rita in. At least with you all I might pick up is something social that's easily cured by the MedUnit."

"Thanks, Lisa. An understanding wife is hard to find."

"You may not believe this, Mark, but I *love* you."

Oh, I believed it. Yes, unfortunately, I believed it. We had been mated according to the best principles of Lifestyle group assessment, namely, we looked good together.

Prior to consulting the head of the Programs Department, I requested Christine Riccardi's personnel file.

Twenty-three years old. Education only through Primary Five. Ten years old at time her father had been declared an Undesirable for traitorous activities during the Maldives rebellion. Regular direct descendant sterilization performed on her two days after her father was sterilized. Withdrawn from school in the City at that time. No brothers or sisters. Mother killed during assault on a policeman when the girl was eleven. Father died of alcoholism when she was fifteen. Entrance tests showed childish handwriting but reading was at final year secondary school level and general information met norm. Not bad for a Primary Five school leaver. Security cleared for unclassified only, and with reservations.

"No problem, Mark," said Eberhardt. "If you need another diskette file clerk, we'll switch a position."

TWO

THE UNDESIRABLE'S DIARY

Be careful of kindness, said my mother. Everything good is paid for. There was a copper coin on the street.... "Don't touch that, child. It will be bad in the end." So we didn't have the coin and somebody else had the good and the bad.

I should have been that way too. Why wasn't I? The coin lay there, dusty, on the rampway crack and offered itself to me. Don't touch that, child, said my mother; you pay before or you pay after.

Coins at least give warning. Mr. Grimal was too handsome to be the kind of coin I could touch. When he helped me from the car that day, his fingers felt like the plastic skin on a mannequin from a department store window. He wasn't my world, he knew nothing about my world. But being polite, he smiled.

In the new job, I stayed behind the diskette files. "Watch out, honey," they said. "Mr. Grimal is an operator." Some girl had left, some girl who had made him property to be scratched at in their whispers. When he passed me in the hall, he nodded, and once he came behind the files to ask how I was getting along. I said fine, thank you. He hesitated, tapping an open fiberglass drawer; then he shoved it in. "Lock them up well," he said. "We can't too careful with the Voice of the People."

With the rest of the staff, things went the way they always go. At first I tried eating lunch with the girls in the cafeteria, but they ignored me. Near the Speakers Division was a flight of stairs leading to the roof; one day I took my lunch up to the roof. It was warm there; the air was clear. After that I always ate on the roof.

By evening the sun was too warm. Summer brought the men out in damp clusters on the ramps when I walked home at night; they whispered and called things and sometimes they followed. Jacques

would stop them at the stairs, not saying anything, just standing
there cleaning his fingernails with the knife that he used on his wood
carving. Jacques is a cook at the Monroe Institute. He belongs to one
of the magic sects. I went to their meeting once and saw a statue of
their god, half naked and pinned like a butterfly to a piece of wood.
It horrified me. But Jacques is a good man.

In July the sun was hot on the roof, even in the half-shadow of a
skylight. Mr. Grimal came up the steps; he didn't see me. He leaned
on the ledge, took his jacket off, lit a cigarette. The smoke coiled
away from him to float across the high, gray city with its block
buildings, scrubbed monthly to remove contaminants, each one
looking like the other, although they say it's nice inside the apartment buildings.... Then the plastic wrap on my sandwich crackled.

"Christie. Do you always eat up here?"

"Yes."

He looked back over the city and flipped the ashes off his
cigarette. "Did they tell you not to eat with them?"

"No."

"You sure?"

"I like eating up here," I said. "I like the sun."

"We'll see," said Mr. Grimal. "When fall comes." With his coat
off, he no longer looked so much like a store mannequin.

That evening when I left the building, his car was waiting in the
circular ramp. He drove me home in silence. Every night afterward
he waited—not like Steve had done, nervously buried in a news
sheet to avoid the glances, but seemingly oblivious to them. He
couldn't have been though. He must have known that the girls in the
department laughed, said, We knew he'd get around to *her*; Grimal
will sleep with anything.

The girls were wrong. To him I was a parcel to be delivered, not
a woman. "Good night, Christie," he would say, very detached and
polite, holding the door. That's the way it always is and not to be
wondered about at all. You are a Thing. The good treat the thing one
way and the bad another.

Like the one called Dresmond from the EcoDev department....
One night Mr. Grimal was late; his car hadn't arrived yet. As I left
the elevator, Dresmond touched my arm. "Two months, Christie.

Where you working now?"

Why that night? Why then?

"Another department."

"That nervous little guy, Maine, doesn't take you home any more, huh? Well, don't worry." He motioned toward an open car ahead. "Get in."

"I don't mind walking," I said.

"Get in the car," he repeated.

There is nothing to be done about the bad coins except take them. If you don't, then you have no chance at any of them.

Afterward he took me home. The windows of the house were flickering light and the Professor's television monitor could be heard above the sounds of the rampway. I tried to push the button that opens the car door, but he held my wrist. "You need more practice, honey. Tomorrow I'll expect you to put a bit more enthusiasm into that tongue or I'll cut it off. Got me?"

"Yes, Mr. Dresmond."

"Dresmond," said a voice outside the car window.

I never cry. I have never cried since the day when they killed my mother. But seeing Mr. Grimal standing by the car, I almost did. Why? Shame is such a part of us that we no longer feel it. Relief? But the worst that could happen had happened and there was nothing to feel relief over.

He said: "I guess you didn't know that Christie works for me now, did you?"

Dresmond slid back to the starter panel. He tried to light a cigarette, but the flame kept missing the tip. Mr. Grimal opened the car door and I got out beside him.

Dresmond shrugged. "O.K., O.K., why don't you stamp your girls so a guy will know which ones are yours? It's her or it wouldn't be so easy. Now if it was that little transmitter girl you used to have, say...."

"Beat it," said Mr. Grimal.

Dresmond left.

There was a fight going on in the bar on the corner and across the street a woman slammed her window, mumbling something in a loud voice. It was nine o'clock.

"Why didn't you tell him I drove you home in the evenings?"

"I didn't think of it."

"You didn't *think* of it?"

"Why, no," I said. "You've been very kind. But that doesn't mean I can...can...."

He said: "Well, you can now."

The flickering lights from the bar daubed his face with blue and red patches. He leaned against his car, hands in his pockets, while the shadow of the street light bristled black across the gaping door to the house. "What a rotten mess," he said.

I didn't know if he meant me or the district or Dresmond or maybe all of it. "That's just the way it is, I guess."

"Why?"

Why? How was I supposed to tell him why things were the way they were? Why some people, like me, were born evil and some, like him, were not. Why it could be a crime to be born. He should know the answers better than me. I tried to remember what I had heard on the Professor's TV, the answers I had never really listened to because they had no connection with anything I knew.

"Well," I said, "the People...."

He laughed. The light from the bar distorted his face. "The People don't exist," he said.

"But the broadcasts say...."

"I write the broadcasts," said Mr. Grimal. "I'm the People. I *know*. Now there's a thought," he added, as though to himself. "Maybe your world wouldn't exist without me. Maybe I made it all up." He paused. "What's the matter?"

"Perhaps you shouldn't think that way."

"Perhaps I shouldn't," he agreed. "But never mind how I think. My wife minds, Security minds, Polyguide minds.... Don't you start minding."

Police sirens were coming from the rampway. A man fell out of the bar, clung, swinging, to the loose screen.

"Poor Christie," said Mr. Grimal. "You must think I'm crazy. Come on, I'll walk you to the door."

Don't touch it, child.

"Mr. Grimal, I...."

Don't touch it...don't touch it...DON'T TOUCH IT....

"Don't call me Mr. Grimal," he said. "Please. Or I'll have to call you Miss Riccardi."

"It's after nine o'clock," I said, "and you've been waiting. I could fix you something to eat. A little sausage or some eggs...."

I am responsible for what happened.

He hesitated on the doorstep, with his hands in his pockets. "I don't want to impose...."

"Impose? After all those hours you waited—"

"Waiting in a place like this gives a man an education." He followed me into the dark hallway. I turned on my pocket flashlight. "Is there a reason you don't have a door on this building?"

"I don't know," I replied; I'd never thought about it before. "Maybe it's because we're not supposed to be living here. It's one of the houses that were abandoned because they thought there were bombs in the garden. There aren't any bombs in the garden. If there were, we'd all have been blown up by now. But if the owner knows that maybe he'd tell us to get out. Maybe that's the explanation."

"Maybe," said Mark Grimal. "But it's easy to check about bombs in a garden."

Going up the stairs, I saw the house with his eyes: the broken railing, the hole that gaped above the landing, the carpet so frayed your heels caught in it, the smell of curry mixed with urine and incense that, in spite of the missing front door, lingered along the hallway. My room was better, or maybe I only thought it was better because I had washed it clean and put up travel posters that Steve had given me. They covered the walls: Switzerland, Tokyo, San Francisco, Nairobi, Kiev, Peking, Florence, Alicante. I liked to lie on my bed and look at those beautiful places. Mark Grimal stared at the posters with a strange expression, then at the window with the crack where I'd put electro glue, then at the two-burner stove, then at the couch with its lumpy mattress, then at the candle I lit on the lid of a coffee can. I shouldn't have brought him here. I knew that suddenly, and, for the first time in twelve years, felt shame.

I cut off the moldy places on the soya sausage and quickly fried it in canned oil while he drank a cup of crystallized coffee, seated in his dark blue suit on the one chair near the metal folding table.

The light from the candle cast grotesque shadows on Nairobi.

"So this is where you live," he said at last.

"It's not so bad."

"I believe you," he said, "but I don't want to see what you consider bad."

"I'm sorry." I put the sausage on the table. My hands trembled when I tried to open the loaf of bread. How could I have been so foolish?

"*You* are sorry?" asked Mark Grimal. "Yes, you would be. We want our Undesirables to believe that, since they deserve their fate, they shouldn't contaminate the rest of us with it."

He took the bread out of my hands, put it on the table, then moved the table over near the bed. "Come on," he said. "You've got to join me. I'm not going to eat your last sausage...."

The next morning Jacques said: "I know it's none of my business but who was that man last night?"

"My boss."

"Bad, Christie, bad. Don't get mixed up with one of Them."

"It's not like that," I said. "He didn't even make love to me. He's a good man."

"Give him time," said Jacques. "He'll make love to you. Then, if you're lucky, he'll get bored. If you're not lucky, he'll stick around until someone reports him and then the police will charge *you* with attempted corruption. Not him, you. That's how the system works."

"He's just trying to be nice."

"Oh, sure," said Jacques. "Well, the nicest thing he could do would be to keep away from here."

Jacques was right of course, just like my mother. But I couldn't be that way. Every night after work I let Mark come upstairs, drink coffee, talk. He brought things: a pane of glass he installed in the window. Two flower teacups with gilded saucers. A case of powdered milk. A miniature orange tree that we put on the back porch. A pair of boots. An oven. A gold necklace.... He wasn't like they said he was at all. He never touched me. I began to wonder if maybe he thought I really *was* unclean, the way the television says we are.

One night I asked him if he'd been to any of those beautiful places on the travel posters. Even if I had the money, UDs are forbidden to travel.

"Tokyo. San Francisco. Nairobi."

"Are they as beautiful as that?"

"Well," he said, "it's different. Those pictures were taken about a hundred years ago. The cities are more like museums now. You go around on little trams and pay admission to all the buildings, the parks, the old temples.... They have guides dressed in the kind of clothes the people used to wear. Maybe we could disguise you as a gold prospector or a Franciscan monk and smuggle you into a Gateways tour to San Francisco."

"That's a joke."

"A bad joke," he said. "Sorry. I could give you one of Lisa's dresses; that way, nobody would guess you were a UD."

He didn't sound as though he were joking.

"I wouldn't be able to get the travel documents."

"We'd use Lisa's."

I was beginning to feel alarmed, but I decided I'd better join him in pretending. "I'd love to," I said. "But it wouldn't work. I'm not small and blonde, and beautiful."

He laughed. "Well, not small and blonde. You're more beautiful. But, you're right: it wouldn't work."

More beautiful? I'd seen his wife. Every month she brought a cake to the department to celebrate the staff members' birthdays. There is no one more beautiful.

Mark picked up the cup and saucer and carried them to the small sink near the stove. He turned the water on, then tried to turn it off. It still trickled. "I ought to fix this faucet. But they don't make them like this any more. I can't find the right washer."

"Why are you doing these things for me?"

Without turning around, he said: "Don't worry, Christie. I know what they've told you about me. If it were all true, I wouldn't have time to do any writing."

"I know that. What I mean is I have a feeling that...maybe I'm part of some bigger problem for you."

He raised his head but kept his back toward me. He continued to twist the faucet on and off. At last he said: "Guilt feelings? Maybe."

"But you've no reason to feel guilty about me."

"You don't think so?"

"Of course not. The trouble with my father happened long ago, during the war. He gave the blueprints on a gun that didn't work to the enemy...."

"The enemy." Mark's voice was bitter. "For a hundred years, maybe two hundred years, maybe longer than that, we haven't had an enemy. If your father thought he'd given the blueprints to an enemy, he was tricked."

I felt a fear begin inside me, like a glass shattering. My father had been a traitor; I accepted that as the reason for all that had happened. "They said it didn't matter that the gun didn't work; it was the thought that counted."

"Yes, they would say that," said Mark. "Treason is in the mind. Disease is in the mind. Everything's in the mind."

"But there *was* a war?"

"So-called. I think it was more a mutiny in the Foreign Interests Department. Some younger officers signed a petition about...well, it's hard to piece together...something about a famine in the Maldives. They were reprimanded and scheduled for restructuring with drugs. About one hundred and fifty of them managed to flee to the Maldives, where eventually they were all tracked down and executed. Or at least so say the records."

I started to cry.

I turned on the bed and buried my face in the pillow, trying not to sob so that he could hear me, to compose myself before he turned around. But maybe it was the silence that he heard.

"Christie, what did I say?" He sprang across the room, sat down beside me on the bed, and touched my shoulder. "I'm sorry. I shouldn't be talking to you like this." I shook my head. How explain that I *wanted* to believe my father had been a traitor? that I wanted a *reason*?

"I know," he said, as though I'd spoken, "you'd like to think that there's justice in this world, some anyway. All right, my dear, maybe it's true: maybe your father *was* a traitor, at least to the foreign Interests Department."

I sat up. He met my eyes, then looked away. He didn't believe it.

"You aren't like the others in the Admin." I brushed the tears off my cheeks. "I'm afraid for you."

"Oh," he said, "I'm safe enough. I have the mind of the People engraved in my brain; I could write a speech in my sleep, I know it so well. Besides, I have this frivolous image: the man who sleeps around. Nobody takes that kind of man seriously."

That night we became lovers. I didn't believe there could be anybody like him.

THREE

Vimalachandra smoked a pipe. That was contrary to Admin regulations. He even smoked a pipe in inter-departmental staff meetings. If anybody objected, he replied, "I have permission." Nobody pursued the matter further. They just opened the air vents.

Monday morning, after seeing Tom Ugaki, I dropped in on Vim, who was sitting in Records behind an enormous tray of diskettes, feet on his desk, puffing away on a pipe made in the form of a fanged god with a feather headdress. Magico-religious symbols are also prohibited within the Admin buildings but Vim said that the pipe was cultural, not magico-religious, that he certainly would never believe in a fanged god with a feather headdress, and that if he *did* believe in one he would have more respect for the god than to smoke with it. The argument was unbeatable.

"Mark, welcome. Sit down. Saturday's speech was a beauty. The things you Program types dream up."

"Inane, right?"

"Entire careers have been built around less."

"Man, you really know how to hurt a speech writer." We laughed. "How about a cup of coffee in the cafeteria?"

Vim glanced toward the corner where tropical plants flanked his ancient ceramic coffee machine, which made coffee from real beans. He raised his eyebrows, I raised my eyebrows. He wrapped his pipe in a pouch. "Sure, Mark. We Records people ought to see how the other ninety-nine percent of you live around here."

We went down the blue corridor to the escalator that descended to the green and black striped patio where a statue by some Afghan sculptor dripped water into a pond. On through the beige room to the green corridor and then into the cafeteria, which was painted off-white and decorated with Associated Territories landscapes done by some of the Foreign Interests employees who had served there. The landscapes were terrible. So was the coffee, but I didn't trust offices—any office, including Vimalachandra's. Maybe, especially, Vimalachandra's.

We picked up the plastic mugs from the dispenser and seated ourselves at a round, glass table near the sandwich bins.

"So how are things with the lovely Lisa?"

"Same as always."

"Tough. You don't know how to appreciate all that blonde hair."

"Two feet of it at last measurement."

"Paradise," murmured Vim,smiling through his pepper-and-salt beard. He wondered what I wanted; I wondered what I wanted. "So, what can Records do for Programs?"

"I'm trying to come up with a good idea for the ninety-fifth anniversary of the People's TV Assembly. None of my material explains how the transition was made from the old representative legislature to universal democratic participation made viable by the global media network. We ought to explain the dynamics. It'd be a good story."

Vim measured liquid sugar into his spoon and dripped it into his muddy coffee. "Probably would, maybe better than you think. That's the trouble with you Program types: you're always coming up with ideas."

"That's what they pay us for."

Vim sipped his coffee thoughtfully. "Someday they'll be sorry. So you want to know what we've got on the Transition? Nothing."

"Nothing?"

"Hard to believe, right? Well, let me tell you. We once had a file, but five years ago Security requested it, then Polyguide requested it, then we got instructions to erase it. You know the bureaucratic mind, Mark: who cares how it happened, so long as it continues forever."

"So Security would have it."

"No chance in getting it from them. You might try Kelly in Polyguide."

I grimaced. I wanted as few favors as possible from Kelly. Vim laughed. "Oh, Kelly's not so bad, Mark. Smart woman. Kind of cute, even...."

"Until she opens her mouth."

"Yes, well, those are power tactics. Just pretend you don't notice the language. Use your masculine wiles on her."

"On *Kelly*? She'd have my head bouncing on the flagpole." We laughed. "O.K., I'll try Kelly, but in case I don't succeed, you didn't keep a backup file, did you?"

"Backup file." Vimalachandra pulled out his pipe and carefully lit it. "Ah, Mark, the things you think of." With dirty glances in our direction, three women at the nearest table pushed back their chairs, clattered their dishes together and moved to a more distant table. He'd kept a backup file.

"As you know, there are two kinds of backup files. There's the kind that's a copy of something specific. Well, that kind would fall under the instructions to erase. But there's another kind. All day long the computers are backing up material in case of a power outage. There's no need to keep those files, but being a super cautious person, I do. Those are my 'bingo' files. It's quite possible that somewhere in the 'bingo' files you might find the Transition file, but it would be quite a job going through all that garbage."

"But if I can't get it from Kelly, you'd let me try?"

Vimalachandra looked steadily at me through his smoke clouds, his brown face expressionless, his yellow shirt unbuttoned at the collar. "My advice, Mark, would be to drop it. Think up another program. But if you don't want to take my advice, sure, you can go through the 'bingo' files. Access them through the DIAG.sys directory. The password is 'rubble.rot.' It'll take you about six months to check them."

The Policy Guidance Department was located on the tenth floor, as close to the reception rooms of Director-General James Francis Finley III as one could get. Kelly Hallihan was buried deep inside it in an office full of electronic equipment, computers, wall charts, clocks that gave the time of day around the world, two bookcases of administrative decrees, policy papers, alternative plans, emergency procedures. Very thin, she was wearing slacks and a loose vest that floated around her nonexistent hips; her hair was pulled back in a ponytail. She wasn't bad-looking in an athletic, stringy way. Probably practiced karate to keep in condition.

When she saw me, she said: "Well, I'll be dipped in shit if it isn't the fucking wordsmith." She smiled, so I knew that must be a friendly greeting.

"Hi, Kelly. Mind if I come in for a moment?"

"Don't be so fucking polite," she said. "This is Kelly, not one of your sweet-talking bimbettes. Of course," she added, plunking into her swivel chair and putting her feet up on the top of a mini-shredder, "you could have buzzed me on the intercom first, but then that would have creamed the frigging surprise, right? I thought you Program hot dogs stayed as far away from Polyguide as the fucking law allowed."

Kind of cute, said Vimalachandra.

I sat down in the dumpy chair alongside her desk. "You know, Kelly, you take a guy's breath away."

She chortled. "That's the idea, Lover-Boy. First strike capability. So come on. What's the angle? Neither of us is getting any younger."

"O.K. I've got an idea for a program to celebrate the ninety-fifth anniversary of the Transition—"

"Oh-oh."

"—and I discovered I've no material on the actual dynamics that were involved in changing the old representative legislature into the People's TV Assembly—"

Kelly was nodding. "So you went to Vimalachandra, and the son-of-a-bitch passed the buck to me. That's Vim for you. Never likes to hard-ass anyone."

"What do you mean 'passed the buck'?"

"Vim knows as well as I do that you're not cleared for the Transition file. He could have saved you a trip to Polyguide."

"What's so secret about that period of history?"

"Nothing secret. Here—" She sprang to her feet and pulled a sheet of paper out of a bin. "In case you don't have it, here's the policy guidance on the Transition." She shoved the sheet into my hand. "Stick to that and you won't get into trouble."

"How does one get cleared for the Transition file?"

"One doesn't," said Kelly.

I saw that we'd come to the end of our conversation. "Well,

thanks anyway."

She let me get to the door before she called out: "By the way, Mark, I never found the officer who cleared your 'Be Kind to Undesirables Week' crap. They all deny it was in the speech when they saw it."

"You want to check the diskette?"

"No," she said. "We'll let it pass. This time. I suppose we could say that Brown cleared that one, right? You were lucky. What you smart-ass Program officers can't get through your fucking skulls is that we're here to keep you from stepping into the dog shit."

"Put that way, Kelly—"

"Just don't do it again, Lover-Boy," she finished with a ringing smile, "or I'll have you busted to an M-3 rating."

By the time I arrived at the round bank escalators, I had cooled off enough to realize that Kelly had done me a favor by telling me she knew I'd bypassed her. Kelly didn't make idle threats; a lot of people could testify to that. The next time I bypassed her it would have to be for the biggie.

Kelly had also pretty well killed the Transition program idea because even if Vim let me go ahead with viewing the "bingo" files, I wouldn't be able to use the information. Still, I was curious. What could be so secret about it?

I rode down the escalator, reading the Policy Guidance on the Transition. There was nothing there I didn't know. The same actions taken, the same infrastructure developed, the same unexplained gaps in the record. On May 23, 2025, the old global world assembly with reps from the 189 nations voluntarily voted itself out of existence, passing all judicial and legislative power to the People's TV Assembly. Executive power was vested in three Chairmen, elected on a yearly basis from the main regions, who were to rotate as world directors once every three months. Day to day administration remained in the hands of the Global Administration.

It stunk like a two-day-old fish lying in the sun in the UD's open-air market. Kelly knew the truth and Vim knew the truth and Danzig of Security knew the truth, but, as far as I could tell, I was the only uninformed person in the Admin who thought it peculiar that a legislature would voluntarily vote itself out of existence.

For the ninety-fifth anniversary of the Transition, I wrote a pious, rhetorical speech that not even Kelly could change. Mallam Ahmed was Chairman that month. After the program, he congratulated me on my "amazing style," so like his own, so subtle, so sub-Saharan. All the official news sheets reprinted it in its entirety, with photos of Mallam Ahmed and the old legislative building, which was described as a conference hall now, and the broadcasting studio where the first People's TV Assembly had been inaugurated. It was pure fiction. Nothing existed. Well, Mallam Ahmed existed. But the old legislative building had been razed decades ago, I knew that for a fact, and the photo of the broadcasting studio had been taken in a corner of the present main building because that made a better visual than the old studio, which had been gutted to serve as a warehouse.

A telephone number for the People's TV Assembly was listed in the official news sheet anniversary editions. I punched in the number. There was no answer.

From the window of my standard Super-Grade II office, I could see the Federation flags billowing around the visitors' entrance. My office had the usual fake wood paneling, maroon carpet, desk lamp, recessed lighting, glass-covered coffee table in front of sectional sofa, computer unit. Only the files were mine, those and the framed poster of a Polynesian beach ("Gauguin slept here."), three merit awards, and a cartoon in French in which a speech writer floated pages of text from the fly deck of a stage down to a robot in front of a microphone.

Wondering if, unlike government offices, other institutions that advertised in the official news sheets ever answered their telephones, I called some tourist hotels, shops that sold virtual reality headsets, a concert hall, an airline company. In only one case did I get an answer, and that was a wrong number.

Penny, my secretary, a woman with shiny black skin and her hair pulled back in a bun, finally noticed that I was doing all this dialing. "Here, let me," she said. "You've probably forgotten how to reach outside." After an hour, she agreed that there was something peculiar about the information distributed in the official news sheets.

For one thing, none of the firms were listed in the Federal Territory electronic directory.

"How come we never noticed this before?"

"Oh, this information's not for us," she said. "We never call those places."

True. Almost everybody in Alternative Four worked either for the Global Administration or for one of the three Chairmen. We had our own in-house communication system. Our Travel Section took care of reservations, Purchasing bought supplies, Housing allocated apartments, Recreation developed film, rented sports equipment, sold discounted tickets, videodiscs, candy bars, flowers, bedding, clothes, luggage, autocycles. The official news sheets listed information for...well, for whom?

I had the feeling that I was on to something, as I had had the feeling that I was on to something with the Transition file.

When I pointed out the mistakes to Julio in Telecom, he laughed and said: "Weird. But then nothing would surprise me about this *manicomio*, Mark. I'll look into it when I get a moment."

On a slow day I visited Blanca Rodriguez, Chief of the Correspondence Section, which was located in the basement between Printing and Garment Cleaning, near an automatic door that opened onto parking level D3. Blanca, a kind, grandmotherly type, was flattered that I should be concerned about her contacts with the People. She showed me her neat statistical charts, kept month by month, year by year, topic by topic. The people who wrote to the Admin were highly articulate, issue-oriented individuals. The South African war was a popular theme, as were contacts with other worlds, funding for space flight, the criteria for selecting Undesirables from the main gene pool, pornography in the schools, the threat from the rebels in the New York subway system, the pollution level of the developed countries' water supply, and the superb job being done by Mr. Brown, Mallam Ahmed, and Comrade Wong.

She found a couple of electronic messages that she had kept, she said, because they were so beautifully composed. I took them back upstairs with me.

The addresses didn't exist and the names weren't listed in any of the directories.

FOUR

THE UNDESIRABLE'S DIARY

Of course Mark and I had no place to go, the way ordinary people do—to restaurants or music shows or even for a drive outside the city, because I wasn't allowed to travel outside the city. After Mark started coming to see me, a woman in the corner front room, who had an old battery-operated refrigerator that she let the rest of us use for things like left-over milk, said: "Let *him* buy you one. I don't want whores in my apartment."

I didn't tell Mark what she'd said because I knew he'd buy me a portable refrigerator, only bigger, and then knock on her door as he brought it in so that she could see it. He was like that. "Reckless," said Jacques. "The Monroe Institute is full of them—popping their pills in the cafeteria, daring anyone to stop them."

"You don't know Mark," I protested.

"I don't need to know him," said Jacques. "I can tell a rich boy slumming without knowing him. What do you think his wife makes of all this?"

But I didn't want to think about his wife. To my mind, she just came with his apartment—cooked the turkey, decorated the birthday cakes, swept the carpet. Mark never talked about her. Had he loved her, he wouldn't have been spending his evenings with me, would he? and so I couldn't see what the problem was. But since Jacques's saved my life twice now, he thinks he has a right to tell me how to live it; and maybe he does—at least live it in such a way that he doesn't have to save it the third time; and so I tried not to get annoyed with him, although there were moments.

Once after we'd arrived home, Mark remembered that he'd left a file in the car and went back to pick it up. He took so long in returning that I got worried. Maybe he'd been mugged or something. But just as I was about to go to look for him, he reappeared, his face slightly flushed, his eyes evasive. He tossed the folder onto the bed and taking off his tie, unbuttoned his shirt collar. "Your watchdog down there almost ate me up, Christie."

"Who? Jacques?" Angry, I started toward the door, but Mark pulled me back.

"Don't get upset. I'm glad someone here cares enough to challenge unscrupulous men for you."

"But you're not an unscrupulous man!"

He kissed my forehead. "Not compared to Dresmond, my dear, but that's not much of a comparison."

Since we couldn't go any place together, on nights when he was free we stayed in my room and talked. I'd fix dinner, although I could tell that he didn't much care for the food I made; he was used to natural, which costs more and doesn't keep without refrigeration. After a while he began to buy ready-prepared from the Admin gourmet market, or bring food from his home. "That's Chinese," he'd say. "Here's Tamil. Try this: it's Mexican." He always wanted to share with me, but that food of his, to him it was great but to me it all tasted differently and yet lacked something, fortifiers maybe; and so while he ate his ham on black bread and his marinated artichokes and cabbage rolled in pastry and speckled cheese, I'd usually just fry myself a couple of reconstituted eggs. No cholesterol, better for you, I'd tell him. He laughed, and said a man had to die of something.

After he had installed the lamp, sometimes I'd crochet or read while he worked on a speech that he had to have ready by morning. It was like being married, almost. I enjoyed that, but he called it a waste of time when he could be loving me; so unless the work was urgent, after dinner we'd just blow out the candles and get into bed and he'd talk, try to make me laugh, told me all kinds of funny stories about trips he'd gone on and studio mishaps and Admin errors, asked me to tell him what my favorite color was or song, what I read, describe my life before the Misfortune, while all the time he was undoing my clothes and kissing each uncovered spot until I'd begin to relax and curl toward him and let him put his hand where he wanted. Even then he'd talk—love words, how beautiful

I was, how I tasted even; I would blush the next morning to think about what he'd said, although I loved to think about it. Sometimes he was inside me before I realized it, but if I tensed up, he'd withdraw and start over again; no matter how long it took, he'd always start over again. I couldn't believe a man would be like that. I guess it was because he'd had all those other women.

But if Mark desired me, then how could I be an Undesirable?

I thought about that a lot because I had come to see that it made no sense, my having been sterilized just because of my father. After all, my father's parents hadn't been Undesirables, so where had the bad genes come from? At the time the People's TV Assembly declared my father an Undesirable, only his mother was living then, in Padua; and when they told her, she had a heart attack in the Plaza del Santo in front of the museum basilica of St. Anthony.

But if that were true with my family, then there must be thousands and thousands of "normal" people in the world today who were really Undesirables, only nobody had discovered it yet. When I left the UD district, I would stare at the people I passed—*Are you one? Are you?* With no blue uniforms to identify them, I'd decide on the basis of whether or not they were polite to me, like if Ramona sprayed her room with disinfectant when I came into it or if Penny loaned me a clip when a button came off my blouse.

Or Dresmond, for instance. "Put a blue uniform on that man and he'd be right at home," said Mark. I couldn't help but laugh, although never before had I considered Dresmond funny.

Or the guard at the cafeteria door who, although he saw me every morning, always held up the line while he called Security to confirm my ID number and then would flip the card at me so I had to catch it.

I've always blamed my father for what happened to my mother and me, since he should have thought about his family first. Why let himself be lured into a rebellion that destroyed us?

But Mark defended him. "If everybody put his family first," he said, "we'd have to stay single to achieve anything. I'm sure your father meant well; he was set up. It never occurred to him that he might end as an Undesirable."

My father of course wasn't there to defend himself, but I don't recall that he ever did so while he was alive either. He just drank. He was a big man, with curly black hair, which he stopped cutting, and freckles across the back of his hands. Where he got the liquor, we never figured out. My mother hid the money her parents sent her, but he never looked for it. He'd go out and come back, drunk, and fall into bed, and that was all we saw of him. After my mother's death, I went to live with the Professor and his wife.

Once the Professor tried to talk to my father. Before the Misfortune, they'd been friends, but the Professor had retained all the careful grooming that my father neglected—clean shirt, buffed shoes, clipped beard, spectacles held together with electro-glue. "One doesn't have to lose one's standards in Misfortune," he would say, as he carefully straightened his worn tie and brushed the dandruff off his collar.

One morning, very early, he went to see my father, hoping he could catch him before my father found a bottle. The Professor found him all right, snoring on top of the mattress, no sheets on the dirty bed, the only food in the room a torn-open loaf of bread on the floor into which bugs were swarming. He almost gave up right then, he told his wife, but he didn't. He woke up my father and gave him what the Professor called "a pep talk," ending with "Your daughter is a nice young girl, Alfredo. Now that her mother's gone, you're all she has. She could help you take care of things You ought to show an interest in her welfare."

To which my father replied: "What good would that do her?"

FIVE

On Wednesday I fell asleep at Christie's and didn't return home until 4:30 in the morning. A bad mistake. The guard at the UD border crossing called Security to verify my ID. Now I was on record for having been in a peculiar place at a peculiar time; Security Chief Danzig would love it.

When I entered the bedroom at home, Lisa was sleeping propped up on her pillow, the light on, with a book about the life of pop singer Damon Vassos open on the bed beside her. Quietly I turned out the light and undressed, but when I opened the closet door she woke up. "Mark?" "It's okay, Lisa. Go back to sleep." She turned the lamp back on and squinted at the clock in the headboard panel. "Almost *five o'clock*! Well, you did have a good time with your UD girlfriend tonight, didn't you?"

In June the girls at work had told Lisa that I was driving Christie home at night, and Lisa drew all the appropriate conclusions, which, in the middle of one of our quarrels, I stupidly admitted.

I hung up my clothes. The curtains at the window shimmered in the opal light from the skylobby fixtures outside. Lisa stared into the wall mirror with hard eyes. From the beginning she had taken the line that my relationship with Christie was somehow qualitatively different from that of any of my previous affairs, something so sordid it hardly bore contemplation, like fucking a chimpanzee or exposing my genitals on the 56th Street rampway.

"What happened to my bottle of catsup?"

Catsup? Oh. Catsup. "Was that the last one?"

"Also the blankets. And the portable heater we kept in the hall. And the turkey I cooked last Saturday. Did you hear me?—the turkey *I* cooked last Saturday."

"I hear you, I hear you."

"Well, at least you owe me the courtesy of a lie. You are so *blatant* about these things."

"I'm sorry."

"Stop lying." Lisa began to cry. "If you meant it, you'd stop seeing that girl. It wasn't so bad before, but an *Undesirable*...!"

"I can't stop seeing her."

"You could with all the others."

"This is different."

"It certainly is. An Undesirable!"

"Undesirables are people too." Why did I have to explain that?

"Well, one doesn't have affairs with them. Mark, what's the matter with you? I suppose you feel sorry for her because we have a roast turkey and she doesn't. Well, give her the turkey if you want to. Give her the heater. I'll...I'll send her cookies when I bake. Anything! Just stop sleeping with her. You *can't* be in love with her! It's *impossible* to love an Undesirable! Listen to the broadcasts."

Did I ever say in a broadcast that it was impossible to love an Undesirable? I never wrote that.

"It is?"

"Mark, I'm not joking. If you don't get rid of that girl before Saturday, I'm going to tell Mr. Danzig in Security, and you can bet he'll do something about it. I'm sick of this; it's been going on since last October. I'll never forgive Steve for passing her on to *you*, of all people. You come into this house, all covered with her secretions and you wash them off in our bathroom where I might pick up a disease...."

Danzig! The name grazed my head like a killer bee. Lisa had never hurled the Man at me before. "Lisa, you're not going to catch anything. You can't really believe that crap."

"Are you saying it's not true? Are you saying Undesirables don't pollute?"

Careful now. "No, Lisa, I'm not saying that. I'm just saying that you're being too literal minded."

"'Too literal minded'? Well, Mr. Danzig can be the judge of that."

She was serious. Her hair cascaded around her shoulders like a mantle, the tie on her nightgown was undone at the neck, her breasts heaved toward me, her cheeks were splotched with tears.... For a moment I wondered what it would be like to wind her hair around her neck and strangle her. Like squeezing a ripe, green grape, I should imagine. I did not need this soft, squishy, whining, weeping woman who "adored" me. But if I let her go to Danzig, they'd fire Christie, maybe even arrest her for attempted "corruption." Danzig thought I was dissolute enough already.

Lisa saw that I'd grasped the situation and she almost smiled. "All things are possible, aren't they?" she said. "Even giving up your beloved Undesirable."

Senior Admin officers do not strangle their wives. All I permitted myself to do was grab her by the shoulders, shake her violently, toss her back on the bed, and fuck her until she was squealing and begging me to stop. That of course was exactly what she wanted. Afterward as I lay there ready to vomit, she told me what a *wonderful* lover I was, what a real *man*. Maybe she would have enjoyed being strangled. Maybe that would have been the ultimate aphrodisiac.

"Don't you dare go near Danzig," I said. "I'll tell Christie this evening."

"Yes, darling," she coo-ed sweetly.

Over the next couple of days I made a lot of mistakes; once you start making them, they pile up, like disposable tissues.

Lisa had done it again. She'd whine and bitch and moan, and I'd tune her out; and then suddenly I'd look up to find her coming at me, knife in hand, straight for the jugular. But threatening me with Danzig was a new one. I didn't understand that. Maybe she thought she could volunteer her services as police informer to help keep me in line; but in that case she didn't understand Danzig, who'd love to get something on me that would make the Clearance Board do more than chuckle. What advantage would it be to Lisa if I got kicked out of Admin?

Not that I thought I would. My affair with Christie was just one more twig for a future fire; however, I couldn't let Danzig's goons arrest Christie for "corruption" nor, on the other hand, could I abandon her. Christie trusted me. All those sweet nothings I'd poured into her ear at night, vowing to protect her and care for her and give her the globe in a basket. I'd only stopped short of promising her sexual fidelity, which would have been a lie, flat out, and I don't lie to women, except Lisa, not for moral reasons but because I like to stay friends with them afterward.

So now how was I going to take care of Christie?

I had to decide fast because, as usual, I'd allowed Lisa not only to dictate the terms but also to set the timing, having gone so far as to promise "this evening" when she'd only asked for "before Saturday." I didn't have time to check all my options. All I could think of was *money*, a lot of it so that Christie would know I was serious; and *cash* because UDs can't have bank accounts unless somebody fronts for them. Perhaps I could have set up a trust fund at the bank, but with a trust fund I would have had to co-sign every transaction, and sooner or later that would have come to Lisa's attention. So it had to be cash, and *not* from our regular accounts or Lisa would notice. I didn't stop to think that giving Christie a lot of money might frighten her or make her feel like a prostitute, or that, anyway, my money wasn't why Christie felt secure around me. Since I couldn't give her *me* any longer, I decided it had to be money.

Fortunately our Telecom International stock was in my name only. I sold most of it.

When I asked the broker for cash, he looked at me as though I'd flipped in from Saturn. Nobody used much cash nowadays, except UDs and drug couriers and rebels in the New York subway system. I could see him trying to figure out which category I fit into. "Eight thousand three hundred and twenty three dolyens in *cash*? Excuse me, sir," he said, "but that'll take two days minimum. Let me transfer the money to your bank account. It'll be faster."

"But I don't want it in my bank account," I replied. I was thinking of Lisa, who occasionally paged through the account on the computer. Besides if the money were in my bank, then I'd just have to get the cash from the bank, wouldn't I?, and the bank would ask questions. But then, having said that, I added illogically: "This is urgent."

"I see, sir," said the broker, deadpan. "Well, I'll try for twenty-four hours, but we don't keep much cash on hand; we'll have to collect it from the branches."

As it turned out I should have taken my chances at the bank, for, although he would have scolded me, at least Jerry Hiraoka would also have warned me that the law required financial institutions to report to Security all cash transactions over 100 dolyens.

On Thursday night, to de-fang her, I assured Lisa that I'd broken off my affair with Christie; however, I didn't actually do so until Friday.

That evening, while Christie washed some clothes in the basement, I pretended to work on a speech about Regional Economic Integration. Working in Christie's room had never been easy, not even with partial summer light still glowing through the windows and under the battery-powered lamp that I had installed to augment the candles; but that night I wouldn't have been able to concentrate if I'd been working under floodlights.

Finally I decided that waiting was only making things worse, and besides I had to get home early enough so that Lisa would suspect nothing. Christie wasn't in the basement. I found her on the roof where she was hanging clothes, her sleeves rolled up to her elbows. The sun was going down behind the parabolic reflector on the Comco Center across the canal. She still had plenty of clothes in the bucket.

"Here's money," I said, handing her a black plastic bag. "I told you I'd take care of you. Put it somewhere."

She took it gingerly in one wet hand, opened the bag, peeked inside, and then gazed at me as though maybe I had manufactured the stuff. "Mark, where did you get this? It's so *much*."

What could I say? I kissed her. A wet bed sheet on the line blew against us with a slap.

"I have to stop seeing you after work; Lisa has threatened to complain to Danzig."

I held her tightly against me. The air was humid, sultry. She said nothing for several moments; then she sighed. "Shall I have to change departments again?" She'd been through this already with Steve.

"No. I want to be able to see you, to be sure you're all right."

She smiled sadly. "Oh, I'll be all right, Mark. Don't worry." She dropped the bag into the plastic pail that held the damp clothes and went back to pinning towels on the line. That disconcerted me a little, but at least any satellite camera watching us would never have guessed the bag contained money. I helped her to finish hanging up the laundry, while keeping one eye on the black bag, because I didn't want to see it blown off the roof and strewn all over the UD district. Then we went downstairs. I knew it was going to be hopeless to try to explain this mess, particularly since I didn't want to make Lisa sound like a bitch; however my tact only deepened the mystery for Christie.

"You never told me your wife was upset about us." Well, no, of course I hadn't. "Mark, you should have told me." Well, perhaps I should have. "Of course," said Christie, struggling to be fair, "I should have asked you, I guess. Jacques warned me." The idea of Jacques's having warned her irritated me enormously.

The threat from Danzig was clear enough, however; Jacques had warned her about that also.

Then we argued about the money: she didn't want it, she couldn't keep it, somebody would break in; it made her feel "bad." Her objections mounted. I couldn't believe this: here she was living in a slum room with one chair and a broken-down bed and a bathroom that she had to share with ten other people and not even a refrigerator to keep her reconstituted food from breaking down into its nasty little chemicals; and she didn't know how she could use my money.

Then I got it. *Oh, shit.* The problem wasn't the money; it was the way I'd shoved it at her, like a rich man paying off a mistress. How could I have been so stupid? I was under deadline; that's how. So much for deadlines. Now I had to spend twenty anguished minutes trying to convince her that the money wasn't a payment for services rendered but rather an attempt to keep my promises to her. But emotions are funny things—once you jiggle a person in the wrong direction, they tend to keep going that way, no matter what happens afterward; and, anyway, Christie had never understood my promises as meaning *money*.

I thought that perhaps making love one last time would help, although that certainly wouldn't get me home early and I'd have to use either my Caveman or my Space Traveller routine on Lisa; however, Christie said, no, she couldn't make love, not tonight— not resisting, just snarled in my arms like a steel mobile, with the lamp turning everything green-hued and bloated. Since sex to Christie was nothing but a symbol—and mainly a bad one—, if I'd needed proof that I'd fouled up, that was it.

So I kissed her on the forehead, said goodbye, sprinted out of the house, and drove back to the city on auto-pilot. I hadn't felt this bad since Fawkesburg.

When I got home I discovered that Steve and Rita and Lisa had been waiting for me to play bridge with them. Steve was simulating a Mars voyage on the computer, while Rita and Lisa gossiped over Chinese checkers. At the sight of me, Lisa smiled, a bit too brightly; she had begun to fear I wasn't going to make it. There were plates of small pizzas, bowls of Oaxacan peanuts, a cream cheese dip for the vegetables, Brazilian chocolate *brigadeiros*. Quickly I drank a couple of Scotch-and-sodas, because if Lisa had told me she'd invited the Maines for bridge that Friday evening, I'd certainly forgotten. However, I didn't mind.

Playing bridge was better than being alone with Lisa.

SIX

THE UNDESIRABLE'S DIARY

After Mark left I sat in the chair for a couple of hours, not thinking, just sitting. The black, plastic bag lay in the bucket, like a package from the open-air market that contained beet-tops or tripe or overripe bananas and would soon start smelling.

About 10:30 I *did* smell it—awful, like burning plastic; but that's when I shook myself and said: *Stop it, Christie. You're beginning to hallucinate the way you did when you were eleven.* I stood up, stiff from having sat so long in one place, and undressed and turned out the light and lay down on the bed. *I'll leave the money in the bucket,* I thought. *Maybe it'll be gone in the morning.*

I couldn't sleep, though. I lay there in the dark, trying to figure out what had happened.

Oh, I knew what had happened. I'd been ditched—for my own good, of course. At least that was how Mark explained it.

But why would a wife threaten to report her husband to Security, even if she hated, really *hated*, him? If the story were true, Mark's wife must be crazy. Was she crazy?

Maybe Mark had made up the story.

But that didn't make sense either, because the night before he'd been so loving. I couldn't figure it out. Maybe he was two people— the one who came across the rooftop, holding that stupid bag of money, couldn't even wait until I had finished hanging up the clothes and gone back inside, he wanted to get away from me so fast.... "Here's money. Put it somewhere." What did he expect me to do? hold it in my teeth?

And then the other Mark, the one who said he wanted to take care of me.

What was it about men and money? They thought it said something about themselves, how good they were, how generous. "Let me know when you need more," he said carelessly, as though he had bundles of it stored away in a closet, as though I could finish even this much in a lifetime. That money wouldn't permit me, a UD, to eat in a city restaurant. If I bought things, I'd have to buy an item here, another item there, otherwise thieves would target me; and anyway who cared whether I owned new clothes or not when I had to wear a blue uniform to work every day? I couldn't put the money in a bank for my old age. I didn't like expensive, natural food. So to me the money was worthless; I couldn't use it.

When Mark saw that I didn't want the money, really didn't want it, a switch seemed to click on in his head and he turned back into the man I loved. But it was too late then; I'd seen the other Mark Grimal.

Maybe that's the trouble with his wife; maybe she only sees the other person.

In the morning when I found the money still in the bucket, I knew I hadn't dreamed it. Maybe a bucket was the best place for it. I left it there and went to work, where I stayed behind the files all day except when I knew that Mark had left the office. From time to time I could hear his voice. The day before he'd been jumping on people for everything that went wrong. But not now. Now he laughed and joked with everyone. Even when Beatrice accidentally transmitted to Tananarive the speech meant for the Ambassador in Yaounde, all he said was: "Quick, honey! Get it back before I'm fed to the monkeys."

At four-thirty he came behind the files. I didn't look up until he was leaning against the side of my desk, hunched down in his jacket, hands in his pockets, as though he were cold. "Christie," he said. "Christie. Why are you hiding back here?"

"It's where I belong," I said.

"Nobody belongs anywhere," he replied. "Sometimes we'd like to, sometimes we don't, but if we didn't step over our boundaries from time to time, nothing good would ever happen to us."

"Or bad."

"Or bad," he agreed. "But I hope it wasn't bad." He paused, as though for me to say something, but I didn't know what to say; and anyway he'd warned me to be careful about talking in offices.

"Just one thing," he said. "I want you to know I've done the best I can. Maybe it wasn't the best possible, but it was all I knew how to do. If I didn't handle it well, blame it on the softness of my spine rather than on the hardness of my heart. If you understand what I mean."

"No," I said softly.

"You're a brave person," he said. "I'm muddled up. Sorry." He was silent, while I continued to paste labels on the diskettes. Then he said: "I've arranged for an auto-taxi to take you home each evening. It will be outside the main entrance."

I dropped the green labels into the red label box by mistake; as I tried to pick them out, my hands were shaking. "Please don't worry. There's a UD bus on Transition Avenue, just down the street."

"The taxi's safer."

"No, Mark. Thank you."

"Christie," he said, "don't make me feel worse than I do already. The taxi will be there, paid in advance. Use it if you want to; don't use it if you don't want to; but it will be there."

I could hear pain in his voice then, and I suddenly realized that I'd wanted him to be miserable because I was, when, if I really loved him, I should have been wanting him to be happy. I dropped the label box and, clutching my arms across my chest, bent over the desk, feeling sick.

"Thank you," I whispered. "You're very kind."

"'Kind' isn't the word," he said. "You know by now that I'm not a *kind* person."

I expected the other girls in the office to make fun of me when they learned Mark no longer drove me home at night, but they didn't. Some of them even became a bit friendly. Nobody mentioned it except Ramona.

Then one day an attractive blonde woman came to the office. Her hair was coiled around her head; she was dressed in a pink suit trimmed in white, and had a rose in her cleavage, like a Lifestyle model. "That's Ingrid Armfeldt," whispered the other diskette file clerk, Nadezhda. We all stared. She was more beautiful in person than she appeared on television, although as she flashed her TV media access card at Penny, she didn't even bother to look at her. "Mr. Grimal is expecting me," Ms. Armfeldt said in a disdainful voice, almost tapping her foot because she had to identify herself, because he hadn't told Penny she was coming and arranged a big reception for her.

However a few minutes later when she emerged from Mark's office with him, she oozed charm, like on television. He was putting on his jacket. They were laughing together. "Don't worry, Ingrid. I won't let them ask you for your autograph." He began to introduce us. Graciously she extended her hand to each of us, even to me, although her eyes were on Mark and her whole body seemed to incline itself toward him like a flower to the window.

"But, darling, you know, I *love* to give autographs! *Please*, somebody, ask me for my autograph or I'll feel *slighted*."

Mark winked at Beatrice; Beatrice asked for the autograph. I crept back toward the files. I wasn't jealous. How could any ordinary woman, let alone a UD, be jealous of Ingrid Armfeldt? She was Mark's kind of woman, her perfect body creamed and manicured and brushed and smelling of roses. Nobody who slept with Ingrid Armfeldt could ever have slept with Christine Riccardi. I had dreamed it all. I stopped feeling bitter then, because you can't fight nature. However I felt sad for him too. Having watched Ms. Armfeldt before, the way she acted toward Penny, and now seeing her pretend to be nice to us in order to impress him, I could tell she wasn't a very good person.

After they left for lunch, the room smelled of roses. Kirsten chuckled. "Wow! He's back to cruising again, isn't he?" Beatrice glanced at me and nudged Kirsten in the ribs. Quickly I retreated behind the files, but in a few minutes, Beatrice joined me. She offered me a candy almond.

"Don't feel bad, Christie," she said. "Mr. Grimal's a nice guy, you know, but he's just that way about women."

SEVEN

It was the end of the month and Lisa had brought a birthday cake to the office. Three staff members had birthdays that month: Penny, Tony, and Waldir. Their names were spelled out in pink curlicues of sugar among the rosebuds and the elegant white candles.

I had forgotten about Lisa's birthday parties until this morning, but even if I had remembered I wouldn't have been able to cancel this one unless a state visit were in the making, and then only for another day, because the staff looked forward to these personal touches that Lisa so delighted in. Since I hadn't admitted to Lisa that Christie still worked for me, at 2 p.m. I sent Christie to the library and told her to stay there until closing time. That was a cowardly thing to do, and, as it turned out, not very smart either.

We were drinking champagne. Or, rather, everybody but me was drinking champagne. I pretended. We toasted the birthday celebrants, we ate cake, we played music. I kept watching the clock. My hands were sweating. "Has everybody got a piece of cake?" Lisa called out. "Hmmm," said writer Ramona, looking around. "Where's Christie?" There was silence.

I knew that Ramona had done this deliberately; she despised Christie and objected to having to work with her. She knew where Christie was; everybody knew where Christie was; but then my staff didn't adore me in quite the same way that they adored Lisa.

Then Penny compounded the problem by muttering, "Shut up, Ramona." She turned the music disk volume up so high that had I intended to answer Ramona's question, nobody would have heard me.

Lisa looked as though she'd received a slap in the face, but, recovering quickly, she exhibited her usual grace under pressure. "We'll save her a piece," she said brightly and cut a large slice of cake with two roses and put it on a glass plate and set it to the side of the table. I tried to open another bottle of champagne, cut my finger, and Waldir took over. Because I was afraid of what might be said if I left the room, I continued to stand there with a napkin wrapped around the cut, feeling ridiculous.

During the drive back to our 22nd floor apartment near the park, Lisa and I said nothing; on the escalator we said nothing. When we entered the living room the sun was setting behind the circular towers of the Global Health Department across the avenue. Lisa pulled the drapes across the picture window. I took the empty cake tray and party items into the kitchen; everything was in the box except the glass plate with the cake for Christie that Lisa pointedly had left on my desk at work. In the kitchen I delayed my return to the living room by washing my finger in the sterilized water from the dispenser. The cut, which had stopped bleeding, looked swollen.

As I stood there, gazing at the blackish-reddish gash, I had a sudden overview of the rest of the evening, of the rest of my life maybe. I had ended my affair with Christie; but now when I returned to the living room, I would find myself apologizing merely for keeping Christie in a job where she wouldn't be harassed. Lisa and I would argue and shout at each other; she'd weep, then threaten. Finally I would give in, as I always gave in, and it would end in a tussle on the floor in which Lisa would emerge, bruised and beaten but victorious. Tomorrow, like Steve, I'd be looking for another department to which I could shunt Christie.

No, I said. No.

I left the kitchen, walked past Lisa, who had seated herself resolutely on a pouf near the china cabinet, opened the front door and went out into the hallway. I closed the door behind me, then headed to the escalators beyond the tropical plants that decorated the reception area. Behind me I could hear our apartment door open; fortunately Lisa was too refined to call after me and alert the neighbors. By taking the escalator at a sprint, I made it down twenty-three flights and into the basement parking area in less than five minutes. I got into my car and drove off.

Not this time, Lisa.

After cruising aimlessly around the rampways for an hour into the twilight, I decided to try to get my mind off my self-loathing by doing some work, a trick that I have used to astonishing effect in my advance up the career ladder and the need for which, in my case, hardly anybody, including my father, believed. The cafeteria in the main Admin building served dinner, such as it was, until 9 p.m. I grabbed something called pasta flan a la king, which was just as bad as it sounded, drank a cup of tea with Mike from Publications, and then headed to my office. I had a pass for night work but the guards knew me; they didn't ask.

Penny had neatly stacked the old Transition anniversary news sheets on one corner of my wall unit. I saw them as I dumped Lisa's cake into the waste basket. What a bunch of crap that speech was! When in doubt, use rhetoric. With a little more information I could have written a memorable program, I knew it. *Somebody*, however, had decided that information about the Transition should not be available to most of us, even most of us in the Admin. So what was the secret about the Transition? I thought again of Vimalachandra's "bingo" files. I had never gone back to him because I figured that Kelly had immediately called and chewed him out for not telling me that I hadn't the necessary clearance. Hard to hold him to his promise after that. Still, he *had* promised.

And who would be in Records at this hour?

There was somebody in Records—Joe Passerman from EcoDev. We greeted each other cheerfully. I sat down at a work station on the opposite side of the room. "Rubble-rot" it was. After ten minutes I managed to locate the "bingo" files. They were formidable all right. After paging through a few hundred documents covering everything from the cost of foam lining to the war in South Africa, I decided I needed a method. Vim had said that five years ago Security had requested a copy; the instruction to erase had come soon afterward. Vim would have made sure he had a copy by then. That being the case, I should be able to narrow the time period down to four, five months, maximum.

Even four, five months were a lot of words in Admin; however, by one a.m., with Joe Passerman long gone, I had come upon a memo from Vim to Security, asking for the exact parameters of their request. By 1:30 a.m. the first documents appeared, and by five o'clock in the morning I had finished reading the Transition file.

I went back to my office, took down my three merit awards and threw them into the waste basket. After ten minutes' reflection, I decided that was an extreme action, as well as a highly noticeable one, so I put them back on the wall.

I, Mark Grimal, hadn't been around at the time of the Transition. I hadn't been one of the Senior Admin Officers who had participated in planning the takeover of the old legislature by the World Chairmen, who had cut off the representatives' communications and utilities, refused to provide food and water, delivered the Chairmen's ultimatums and, backed by the military, forced the representatives to liquidate themselves (quite literally) after signing a document that turned power over to the People's TV Assembly, which, the best I could figure out, at that time had been nothing but an interactive TV chain with punch buttons.

Not me. I hadn't been there.

At six a.m. I had my first visitor.

After my all-night session at the computer, I was trying to decide how to recharge myself without going home. Breakfast in the cafeteria or a shower in Recreation? It was going to be a long day. None of my staff had arrived yet. The corridors outside Programs were still empty enough so that I could distinguish rare, individual footsteps as they clunked by. I heard someone enter the reception area, then come in the direction of my office.

"You're here," said Kelly Hallihan in a flat voice, as though she couldn't believe it.

"Been here all night. Where else should I be?"

Kelly looked at me as though she'd never quite seen me before. "Been here all night," she repeated. She had on her usual pants-and-vest outfit, with blouse sleeves rolled up to her elbows. She was carrying a rope bag stuffed with documents. "Well, do us all a fucking favor and call your wife to let her know. She must think you've got your pecker engaged elsewhere."

"My wife?"

"Yeah, you know, Blondie. She's been calling people all over the Admin. Even got me, the crazy bitch, excuse my language, I don't usually call wives names; however, none but yours has ever called me at three o'clock in the morning."

I closed my eyes. I couldn't believe that Lisa had done that, but then I had never walked out on her *before* a fight either. I slammed one fist against the desk. "Oh, *shiiiiit!*"

Kelly laughed and smacked her hands together. "Hey, the man swears! I never thought I'd hear it."

"I'm sorry she disturbed you, Kelly."

"Not your fault; she's of age. You ask me, she sounds as though she needs psycho counseling at the MedUnit. Better get her over there." I looked at Kelly with astonishment. This was the first time in my life that anyone had suggested that Lisa rather than I might be the one at fault. This was better than breakfast.

"Don't look so fucking surprised, Lover-Boy. I'm serious. If Blondie isn't always like that, then you sure scared the shit out of her last night—by coming to work yet." Kelly shook her head and laughed. "Come to think of it, that scares the shit out of me too. You keep on this way, I'll have to change my image of you."

"Aberration, Kelly, aberration."

"Look—" She leaned across the desk. According to BioFacts, she was thirty-seven years old and the toughest administrator Polyguide had ever had. I could believe it. "This is none of my fucking business, I'm not Security. But it doesn't sound as though you two have exactly what Lifestyle calls—" Her voice went into a wobble parody. "—'a trusting, loving, fulfilling relationship.' Of course, those of us into singlestyle can't imagine how you doubles manage anyway. Shit, I don't trust my dog, I should trust a *person*? But I try to be broad-minded. Has it occurred to you that you might be mismated? Maybe what Blondie needs is the tinkering-around-the house type. Maybe you're too advanced for her concepts. Those things happen. They're not supposed to, but they do. You could check it out, have some new tests. When they fuck up in Lifestyle, they call it 'unassessed variables.'" Around Kelly's eyes the skin looked as though it were being pulled back into her ponytail.

I wasn't sure what to reply. Kelly might not be the last person in all the Admin that I would have thought of going to for marriage counseling—Danzig had that honor; however, she certainly ran him a close second.

"It's...bumpy sometimes, but then I suppose so are most marriages."

"Ah, shit. I knew you'd be a gentleman." She flipped her ponytail up and down. "Well, Blondie sounds more than bumpy to me. But then I may be prejudiced: anyone who calls me at three o'clock in the morning had better have a fucking good reason." She slung her rope bag over her shoulder. "However, don't worry, I doubt she'll do *that* again. I pretty well ripped her apart. Sorry."

"I can imagine." I wasn't sorry either.

"No, you *can't* imagine," said Kelly. "You've never called me at three o'clock in the morning." She turned to go. "Tell you what, Lover-Boy, I'll send you some policy guidance on Choosing and Changing Lifestyles; I think you could use it."

"You've got policy guidance on *that*?"

She grinned. "Shit, we have policy guidance on *everything*."

After Kelly left, I dialed the apartment. Lisa answered. She sounded as though she had a bad cold.

"I have instructions from Polyguide to let you know that I have been at work all night. If you had to call anybody, why didn't you call here?" Then I hung up.

Thirty seconds later she called me back, whimpering. "Mark, I'm sorry. I just panicked. I never thought you'd be at *work*. Please don't be upset!"

"How can I not be upset? Those people you called are my *work* colleagues. Are you trying to ruin my career?"

Oh, no, no, *that* wasn't what she'd been trying to ruin. My sanity, maybe; my extra-marital sex life, certainly; but the idea that she might have put my *career* in jeopardy set off a bout of hysterical weeping punctuated by abject apologies that made me understand why Kelly thought Lisa needed psychological counseling. Careers were serious stuff; they provided high rise apartments, gold jewelry, genuine roast beef instead of soya, tickets to the multi-sound concert series at Highland Crescent. "All right, all right," I said. But she kept sobbing. "Look, stop that or I'll take Kelly's advice and get an appointment for you at the MedUnit."

The sobbing burped to a stop. "That *horrible* woman," said Lisa.

"Do you know what she said to me?"

"No, and I don't care. There is *no* reason *you* should ever call Kelly Hallihan at any hour." Then I added: "Just for curiosity's sake, did you also call Danzig?"

There was a brief silence. "I didn't tell him anything."

"But you called him?"

"Yes, but, honest, Mark, I didn't say a *word* about..."

"Watch it." The phone was probably bugged.

"...Well, you know...."

"Yes."

"She's still there...."

"She works here," I said. "She's going to continue to work here where she's safe. Do you understand that?"

"Safe from everyone but you," Lisa replied sweetly.

She'd recovered.

I slammed up the receiver. I didn't have to go home; I could stay here forever. Within the Admin complex, we had banks, shops, restaurants, dry cleaners, a video viewing room, three bars, and even a theater. I could sleep on the sofa.

But before I could get out of the office to go to the cafeteria, Lisa called back again in tears. She hadn't meant it that way. *Of course* she understood; it was so *good* of me to be *concerned*; I was such a *good* person. Why, most men would simply have *discarded* the poor thing. Mark Grimal, however, was *different*. That was why she loved me so much and why she always got so upset when she thought I didn't love her....

Kelly was right. But breaking away from Lisa wouldn't be easy: she had too much on me.

It was now seven o'clock. On my way down to the cafeteria I met three people who had been telephoned by Lisa. "Hey, Mark, call home!" "Your wife wants you, Tiger." "Interesting evening, Mark?" They laughed, winked. I shrugged, rolled my eyes, and kept going. The only one I dreaded having to deal with later was Danzig, with his little computer notebook, because once he had the notebook open, he liked to bring up whatever happened to be floating through his mind—sex, drugs, alcohol, politics, other people. I'd need plenty of coffee to be able to cope with Danzig.

In the cafeteria, Christie was sitting at a table by herself, eating breakfast, a side benefit of working at the Admin. I grabbed a mug of coffee, a sugary roll, and something that looked like yogurt but probably wasn't, and sat down at her table. "Good morning, Christie."

She smiled tentatively at me. "How was it yesterday?"

"Rough. You'll hear them talking. Ramona decided to be disagreeable."

She nodded. "She likes you, that's why."

"Ramona?!" I was startled at the notion. Ramona had dyed red hair and a subscription to Great World Video Drama. "Well, I'd hate to be her enemy if that's what she does to the people she likes."

"She thinks *I'm* her enemy. Even now."

"I'll have her transferred to Publications."

"No, no, Mark. You can't start transferring people because of me." She was right; I'd have to think of another reason. "What happened to your finger?"

"Cut it opening champagne."

"You didn't put anything on it. You'd better go to the MedUnit."

"Yes, dear." I smiled at her. Her curly black hair puffed out on both sides of her pale face. I thought of her fragile body underneath that ugly uniform. At my glance, she bit her lip, blushed, and looked away. "Don't, Mark. Someone will notice." I discovered I had a hard-on.

Time for a shower.

There was no one in Recreation except the jogging contingent, nineteen of them panting around the mini-racecourse in grey and red sweatsuits; if Lisa had called any of them last night, they were too out of breath to needle me about it. The shower room was empty, the water hot if somewhat rusty, the dispenser tray provided razors, lotions, deodorants. I put on fresh underwear and a clean shirt from my locker. I was ready for Danzig.

And he was ready for me. We were good at anticipating each other this way. When I got back to Programs, Penny was seated at her desk; she tilted her head toward my office and mouthed his name, then whispered: "Where were you last night?"

"She called you too?"

"Lisa called everybody she ever heard of, I guess, except the World Chairmen. Good luck."

"For once I'm innocent. I was right here all evening."

Jake Danzig was seated on my couch, dressed in his usual brown safari suit. He had undoubtedly gone through everything on my desk, just in case, but since I kept a clean desk in his honor, he had been reduced to reading an old anniversary news sheet from the top of the pile.

"Morning, Danzig. Sorry to keep you waiting."

"Morning, Mark. No problem. I guess you're a little tuckered this morning." He winked at me in his buddy-buddy way. He wore a gold name tag around his left wrist and a decoration for valor on his breast pocket, earned while he was a young Security officer on personal protection detail with the Chairmen. Since those days he had grown slightly overweight, but I still wouldn't want to tangle with him in a basement corridor.

"I sure am," I replied. "Working all night long just isn't my style."

A little crease appeared in Danzig's forehead. "You call *that* work?"

I laughed. "Don't jump to conclusions, Danzig."

He gestured mysteriously toward the outer office. "Let's close the door."

"Oh, I have nothing to hide from my trusty secretary," I replied in a loud voice, as I always replied in a loud voice whenever Danzig wanted to close the door. We heard a muffled giggle from Penny. Danzig shook his head.

"Mark, do we have to go through this routine every time we get together?" He made it sound like a social occasion. He forced a smile. "Your wife called me at two-thirty this morning." No wonder he sounded so plaintive.

"Sorry, Danzig. I had no idea she was going to freak out that way."

"Close the door, Mark," repeated Danzig. This time he frowned. I closed the door. Pleasantries were over; we were into the serious stuff. Damn Lisa. I sat down in my swivel chair and put my feet up on my desk. He hated that, but after all, it was my desk.

"There are two aspects about last night that I want to go into," said Danzig. "One is where were you? And the other is why did your wife, as you put it, 'freak out' when she couldn't find you?"

"I can tell you about the first," I replied. "Ask her about the second."

"I'm asking you."

"I don't know. She's never done it before."

He entered something in his notepad computer. "Never, hmm?"

"I'm sure I would have heard about it if she had."

"Then something unusual must have occurred earlier in the evening."

"I don't know."

"Don't bullshit me," said Danzig. "You *know*." His finger was poised above the keys like an armed space missile.

I replied: "Do you think I *wanted* Lisa to take the Admin directory and start punching numbers? If I'd known anything unusual enough had happened to get *that* going, I would have stayed home and sat on her."

Danzig saw the point, or at least pretended to. He entered something in his notebook. "So where *were* you?"

"Right here."

"Mark, Mark...."

"Well," I said, "ask your guards. Check the log. Call Mike Schultz in Publications, Joe Passerman in EcoDev; they were here too." He was looking at me in amazement, just as Kelly had. I grinned. "Danzig, your lack of trust hurts. After all the in-depth discussions we've had in the past, would I lie to you about something you could check at the front entrance?"

He folded his computer and put it back in his pocket. "No, I guess you wouldn't. Mark, this has been a most interesting chat; it always is with you." But he wasn't finished; he was just pretending to be finished. "Lisa is obviously disturbed about something and if you don't know what it is, for your own good I think you'd better try to find out."

He stood up. "You know, Mark, just between us men—" He winked again. "—women can be worse than drugs, alcohol, you name it, in wrecking a career. As I've told you in the past, each year when your security clearance comes up for review by the Board, I have to explain why a Senior Admin officer can have such a poor record in, ahem, how shall I put it...?"

"Crudely."

"All right. In keeping his pants zipped up. I always point out that your wife is stable, supportive, knows how to handle the situation; and this helps in the overall assessment. If Lisa starts, as you say, 'freaking out' because of your abnormal sexual activities, then we're going to have a lot more trouble keeping you cleared. You understand me?"

"Yes." I'd heard the lecture before. There was no sense in arguing with Security about what was normal and what wasn't; they had their own definitions.

He turned to go. But I knew he still wasn't through. He always saved the zinger for the last.

"Oh, yes, and, Mark, do you still drive that UD employee, what's her name?, Christine Riccardi, home in the evenings?"

He'd hit the target.

"No."

"Good." He nodded. "Glad to hear it, Mark. You know, people were beginning to talk. Your record's bad enough with normal women; you don't want to get mixed up with the kinky, sick ones like the Riccardi UD."

I gripped the arms of the chair; the knuckles were pure bone.

Danzig smiled. He removed the notepad from his pocket and recorded something. "I'll bet Riccardi was grateful that you went all that way to take her home, Mark. What was in it for you? A good-night kiss, maybe?"

"Danzig," I said, "you're obscene."

Danzig laughed. "Rubs off on me from the people I associate with. Just answer the question: did you or didn't you screw her?"

"Why would I screw a UD when I can screw a TV star?"

"Beats me," said Danzig. "It's your trip. Yes or no?"

You can't win with Security. The best you can hope for is to break even.

When I applied for the Admin fifteen years ago, my past hadn't

been as colorful as it is now, but still there were a few things that
Security was interested in—like Maggie and Odette and Miss Hansen,
my university English teacher. To all Security's questions, I replied: "I never talk about women." When they got down to naming
names, I said: "Ask *them*." When Security threatened to hold up my
clearance if I didn't cooperate, I shrugged. "Suit yourself." They
cleared me.

That was the last time I won anything with Security, because then
I was in the Admin and the rules were different. When I discovered
that, I should have resigned; however, by then I enjoyed my job, I
was good at it, and I quickly rose into an income bracket far beyond
that of the ordinary academic's son from Austin Hills. My father
might say: "Abide by the rules or get out of the game," but that was
the sort of self-righteous thing my father always said, and I didn't
see it that way.

So I just got deeper and deeper into trouble. To "yes or no"
questions, you couldn't say "yes" without framing yourself or
someone else; and you couldn't say "no" unless, of course, the
episode never happened, because then they had you on record for
lying, and for that you could be dismissed or even prosecuted. That
left feinting and dodging, but to Security feinting and dodging
meant simply that the charge was true, but, since you didn't want to
admit it, the truth must be even worse than they suspected. When
that was entered in your record, you broke even, provided they
didn't investigate; however, every time you came up for promotion
or a new job, your Security file went skimming from hand to hand,
filled with comments and recommendations; and a lot of people
never guessed what had hit them. I knew what had hit me. I knew I
was never going to get any higher in the Admin than Chief of the
Speakers Division.

I took my feet off my desk. "Are you making one of your usual
innuendos about my sexual behavior?"

Danzig faked surprise. "Of course not, Mark. I'm just trying to
figure out what you could find to do in the UD district until four-
thirty in the morning."

"Oh, that night. My car broke down that night."

"You remember the night?"

"Of course I remember the night."

"It took ten hours to get your car fixed?"

"Right."

"Why didn't you phone a towaway?"

"Couldn't find a phone. UD district, remember."

"Car phone?"

"Out of order."

"Watch phone?"

"Awful gadgets. Don't own one."

"Bad night all around, I see. So who finally fixed the car?"

"Little guy named 'Happy.' Short, red-haired, free-lance mechanic. Works out of a pub on—"

"Save it," said Danzig. "Save it for the cameras." He folded his notepad and put it back into his breast pocket. "Got to hand it to you, Mark: you're an original. But watch it; you're pushing your luck. Getting involved with a UD would be sufficient cause for Lisa to crack up. I thought of that last night. UDs are the scum of the earth, Mark. This one's father was a traitor; her mother assaulted a policeman. The genes are all there, both sides of the family."

He moved another step toward the door. My merit awards, which I had carelessly stuck back up on the wall, were hanging crooked. Danzig paused to straighten them. I could tell he and Lisa had one or two things in common.

"Personally, I don't think we should hire UDs in the Admin, period, but I've been overruled on that by the broad-minded Chairmen. They're thinking of the efficiency angle: you can pay UDs next to nothing for grunt work nobody else wants to do. Unfortunately, what the Big Three don't realize are the temptations for some of you less stable officers."

He knew he wouldn't get a rise out of me because, if I said anything, the words would go straight into his little computer notebook. I braced myself for the final shaft.

"Tell you what, Mark, if you ever want to sample UD tail, just contact me and I'll give you a list of the men this Riccardi dame has fucked since she was eleven. *Eleven*, Mark, *eleven*. I'd hate to add your name to the list." He opened the door. Smiled. "Keep clean, old buddy. We don't want to lose you."

For all I knew, Security might have micro-cameras installed in my in-basket. After Danzig left, I very slowly unclenched my hands, got to my feet, picked up a draft of this Saturday's speech, walked past Penny and the Speakers Division staff, and went to the library. There I sat for an hour in front of an electronic document entitled *An Abstract of Legislation Concerning Refugees from South Africa* without seeing a word. My breath was labored, as though I'd been running; I was conscious of my lungs expanding, contracting; and there were red lights beneath my eyelids. With every breath I loathed myself more. How could I have sat there in front of that son-of-a-bitch and let him talk that way about Christie? I was sure now that he'd had us followed every evening. He knew what time I had entered Christie's house and what time I'd come out; he knew exactly when I had stopped taking her home. He probably knew the gifts I had given her; he might very well know about the stock. Why hadn't I thought he would? I was not using my head very well. Keeping track of the UDs in the Admin was part of Danzig's job. Now all he needed was a pretext to pick Christie up for "corrupting" me.

I breathed slowly, as though the air were syrup.

EIGHT

At ten o'clock Penny finally tracked me down in the library. Comrade Wong's office wanted to talk to me. I hurried back to Programs.

Wong's secretary, Fairouz Moked, told me that Wong had been invited to speak about Ethnic Diversity in the Cultural Renaissance of the 21st Century to a group of oral traditionalists in San Francisco. Although he had received the invitation only this Tuesday morning and the event was on Friday, he had decided to accept, because it was a topic that particularly interested Comrade Wong. He realized that this was short notice. Although he would like me, personally, to write the speech, if I were working on a priority from one of the other Chairman, he would accept a draft from Waldir Souza, provided he could have the text by noon tomorrow.

"I'll be happy to do it, Fairouz." Perhaps I should have given Waldir the opportunity, but I liked writing speeches for Wong. Of all the Chairmen he was the only one who actually read them. Ahmed skimmed the speech an hour before the event and added a rhetorical flourish or two. Brown winged it. When I wanted to experiment, I chose Brown because, even if he didn't like the speech, all he could do was blunder through it, jumping over a word he couldn't pronounce, or abandon the script entirely, ad lib, and complain afterward. But Wong had definite ideas about what he wanted; he worked the draft over the day before himself; and he was always speaking to some strange group on an exotic topic about which I knew nothing; therefore I learned things.

"Any guidelines, Fairouz?"

"He would like to discuss those with you himself. Can you be here by two-fifteen this afternoon?"

"Certainly."

I hung up, jubilant. The tight deadline, the unfamiliar topic, the demanding client; I certainly wouldn't have any time to brood over my problems for the next twenty-four hours.

"You look better," said Penny with a smile, as she handed me a stack of messages that had come in during my absence. She was an attractive woman, I noted; profile like Nefertiti. She had arranged the small yellow slips in what she considered priority order. Vimalachandra's name was on top.

I buzzed him on the intercom. "Good morning, Vim."

"Good morning, Mark. I hear you had the circuits over here burning all night long. Did you find what you were looking for?"

"Yes."

"Is it what we discussed once in the cafeteria several months ago?"

"Yes."

"Good." Good? "Then I have to take you to lunch. Are you free today?"

"I have to be at Comrade Wong's at two-fifteen."

"We'll go early. Is 11:45 all right? See you at the underground near the Cashier's office." Although I was sure that Lisa must have called Vim last night, he never mentioned it.

At eleven-forty-five I was at the underground subway that connected the Admin buildings all over the Federal Territory. We were going, Vim said, to a restaurant called The Sub-Orbital, "and be forewarned: Kelly Hallihan will be there."

"Kelly eats lunch?" I wasn't sure I could cope with Kelly twice in one day.

Vim chuckled. He was wearing a white Nehru jacket over baggy tweed slacks. "On special occasions."

"What's so special about this occasion?"

"You've joined the Club, Mark, the only club that matters in the Admin: those who know about the Transition."

He smiled encouragingly. I had been prepared to apologize to him for embarrassing, or maybe even compromising, him by overstepping my classification, but it seemed no apology was expected. The maglev subway glided softly on monorails into the station. We boarded. The trip took two minutes forty-five seconds to the Western Contact station.

The Sub-Orbital was an expensive, space-motif restaurant that served organically grown rather than reconstituted food and catered to the scientists who worked at nearby Grosset Labs. There didn't seem to be another Admin type in the place until we took an elevator to the nineteenth floor tower, entered a private dining room and found Kelly Hallihan. Kelly had a notebook computer on the table in front of her. When she saw us, she dumped it back into her rope bag. "Well, Grimal," she said, "you sure don't believe in wasting your time at night, do you? Welcome to the Club."

I saw my status had gone up; I had a name now, I was no longer "Lover-Boy."

Vim and I seated ourselves around the table. Kelly punched a button. The floor started revolving; we were on a turntable. Another button and the wall curtains swished back: the entire Federal Territory capital as far as the Transport Cabins and the air shuttle testing fields to the west came into view. It was a grey, monotonous, geometric erector set, but it controlled the world. I was impressed.

"Sure beats the cafeteria."

"Nothing's too good for a Club member," said Kelly. She turned to Vim. "Well, I broke the fucking news to Danzig."

"Oh, my dear, I am sorry," said Vimalachandra.

"Better me than you. He bust a gut. Grimal, of all possible Admin flakes, he yelled, only he didn't say 'flake.' Threw things, broke a six-foot palm tree in half. I thought I was going to have to call MedUnit. He wants your head but he'll settle for the 'bingo' files."

"A good compromise," said Vimalachandra. He didn't try to hide his smile.

Kelly swung around to punch another button. "I assume you've taken precautions, because he's in Records right now, erasing like a wild man."

"I have."

"'Bingo' is now 'bongo'?"

"That would be telling."

"Yeah," said Kelly. "It's more likely 'appalachia.'" She grinned at him. Her language, while not purified, had bleached itself considerably. She was treating Vim like an equal. I saw that belonging to the Club must have its benefits.

A door opened and a bald waiter in a tuxedo slithered in. Kelly introduced us. "A new member of the Club, Jerome. When Mr. Grimal comes here, take good care of him."

Jerome bowed. "Welcome to the Sub-Orbital, sir."

We ordered. "Whatever you want, Grimal," said Kelly. "It's on us this time." After two meals in the Admin cafeteria, I was ready for the steak and fettucine at thirty dolyens. When the waiter had gone, she added: "Jerome's an Undesirable."

"No blue uniform?"

"In his case not necessary at work, because he's also a Club member." At my startled look, she nodded. "Yeah, an Undesirable who knows about the Transition. Inadvertently, of course. Some asshole at one of these luncheons shot off his fucking mouth over a frozen daiquiri; we had to hire Jerome on the spot; now he only waits on Club members, so we can all be assholes. Jerome's a good guy. We take care of him."

Evidently Danzig had managed to swallow the inclusion of Jerome in the group. I wondered if I had been meant to note that.

Jerome brought back three club sodas with lime. Vim didn't drink, Kelly wouldn't at lunch, and, after thirty hours without sleep, I knew I'd fall on my face if I tried to.

"And now to you." Kelly turned to me and raised her glass. "Congratulations. You're Vim's boy, Grimal. I can't say I would have approved if he'd asked me. You know what I think of you Program hot dogs: nothing personal, but you give me more headaches than anybody else in the Admin, with your 'Be Kind to Undesirables Week' crap and such like."

I grimaced. My success in getting past her on that occasion obviously still rankled. I figured I'd better apologize and start anew. "I'm sorry about that, Kelly. I was—"

"—testing. I know. To see if it were possible. Well," she said, "it's you guys who test the rules who usually self-select yourselves into the Club, right, Vim? The plodders never make it. That doesn't make me love you any more, but I'm prepared to cope because I've got to. Common sense is what fuels me, fuels the Club.

I'm not too sure how strong you are in that department, Grimal. Vim thinks your other assets make up for it."

I wondered what my other assets were.

"Look, you guys," I said, "I haven't slept for thirty hours. Maybe you should talk more slowly or something."

Kelly laughed. "Over to you, Vim. Explain the Club. You do it more nicely than I do."

Vim was chewing on the lime from his club soda. "Sorry, Mark." He dropped the rind into an ashtray. "I know you're tired but it's important to lay out a few things. Stumbling onto the Transition file can be a shock to anyone. That period of history doesn't show the Admin personnel in the best light. Even from the official records, the coup by the regional chairmen was a nasty business. If any Admin personnel objected to it, their names are not recorded in the files. The top officials all performed their jobs with enthusiasm, and, as a result, were rewarded with extensive powers in the new government...."

I looked at Kelly Hallihan. She was staring moodily into her club soda.

"...In fact it had to be that way. With the global legislature gone, the People's TV Assembly in its infancy, and the Chairmen in their own power struggle backed by different branches of the armed forces, the Admin was the only body left to govern. In that, we did as good a job as could be expected. But it wasn't good enough. You can't expect bureaucrats like us to incite much enthusiasm from the masses. Ah, here it comes."

The door opened and Jerome brought in lunch—a leafy salad with anchovies and olives for Kelly, a plate of fried prawns for Vim. My steak tasted as good as one of Lisa's.

When Jerome left, Vim continued. "Finally, as you read, in the best tradition of the professional civil service, the heads of the departments got together, negotiated peace among the Chairmen, merged the military under Security, and set up a mechanism whereby the People could ratify decisions taken."

"'Ratify decisions taken'," I repeated.

"That's correct," said Vim. He poured liquid sugar into his club soda. "The People's TV Assembly, even now, is much too diffuse an organization to function as a genuine policy-making body. What you have to deal with is a bunch of push buttons. There is no way that the People can initiate an action, although at times a few radical groups have attempted it; the world-wide support's not there, nor even access to the global studios to start the system operating. Decisions are made by the Chairmen or the Admin; the People agree or disagree. We provide policy guidance, including the Saturday public service program in which the Chairmen participate. Thanks to the public opinion polls, we know how to tailor the issues; since we never try to go too much against the polls, we can predict to one-half of one percent what the decision will be in any given vote."

Kelly was eying me ironically from across her shredded lettuce leaves. "Grimal doesn't like this part."

Unperturbed, Vim speared a prawn with his fork and dipped it into the sauce. "The Transition history is not too pleasant a story, all told, so you can see why it might have been suppressed all these years. But the real reason, of course, is that the arrangement set up in those days continues into this one. The Chairmen cancel one another out, the People have the illusion of participation, and the Admin runs the government."

I had lost my appetite. I pushed back my plate and said: "Well. Well, well, well...."

"Go on," said Vim, with his encouraging smile. "Say what you're thinking."

"That's mighty cynical, Vim. You're stating that this whole facade of universal democratic participation is...is—"

"Screw the People," contributed Kelly. "Hey, Vim, I think he may prefer my version."

"—that we're putting on some gigantic show to hide the puppet strings we're pulling."

"You're getting there," said Kelly. She picked up an anchovy with her fingers and studied it in the light, as though it might have sprouted ringworm.

Vim chewed meditatively on a prawn, then went to work removing the tail from another one. "Your reaction is a normal one for an idealistic officer, Mark. I've had 15 years to get used to the notion. And to see the benefits. For there are benefits. Limited participation is better than no participation at all. Knowing the People have to ratify an action at least makes the leaders think before they do it. And, basically, the system works. The world is at peace, has been for years—"

"What about the war in South Africa?"

Kelly crumbled a cracker over the lettuce leaves. "There is no war in South Africa."

"Kelly!" Vim twisted in his chair. "Isn't the Transition enough for one day? Do we have to include the war in South Africa?"

"Shit," said Kelly. "Grimal has been nosing around the Admin for weeks now trying to come up with answers to questions like—" Her voice went into a parody of my own. "—how come the telephone numbers and addresses are all wrong in the official news sheets? Right? You don't think he would have missed South Africa."

"It looks as though Danzig is not the only one who has my office bugged," I said. She was wrong: I'd missed South Africa.

"Relax," said Kelly. "I've got better things to do. Blanca Rodriguez confided that you'd been to see her." I had forgotten about Blanca. "You're right, Vim. Better to have your boy in the Club where we can watch him than outside smelling the crap from beneath the door."

"Let's see if I've got this correct," I said. "The first advantage to our governing the world is that peace has broken out all over. What's the second advantage?"

Vim pushed aside the remains of the prawns and pulled out his pipe. "The second is that we have a large number of public-spirited experts who are concerned to do the best they can for world-wide economic development. We're rational; we work by consensus. Few of us are tempted by power, the way the Chairmen are. Nobody elects us so we don't have to worry about pursuing demagogic policies in order to be re-elected. The People don't know who we are and don't care so long as their sewage pipes get laid, their children receive free milk at school, their elderly are taken care of in medical housing complexes. We have boards that monitor our own ethical behavior; we have stringent policy controls to enforce human rights standards. Would the people be better off under any other arrangement? They weren't before, Mark. Read what it was like under the old legislative assembly. I'm not trying to justify what happened—"

"Only what happens now." I swirled some cold fettucine around with my fork on the butter-smeared plate.

"Well, yes," Vim agreed. He lit his pipe. "This is reality, Mark. This is how things work. You may not like it, but you'll have to live with it. Therefore, you might as well focus on the good points of the system rather than regret the loss of our great myth of universal democratic participation."

Kelly cut an olive in two. "I don't think Reality is your boy's strong point, Vim. He wants to live in a fucking Utopia."

To gain time I ate some lukewarm steak. Three air shuttles took off in the distance. A glidercopter skimmed over the vegetation planted on the roof of the EcoDev building. I hadn't joined the Club at all; the Club was composed of Realists, and Kelly was right: I was not a realist.

"How do the Undesirables benefit from all this?" I asked.

The question thudded into the room. Vim raised an eyebrow. Kelly said, "Oh, yeah, the Undesirables. Danzig told me you have one."

Something exploded inside me. What was it that gave people like Danzig and Kelly and Lisa the right to talk about Christie as though she were a thing, a novelty item for my jaded sexual appetite? "I do not have one!" I shouted, simultaneously slamming my knife and fork down on either side of my plate. The club soda glass jumped. From the expression on Kelly's face, I could tell I'd made my point, not a swear word in it. I was shaking.

"Had one?" asked Kelly tentatively, leaning forward.

I covered my eyes with one hand.

Vim interjected: "Kelly, don't repeat Danzig's gossip. You lack sensitivity."

"I'm not a natural," she admitted. "In fact, I'm a real shitass sometimes. Like now, it appears." She whistled. "But, for gossip, that sure did get a reaction." She reached across the table and patted my arm. "Sorry, Mark. What I was trying to say was that you probably have a clearer view of the conditions under which the Undesirables live than do those of us who don't know any, and therefore it must bother you more."

"And rightly so," added Vim. "The existence of the Undesirables is a holdover from a more primitive age. It's a sad commentary on people's need for an underclass in any society."

"But it's policy," Kelly went on to emphasize. "We're stuck with it until all three of the Chairmen decide to change it, and those guys can't even agree on a breakfast menu."

"So it's policy," I agreed. "But why can't we at least provide them with humane living conditions since we say it's not the UDs's fault that they were born with faulty genes?"

Kelly cleared her throat. Vim took a puff on his pipe.

"We're talking millions of dolyens here, world-wide," he said. "The short answer is that it's not in the Budget. The reason it's not in the budget, of course, is that UDs don't vote, and since befriending a UD is a risky activity, they have few supporters within the Admin."

I could vouch for that. Oh, Vim and Kelly had their answers ready; they patched together the fractured luncheon; they were understanding, compassionate, ready to listen, even to agree. I took a deep breath. I knew I had shouted at Kelly because that morning I had been afraid to shout at Danzig. There was a pain in the middle of my forehead. If Vim and Kelly had been worried about me before the outburst, they would be even more worried about me now.

"Sorry I blew up. It's...it's been a very long day already." I looked at my watch. The time was 1:45. "I have an appointment with Comrade Wong at two-fifteen."

"Wong," Kelly mused. She punched a panel button. The room stopped moving. "What's he tackling this time?"

"'Ethnic Diversity in the Cultural Renaissance of the Twenty-first Century.'"

She screwed her lips, thought for a few minutes, then shook her ponytail. "Was there one? Cultural Renaissance, I mean...."

"I don't know."

"Glad to hear that. I thought I was slipping."

Vim smiled. "No policy guidance, Kelly?"

"Not a shred."

Thinking about the speech made me feel better. "If Wong says there was a Cultural Renaissance, there probably was one."

"Yeah," she agreed. "A local phenomenon, maybe. He's solid on those weird topics. Drives me crazy on policy though when he accidentally touches on it. Tell you what, Mark, I'll send you something on Ethnic Politics. Maybe that'll help."

I doubted it, but I said "Thanks."

"Oh, and, here—" She thrust her hand into her rope bag and pulled out a policy guidance paper. "Here's the other stuff I promised you." She smiled. It was the Lifestyle paper.

We left the restaurant. Back in the underground, Kelly and Vim went in one direction, I in another. As I rode to the Board of Government building where Comrade Wong had his office, I was developing a theory about the lunch, the Club, my newly frank and friendly colleagues. Maybe I was just tired, but I kept seeing a net drop. A nice net, a helpful net, a net to protect me but, of course, to protect them as well. In the future, Kelly would call me "Mark," Danzig would force a smile, I'd be introduced to the other members of the Club, we'd discuss the past, deplore injustice, meet for drinks after work, plan ways in which we could improve the functioning of the Admin, count the number of wells dug in Somalia, laugh at Mr. Brown's foibles, draw up a new studio backdrop for the People's TV Assembly. Vim would keep in close touch. If I wanted to file a mismating petition against Lisa, they'd probably help me do it. I might even be able to see Christie again after work hours because my new friends knew that Undesirables didn't pollute and they'd muzzle Danzig. This was all fine, comforting even, and I needed a little comfort at the moment. But a net was a net, steel or mesh, it didn't matter.

NINE

THE UNDESIRABLE'S DIARY

After the Misfortune, when they destroyed all Professor Zilke's electronic data, they allowed him to keep his books, and so the Zilkes' apartment was full of books, piled on shelves, in corners, on the floor, one whole side of the dining room table, even in the bathroom. His books were boring, nothing but equations and diagrams; however, some of his wife's books were interesting, if you like reading, and as a child I learned to like it since there wasn't much else to do. It was a substitute for school. "You can learn a lot from books," Aunty Flo said, and I guess she was right because when I took the Admin entrance exam I passed it just as well as anyone.

Aunty Flo is an old woman now, almost seventy. Since I didn't dare confide in Jacques, and the black bag full of money couldn't lie forever in the bucket, I decided to ask her advice about what I should do with it.

I invited her to have a cup of tea with me in my room. When she came up the stairs, wearing a nice grey silk dress that she'd owned from before the Misfortune, I was glad I'd purchased some raspberry-flavored biscuits to go with the tea. We sat on the bed with the table in front of us. That was a little awkward, because she had trouble picking up the cup, and, since she didn't want to move to the chair, each time she wanted to take a sip of tea, I had to pick up the teacup for her, and then put it back on the table. Of course she commented on how pretty the teacups were, and that gave me the chance to tell her about Mark, who had given them to me, because although I'm sure that she and the Professor must have suspected we were lovers, they'd never said anything.

"Yes, dear." She nodded sympathetically. "I'm sure he must

have been a nice man. Most men would never have thought to buy a girl teacups."

"He gave me something else, though, Aunty," I said, "and this I don't know what to do with." I opened the bag of money and laid it out between us on the bed—all the purple and brown notes with the photos on them of Government House and a pine tree crossed with a palm and Commandant Pendleton Warner.

"Dear me," said Aunty Flo. "How extraordinary."

She stared at the banknotes and I stared at the banknotes and for several minutes we didn't say anything. Then she picked up a bundle and turned it around in her shriveled hands. "Are you sure, my dear," she asked delicately, "that your young man isn't involved in some illegal business? Why, that would be nothing to hold against him. Some of the nicest men end up in such endeavors. Look at the Professor!"

I couldn't help but smile. "No, Aunty, he's an important official in the Admin. He told me he sold some stock."

"Ah, stock," said the Professor's wife. "I remember. We had some once, before the Misfortune. I used to look at the screen each day to see whether it had gone up or down...."

I imagined small pieces of paper blowing up to the ceiling and then falling like confetti. She laid the money back on the blanket. "Well, dear, and so what are you going to do with this?"

"That's the problem, Aunty. I tried to give it back to him, but he said no."

"Well, I should hope he said no," said Aunty Flo. "He couldn't take back what he gave you, could he? That wouldn't have been proper. Why did you try to give it back to him?"

I was confused. I had expected her to be disapproving. "I...I felt like a prostitute."

"My dear child," said the Professor's wife, patting my hand, "nobody would ever take you for a prostitute, certainly not the kind of man who'd buy teacups. I can't imagine what gave you that idea. Your young man was just being nice, I daresay."

"But it's so much! Eight thousand dolyens!"

She shrugged her shoulders. "I suppose you think that's much. Well, dear, it isn't really. Not for a top Admin official. Why,

I recall before the Misfortune we knew people who would spend that much alone on a vacation to Europe. Not the Professor, you understand, never. He insisted on staying at university guest houses when we travelled, although I would have loved to have stayed in a grand hotel just once, but, no, he said it was exhibitionistic and of poor value. You'll see. The money will go just as fast as anything once you start to spend it."

"'Spend it?'" I was still trying to comprehend Aunty Flo's unexpected attitude toward the money.

"Well, what else can you do with it?" said Aunty Flo. She frowned a little. "Suppose the house caught on fire or something? That would be the end of it, wouldn't it? Really, Christie, sometimes you surprise me."

"But what will I spend it on?"

The Professor's wife blinked. "My dear child," she said, "is that a real question?"

"Yes. I just don't see what I can do with it."

Aunty Flo gazed up at the ceiling and addressed my deceased mother as though she could see her floating there. "Angela Riccardi, you see? What did I tell you? This is what comes of scrimping and saving and hiding your money in the toilet tank. Your daughter doesn't even know that she needs two chairs at a table, or a TV set, or curtains at the window, or a refrigerator—Now wouldn't that be nice, Christie?—or a pretty dress or a rug on the floor or a bed with a headboard and a mattress that doesn't have lumps in it.... Your young man must have been quite astonished at you, Christie."

I bit my lip. For the first time I wondered if maybe I hadn't been the one in the wrong, really wrong, about everything.

"He's not young, Aunty. He's—oh, almost forty."

The Professor's wife wiped her lips on the paper napkin. "Ancient indeed.... Does he have grey hair, my dear? Wrinkles? Joints creak when he moves? Tells you the same story twenty times over?"

I had to laugh. "No, no, Aunty. He's still very handsome."

"I should think so; I saw him once from the window. Better make me another cup of tea, dear. I never expected to have to tell a young girl how to spend money."

The Professor's wife accompanied me to buy the furniture because she could see I knew nothing about how to do it; and the Professor came too—to protect us, he said, which was nice, although he's too frail nowadays to protect anybody. They enjoyed the shopping more than I did. We browsed through the used furniture stores that line the open air market, and although to me it was all just, well, furniture, some heavier than others, some with fewer scratches, some with more decoration, if I'd left Aunty Flo to herself, she would have finished the eight thousand dolyens in a couple of weeks, buying brass headboards and glass china cabinets and reproductions of old paintings to replace my posters. I like my posters. The Professor backed me on that. "Now, Flo," he kept saying, "it's Christie's apartment." I refused to pay much for anything and we were careful never to buy more than one thing in one place on any one day, for fear thieves might think we had a lot of money and follow us home to rob us.

After we completed furnishing the room, we celebrated with a dinner to which I also invited Jacques Laye, because I wanted him to see that the Zilkes thought it was all right for me to have nice furniture. I wore the dress Aunty Flo had insisted I buy—a long one, white, with a gathered bodice. Jacques was astonished—I could see that; but he didn't say much until after dinner, after we had helped them back down the rickety stairs in the dark and made sure they were safely in their apartment, and then Jacques and I were standing once again before my door in the hallway on the second floor.

"Do you think it's terrible, Jacques?" I asked. "That I have nice things?"

"He gave them to you."

"He gave me the money to buy them."

"Well, I'm glad at least that he felt guilty enough to do something for you," said Jacques. "So he's gone, is he? Thank God for that."

I ignored the question. "He did it from love."

"Oh, all right," said Jacques. "Love, if you wish. I hope you're not seeing him any more anywhere."

"Only at work."

"At work?" Jacques's voice rose. I tried to shush him.

"You're still in his section? For God's sake, Christie, ask for a transfer! Do it, now! Immediately!"

I hesitated. "But why? I don't see.... He wants me to stay there. He says I'll be safer—"

"He doesn't know yam from cassava," snapped Jacques. He tapped his flashlight in the palm of his hand as though he'd like to hit Mark with it. "Haven't the Security people gotten on to you yet?"

I said nothing.

"Well?" He grabbed my shoulders and shook me, once, hard, as though he were trying to jolt catsup out of a bottle.

I caught my breath. Jacques has killed men, they say, although not since he joined the magic-makers. "Two agents came around the other day asking questions about him."

"Uh-huh. And?"

"I didn't tell them anything."

"You lied?"

"Of course."

He loosened his grip and let me tremble back against the door frame. "Okay." Then he patted my arm. "Well, what else could you have done? Maybe it's too late now to get out of his section."

One of the men had been rude and the other kept saying, "Now, Charlie, don't frighten the girl," but I knew they both came from the same office.

Afterwards I thought I should tell Mark, but I didn't know how to go about it now that Security was watching us. Maybe somebody else could tell him, somebody they wouldn't suspect, but who?

First I thought of Mr. Souza, his deputy. Mr. Souza is very reserved, very quiet, but one morning when the cafeteria guard was giving me the usual trouble, Mr. Souza, who had been waiting in the line far behind me, suddenly stepped forward and said to him: "This young lady is named Christine Riccardi. She works in the Speakers Division. Now, look at her face very carefully because if you don't recognize her tomorrow, then I shall have to report to Security that you're not very observant." The man gazed at Mr. Souza, and then he handed, not threw, my ID card back to me, and he turned away without saying a word; and after that he never bothered me again. However Mr. Souza said that if I had any more trouble, I should tell him.

So I thought about telling Mr. Souza about the agents; however I didn't know if Mr. Souza knew about Mark and me and I decided it might be awkward, their working in the same office.

The only other person I could think of was Steve Maine. Steve had told me that I could always count on him for legal advice if I needed it. Besides he was a friend of Mark's and could see him any time he wanted to.

Since I didn't want to telephone, I walked over to the Human Rights Legal Division, where I used to work; and although Steve's secretary told me to go back to Programs, that she'd have him call me, I waited. Finally she gave up and told him I was there. He came out of the office, coughing to cover his surprise. "Christie! I was just heading for the cafeteria. Come join me."

When we got to the cafeteria we carried our coffee out to the interior courtyard and sat down on a plastic bench in the late afternoon sun. I told him what had happened, and he said: "Shit! shit! shit!" and bit a fingernail.

"I guess Mark ought to know that they were asking about him."

"Oh, they've probably interviewed him now too. I just hope your stories hold together."

"It won't mean trouble for him, will it?"

Steve gave a short laugh. "For him? Don't worry. Mark's fast on his feet. He's had a lot of practice." I guess I must have looked unhappy at that, because he added quickly: "Sorry, Christie. This is all my fault. I knew Mark's reputation, but I never thought—"

"That he would be interested in a UD." I tried to keep the bitterness from my voice. To Steve, I'd always been a package, not a woman.

"Well, yes," said Steve. "I guess so. I didn't think Mark would take advantage of you."

"He didn't take advantage of me. It was all right. Really."

Steve smiled at me. "You're out of this world, Christie. Out of this world...." He put the empty coffee mug down on the ground between his feet and, leaning forward, clasped his hands' in front of him. "Now, listen. I wish I'd known about this before they talked to you, but don't worry. First, go to the library and look up Section Seven, 9-17.01, in the Admin Operating Guide. That will let you know what your rights are. They can't just fire you, although they'll try to give you that impression."

"Even UDs?"

"Any Admin employee, even UDs. They have to follow certain procedures. Say as little as possible. Often Security will just drop the case because it's not worth their time to follow through. If they proceed, as a last resort we can always file a grievance. That would tie them up for weeks trying to prove their allegations. Meanwhile the Admin has to go on paying your salary, all benefits intact, etc., etc."

"But wouldn't it be terrible for Mark if they could prove the allegations?"

"Not fatal. Not unless he does something so far out he could be dismissed anyway, and then they might try to blame it on your influence."

"Oh...." I covered my mouth with one hand.

"Don't worry." Steve frowned. "Mark's not crazy. He just acts like it sometimes. I'll warn him."

TEN

Comrade Wong's secretary, Fairouz Moked, was a willowy, six-foot-tall beauty who painted broad strokes of emerald eye shadow around her green eyes and spoke as though she had learned English at an air hostess training school. "Please be seated, Mr. Grimal. The Chairman will be with you when he finishes his session with the Afghan ambassador." She was as remote and inaccessible as the telecommunications panel outside Comrade Wong's office. Taking my cue, I waited silently, with an occasional admiring glance at her long fingers pressing buttons and lights, her frigid profile etched against the beige panel. Every woman has her rhythm, and if there is a secret to my success, it's that I always let her follow it.

The Afghan ambassador finally emerged, accompanied by his three-member entourage, all of them dressed in their traditional robes. "You may go into Comrade Wong's chamber now, Mr. Grimal."

"Thank you, Fairouz."

Four feet ten inches tall, Comrade Wong was standing behind his ornate desk, ripping in half a computer print-out, which he then stapled together and tossed into his out-basket. "Mark. Good to see you. Sit down. The language policy is a disaster. I warned them. You can't make every village tribesman learn English." Whose language policy? But Wong was talking to himself, not to me. Coming over to the sofa, he perched himself on a leather armchair, and started defining what he wanted in his speech.

As Kelly had suspected, the "Cultural Renaissance" was a San Francisco Bay Area flowering between the years 2045 and 2055, based upon a renewed interest in forms that had evolved in the 1950s. "Get the names right," ordered Wong. "The audience will know the subject. Brimacelli, Fontaine, Togami, Novak in music, who else? Martinez, don't forget Martinez...."

I had no idea what he was talking about, but I took notes furiously.

"What I want to emphasize is that both the cultural flowering and its decay were due to the ethnic component. Are you following me?"

"No," I answered honestly.

Wong smiled. He liked being told that he was way ahead of the rest of us. For the next five minutes he gave me his theory of culture: diversity stimulated response; responses coalesced; the resulting culture glowed for a brief period, then collapsed under attacks from those who wanted a return to traditional ethnic cultural values; decay set in. "I want them to think about how cultures are created. I want arguments," said Wong.

"How long?"

"An hour."

One hour was a lot of words when you didn't know what you were talking about; I'd have to give Waldir the Saturday public service program on South Africa to complete. Just as well, since I now knew there was no war in South Africa. "May I have until three p.m. tomorrow to get the first draft over here?"

He hesitated, then said, "Since it's you, yes."

I went back to the office and set the staff to researching the information in my notes. Tony made bios for the leading writers, artists, and musicians; Ramona summarized the basic facts; but I needed quotes, strong ones, and for that there was no substitute for reading through the literature. By 4:00 p.m. my head was throbbing and the walls looked rosy. I talked the MedUnit out of four stimulant pills—two for now, two for when I got up at 3:00 a.m. to start the writing. I stayed working at the office until 6:30.

When I arrived home Lisa greeted me in a long, backless, satin gown that clung to her bare buttocks and scooped into her crotch. She was floating in a cloud of perfume and the smell of roast beef from the kitchen. Exhausted as I was, this struck me as wondrously comical, something out of the poetry I'd just been reading. To her consternation, I collapsed in laughter on the living room couch. "Lisa, I've got to go to work tonight!" That was a tactical error on my part because, infuriated, she leapt on top of me and started pummeling me with her fists. I defended myself, one thing led to another, and we ended up screwing on the floor, just as she had intended. Afterwards I was so tired, I couldn't even stay awake for the roast beef.

At 2:30 the next day the transmitter operator Beatrice faxed the first draft of the speech to Comrade Wong's office in the Government House Building. By 5:30 I had it back from Wong, robot-delivered, all scratched up, but with "Good" written across the top. Not all of his corrections were stylistic improvements from my point of view, but I wouldn't argue: it was his speech. I gave the text to Beatrice to revise and re-print. A few minutes later Fairouz Moked called me.

"More changes, Fairouz?"

"No, Mr. Grimal," she replied coolly. "Comrade Wong has asked me to check to see if you would be able to accompany him to San Francisco. It now appears that he will need you there. On Saturday he has been asked to deliver a short address at the opening of a bicultural exhibit on media resources. On Monday, the Department of Foreign Interests has proposed a lecture at one of the universities on the historical origins of the Pacific fishing industry. Unfortunately he does not yet have complete details on these events and the university topic may change. We shall be departing the Transport Cabins at eight-thirty p.m. on Thursday evening, that is to say, tomorrow."

"I'll have to get clearance. You know, the Saturday public affairs program on GTV—"

"Comrade Wong has thought of that. As you know, he will participate via satellite. From Headquarters in San Francisco we can take care of any coordination that you might need to do in connection with the program. I shall be sending you first thing tomorrow an offical note to expedite the clearance of your travel documents through Security. May we count on you, Mr. Grimal?"

I liked the use of "we" in Fairouz's cool voice.

"Of course. Ah...just one thing, Fairouz. My wife will ask if she can come along...."

"I very much regret to inform you that Comrade Wong does

not permit the inclusion of spouses in his entourage. He says it detracts from the work atmosphere."

"I understand. I'll break the news to her."

Definitely Comrade Wong was my type of client.

On Thursday morning Steve Maine buzzed me on the intercom to suggest that we have a drink after work.

"Sorry. I'm leaving for San Francisco at eight-thirty."

"A fast one, then," said Steve. "It's moderately urgent."

Since "moderately urgent" was Steve's code for "you've done it again, dummy," I groaned and agreed, then called Lisa and asked her to pack the suitcase for me.

At 5:30 Steve and I went to a quiet neighborhood pub near the Federal Planetarium and ordered Mexican beer. The pub was decorated like an old parish church. In the rear near the dart board a bank of candles burned before a mural celebrating the Federal Territory football team's 2076 victory over Brazil in the World Finals.

"So, what's up?"

"You know what's up," said Steve. He looked annoyed, or at least as annoyed as Steve would ever allow himself to look—frown, clenched jaw, tie askew, fingers tapping the table. "What maybe you don't know is that now they're after Christie."

"Oh, shit!" I closed my eyes and slumped back on the bench.

"A surprise maybe?" Steve's voice oozed sarcasm. "You've got the entire Federal Territory to choose from and you had to mess up some poor dumb UD kid—"

I jerked to an upright position. "Hold it!"

Steve cleared his throat and drew back slightly, pulling his beer glass across the table toward him. Usually I let him rant away, but this time, since I knew that Lisa had told Rita months ago about Christie and me, I was certain he had long known, and therefore I found his sudden outrage particularly hypocritical. "You don't know what you're talking about so just shut up for a few minutes."

That impressed him. He poured the balance of his bottle into his glass. The beer foamed up, glowed in the light from the stained glass window above us. Steve leaned back against the carved mahogany bench and rubbed the side of his forehead. "Okay, so I don't know shit. So tell me."

I trusted Steve, as those things went in the Admin, but we weren't exactly—or even remotely—alike. I had met him during my first big encounter with Security. Since then he'd tried to keep me out of trouble, or at least to mop up afterwards, and our wives had become friends; but most of the time we just talked past each other. As a lawyer, Steve was considered a good one. The reason he hadn't risen as high as he should have in the Admin was because he'd lost the Balthazar De Jonge case eight years before. But then any lawyer would have lost that case. Balthazar De Jonge was the EcoDev Assistant Director who had been caught by Security funneling development money to the rebels in the New York subway system. De Jonge was definitely wacko, but the Admin couldn't hush things up by restructuring him with drugs and then tucking him away in some damp, bureaucratic corner, because this was no administrative error; this was treason. Not only did Security have proof, but also De Jonge himself kept bragging about how he'd done it all in the name of the Liberation Struggle. The lawyers ran for cover. Someone, though, had to defend De Jonge before the People's TV Court or he couldn't be tried; the Government chose Steve. Human Rights types get all the garbage.

Steve entered an insanity plea. That should have worked; after all, De Jonge had been making his immediate staff write memos to one another in crytograms based on ancient Egyptian. Unfortunately, during the trial he started to rave about the noble Liberation Struggle, and although Steve tried to pull the plug, Security insisted the tech crew play the whole thing through with closeups of Balthazar De Jonge's foaming mouth. After that, one could say, as Steve did, that De Jonge's speech proved he was crazy; however, the People voted for Execution, and the Chairmen refused to consider Steve's appeal for a stay.

What happened afterward was that Steve, who had been furious with Security for exhibiting a sick man on television, began to take on cases that Security would have preferred to have come up only in a late night TV slot or bunched together for mass disposal in a weekend court menu. He was particularly good at "widows and orphans." If a charge was dropped and you examined the fine print, you'd often discover Steve's name listed as defense attorney, and usually free of charge. He also got a reputation within the Admin of being the man you went to if, like me, you needed help fast. None of this aided his career, which froze solid at an M-18. He could have unfrozen it by changing sides, but he didn't. I respected him for that, and even though I didn't anticipate ending up like Balthazar De Jonge, I figured Steve had the experience to cope should I need it.

But what could I possibly tell him about my relationship with Christie that he'd understand? Despite Rita's suspicions, Steve most certainly had never had an affair with Christie, nor could he imagine any normal man wanting to do so. Maybe I wasn't normal.

"Christie's a wonderful person. I'm extremely fond of her."

"Uh-huh. Go on," said Steve.

"I intend to take care of her for the rest of her life."

Steve blinked. He drained the beer from the glass, and, twisting around in his seat, gestured to the waiter who was standing at the bar. "Two more beers, please."

"Not for me," I said. "I've got to stay alert for Comrade Wong."

"One," said Steve. We stared at each other across the table until the beer came and the waiter withdrew.

"Don't give me the details," said Steve. "At this point I don't want to know. Just one question: how do you think you're taking care of Christie when you've got Security on her tail?"

"Score one for you, Steve."

"Dumb, Mark. Dumb."

"No argument." I swirled my glass around in watery figure eights on the table top.

"Well, all you can do now is be very careful, because you know who'll be blamed for—"

"Corrupting me. I know. Danzig's on it."

"The Man himself? He ought to have more important things to worry about than your sex life."

"What could be more important?"

Steve shook his head. "I don't get you." Then he croaked out a small laugh. "All these years. I still don't get you."

It was a good thing that I had once visited San Francisco as a tourist because traveling with Wong gave me no chance to see any of it but glimpses on the in-house monitor as a backdrop to the Chairman's activities. The four days we were there I was holed up at Headquarters on Twin Peaks, writing and revising with the help of only one transmitter operator, a native Hungarian speaker named Desirée, who was a computer whiz but, as far as I could tell, practically illiterate in English. Wong had surrounded himself with staff people like that. There was the cool Fairouz, who talked like a recording; the Colombian staff director, rattling away in Spanish to the local politicians; a Vietnamese economic adviser; a Yoruba program coordinator, who spoke formal English on the phone but, in person, pidgin; and a French media officer. They all seemed to understand one another, but I could see why Wong had asked me to come along to write his speeches.

The text for the opening of the bicultural exhibit on media resources was simple; however, the university lecture, which suddenly became a major address on "The Historical Origins of East-West Trade," was one of the most difficult I'd ever tackled, flung there alone without a staff. Although I could plug into the Admin resources by computer, Desirée was no help as a researcher. It was simpler to do it myself. The Vietnamese econ adviser was amiable about providing leads and he checked my facts afterwards, but I didn't want Wong to sound like an economist: he was a politician relating to academicians—"Look, you guys, this is what it means in the real world." The trouble was I wasn't sure what it did mean in the real world; I was no longer even certain what the real world was. On Sunday morning at 7:00, with a 10:00 a.m. first-draft deadline looming ahead of me, Fairouz noticed my dilemma and offered to help. Her English might be stilted, but it was English, so I gratefully turned the editing and proofing over to her. We made the deadline, just barely; however, Wong decided he didn't like the angle and I had to rewrite the entire thing by 3:00 p.m.

Unfortunately Fairouz was gone for most of that time because Wong was touring the naval works and he liked her to carry his briefcase. It was one of the peculiar touches I had noticed from the time we left the Transport Cabins on Thursday and she declined to let me do it for her. "Thank you, no, Mr. Grimal. Comrade Wong prefers that I carry it." Maybe she was the only person he trusted; maybe he liked having a six-foot, exotic beauty as the handmaiden to his four-foot-ten power package. They did make quite a picture, as from time to time I glimpsed them on the Headquarters monitor: diminutive Wong flashing his set smile, somber Fairouz looming behind him. When they got back to Headquarters at 2:30, Fairouz rushed in to help me put the last touches on the second draft. She was as cool, efficient, and remote as always, but after we handed over the text, she said: "It appears, Mr. Grimal, that you have not eaten lunch. Permit me to order you something from the dining room."

"Yes, I'd better re-fuel before I have to write the third version."

She almost smiled. "Comrade Wong is very demanding, but he considers your work to be of the highest quality. If you were not a member of the Admin, he would ask you to join his staff."

"I'd like that."

"I think you would. Unfortunately, as you know, there's a regulation forbidding the Chairmen to 'raid' the Admin personnel. You would have to work elsewhere for two years before we could hire you."

She appeared to be passing the word. The regulation that Fairouz cited was based on the idea that the Admin was a neutral, problem-solving institution that should be above politics. If competent Admin people could be hired away by the highest bidder, then one Chairman might collect the greatest number of experts, the balance of power would shift to him, and the world might be plunged into chaos once again. It was one of those regulations that sound very sensible until you discover that they affect your career personally. I was chagrined. Although, under any circumstances, I'd be tempted by an offer from Wong, if I left my career status job in the Admin, where would I spend the intervening two years? And supposing I did locate something comparable, by the end of two years, Wong might no longer be a Chairman.

After approving seventy percent of the second version of the speech on East-West trade, Wong left to discuss the local Chinese-language curriculum with the global educational consultant. "Almost there, Mark," he called out cheerfully. To my surprise, he left the briefcase and Fairouz at Headquarters. As she sat down at a work station beside me, Fairouz solemnly explained that she did not speak Chinese. "In Comrade Wong's opinion I might be more useful here working with you."

She was indeed helpful. After an hour of editing, she suddenly said, "Mr. Grimal, would you permit me to make a few comments? I think I see where your mind and that of the Chairman are not meshing."

Meshing was a great word. "Please do."

"I think Comrade Wong has been too busy to explain fully his thinking on this topic. You are looking at it from the economic point of view. Comrade Wong does not consider trade primarily an economic issue."

"He doesn't?"

"No. Comrade Wong looks at it in a larger context as a point of contact between differing cultures. He says pots are like seeds, oil is like semen. He calls the process 'fertilization.'"

I didn't dare to laugh, or at least not until she did. "Those are direct quotes, I assume?"

She did, then, smile faintly. "Yes, Mr. Grimal. I could not make it up that way."

"Too bad we can't use them. Thanks, Fairouz." But then I wondered, Why not use them? He'd cut it out if he didn't want to say it. So we used them, and he loved it.

By 9:00 p.m. I had completed what I thought was my final job on the trip. However, at 10:30, as I was about to step into the shower, the phone rang. The French media assistant had convinced Comrade Wong to attend a media association group meeting at 5:00 p.m. the next day. Jean-Paul was apologetic; he said he usually wrote the Chairman's remarks in French, which Fairouz then translated into English: however, since I was here with no other commitment tomorrow, Comrade Wong had suggested that perhaps I wouldn't mind throwing together, oh, say, about twenty minutes on the role of the media in a democratic society, spiced with references to local organizations, both modern and historical.

I wondered how Wong managed when he didn't have an
English language speech writer with him. Did Jean-Paul do everything in French first? Or did they divide up the job—Babatunde in
pidgin, Carlos in Spanish, Nha contributing his economic input in
Vietnamese, Fairouz recycling it all into air hostess English?

I told Jean-Paul I'd be delighted.

Seated in front of the Headquarters monitor on Monday
afternoon, I watched Comrade Wong at the media group meeting.
Ninety percent of the members of the association worked for the
government, directly or indirectly, and there he was discussing the
role of the media in a democratic society. On this occasion he
dutifully said what they all said; he stuck to policy: the media was
the Voice of the People.

Tonight Jean-Paul was carrying the briefcase; they were
going to a dinner afterward. Fairouz said she did not attend dinners
with the Chairman; that would not be appropriate. Behind me she
was shredding, filing, packing up in anticipation of our 6:00 a.m.
departure tomorrow.

Suddenly I thought: airport. World Chairmen always made
speeches at airports.

I abandoned my chair, sat down at a work station, and turned
on the computer. Fairouz stopped shredding papers. Over my shoulder I heard: "Are you not finished, Mr. Grimal?"

"He may need some remarks at the airport. I'll keep it
simple. We don't want to hold up the air shuttle."

She came over to my side and watched for a moment in
silence. The formal stuff like this was easy to do: there was a limit
to how creative even Comrade Wong could be at an airport.

Then Fairouz said: "You do like to work, don't you, Mr.
Grimal?"

"Well, there's work and there's work," I replied. "I hate
writing speeches for people who don't care what's in them, who
have no ideas of their own. They tempt me to do mad things, like
make up a phony event or contradict a policy statement or mock the
eternal verities, like Universal Democratic Participation. Then I
wait to see if they'll notice. Often they don't."

The mascara was slightly smudged around her big green eyes; she had lost an earring. "Doesn't that get you into trouble?"

"Occasionally." I grinned up at her. "I once was suspended for a week after describing the Central African Republic as a fascist dictatorship located off the coast of Finland. The Chairman happened to be in the Central African Republic at the time he delivered the speech. They couldn't prove that I did it deliberately; they just nailed me for proof-reading negligence."

She looked genuinely alarmed. "But that's terrible, Mr. Grimal. Someday you will make a dreadful mistake, and they will not be forgiving. Promise me you won't do that any more."

Promise her! She sounded like my mother. But she wasn't my mother, or my sister, or my wife, or my mistress, or even a friend yet. She was delicious. I restrained an urge to kiss her.

"You're right," I solemnly agreed. "It's immature, adolescent behavior, and could be fatal. I promise to resist temptation."

She went back to her work while I finished the airport remarks. As I was running off copies, ancient jazz music came on in the background and I smelled marijuana. I looked in the direction of her now clean desk; she was bent over it lighting a reefer. She tossed back her thick black hair and took a deep puff, then stood up and came toward me, holding out the cigarette, with its smudge of raspberry lipstick.

Ordinarily I avoid drugs; they don't do a thing for one's literary style; but work was over and this was an offer of more than marijuana. I took a short puff and handed back the cigarette; her lipstick had a creamy taste, like a soda. "Speaking of work, you're a super-woman. Thanks again for the help on the lecture."

She smiled. "I suppose there are many people who would not believe that either of us work."

It was a personal comment, the first to indicate that she knew anything about me beyond the fact that I wrote speeches. I put the airport remarks in an envelope and tossed it onto the top of my briefcase. "It's strange about people. They'd rather believe that they too could do what you do if only they had your wit or beauty or ability to manipulate, rather than think you achieve it through work, which is open to everybody."

She drew on the reefer. "In my case, Mr. Grimal, they usually put it more crudely. No, I do not sleep with Comrade Wong, in case you too have been wondering."

Of course I'd been wondering, but since it obviously annoyed her, I didn't admit it. "I'm glad you don't, but if you did, I'm sure that wouldn't be why he hired you."

"That was diplomatic." She smiled and sat down in a contoured work station chair. Marijuana was affecting her personality; she had become ironic, intense, aggressive. Was this the real Fairouz or was it the air hostess? She leaned far back in the chair and stretched like a cat. I kept hands off.

"Do you want to sleep with me?"

I replied: "Of course. Wouldn't any man?"

"Why, no," she said. "Quite a few men don't want to when they know anything about me. Why don't you sit down, Mr. Grimal?"

I sat down. "Call me Mark."

"Oh, I can't do that. I might forget and say it in front of the Chairman. Comrade Wong believes that proper respect should be maintained at all times between staff members and the rest of the world."

"Then I'll have to call you Miss Moked."

"Mrs.," she corrected. "My husband is an Undesirable. I abandoned him." She was watching me closely with her ironic green eyes. "I tried living one week in the UD district and I thought, 'I can't do this,' and so I abandoned him. If we'd had children, I suppose I would have been trapped in that nightmare; it's harder to abandon children."

None of this was what I expected to hear; I became wary of where the conversation was heading. "No one could blame you for that. The UDs live a rotten life."

"Don't they?" she said. "But he blames me anyway. Never mind that my salary pays for his medicine, his food, everything. I have to sneak it to someone in the district who takes care of him. He won't speak to me. He won't look at me. He's right: what kind of love is it when you can't go down into the sewer with someone to spend the rest of your life?"

"Mrs. Moked, why are you telling me this?"

She leaned forward. The cigarette was now a stub. Her voice sounded huskier. "For two reasons. One is that if you want to make love to me, it is only fair to both of us that you should know about my husband. He was declared an Undesirable because he has a contagious, incurable disease—not sexual—and I have tested negative for it every year for six years. Still many men find the situation not conducive to a relaxed performance in bed."

I took her hand, removed the cigarette, and extinguished it in a coffee mug. I didn't say anything; I just held her hand. The fingers doubled up, but she didn't pull away. She looked at the monitor. Comrade Wong and Jean-Paul were riding an antique cable car up Powell Street while people cheered.

"And the second reason?"

"The second reason," she said slowly, continuing to watch the monitor, "is that I understand you know what it's like to love a UD. That's what people tell me."

I didn't move. We watched Comrade Wong and Jean-Paul enter a restored, twentieth century hotel, called the Fairmont. They moved through the lobby, went to a dining room. People stood to applaud. The doors closed in the face of the cameraman. The footage shifted wildly around the hotel, then went blank. Fairouz reached over with her free hand and turned off the monitor. We were in the Headquarters with only the distant sound of jazz and the computers humming. I knew that my silence was as much a confirmation as though I had spoken, but Fairouz had used the word "love," a word that meant so many things that it was worthless. Did I love Christie? I was drawn to Christie, but when I thought of her I thought mainly of an injured child whom I wanted to help, someone who had the right to make just demands on me, someone to protect and care for. Certainly I had told Christie I loved her; therefore, I would never deny it; but making love to her was like trying to pour medicine on a wound. If she had an orgasm, I was as proud as a doctor noting an improvement in a patient's condition. I liked myself better, I felt more like a decent human being, when I was with Christie. Under her adoration I swelled into a gracious, benign deity. Was that love? Or wasn't it something rather more self-centered?

And "love" was not the word that those faceless ones who talked about "Mark Grimal's UD" had used when they told Fairouz about Christie.

"Alternative Four, the capital of the Federal Territory, is a city of seven million, three hundred and six thousand people," I said bitterly. "It contains the highest per capita collection of experts in all fields of human endeavor, with the exception of the artistic, which prefers a more intimate mud. The International Library has a copy of every book ever printed in any language; the theaters and video viewing centers show innumerable productions. There are restaurants, parks, sports facilities, concert halls, one hundred and six museums. And yet, and yet, at any given hour of the day or night here, it seems that to some people one of the most fascinating topics in the entire Federal Territory is my sex life."

"I didn't say 'sex life,'" said Fairouz.

"No, but the people who told you said it."

"Mr. Grimal," she said, "I apologize. I didn't mean to upset you." She tried to withdraw her hand but I kept hold of it. "I mentioned it because...there are times when I think how good it would be to be able to talk to somebody about this—this—" Her voice broke off, then recovered. "—this vicious, disgusting system of, of slavery that we justify by scientific explanations and call it the will of the People."

The gossips were right: we had a lot in common.

I brought her hand to my lips and kissed it. "The science is fake. Maybe in the old days when entire races were held as slaves and considered genetically inferior, things were worse, but now, since we all work together, play together, and despise the same things together, officially discrimination no longer exists. Therefore, if a person is declared an Undesirable, he must deserve it. No group will complain on his behalf. Nobody is interested."

"My husband didn't choose to get his disease," said Fairouz.

"Fear is another element. Isolate them."

"And your friend?"

I didn't want to talk about Christie, but I saw I had to.

"She's one of those 'innocent victims' whom people point to as an unfortunate byproduct of the genetic policy: the child of an

Undesirable. Her father was involved in the Maldives rebellion. Her mother stayed with the family and was killed trying to protect her daughter from rape at the age of eleven. You're lucky you didn't have any children...."

Fairouz squeezed my hand tightly. "And now?"

"Someone threatened to go to Security. Now I try to take care of her at a distance."

"It isn't easy," said Fairouz. "It isn't easy."

This was not how I had imagined us falling into each other's arms. This was nothing like it at all.

Although we briefly considered going out, to save time we had dinner together in the Headquarters dining room. Then we went to Fairouz's room, where we spent the night, with the curtains pulled open and the moonlight sifting through the fog outside her window. She was elegant and unpredictable and tasted like almond-flavored whipped cream. We "meshed" together very well, two times in bed, once in the chair, the last time in the shower at four o'clock in the morning with her long hair plastered around us by the water. At 5:00 a.m. when I climbed into one of the official cars parked in front of the Headquarters, I felt tired but invigorated. It had been the best working trip that I could remember. From the Headquarters' bronze doors Wong emerged, Fairouz behind him, cool and remote, carrying his briefcase. Below us San Francisco was still blanketed with fog. I handed Wong the draft airport remarks. "Good thinking, Mark." Maybe the Admin would be happy to get rid of me; maybe I could get an exemption from the rule and go to work for Wong.

It was a nice thought but it only lasted until the air shuttle stopped at Minneapolis. There Jean-Paul disembarked and returned with an armload of news sheets from around the world. Jean-Paul was all smiles; he had done his job well. Every front page carried Wong's picture at the university, with banner headlines acclaiming the speech on East-West trade. Inside were expanded biographies of Wong, commentaries on Wong, photographs of Wong waving from the cable car, excerpts from the speech, quotes from Wong's book on ethnicity, even a poem by an eight-year-old Asante schoolboy calling Wong "a star in the murkiness of mendacity." I sank down

in my seat and pretended to be asleep. The other Chairmen were
going to be furious.

ELEVEN

THE UNDESIRABLE'S DIARY

After what Steve had said, I was frightened to think that somebody might be watching me all the time; however, the only one who seemed to be doing that was the guard from the cafeteria, who had been transferred to our floor. He didn't give me any trouble; I just didn't like the idea of his being stationed there near the stairway to the roof. I wondered if maybe I had been doing something illegal by eating lunch on the roof, although surely Mark would have told me.

When the guard was there on Thursday, I decided to go to the cafeteria for lunch. The next day I delayed lunch until 1:15. Since the guard wasn't in the hall when I came out, I went up to the roof as usual; however, on returning to work at two o'clock, I had to brush by him at the foot of the stairs.

He glared at me but he didn't say anything.

TWELVE

When I got home Tuesday night, Waldir Souza called to warn me that a furor had broken out in my absence. "Mark," he said, "you lucky dog. There you were in San Francisco—"

"Working."

"—Oh, yes," said Waldir, "we could tell you were working. Wong hit the television news every night and the news sheet headlines every morning. Why don't you act like other people on these trips and enjoy yourself?"

"Working's how I enjoy myself. What happened?"

"To begin with, Brown was miffed that you weren't at the Saturday program—"

"That's ridiculous. You did a great job with the speech." Waldir was an excellent writer. He used more adjectives and adverbs and elaborate little phrases than I did, but some people, like Mallam Ahmed, preferred his style to mine.

"Thanks, but, well, you know how Brown is: likes to have the head of section bowing at his elbow. So after the program he called Danzig and demanded to know why Security had given the chief of the Speakers Division clearance to write personal speeches for Wong in San Francisco—"

"Personal!"

"—when an important public affairs program was scheduled in the Global Studios. Danzig told Brown the clearance was in order. However, afterward he came down and implied that you shouldn't have accepted the assignment even if Wong had requested you do it..."

"My pal, Danzig."

"...Then came the East-West trade speech. Nobody knew Wong was going to give the speech except some Foreign Interests officers—you know how they are—who forgot to clear the concept with Polyguide."

I groaned. Chairmen didn't clear speeches with Polyguide but if an Admin department proposed a speech, the department was supposed to clear the idea first. Kelly Hallihan's obscenities must been blanketing the Admin building. "The poor guys."

"Yeah, Kelly's out for blood. Wong's going to have to intervene personally to save their necks. Nobody blames you for that—"

"That's a relief."

"—Only for writing the best speech Wong has ever given, that's all. Who usually handles Wong's personal speech writing?"

"I think it's a group effort."

"Well, if it isn't, it sounds like it; and that's just fine with the other Big Two. But now, all of a sudden, Wong sounded literate for a change—"

"He's always literate."

"No, Mark. Informed, yes. Literate, no. The speech was a blockbuster—"

Despite everything I was pleased.

"—and that even annoyed Ahmed, who had tried to calm Brown down about the Saturday program embroglio. You know, the most outstandingly favorable coverage of the speech was in the Associated Territories, and a lot of them are in Ahmed's region. Ahmed keeps saying: 'Perhaps Mr. Grimal might be so kind as to compose a speech like that for me some day.' So, you see, everybody's mad at you for doing a good job."

"Except Wong."

"Right. And he's laughing all the way to the December election."

"Well, thanks, Waldir. I'll try to get things straightened out tomorrow." I didn't anticipate much luck.

"Mark—" Waldir wasn't finished. "There's another problem, not connected to this one. I don't want to tell you over the phone. First thing tomorrow, okay?"

"Sure." What a great sleep I was going to have this evening.

I hung up the phone. Lisa had been sitting across the room in a corner of the couch, pretending to read a historical novel that had a helmeted warrior from the Western Dark Ages on the cover. She had been unusually cool this evening. She had not thrown herself at me as I walked in the door, nor had she asked whom I had slept with in San Francisco, nor had she prepared a special dinner to welcome me home. In fact, she had prepared no dinner at all. This undoubtedly portended bad news, and I had had enough bad news for an evening. I went into the kitchen, fixed myself a tall Scotch-and-soda, dumped some crackers and slices of Gouda cheese on a plate, and stretched out on the bench in the breakfast nook. I thought of Fairouz Moked lifting her slip above her head in the foggy moonlight. I thought of her darting tongue on my cock. I thought of how we were going to meet tomorrow night at the Sub-Orbital.

"Pleasant dreams?" asked Lisa. I opened my eyes. She sat down on the bench opposite me. She was wearing a Japanese kimono with purple birds on it. "Must be a new woman. Nothing else gives you that expression."

"Lisa, I worked hard in San Francisco. Lay off."

"I know, I know," she said sweetly. "You worked hard. So, like a good boy, you deserved your dessert. Isn't that how you always justify it?"

"Do we have to fight my first night home?"

She smiled in a nasty, sweet way. "Depends on whether or not you can answer some questions."

I took a swallow of my drink. "Go ahead. Get it over with."

"Why did you sell our Telecom International stock?"

Oh. I swung my feet to the floor. For moment my mind went blank: I could't remember how I had planned to answer this question, which I knew, sooner or later, she would ask, at tax time maybe, but this wasn't tax time.

She acknowledged her victory. "My, we didn't expect that question, did we? Sometimes these questions about our finances just pop into my head." I didn't believe that. Ordinarily Lisa's idea of financial planning was to update personal ID access codes.

I fought for time. "I've been meaning to tell you. It just kept slipping my mind."

"Sure you meant to tell me."

"The price went up. It seemed like a good time to sell."

"Then we made a nice profit, right? Where's the money?"

"I, ah, I invested it in a housing project."

"Really?" Her nasty smile got nastier. "Where? In the UD district?"

"In Saudi Arabia. Look, Lisa—"

She leaned forward and practically whispered the words: "Lies, lies, lies! You gave eight thousand dolyens of our money to that UD slut you're keeping."

Methodically I put a piece of cheese on a cracker. I took a sip of Scotch. I stood up and went to the bedroom. My suitcase was still packed. From the chest of drawers I extracted three clean shirts and some underwear and put them in the suitcase, took my grey suit out of the closet, and picked up the photograph of my parents that was taken on their silver wedding anniversary in Ontario. Lisa was standing in the doorway watching me.

"What do you think you're doing?"

I didn't answer. I shoved past her into the living room and removed several books from the bookcase behind the leather sofa. I piled them on the coffee table. From the media unit storage compartment I chose six discs of eighteenth and nineteenth century chamber music, three classic twenty-first century videos, and a documentary on Iceland. I was doing all this as though I had planned it, but I hadn't planned it, and I had no interest in Iceland. Lisa was screaming my name in the background. I continued to ignore her. In the kitchen I picked up the Gouda cheese, the box of crackers, the bottle of Scotch, and some instant soup mix in a container that plugged into a wall outlet. She grabbed my arm. I pushed her aside. These things weren't going to fit into my suitcase. From among the baskets with dried flowers set beneath the picture window, I grabbed one, dumped the flowers, and tossed books, discs, food, into it.

I turned again to the bedroom—just in time to intercept my blue shirt as it came whirling out. Lisa had ejected the contents of my suitcase onto the floor. She was tossing things in every direction. The bedroom lamp crashed over. I leapt to catch a can of deodorant which was zooming toward the picture window. The photograph of my parents crashed at my feet. I hurtled toward the bedroom. "Lisa! You crazy bitch! Stop that!" A shoe brush bounced with a crack off the mirror. She hurled a handful of underwear into my face. I grabbed her and pinned her arms to her side. She bit my wrist, but I hung on, pushed her back onto the bed and held her there until she stopped strugling. Somewhere a telephone was ringing.

We both sat up, breathing heavily. One sleeve of her kimono had been ripped. Blood was oozing out of the punctures on my wrist. Since I was the nearest to the phone, I picked up the receiver. "Hello."

"Mr. Grimal," said a raspy feminine voice. "This is Betty Doherty next door. Are you two all right?"

I closed my eyes. "Yes, Mrs. Doherty. Sorry. We'll turn down the video."

"Oh, was that noise the video?" she asked, knowing it wasn't. "I'm so relieved. Well, welcome back from your trip, Mr. Grimal."

"Thank you, Mrs. Doherty." I hung up. We were now the scandal of the Atlas Towers West, and just lucky that we didn't have a shattered picture window as outside evidence. I lay back on the bed, crushing my grey suit beneath me. Lisa put her face in her hands and wept.

"Lisa, I want a mismating decree."

"No!"

"I'm going to file a petition tomorrow."

"No, you're not."

"Yes, I am, Lisa." I closed my eyes. How had we gotten to this stage? I seemed to remember that in the beginning we had enjoyed each other. "I agree with you that it's all my fault. They made a mistake with the tests. You need someone who is faithful and truthful and kind and loving. I'm none of those things, as you continually tell me. And you're right: I'm not. So let's not wallow in it. Let's break up and get on to something better."

She said: "You'd better think twice. Mr. Danzig tells me that you would have been kicked out of the Admin years ago if you hadn't had a stable doublestyle relationship."

Danzig! She'd been talking to Danzig. I sat up. "When did you see Danzig?"

"Friday he called, said he needed to update our security clearances, and came by. We chatted for an hour or so."

"And I suppose he said to you, 'Mrs. Grimal, I don't want to raise questions in your mind, but I think maybe you'd better find out why your husband sold a large amount of stock recently.' Isn't that how he said it?"

"Well, what's the answer, Mark? Give me the answer."

"I'll do better than that," I said, standing up. "I'll find eight thousand dolyens and give them to you."

Fully dressed, I spent the night on the couch in the living room, wondering between fitful bouts of sleep how I was going to come up with the money. If I had known where to find eight thousand dolyens easily, I would never have sold the stock. Whenever I woke I heard Lisa whimpering in the bedroom. At 5:00 a.m. she came in and crawled up on the couch beside me. She laid her head on my shoulder. I pretended to sleep. She started trying to undo the belt buckle on my pants. I turned my back to her. "Please, Mark this is terrible. Let's make up."

"Fucking is your idea of making up," I said.

She drew away. After a few minutes she got up. I could hear her tidying the room, putting the cheese back in the refrigerator, the books on the bookshelf, the dried flowers in the basket. She was sweeping up the glass. "I'm sorry about your parents' photo, Mark. I'll get it reframed." "O.K." At least now we were being polite to each other. When I went into the bathroom, I locked the door to make sure she didn't join me in the shower.

THIRTEEN

At 8:30 a.m. when I arrived at work, Program staff people were standing around in little clusters, whispering to one another. They greeted me in a subdued though friendly manner and scattered to their work stations. Penny had stacked my correspondence neatly in the middle of my desk in a folder marked "Private." The top item was a memo from Mr. Brown requesting my presence in his Board of Government chamber at 11:30 that morning. I started reading through the mail, then realized that Penny and Waldir had come into my office and closed the door behind them.

This must be the "other problem." I closed the folder. Penny sat down on the sofa, Waldir perched on the arm of a chair. Only three years older than I, Waldir, who was short and bearded, appeared so much older that visitors often took him to be the chief of the division. I wondered why it took two of them to tell me.

"Mark," said Waldir, "you know, I mentioned last night that something else occurred while you were gone." I nodded. His spectacles glinted in the reflecting light from the window. "I hate to upset you before your meeting with Brown this morning, but we want you to find out from us before somebody else mentions it."

"That bad?"

"That bad." He and Penny exchanged a look.

Penny said: "Something happened to Christie."

I took a deep breath and coiled one hand around a green, sandstone pencil holder labeled "The Voice of the People."

"She's in the hospital," said Waldir. "We took her on Monday to the MedUnit station near the Health Department building."

"What happened?"

Waldir cleared his throat. He looked beseechingly at Penny, who clamped her hands around her knees and leaned forward.

"Well, you know, Mr. Grimal, how Christie always goes up

to the roof to eat her lunch?" I nodded. "Yesterday...about two-thirty, she wasn't here. We needed her to find a diskette. That's not like her, you know; she never takes long for lunch—"

I said quietly: "Go on, Penny, tell me."

"—So I went up to the roof, and...she was, she was lying there unconscious—"

Waldir brusquely interrupted: "It's like this, Mark, some-body evidently followed her up there, raped her and cut her up pretty badly. That's what happened." Penny covered her eyes with her hands and shook her head back and forth; she gave a little moan.

He was still talking, but I didn't hear anything. I shoved back my chair, got to my feet, and headed for the door. Waldir pushed in front of me. "Uh-uh, Mark. Hold on." I tried to thrust him aside but he was amazingly strong for a short guy. "Take it easy, Mark. Use your head. Where are you going? The hospital?" I nodded. I was still gripping the pencil holder in one hand. Slowly I set it down on an end table. "O.K., fine, but take Penny with you. Maybe it's you they're after, man. Don't give them reason."

When Penny and I got to the MedUnit station we discovered that on Monday night they had transferred Christie to the hospital in the UD district. The receptionist was frosty. "We can't keep those people here, Mr. Grimal. Only in emergencies do we take them in. They belong with their own kind." I restrained an urge to punch her.

We darted back to the car and headed for the UD district. Penny had never been in the UD district. "Are we safe?" she asked, fidgeting in her seat as the vehicle spun along a street that had been torn up with what appeared to be metal meteors.

"Just keep your door locked." Three dogs leapt out of a side rampway and ran, barking, after us. I swerved to avoid hitting an old drunk as he reeled off a curbstone. Broken panes glittered above us. A woman in a torn robe emptied a pail out of a third story window. She shouted something at us.

"Like another planet," said Penny.

At the MedUnit branch hospital, an old brick building with beggars sitting on the front steps, they told us that Christie had been discharged on Tuesday. "Discharged?" shrieked Penny. "How did she get well that fast?" The receptionist, a man this time, pulled back from the counter. "Lady," he said, "we got a lot worse cases than hers here. Beds, lady, beds. We ain't got beds."

"How did she get home?" I asked.

"How should I know?" grumbled the man, waving his arm toward the street. "I just sign the papers."

We drove to the house Christie lived in.

I knocked on her door. There was no answer. Penny was looking around the hallway, muttering: "Jeez, jeez. What a dump. Jeez." I knocked on the door across the hall. No answer there either. I descended to the ground floor and started banging on doors left and right. Finally one opened cautiously, a chain across the slit. An old woman I didn't recall ever having seen before peered out. "Oh, it's you," she said, recognizing me. She took the chain off the door. "Christie's young man. The one who got her all those nice things." Penny was behind me hearing every word of this.

"Is she in her room? She doesn't answer."

"She can't, poor dear," said the woman. "Can't walk." She dipped into a deep apron pocket and pulled out a key. "I'll let you in; she'll want to see you." The woman carefully closed and locked her own door behind her and tottered to the stairs, keys jangling. "They threw her out of the hospital, you know that?" I nodded my head. I was trying to keep all these details iced away. "Somebody stole her purse there. She didn't have any money. Had to walk home—"

"Jeez," Penny breathed. "How could she have done that?"

The old woman looked at Penny's crisp, lace-trimmed blouse and large hoop earrings. "Well, when you have to do it, miss, you do it. Only she tore all the stitches, so we got the Mystic Doctor down the street, he knows those things, and he sewed her up again."

I took a deep breath. The upstairs hallway was very hot. The old woman inserted the key in Christie's door and opened it.

Christie was lying in a bed I hadn't seen before, a bed that she'd purchased with the money I had given her; it had a headboard and was covered with a new spread. Beside her was a nightstand. There was a rug on both sides of the bed. Curtains hung at the windows behind the bed. She was lying very still. I was afraid to look at her, but I drew near behind the old woman, who was calling

out in a cheery voice: "Christie, Christie, dear, you have visitors!"
Christie turned her head slightly. There was a bandage above her
left eye and one that started beneath her chin and covered the right
cheek. She wet her lips with her tongue. "Mark," she whispered,
jerking one hand toward me. I took it between both my own. Her
hand felt hot and dry.

On the bedside table stood a large, framed photograph of
Mark Grimal smiling at the camera.

Penny asked: "How are you, honey?" She must have seen the
photograph.

Christie tried to smile. Her mouth formed the words, "O.K."

I asked the old woman: "Who's taking care of her?"

"We all try to help a bit. The cook downstairs got one of the
magic sect attendants to come in the evenings." Christie confirmed
this by nodding her head. The toilet was down the hall. I didn't see
how she could even reach the pitcher of water on the table let alone
the toilet. In her condition, could she even use the toilet? She needed
to be in a hospital. Yet if I took her back to the UD MedUnit branch,
they'd only accept her provided I shouted and threatened and
demanded to see the director; and then, as soon as I left, they'd
discharge her again. My chest felt as though it were plugged with
cotton.

"Mr. Grimal," said Penny, "I'm going to wait in the hallway." She pointed at her wristwatch. "Remember, you've got an
appointment with Mr. Brown at eleven-thirty. It's ten-fifteen now."
I grimaced. Screw Brown. But, like a good secretary, Penny knew
what I was thinking. "Right, Christie? He's got to be there on time."
Christie nodded at me. "Very important," she whispered. Penny
opened the door. "Get well, honey. We miss you." The old lady
followed her, telling me to knock on her door again when I wanted
her to lock up.

I squatted down beside the bed and touched Christie's hair.
I hadn't said one word directly to her yet. The cotton in my chest
wouldn't let me.

"Chair, Mark...get a chair. We have chairs now."

I kissed her hand. It was true: she had two large upholstered
chairs and an entire dining room set for four. I pulled one of the

straight chairs over to the bed. There didn't seem to be anything appropriate to say at all. I picked up her hand again. "I have to...have to get someone here to take care of you." Who would come? Only a UD nurse, and the few there were must be in great demand already. Christie looked dubious. "Don't worry," she whispered. "Mark, don't worry...".

"'Don't worry'? How can I—" My voice cracked. Quickly I pressed the back of her hand against my forehead, hiding my eyes. I wanted to ask her who had done it, but how could I remind her by asking? Not now, anyway. She tried to sit up to comfort me. I settled her back. I pulled myself together. I gave her a glass of water. I promised her I'd return soon, with medicine and doctors and nurses and ginger ale and Penny as chaperon. Promises, promises....

Mark Grimal was good at promises.

FOURTEEN

Mr. Brown's secretary, Evelyn Thompson, was robust and cheery. "Nice to see you again, Mr. Grimal. Go right on in. Mr. Brown is waiting." I was two minutes late. I had dropped Penny off at the main Admin building and had then driven directly here, only to find the Government House underground parking garage jammed with departing early lunchers.

Mr. Brown was seated at his desk, which was decorated with miniature flags from all the countries in the Northern region.

"Sorry I'm late, Mr. Brown. Traffic problems." Then I saw Helmut Eberhardt, the director of the Programs Department, seated at one end of the couch. Eberhardt was technically my supervisor, although he believed in decentralization to such an extent that I only saw him about once every three months at a program review staff meeting. Eberhardt greeted me affably enough; however, his presence was as reassuring as finding a piece of glass inside a soda container. I could see that Brown had decided to escalate the meeting into a confrontation.

"Sit down, Mark. Sit down." The Chairman stood up and waved me to the sofa. He was dressed in a trim suit with gold chains looping out of the pockets—a bizarre yet trendy effect that, aided by the sideburns and goatee, made him look like a male model for a Lifestyle journal. I have never understood Brown's appeal to the northern countries; yet in spite of repeated predictions each year that he'll lose, he always emerged a winner.

"Mark," said Mr. Brown, sitting down in a chair made out of fiberglass and alpaca, "I've been telling Helmut how disturbed I was at your not being present at the program last Saturday."

"Good program," I replied. "I liked the way you handled the South African refugee issue. The humaneness of it, the wisdom of the People's approach came across very well."

Eberhardt gave me a reassuring smile. "I agree with Mark; it was one of the better programs. Mark has an excellent staff, very high morale. As I've often told you, Mr. Brown, if the chief of a division is doing his job properly, he shouldn't have to supervise every detail in a program, particularly not a program that's been on the satellites as long as the 'Voice of the People.'"

"That may be true," snapped Mr. Brown. "We're all aware of Mark Grimal's technical competence—"

Technical! The son-of-a-bitch.

"—but what I'm getting at is a question of priorities. To have the chief of the Speakers Division writing airport remarks in San Francisco and little introductory speeches for exhibits and off-the-cuff comments to media groups at a time when an important policy statement is being broadcast here, strikes me as the height of poor judgment. At best. At worst it's blatant favoritism!"

"Now, Mr. Brown," said Eberhardt, "in my sixteen years as head of the Department I have yet to find a program officer playing favorites among the Chairmen. I'm not saying it doesn't happen; it may; but when problems occur, it's more often because you Chairmen, naturally enough, have your own favorites among our officers...."

Mr. Brown clicked his tongue in annoyance. I looked at Eberhardt's clean shaven, jowly face with new respect. I hardly knew Eberhardt; he'd never taken any interest in our section; but part of his job description must be defusing accusations of unfairness from the Chairmen.

"...Individuals click for all sorts of reasons," said Eberhardt. "'Writing style' or 'outgoing personality' or 'good tennis partner.' One of your predecessors always wanted a junior female cultural officer to accompany him to art exhibits because she could 'read his mind....'"

"Now, Helmut," said Mr. Brown, squinching his mouth distastefully, "let's not get into sexual dalliance."

"I don't think it was. She said she really could read his mind; she'd taken lessons from the telepathy people...."

I hid a smile behind my hand. Utterly deadpan, Helmut Eberhardt, with the sagging pockets beneath his eyes, had said this hundreds of times before in defense of dozens of other program officers to a score of Chairmen.

"...I've checked with Comrade Wong. He confirms that he requested Mark Grimal to accompany him to San Francisco because Mark had already written one speech for the trip. When my people get a personal request from a Chairman, it's pretty hard to say 'no.'"

"But a head of an entire section!"

"Mark is a hands-on type, not primarily a manager," said Eberhardt. "He's good at writing speeches and nobody wants him to stop doing it."

I cleared my throat. Wait a minute. I was a damn good manager—a bit free form perhaps, but it worked, didn't it?

Mr. Brown shook his head. "You always defend your people, Helmut. If Mark doesn't want to be a manager, maybe he's the wrong person in the job." With his gold chains tinkling every time he moved, he reminded me of a puppet from some traditional cultural show.

"Mr. Brown," I said at last, "is there anything you would like me to do that would make you feel better about this situation?"

Silence. Nothing had occurred to him. He just wanted to complain.

By 1:00 p.m. we finally managed to escape from Brown's office.

"Nothing to worry about, Mark," said Eberhardt, as we rode down the escalator past the stained glass windows that turned the Government House lobby into an awesome setting for international gatherings. "A minor flap. It'll blow over. I'm perfectly happy with the way you guys have been operating, but you are a part of Programs. We ought to keep in closer touch. Come to our eleven a.m. Monday morning staff meeting and you'll see what the other divisions have to contend with. Denise in Performing Arts has trouble with one or the other of the Big Three at least twice a month."

"Thanks for your help." I could tell he didn't want any more surprises. I wondered if he were a member of the Club.

Eberhardt stopped at the entrance to the underground. "Just one caution. No matter what we said in the meeting, Wong is your favorite Chairman, isn't he?"

I shrugged. "Well, he's the most challenging to work for."

"I know," said Eberhardt. "But remember: in this business it's not your enemies who do you in; it's your friends. Wong's a sharp guy. He'll try to get the best. Just don't let him monopolize you."

After Eberhardt had left, I paused near the auditorium, whose carved wooden doors depicted village scenes from countries of the Associated Territories. In front of me loomed a large, wrought-iron statue of an armed warrior in his death throes, entitled "Disarmament." Government House officials, gawking tourists, and wary security guards swirled past. Fairouz was the only person I could think of who might know how to find somebody to take care of Christie. Wong's chamber was nearby but, given Brown's present paranoia, I didn't want to be seen leaving Brown's office to hurry to Wong's. Finally I approached the information desk and convinced the pretty girl guide to let me use her in-house phone to call Comrade Wong's secretary. Fairouz agreed to meet me in the lobby.

From a distance I watched her get off the third bank of escalators, her hair billowing down her shoulders. She towered above most of the individuals in her path as she floated among the stained glass and marble, past the bombastic murals illustrating the victory of the People, under the abstract mobiles dangling over the balcony. She ignored the admiring glances from the men. When she saw me a faint smile formed on her lips; I wished we were meeting for something less terrible.

"Do you have a problem, Mr. Grimal? We heard Mr. Brown is unhappy that you accompanied us to San Francisco."

"To put it mildly, Fairouz. Tell Jean-Paul not to dig my grave so deep on the next occasion."

She smiled, truly, this time. "I am sorry for you, Mr. Grimal, but I am not sorry for us that you accompanied us to San Francisco."

"I'm not sorry either." I took a deep breath. "Well, now the bad part. I'm sorry to have to ask your help on this. I don't know who else to ask. It isn't the sort of thing that a man should have to ask a beautiful woman to help him with." "I didn't know," she said, "that there are things for which a man shouldn't ask help. What is this request, Mr. Grimal?"

I told her about Christie. She listened with an expression that grew markedly more tense each minute. Her lips pinched together, her eyes narrowed. When I finished she folded her arms across her chest. "The poor child. It is not easy to make arrangements, Mr. Grimal, but I shall find out from my husband's caretaker and give you the information this afternoon by telephone."

"Thank you, Fairouz."

She shook her head as though to brush off cobwebs. "Is Security making an investigation? But of course they will say they are, and they won't, because what difference does it make? this is only an Undesirable. It was probably one of the guards anyway. They are all animals." She looked at me. "I am sorry," she said more gently. "It is hurting you very much, I know, because you weren't here and because you can't help her. But we shall help her the best we can. I shall call you."

"You are a wonderful woman, Fairouz."

"No," she replied. "I am not. There is nothing wonderful about trying to help somebody in pain." She started to go, then stopped. "Please do not take this in the wrong manner, Mr. Grimal, but I think we should postpone our meeting at the restaurant until tomorrow evening."

"But I've been looking forward to it. That's what's been getting me through the day."

"Yes, I know. So you think now. But if we meet tonight I shall want you to make love to me; and when you finish taking care of the arrangements for your friend, you will not want to make love to anybody, believe me. So you will be embarrassed. And then we shall be unhappy. Let us wait until tomorrow evening."

"What can I say?"

She smiled. "Trust me. I'll talk to you later."

Back at the office I told Waldir about the meeting with Brown and Eberhardt. "Unfortunately Eberhardt now knows we exist, wants me to attend staff meetings, let him know what we're doing so he won't have to mount hasty rescue operations. Read between the lines—I should be more of a bureaucrat. I suppose it was inevitable. Want to trade places? Or rotate. We could rotate like the Chairmen in the division chief job."

Waldir made a face. "No thanks. I guess we'd better start giving more major assignments to Tony and Ramona, unless you can figure a way to write speeches during staff meetings."

Alone in my office, I picked up the intercom and buzzed Danzig. Danzig's secretary had trouble finding him, or she pretended to, but at last Danzig's rumbling voice came on the intercom. "What can I do for you, Mark?"

"Just wondering how the investigation's going into the incident that occurred last Monday in the Speakers Division."

"You mean the rape of the UD on the roof?"

I closed my eyes and kept my voice even. "Yes."

"Sure, we're looking into it," said Danzig. "But what I don't understand is why was she eating her lunch on the roof? Doesn't she know about the cafeteria? Nobody's supposed to be up on the roof. That's asking for trouble."

Right—blame the victim.

I enunciated each word as carefully as possible. "I don't see that, Danzig. This is supposed to be a tight security building. The stairs are near our section. We all go up there sometimes. If you don't want people on the roof, lock the door, put up a sign, station a guard, let us know."

"Well," said Danzig, "this ought to be warning enough, right?" Then he must have decided he was being too flippant about security. "Sure, you've got a point, Mark. A lot of people can't use their heads; they need things in writing. We'll declare it off limits. I'll tell you if we turn up anything on the case."

"Thanks. I'll be checking back."

There was a pause. Then he said: "By the way, did you get the fuss with Brown straightened out?"

"More or less."

"You're lucky to be working for Eberhardt," said Danzig.

At 3:10 Fairouz called to tell me that I should meet Vilma Thatcher, the person who was taking care of her husband, at 15 Avenue Coal Station as soon as possible. "She knows a para-medic who may be able to help."

Polyguide always sent down the topic for the Saturday program by noon on Monday; it had been sitting on my desk; I was certainly not going to get to it today. They wanted us to feature efforts to resolve Antarctic pollution. "Sounds like a Ramona topic," suggested Waldir. "Let's try her on it. But you ask her; if I do, she'll think I'm trying to foist work off on her." So I laid the charm on thick, or at least as thick as I dared lay it on with Ramona, and she grabbed at the chance for the big time. Relieved, I dashed out of the office, with Penny in tow. If we were in luck, Ramona would turn out to be Brown's favorite speech writer.

We headed back to the UD district. "Sorry to have to drag you through this, Penny."

"It's all right," said Penny. She was calmer this trip, although at the bridge checkpoint we saw a guard beating up a man who was trying to cross into the main City without wearing his blue uniform. Going into the UD district was easy. Coming out you had to prove you lived elsewhere or were working in the City.

I manoeuvered the car down a street with a dirty canal running alongside it. There were about twenty men fishing in the canal, although if the canal had fish, they must be poisonous mutants.

"I never guessed the UDs live like this, you know," said Penny. "I mean, I knew they were supposed to be really crummy people and that one should stay away from them; but now take that little old lady we met this morning at Christie's, well, what's wrong with her? I mean, she acts just like a lot of little old ladies I know. And Christie's a nice girl. We haven't been as friendly to her as we should have, I guess. Maybe if we'd tried to include her in things, she wouldn't have gotten into the habit of eating her lunch on the roof. I thought about that. It really bothers me. I don't know. They just look so funny, in their baggy uniforms; and then you hear the stories. You get kind of scared. You sure wouldn't want to become one of them, and go to live in a place like this."

"Well, some of us aren't so great either, are we?" I replied. "And yet they let us walk around disguised as normal human beings and wreck people's lives."

We turned into a street with tacky looking restaurants, bars, and shops lining both sides. There was a large gathering of people at the end, with a raucous band playing popular music. A banner strung between the roofs of two buildings carried words written with umlauts and wedges and cedillas—no language I knew. Best to divert. I swung to the left into an intersecting road strewn with smashed cans, as though a recycling truck had dumped them there. Avenue Coal Station finally emerged out of the litter—a fairly clean street, with brick rampways and shrubs growing around the cellars of old houses. Number 15 was newly painted a cream color with grey doors and window frames. This must be where Fairouz's husband lived. I hoped the caretaker would come to the door. I didn't want to meet Fairouz's husband; I don't like to put faces on my rivals, even when, as in this case, they weren't currently rivals.

Penny stayed in the car while I went up to the house. There was an old buzzer on the doorjamb, but when I pushed it I heard nothing, so I knocked. Vilma Thatcher came to the door. She was about forty and wearing a blonde wig; the seams showed above her left ear. She gave the hairpiece a shove on top rather as though she was punching down a lid. "You the man the missus says needs a nurse?"

"Yes. Mrs. Thatcher?"

"You can call me that," she said. "Well, the only one I know is a paramedic, but he's pretty good, they tell me. It'll cost you— about one hundred dolyens a day, maybe more, since he needs it and you look as though you could afford it."

"No problem." A lie. Rapidly I calculated. One hundred dolyens a day for ten days, if he had to stay that long, would set me back a thousand dolyens, which, added to the eight thousand I'd promised to give to Lisa, was a hefty sum. But I wouldn't bargain over Christie's health, and, anyway, what the hell, nine thousand dolyens wouldn't be any more difficult to come up with than would eight thousand.

"Also," said Mrs. Thatcher, determined to get everything in, "the boy's a homosexual, if that bothers you."

I shook my head impatiently.

She was pleased. "Well, if you weren't broad-minded like the missus said, I guess you wouldn't be roaming around down here.

But it's good to check: even some of the other UDs don't like homos. Hold on a minute till I grab my purse and tell the mister I'm going out."

She left me standing on the porch, with the front door open. Broad-minded. Fairouz had said I was broad-minded. I wondered how contagious was contagious in the case of Mr. Moked. Inside the house a strip of worn carpet led down a dark hallway. I heard a querulous male voice demanding something.

When we returned to the car, Penny moved to a seat in the back. Mrs. Thatcher directed me to an area called Diamond Square, which was where the UD homosexuals lived, a district within a district, on the whole a rather better looking one, with painted houses and trimmed grasses. The paramedic was a scrubbed young man with freckles who said that, speaking frankly, feminine rape cases were not his preferred specialty, but that for one hundred and twenty dolyens a day, he'd do it. Since there seemed to be no alternative, I agreed. After that he told me he'd need medical equipment, but here Mrs. Thatcher intervened. "Stop trying to rip off the man, Ambrose. You've got all the equipment you need." Ambrose gave a little laugh. "Oh, all right, Vilma, because it's you." I was beginning to get a pain in the middle of my forehead. I wasn't sure this was a good idea. Ambrose did not inspire confidence.

By 6:00 p.m. we were finally at Christie's place, after dropping off Mrs. Thatcher and stopping to buy antibiotics and other medicines that Ambrose insisted, even without seeing Christie, would be necessary. Ambrose obviously had me figured for a patsy, and he was right. If Mrs. Thatcher hadn't intervened, I probably would have bought him an entire mobile medical unit. I just hoped some of the medicine actually would go into Christie; he could keep the rest for his supplies if he wanted to.

The door to Christie's room was open when we arrived and inside, gathered around Christie's bed, we found the African cook, Jacques Laye, along with a thin woman wearing a veil, who turned out to be the magic sect attendant. Candles were set up all over the room in front of Jacques's carvings Incense burned on top of Christie's new, battery-operated refrigerator. An instant transformation came over Ambrose. Perhaps it was only the straight world, the right-minded, in the form of Mark Grimal that he had wanted to rip off. Now, with these people, other UDs, he became a compassionate professional, anxious to prove his credentials. He spoke soothingly to Christie, asked her questions in a gentle voice. I was relieved. Anyway not much was going to get past Jacques Laye, whose presence inspired rectitude. I knew I was not Laye's favorite person, but tonight he was civil, even respectful. Accompanied by my secretary, I was no longer Christie's irresponsible lover but a Concerned Supervisor, a more principled role.

Considering the candles and the incense and the statues and the smell of antiseptics and Christie's occasional moans, Penny was bearing up well; however she suddenly asked me where the toilet was. I took her down the hall, handed her the flashlight, and waited outside the door. I could hear her vomiting within. When she came out, she was shaking. "I'm sorry, Mr. Grimal. This is really something. I've never seen anything like this." I put my arm around her shoulders. "I'm sorry, Penny. We'll leave in a few minutes. I just want to hear Ambrose's report on Christie's condition." There was nothing else I could do for Christie.

Christie tried to smile at me when I came near the bed, but her face was flushed and her forehead hot to my touch. She was worse now than she had been in the morning. Ambrose told me that she was running a high fever, which indicated infection, and that worried him, but he'd given her a massive dose of antibiotics and we'd just have to wait and see. It was not a very reassuring diagnosis; however I was grateful for anything that sounded the least scientific. I left my work telephone number with him and told him I'd be back the next afternoon if I didn't hear from him before. I kissed Christie on the forehead, endangering my new status with Jacques Laye; then I took Penny by the arm and escorted her down the dark stairs into the street, where the last rays of the sun were spilling over the rampway behind us. Some children were hovering around my car; when they saw us, they scattered. As I went to open the door on the driver's side, I discovered that the lock had been pried loose with a knife. The music disc was missing from the panel. "Oh, Mr. Grimal!" cried Penny. There went another 800 dolyens.

On the ride back to the City, Penny was silent until, after showing our ID cards, we had passed the bridge checkpoint. It was now 7:30 p.m. I was glad that Fairouz had had the foresight to cancel our date for the evening; she had been right—I didn't want to make love to anybody. I volunteered to buy Penny dinner because I felt that was the least I could do for her, but she declined. "I don't think I could keep anything on my stomach, Mr. Grimal."

I suggested that perhaps one of the other division employees might accompany me tomorrow. "You've more than served your time, Penny."

"No. I'll go," said Penny. "I'm learning things. Jeez, am I learning things! Besides," she added, "it's just as well nobody else sees the photograph."

I said nothing. I turned down Transition Avenue, the eight-lane boulevard that bisected the City. Massive arc lamps illuminated vehicles, buildings, the ornate Highland Crescent hall, the Government House, the Monroe Institute, flowering shrubs, the statue of Commandant Pendleton Warner, the roundabout in front of the main Admin building, the global broadcast studios with their wheeling transmitter-receivers, the air shuttles taking off in the distance. The air was fresh. I didn't know how much longer I could stand my life.

"You take care of Christie, don't you?" asked Penny.

Lisa knew, Danzig knew. Let the whole world know. "I try."

"Why?"

Why? I thought: because it makes me feel good to help her; because she's my lifetime redemption project. But all I said was: "She doesn't have anybody else."

"Do you love her?" I took a deep breath. Penny added quickly: "I don't mean screw-love, I mean love-love."

"Yes, I guess I do. She's the best person I've ever known."

I turned into Penny's street, Independence Place, and stopped before her cheery apartment tower building, where the doorman was joking with one of the tenants.

"I guess we had you figured all wrong," she said. "We didn't know you were serious about Christie. We just thought you were having fun."

"Fun?" Had she used any other word, almost any other word, except fun.... I exploded: "What kind of a shit-ass do you think I am? Do you really believe that I have to screw some defenseless girl to get my kicks?"

Penny covered her mouth with one hand. "Sorry, Mr. Grimal. Fun's the wrong word. I mean, we just thought she was another one of your women."

Another one of my women.... I managed a laugh. "Okay, Penny. I deserve that one. But not 'fun.'"

"No," said Penny. "I can see it wasn't any fun going to that place. All I'm trying to say, Mr. Grimal, is that, well, everybody likes you, we always did, but we never realized you were the kind of guy who'd be taking care of someone like Christie."

I drove back to the Atlas Towers West.

Although my salary was a top one for a Senior Admin official and I'd always been able to afford what I wanted, neither Lisa nor I was the type who piled up money for a rainy day. Lisa had her stash of jewelry in the bank vault. If I lived long enough to retire, the Admin would take care of me. I didn't expect to live that long; I didn't even want to live that long. I wanted to have it now while I could enjoy it. Or at least that was how I'd always felt until now. Financial problems when you're eighty-four and falling apart— that was normal, who cared? What could you enjoy at the age of eighty-four? Not even a good steak. But financial problems at the age of thirty-eight, well, that was different. That was a chump's trap. If I wanted to afford the luxury of compassion and responsible behavior, I was going to have to change my way of living. I was going to have to give up the best liquor, the genuine beef steaks, the top-of-the-line media unit, the first rated power vehicle, the annual vacation at an expensive resort, and the women who were impressed by those things. Well, I could give them up; but I wasn't sure I could give them up fast enough to locate ten thousand dolyens.

I parked in the garage and rode up the escalators to the twenty-second floor. When I opened the door to our apartment, I discovered the place was dark. I switched on the lights, went from room to room. No Lisa.

No Lisa? That was hard to believe. I searched for a note,

telling me where she'd gone. No note. The photograph of my parents had been reframed; it was standing again on the bedside table. But there was no Lisa and there was no note to explain why there was no Lisa. This had never occurred before; she was always there, waiting for her erring husband to wander back into her arms. For a moment I wondered if something had happened to her, but then I thought, no. The leather suitcase was missing from the bedroom. When I checked the closet, I found a gap where four or five of her dresses should have been. She'd left me!

For a moment I was chagrined: in the scenario I had planned, I left her. But it was unlike Lisa to have left permanently without a spectacular farewell scene or at least a note denouncing me, and in fact she had taken only enough clothes for a weekend. No, it was a ploy to find out if I "really cared." She expected me to panic, to call her mother in Porto Alegre, her Aunt Julia in Melbourne, her father in Kuala Lumpur, to try to remember who she went shopping with— Janet and Rita and Clarice and Esther—and contact them. Phone all the hotels, maybe even a possible lover or two, if I could think of any, which I couldn't, although maybe that was just because I was so self-centered that I'd never noticed, since men were always telling me how beautiful my wife was. In short, I should act the way she had acted the other night: I should let the world know that I'd lost her, and when at last I located her, I should beg her forgiveness and ask her to come home again. That was how Lisa had it figured.

I fixed myself a Scotch-and-soda, made a roast beef sandwich, and sat down on the living room couch with my portable computer on the coffee table before me and the account books spread out around it. Nine thousand, make that ten thousand, dolyens was what I needed to come up with. The apartment was quiet without Lisa. No questions about where I'd been or what I'd been doing. No queries about why I was going through our bank accounts. No tears, no hysterics, no snide remarks. I stretched. I put a music disc on the unit. My headache was beginning to vanish.

The nicest thing that had happened to me all day was that Lisa had walked out on me.

FIFTEEN

I had barely arrived at work on Thursday morning when Julio Meza from Telecom appeared, making mysterious gestures with his hands and eyebrows for me to follow him into the Telecom center.

Dressed in a green corduroy outfit and sporting a handlebar mustache that hid a third of his face, Julio strode down the corridor, making me look like a brown pheasant alongside a quetzal bird. He must have been older than he appeared or he wouldn't have been in charge of Telecom. All Admin non-classified communications floweᴄ through Telecom, all the official news sheets, radio and TV broadcasts, letters, reports to and from the global Admin branch offices, telegraphic messages, telephone communications, training programs directed by satellite to the Associated Territories, global computer networks. Through Julio's section they flowed into Telecom International, which relayed them to the world. Twenty-four hours a day four of his employees did nothing but monitor other material carried on Telecom International and record what appeared to be of interest to the Admin. If it wasn't classified, Julio had it and even if it were classified, Julio might have it, so long as it was a question of pushing the right keys on the computer. He could read into all of our sections at any moment to see what the transmitters were working on. If he had had the time and inclination, he probably could have blackmailed half the Admin; but he was pure business. Therefore I was surprised at all this mystery.

"Remember your question about the addresses and phone numbers in the official news sheets?" I nodded. "Well, man," said Julio, "you're going to love this."

He took me into his inner office, where I'd never been before since Julio was nearly always outside checking the monitors and unscrambling foul-ups. Closing the door behind us, he directed me to his own computer. The screen showed a page of ads for the news sheets being relayed to the publications section. He pointed his finger at the source line at the bottom of the screen: "Secur.5/10." I glanced at Julio, who, grinning, bobbed his eyebrows up and down at me. He waved one finger, pointed again at the address of one of the ads, a theater called the Monarch—"19 Roundabout Way" in the Federal Territory capital. As I well knew, there was no Roundabout Way.... Now, wait a minute, I didn't check "Roundabout Way," I checked "Roundabout Crescent." Right. He had the copy of the old news sheet that I had given him. We went through three other ads, which also ran in the earlier news sheet. In each one there were small changes, often just one number out of six or "Free" became "Gratis" or "Babylon" airlines turned into "Babtron."

Motioning toward the door, Julio punched a button and the screen switched to an EcoDev office. We left Telecom and headed toward the escalators that led to the cafeteria.

"I've got a hell of an interesting job," said Julio. "Only trouble is I never can talk about it to anyone. But if you hadn't asked your question, I never would have bothered with ads, so I figure it's legit to let you know what I discovered." He shook his head. "The things that go on in this building, you wouldn't believe."

"Why would Security be clearing ads?"

"Not clearing ads, man, designing them."

"I'm slow, Julio," I said. "I don't get it. Is it a code? And if so, why do they have to do it that way? They've got better resources than using news sheets."

Said Julio: "I can see you don't have the proper cast of mind, Mark. The Security guys love this kind of thing. To them it's like playing computer games." We came to the cafeteria. "Now be careful what you say until I check things out."

Check things out? We grabbed our coffee mugs, Julio chose a table, kicked it, chose another, tipped it up on one side, moved to a third in the center aisle, felt underneath it... He finally located one to his liking. "Looks okay," he said, "though you never can tell. They like to experiment."

In the future I was going to be a lot more careful what I had to say in the cafeteria.

We sat down. "Are you a member of the Club, Julio?"

Julio poured half the liquid sugar into his coffee. "Man, I've got to be. They can't do anything without me.... I heard you joined us. In fact I've got a picture of you sitting at the computer in Records."

"That gives me a real warm feeling."

"I figured it would." Julio grinned. "You know, for a nice guy, you have some people rattled around here. The kindest thing I've heard said about you is that you're a 'loose cannon.'"

"Me?"

"I know," said Julio. "To see ourselves as others see us, right? Actually the phrase is usually 'a fucking loose cannon.' Why, I'm risking my reputation to be seen with you, man. And I am being seen with you. Don't look now, but there's a little guy sitting over there by the air conditioner who's probably been seated there since six a.m. just checking things out for Security."

"You know, Julio," I said, "associating with you could turn me into a nervous wreck."

Julio nodded at me. "Seriously, be a bit more careful than you have been, okay?, because you can count on it, man, you're wired." He grinned broadly. "Let's have a cheerful conversation."

I glanced to the corner where the air conditioner was located, and, sure enough, there was a tired looking man in a seersucker suit cuddling a mug of coffee and looking directly at us. I smiled back at Julio.

"Oh, shit. Don't they have better things to do?"

"Like I tell you, to them it's fun and games. Two kinds of characters go into Security: the bang 'em up guys and the trot-through-the-maze guys. The maze guys can be interesting in a weird way, though lethal, Mark, lethal. The bangers are worse though, on a day-to-day basis. Danzig, now, is basically a banger. Don't get trapped with him alone without witnesses."

"You know, it's funny," I said, "but recently people seem to be going out of their way to warn me about something."

"We like you, Mark," said Julio. "We read the signs. They're waiting for you to make a mistake; you're that kind of guy. No offense meant, man, but you are. However, you're in the Club now, so you've got some protection. Just think twice or maybe thrice before you do anything, huh? Now—" He slammed his hands together. "I've solved one mystery for you, right? Security is communicating with agents via coded ads in the official news sheets. Why? We don't know. We probably never shall know."

I told him what I had discovered about the Correspondence Section letters. "Would that be tied into these phony ads?"

"I doubt it. Sounds more like Polyguide skewing the polls or preparing the ground for some action it wants to get adopted. You know,—'three hundred letters support such-and-such, twenty-nine thousand are in favor of such-and-such,' that kind of thing."

I could see that Julio was quite a fund of information. "Know anything about the rape in my section?"

"Not for repeating," said Julio. "But they let her live. Something weird there, man. She could identify the attacker. A mistake maybe. Play it low cool, sub-zero. And keep her out on sick leave for a few weeks until you get a feel for the canvas."

I didn't have time to think over what Julio had told me because when I got back to my office that morning I found I had to edit a speech by noontime for the Economic Development director, Vasili Rublev, who filtered his department's peculiar jargon through a formidable accent that reminded me of zaranga music. Tony wrote his speeches because, of all of us, only Tony could figure out what Rublev was saying. I hoped Tony had checked the graphs. Vasili Rublev didn't care about style, but an error in a graph meant at least an hour of recriminations.

At eleven o'clock Steve Maine called.

"If you're missing anything at home," he said, "you can pick it up at my house."

"It's all yours," I replied. "Keep it."

"Oh-oh," said Steve. "I gather this means you don't intend to come by after work."

"You gathered right. Put it on a plane and send it to my mother-in-law in Porto Alegre."

"Mark," said Steve, "cool off. None of us needs this."

"Certainly not me," I agreed, looking at the clock above the doorway. Eleven-twenty. I stacked the pages I'd read to one side, on top of the dictionary. "I've got a few other problems over here too."

"So I hear. Poor girl. Let me know if I can do anything."

"Thanks."

"And think about dropping by tonight."

"Sorry. I'll be elsewhere."

"You can't stay elsewhere all your life, Mark."

"I can tonight, though," I replied, tossing my pencil onto the desk.

After finishing the speech, instead of going to lunch I stayed at my desk and filled out the bank application form for a signature loan, which, in case Lisa found out about it, would be better than pledging the vehicle as collateral. By midnight last night I had decided I could squeeze one thousand dolyens out of our regular accounts and that if I returned four thousand dolyens to Lisa, rather than eight thousand, I could get by with requesting only five thousand dolyens from the bank. After all, the stock had been our property; I was entitled to fifty percent of it, and to give all of the proceeds to Lisa would be stupid of me.

The form line I had trouble filling out was "Purpose." What purpose could I put down that would convince Jerry Hiraoka, who was always wagging his finger at me anyway, that he should loan me five thousand dolyens without substantial collateral behind it? The truth, of course, was out of the question. Although I suspected that Jerry himself had a mistress tucked away in a penthouse, borrowing money to give to a woman, even your wife, was not what he'd consider a legitimate expense; and besides I didn't want to get involved in trying to explain the complexities of that one. Car loan? My vehicle was almost new. Stock purchase? He'd tell me to do it on margin. Property was a possibility, but then he'd want to know where and at what interest rate and how come I didn't have any documents. Medical expenses? Why didn't the Admin insurance cover it? I finally decided to put down "vacation," even though I knew this would mean having to listen to his lecture about financing pleasures before you enjoyed them. I have never defaulted on a loan from the Nobutaka Bank; I've never even been late in making a payment; but Jerry can't understand how someone earning my salary doesn't show little piles of money earning more little piles of money on his net worth statement.

At the last minute I decided to ask for seven thousand dolyens instead of five thousand, because he'd probably knock the figure down anyway.

He did. "Mark! Mark! Mark!" he cried imperiously, waving his hands above my application. "How can you spend eight percent of your annual salary on a vacation?"

"Second honeymoon, Jerry. I want to take Lisa to a white sand beach with palm trees, somewhere in the Pacific—"

"Nonsense," he said "Go to Cape Winnemucca. It's got the same thing. Five thousand dolyens will keep you in debt through the year 2122. Seven thousand will mean you won't take another vacation until 2124. I'm thinking of you, Mark. No more than five thousand on your signature."

I let myself be talked into agreeing to the lower figure, and returned to the Admin building, feeling better than when I had left it.

At 2:30 the staff gathered in the reception area and Penny presented me with two hundred and fifty-three dolyens that she'd collected from the Speakers Division personnel to help pay for Christie's medical expenses. They also wanted me to add my name to a "Get Well" card for Christie, which had been signed by everybody, including Ramona. I was so surprised and touched that, although I tried, I couldn't say anything; and I settled for kissing Penny while everybody applauded.

When we reached Christie's place at 3:30, we found that her fever had gone down two degrees, but she seemed very weak and Ambrose was vocal about what he considered the inadequate, if not outright criminal, qualifications of the Mystic Doctor down the street when it came to sewing up people.

The unexpected card from the office staff pleased Christie. She and Penny talked while I sat in one of the new upholstered chairs, comparing the small room with the place that I had first seen over six months ago. What my money had wrought. Our money; sorry, Lisa. Christie hadn't had much chance to enjoy all this though, I thought. I looked across the room to the bed where she lay. Her head rested on the pillow against a pattern of pink flowers, the black hair matted from perspiration, a weak smile on her face. My photograph was still on the bedside table. Penny was telling her some story about the computer terminals being reprogrammed to play classic High Rock at the menus. For a few moments Christie had forgotten what had happened to her on the roof. I wanted her to forget it forever, but I couldn't let her do that. Julio's words came back to me. If I didn't ask her, I'd never know whether they had botched the job or had just wanted to goad me; if they'd botched the job, they might be back.

Abruptly I got to my feet and, pulling a straight chair over to the bed, sat down beside it. I took Christie's hand. Penny started to rise, but I stopped her.

"Christie," I said, "I don't want to ask you this but I have to. Did you recognize the person who did it?"

Her hand stiffened in mine. I closed my eyes because I didn't want to see the horror on her face. Then softly I heard her whisper: "No, Mark. He wore a mask."

I sighed in relief.

It must be me they were after.

We got back to the City by 5:30. After dropping Penny off at her apartment, I went home to change clothes before meeting Fairouz, whom I had been too busy to call to confirm our date. The apartment was as quiet as the Admin building's "Meditation Gallery." In the living room I dropped my briefcase beside the coffee table, where the remains of last night's sandwich sat beside a dirty glass and crumpled papers. The afternoon sun poured through the window onto the carpet, which needed vacuuming.

I picked up the phone and punched in the number for Comrade Wong's office. Fairouz had left for the day but I managed to talk the switchboard operator out of her home phone number. Fairouz answered immediately.

Without identifying myself, I said: "You were right. Last night I didn't want to make love to anybody."

Fairouz laughed, a husky sound that hit me in the stomach. "And tonight?"

"I want you."

"Do you still prefer going to the restaurant first? I have

houmous and Syrian bread and lamb kebobs and a red Algerian wine that tastes superb with it."

"That's better than the restaurant."

She gave me her address and I told her that I'd be there in thirty minutes.

Then I hung up, turned around, and saw Lisa standing in the doorway to the bedroom.

The truth is always a shock, the confirmed truth, that is, the visual, auditory, sensory truth, rather than the fertile imagination or the candid admission or the report to the Inspector General. For a full minute we could think of nothing to do except stare at each other. She must have arrived only a few minutes before me because she still had on her high heels and a trim green dress with white cuffs and collar. She had heard every word of my conversation. She knew whom I was meeting and she knew where and if she hadn't memorized the telephone number, she could get it off the machine. How could I have been this stupid? For her part, Lisa undoubtedly hadn't wanted to find out how well I was coping without her.

"Welcome back," I said at last. I brushed past her into the bedroom. She said nothing. When I came out of the shower she was still standing in the doorway. I dressed more quickly than usual and checked to be sure I had the right money access cards in my wallet. As I grazed past her again back into the living room, she said: "Thanks, Mark. Now I see myself the way others see me."

I sprinted down the escalators to the garage, feeling as though I had just won the Prick of the Year Award. To imply that my way of living humiliated her when I had never intended to humiliate her but undoubtedly had and undoubtedly would and was most certainly doing so right this minute as I climbed into my car and headed for Fairouz Moked's apartment threw the burden of guilt for our lousy relationship back to where it belonged, on me. If I must screw other women, why couldn't I do it discretely, like Jerry Hiraoka? Why must I flaunt it in her face, perform impetuous acts, drop clues, fail to take necessary precautions, win a reputation as the Don Juan of the Admin? There must be a name for men like me, but I didn't want to hear it.

SIXTEEN

Since I knew I couldn't go to Fairouz Moked's apartment feeling the way I did then, I spent the next twenty minutes driving around and through Iroko Park, as fast as I could do so safely, while I blocked the scene with Lisa away in storage. Later, later.... For if there was one thing I'd picked up about Fairouz it was that she had no patience with masochism, hers or anybody else's. If you intended to do it, do it.

At last I found her address, a modest looking building near the park. The flat was in the basement. A large percentage of Fairouz's money must go to support her sick husband in the UD district.

She opened the door, wearing a cotton caftan with swirls of purple on a blue background. It was almost seven o'clock.

"Sorry I'm late."

"It is no problem, Mr. Grimal. I knew you'd get lost when you came out of the park. I have been working. It is more comfortable to work at home."

I walked into a small room, its walls covered with paintings. On the left was an enormous collage of stylized circus performers riding on bicycles, swinging from trapezes, jumping through hoops, prancing on elephants, sprawling in the sawdust. A unicycle jumped on a spring out of the canvas; a somersaulting lady kicked her feet in my direction; a clown dripped paint past the bottom frame onto the floor. I'd never seen anything like this painting, even in a museum; and the impact was such that for a moment my mind didn't register that she'd said "working."

"Working?"

"We are a small staff, and Comrade Wong never rests. Please be seated, Mr. Grimal, while I prepare you a drink of something good and then our food, which is ready except for the warming."

"You know, Fairouz, this 'Mr. Grimal' business makes me feel very old. Can't you try 'Mark'?"

"In bed," she replied. "I agree there the name will be more appropriate. Although I have not yet figured out whether you are the lion of the Christian Evangelist or the wolf of the Roman god of war."

I had only the vaguest idea what she was talking about. "A lion, Fairouz, definitely a lion."

"We shall see." She smiled at me. "Wolves are unjustly criticized simply because they are wolves, but one must fulfill one's nature."

She went to the kitchen.

I wondered what it was going to be like making love to her, flanked by a circus.

"This is what you like, is it not?" She handed me a tall Scotch-and-soda.

"You remembered."

"We women are supposed to remember such things," she replied. "We juggle many balls as we walk the tight rope. Do you see that small lady up there in the corner of the painting, Mr. Grimal? The one who is stepping out on the rope in her ballet slippers? That is me. That really is me; I modeled for the figure when I was fourteen years old."

Since the people in the painting were all very stylized, I could see no resemblance between that tense face and Fairouz's.

"The artist of this painting was once very famous in certain circles. Not yours, forgive me, Mr. Grimal. Artazio Colonna was his name. He painted many exciting pictures and his work was hung in all the museums of the northern countries, as well as in some of the south. But then he did an unforgivable thing, Mr. Grimal. He stated in an interview on a live, around-the-world satellite broadcast that whoever spoke about art as being the collective expression of the People spoke trash; that in fact art was made by individuals and approved by individuals within the Admin, some of whom knew something about it and some of whom didn't, and that those who did not know anything about it came closer to the taste of the People than did those who knew. But none of that mattered, he said, because the Admin officials could get anything they wanted approved simply by shutting off a segment of the punch buttons on the People's TV Assembly."

"That's true," I said. And instantly realized that I shouldn't have said it.

"Of course it's true," said Fairouz without changing her expression. "The Chairmen all know they can get nothing approved by the People unless someone in the Admin decides to slant the issue. But the point is, Mr. Grimal, Artazio Colonna said it on the satellites."

"And what happened?"

"A sad story. He was tried before the cameras and condemned by the People to be 'restructured,' because he was too important to be made an Undesirable. MedUnit injected him with drugs and now he sits in some cultural center in Bolivia making wood carvings of llamas. All of his works were removed from the museums and stored in a leaky garage in New Hampshire. That's where I rescued this one. Or, if you prefer, stole it."

"It couldn't have been easy to steal."

She shrugged. "There were no guards. By then nobody knew who he was or cared. Some UD road workers helped me cart it off. Everybody who saw us, including the policemen, thought the scene hilarious: a tall woman, three blue UD uniforms, and a circus going down the road. So you see, Mr. Grimal, you are sitting in a room with a subversive painting, except that nobody knows it."

She disappeared into the kitchen.

I determined that first thing tomorrow I'd check on Artazio Colonna.

Scotch in hand, I went over to the canvas and examined the details. Although I was one of the Admin types who knew nothing about art, I doubted that the People would have approved this collage easily, in spite of its fertile invention. It was not a happy circus. Faces were tense, muscles strained, arms grabbed at the air before falling. The performers were poised on the edge of catastrophe. They were not right-minded people. I knew Fairouz hadn't told me this story simply because I was astonished by the painting. There was an object lesson somewhere in this. I thought of Artazio Colonna carving llamas.

She brought in the food and set it on a table, which was located beneath a more cheerful drawing of three drunks in a bar. We sat down next to each other on a window bench. Since I hadn't eaten anything all day, I was hungrier than I had thought, and the kebobs disappeared rapidly.

"Do you have to finish your work tonight?" I asked.

"I shall complete it before going to the office in the morning. It is a speech by Babatunde that I must fix up the English."

That I must fix up the English.... I cleared my throat. "Fairouz, would you like me to take a look at it?"

"No, no, Mr. Grimal. You are not supposed to work this evening."

"I won't work," I promised. "I'll just look, make a few marginal comments. What's it about?"

"Urban development in Abeokuta, where Babatunde was born."

"Even if I want to work on that one," I said, "I don't know anything about it." Comrade Wong!

While Fairouz put the dishes in the machine, I read over the four page speech; it was easy to correct, except in the places where I was not certain what Babatunde was trying to say. When Fairouz returned, we went over those places together and she explained the best she could. I completely recast the ambiguous sentences. But then, of course, the rest of the text didn't go with the revised sentences and I needed to rewrite that as well. It was nine p.m. before I had finished.

Fairouz, still wrapped in her purple caftan, was sitting in a corner of the couch. "I am glad you decided not to work," she said.

"Sorry. Professional ego."

"Comrade Wong will know that this speech is not edited by me. I shall have to tell him that you helped out."

"Will that bother him?"

"Bother him?" She laughed. "He will try to get me to persuade you to rewrite all our speeches, in your spare time, for free, and because it's such fun for your professional ego. You must not do it."

Although tempted, I had to admit that Admin rules prohibited my doing so. "Of course, if I didn't accept money for it, they might just fire me rather than indict me for corruption."

Fairouz paled visibly. "Mr. Grimal! You knew that and yet you still rewrote this speech!

"It's only one little speech, done for love. What they look for is a pattern of behavior...."

"Mr. Grimal," said Fairouz, "you think you live a charmed life. You take these rash chances because you think always at the last minute you will survive. Didn't you understand what I was trying to tell you about the painting?"

"Yes," I admitted, curbing my wit. "You think I'll end up in Bolivia."

"No, not Bolivia," she said. "They will keep you in the Admin because you know too much. They will set you to work processing figures for EcoDev loans or proofreading others' publications. When you remember that you once knew how to write and now no longer can, you will want to kill yourself, but since you have been 'restructured,' you won't do it, because you are too stable, too responsible, too grateful to them for having saved you from your madness."

I had to admit that she had succeeded in impressing me, if not positively chilling my blood, but considering that we hardly knew each other, I didn't understand why she was so concerned. I took her hands in mine. "Why do you think I'll do anything so foolish as to get myself 'restructured'?"

She smiled. "Because, Mark—you see, it is time for bed now; I am calling you 'Mark'—you will not think it is so foolish, and you will do it, like the speech, out of 'love' or professionalism or respect or because you get annoyed at somebody important. And you will think it is all quite humorous until they start jabbing you with needles."

I fingered the neck of her caftan. "How do I get this thing off you?"

She raised her arms above her head. "Lift."

She had nothing on underneath. I ran my hands lightly over

her body, then again and again with increasing pressure. She undid my buttons, buckle, zipper. We moved slowly, took time. I was poised with her on the tightrope high above the ring. Below us was sand and buckets of water and cages and pedestals and a horde of hungry tigers jumping through flaming hoops.

And no safety net.

When I got home at 1:20 a.m. Lisa was asleep in our bed with the light on. I stood at the foot of the bed looking down at her. Her blonde hair was coiled around her head, which lay on one side of the pink pillow. Her mouth was half open, her eyelashes caked with mascara. She looked vulnerable and aging. The beginning of a double chin, the wrinkles on her neck, the bare arms loose and slightly flabby, a faint sag to her breasts. But I had just come from the arms of a woman whose defects I hadn't noticed yet, and anyway living with me would be enough to age any woman. Briefly I considered sleeping on the living room couch, but the couch was not all that comfortable. I undressed, turned out the light, and very carefully eased myself onto the far side of the bed. Instantly she awoke. "Mark?"

No, I wanted to say, Artazio Colonna. Instead I just grunted. I expected some bitter diatribe; however she was silent for so long that I almost fell asleep, and when at last she decided to speak, it was in an ordinary, conversational tone of voice.

"There has to be a reason why I stay with you," she said. "I thought it was love, but Rita says, no, it can't be love; it has to be something else, that I have a poor self image and that you probably have one too and that's why the Lifestyle Department paired us, because they figured at least we'd have that in common."

The remark was so outrageous, especially coming from that scrawny, sharp-chinned Rita whom only a man like Steve would ever want to lay a finger on, that I sat right up in bed. "Screw Rita," I muttered. "She's been reading those pop psycho books again. There's nothing wrong with you that living with a better man wouldn't cure."

"But I don't want a better man," she said. "I want you. That's the point, you see: I want someone who turns me into a screaming bitch because he doesn't love me. That's not normal. And yet we're supposed to be normal people, aren't we?"

I rested my head against the panel behind the bed. Without looking, I reached above, choose a music disc from the holder, and inserted it in the unit. Pop music sung by Damon Vassos flowed into the room. Damon Vassos was hardly my favorite singer, but so what? he was Lisa's. Slowly I took her hand in mine. We lay there silently. I knew she'd feel better if I made love to her, but not only did I not want to make love to her but after three hours of sex with Fairouz Moked I didn't have the resources.

SEVENTEEN

Fairouz was leaving that evening for Australia with Comrade Wong and wouldn't be back until next Wednesday. Her cool voice answered the phone. "We were just talking about you here, Mr. Grimal, how we wish you could go with us."

"How I wish I could too."

"When we get back, Comrade Wong would like to discuss a project with you. Is next Thursday afternoon at three p.m. a convenient time?"

A project? A project sounded like something Eberhardt would tell me to stay away from, but we'd see. My calendar was clear. "Looks fine, Fairouz."

When Penny and I arrived at Christie's place that afternoon, we discovered that her fever had gone up again in spite of all the antibiotics. Ambrose was giving her small sips of water every ten minutes. Outside in the hallway he confided to me that, although it was true that fever usually rose in the afternoon, he didn't like the way things were going. He suggested that a friend of his, someone who had spent two years at medical school, come to give his opinion. Although secretly I thought the Mystic Doctor might do just as well, I drove Ambrose back to Diamond Square, while Penny stayed with Christie, and we picked up his friend, an older man named Harrison, who brought along an enormous medical tome, which, after examining Christie, he solemnly consulted. Other than recommending a different antibiotic, however, Harrison didn't have much to offer. I paid him fifty dolyens and returned him to Diamond Square.

It was now 6 p.m. I sat down beside Christie and attempted to persuade her to drink a glass of apple juice. To please me, she tried. Her lips were cracked. She had trouble swallowing.

"Mark...," she whispered. I lowered my head to her mouth.

"I want to talk to you privately."

That didn't sound good. I asked Penny and Ambrose to leave the room for a few minutes. I sat back down beside her and took her hand.

She said: "The rest of the money you gave me is wrapped up in the freezing unit. Take it with you. I don't want to trust it with anybody. In case something happens...."

"Nothing's going to happen."

"Of course not. I know." She forced a smile. "But in case it does, you will need it. It isn't cheap to die, even in the UD district."

"You're not going to die, Christie. What are you talking about?"

"He's worried." She looked toward the door to the hallway. "He says I'm all messed up down there, and that he's not a doctor; he can't fix it properly."

"Maybe I should take you back to the hospital."

"Oh, that place...." Her voice trailed off. "No. I never saw a doctor there. I don't know if they even have them. At least here it's more comfortable. Nobody's screaming, nobody's vomiting, nobody's urinating on the floor...."

I pressed her hand. What was I to do?

"Mark...."

"Yes, my love?"

She smiled faintly. "Am I still your love?"

"Always."

"If I do die, please remember: You've done everything you can. Don't blame yourself because I didn't live, promise me."

I shook my head. "You're not going to die, Christie."

Her cracked lips felt like sandpaper when I kissed them.

As she directed, I took the money. There were three thousand six hundred and twenty-two dolyens left. Since tomorrow was Saturday, I left my home phone number with Ambrose, although this might create all sorts of future problems I didn't want to think about, and then drove Penny home. We agreed to check on Christie in the morning.

I'd have to be careful or Lisa would get the idea that I was having an affair with Penny.

Lisa was astonished to see me home so early on a Friday evening. She prepared cannelloni for dinner. Seated at the table, we watched Ingrid Armfeldt, draped in a black sari with gold bangles dangling around her midriff, deliver the evening news. Comrade Wong was departing from the Transport Cabins for Australia. Ahead of him on the mobile passenger escalator floated Fairouz Moked, carrying his briefcase. The cameraman couldn't resist a quick closeup of her elegant profile. "Now I understand," said Lisa, as she handed me the salad dressing. "You've been abandoned for the sex dens of the Orient."

"Hardly in Australia."

"Don't you hope. Australian men are even taller than she is. Handsome, dominating, athletic...."

"Knock it off, Lisa. You're sniping."

"I suppose so," she agreed. "I suppose for once I'd like to see a woman leave you rather than the other way around, just to find out how you'd react. But that'll probably never happen."

After dinner I took a Nobutaka Bank draft for four thousand dolyens out of the bank envelope and tossed it into her lap as she sat in front of the media unit, watching a documentary on China.

"Half and half," I said shortly. "There's yours. What I did with my half is my own business. Take a trip to Australia if you want to. Fuck the natives." I plopped into a viewing chair alongside her.

She sat there, the bank draft lying on her long jersey skirt; she didn't touch it. Tears started dripping down her cheeks. The Great Wall of China was being destroyed by industrial pollution. Global experts examined green chunks of it. A glidercopter blew dust across the factories of the Mongolian plain. I closed my eyes and wished I were in an airplane high above the Pacific Ocean. I should feel happy because I'd evened the score with Lisa, but I didn't feel happy.

"Sorry," I said at last. "I didn't mean the part about Australia."

My father had warned Lisa not to marry me. A vigorous old man with lots of white hair, who taught mathematics at a university in Ottawa, he was the only one who warned her. "Mark doesn't belong to this era of scientific mating and genetic testing," said my father. "He's a throwback to King David...the Caliphs...Don Juan...a twentieth century pop star...." At the time Lisa had been shocked: how could my father talk that way about his darling son, who'd been faithful to her for all of six months? Why wouldn't it go on forever? Even my mother thought so, but then my mother was a romantic soul who chose to believe that what my father called my "promiscuous behavior" was really the search for the perfect woman; and in Lisa I had found her. Well, not quite. I wanted Lisa, true, but, once married, well, I became more critical. Her reading tastes, for instance, her conformity with established opinion, her assumption that superb food and sex were enough to keep me at her feet every evening. Food and sex aren't everything, not to me, not, anyway, once I had them. Three weeks after our marriage, I took up with a mousy woman named Jennifer Fitch, the curator of a paleontology museum on Valdez Boulevard, who fed me ham sandwiches and gritted her teeth during intercourse and taught me more than I really needed to know about dinosaurs. Lisa had her first attack of hysterics. She went home to my parents, her own not being readily available, but all my father said to her was "I warned you." To me he wouldn't speak at all; however my mother scolded me at great length over the telephone until I finally agreed to give up Jennifer, whose gritting teeth were beginning to annoy me anyway; and Lisa came back to me. And then two months later I met Anabel, the poet.

This time Lisa didn't leave; she stayed and railed at me when I came home in the early hours of the morning. She wept; she tried new sexual positions, recipes with orange pasta, literary book reviews, word games, black and yellow sheets. I began to dread coming home because I was never certain what I would encounter. Anabel was quite flaky enough without having to cope with a flaky wife as well. Finally I caved in and broke with Anabel. Lisa glowed. But not for long. Others followed—research assistants with button-down collars, theater actresses, engineering professors, television announcers. They always followed, they always will, unless some day women become clones, one just like the other, and then there'll be no reason to explore them.

I realize that this doesn't make me much of a husband.

When Penny and I saw Christie Saturday morning, she appeared slightly better; the new antibiotic was working. She drank some bouillon, opened the magazine Penny had brought her, asked me to turn on her radio. Though Ambrose still appeared glum, I left the house more optimistic than I had been the day before. I could now concentrate on revising the script Ramona had written for the afternoon's public service program. It wasn't bad; Comrade Wong could have handled it, but it was too technical for Mr. Brown, who would find many words he couldn't pronounce, have to skip them on camera, and then would complain afterward that I had foisted the speech off on the number three writer in the section. Ramona would be hurt less if I edited it now and explained to her on Monday about Mr. Brown's difficulty with words of more than three syllables.

I worked in my office until 3:30 p.m., with a break only for a stale soya-chicken sandwich in the cafeteria, and then took the underground over to the Global Broadcasting Studios on Transition Avenue. The floor manager, Magda Rostowski, was already in the studio. "Mark! Praise the heavens!" Grabbing my arm with one hand, she tucked her loose, salt-and-pepper hair behind her ear. "Never, never, never will you be allowed again to travel on Saturday when Brown is chairman. You cannot believe what poor Waldir went through last week. And me too, poor me, you cannot believe it." For ten minutes she filled in the dramatic details, acting out all the parts. She did Brown especially well—his precise voice, his stiff posture at the microphone, his incoherent outrage. We were collapsed in laughter in the production control room when Brown's media assistant, a brisk young man named Harvey Milliard, arrived. "Welcome back," said Harvey, taking his copy of the script from me. "What's so funny? Things sure weren't funny around here last weekend."

"I didn't know your boss thought so highly of me," I said. "All I do is hand him the damn script."

Harvey repressed a small smile; Harvey was not really a smiler. "You're tall. You're relaxed. You reassure him. He doesn't like surprises." He looked over the first page. "Antarctic pollution! Shit! Why give that to him? Why not to Mallam Ahmed?"

"I don't pick the topics."

"Yeah, I know, but you can expect grumbling. Penguins don't vote." Leafing through the speech, he moved out into the studio to sit down in one of the chairs in the visitors' section. I was glad somebody on Brown's staff read the text before the program, although Harvey never questioned details; he just wanted to know how it would play to the media.

When producer George Abish came in, we checked the visuals. They were heavy on penguins, all right—penguins, research centers, snow, penguins, shots of the flapping World Federation flag, sea leopards with black dots, more penguins. I explained Mr. Brown's problem. George superimposed a slide of a voter registration card onto a penguin's flipper. The penguin waved it in the air.

"Good try, George, but that's still a southern region voter."

By the time Mallam Ahmed arrived at 5:15 p.m., all of the production and floor crew staff were present and I was waiting alongside Billy, the propman, for the appearance of Mr. Brown. Mr. Brown was cutting it close today. Mallam Ahmed seated himself at the triangular desk in front of the global backdrop. An impressive figure—tall, dressed Hausa-style in a flowing white robe, a red cap on his head—, he greeted me graciously. Of the three Chairmen, Ahmed was definitely the most pleasant to work with. I hoped he'd gotten over his pique at my speech writing efforts on behalf of Comrade Wong.

At 5:27 p.m., when Magda was beginning nervously to slap her script against her thigh, Mr. Brown breezed in. "Oh, hello, Mark," he said in a fake-friendly voice as I hurried over to the desk with the red Admin binder containing the speech. "I was wondering if you'd deign to join us today. What's the topic?"

"Efforts to clean up the Antarctic."

"Oh, my blessed grandmother." Mr. Brown beamed beyond me into the camera. "Doesn't Polyguide know which region of the world I represent? South African refugees one week, Antarctica the next."

"Well, sir," I replied, "I guess Polyguide just wants to associate you with some of the more noble, world-wide causes."

Magda was making wild gestures at me to move out of camera range. I stepped back quickly but not before I heard Mr. Brown snap, "Smart ass"; and I guess he meant me, not Polyguide.

The program went off well. In the production control room I watched Comrade Wong relayed by satellite from the entrance to the old opera house on Sydney's waterfront. This was the last Saturday of September and next month Wong would be Global Chairman, and then Ahmed, and perhaps by the time Brown was Chairman again in December, Eberhardt's prediction would come true, and the "minor flap" would be over. Maybe. Personally I saw difficult days ahead. Brown struck me as a grudge-holder.

EIGHTEEN

I went to bed early that evening, which turned out to be a good thing, because at 3:00 a.m. the telephone rang. Both Lisa and I fumbled for the receiver at the same time. It fell down on her side. She tucked it under her hair. "Hello?" Then "Just a minute," and handed it to me. "Somebody named Ambrose Fitzhugh."

"Oh, shit." Groaning, I sat up. "Ambrose, what's wrong?" Lisa switched on the lamp.

"Mr. Grimal," said the voice. "Sorry to wake you at this hour, but Miss Riccardi is much worse. An hour ago she went into a coma...."

Coma! I shook my head to clear it. "I'll be right there."

I flung the covers back on top of Lisa and, standing up, started pulling on my clothes. It was too late to call Penny; I'd have to go alone.

"What's the matter?" asked Lisa. "Where are you going?"

"The UD district."

"At this hour?"

"Christie's in a coma."

"What? What are you talking about?"

Suddenly I realized that Lisa might not know what had happened to Christie. Lisa hadn't come to the office the past week and with the new solidarity among my staff, maybe nobody had called to give her the gossip.

"It's a long story...."

"Perhaps you'd better tell me."

I tucked my shirt into my suit pants. I'd decided to wear a suit since looking like a Senior Admin Official might be necessary if I had to cope with hospital personnel. "Later, Lisa, later. When I get back."

"You can't just dash off to the UD district at three o'clock in the morning, Mark. I swear, you're the most irresponsible man—"

I exploded. "Irresponsible! Christie may be dying and you call me irresponsible for trying to help her? That's a new definition—"

"Sshh." Lisa made wild gestures at the wall. "Betty Doherty...."

I lowered my voice. "Shit on Betty Doherty. You want to see how much fun I have in the UD district, come along! Broaden your horizons!" I pulled on my jacket, removed a thousand dolyens from the bank envelope and stuffed them into my wallet, leaving the money Christie returned in the closet.

"All that money—"

"That's what people use in the UD district."

"You're not going to spend all that—"

"Lisa," I said, "you have the most limited mind—"

"I do not!" Lisa was getting out of bed, Lisa was pulling off her nightgown, Lisa was putting on her panties and bra.

I stared at her. "What are you doing?"

"Coming with you," she said.

"What?"

"You invited me. You want me to 'broaden my horizons,' don't you? Fine." She dragged a blue chemise from the closet. "I'll broaden my horizons." Stunned, I watched her pull the dress over her head. "Here. Zip me up." I zipped her up. She turned and patted my cheek. "Called your bluff, Mark baby. Let's go. You can explain everything in the vehicle."

I explained everything in the vehicle, that is to say, I told Lisa what had happened to Christie and what I had been trying to do to help her, but what Lisa understood about this explanation I didn't know since she said nothing, just kept glancing sideways at me as though I were some new form of maritime plant life in an aquarium. The streets were well lit but empty. Bureaucrats sleep early, particularly well-cared-for, rational, problem-solving bureaucrats, which is what we were, or anyway what they were. I was beginning to think that it was pure fluke that I'd ever entered the Admin, let alone risen to the upper ranks of it. Who else in the Admin would be driving to the UD district at 3:30 in the morning? Not Vim, not Julio, not Waldir, not Kelly, not Eberhardt, not Vasili Rublev or Blanca Rodriguez. Steve maybe, in his Human Rights defender role. Or Danzig. Yes, Danzig might meet Mark Grimal in the UD district.

When we arrived at the bridge checkpoint, we were the only car, and the guard was curious enough to stop us and ask to see my ID. He studied the ID, shook his head, looked into the car and shot a focal light into Lisa's face. "Who's that?"

"My wife."

"You're taking your wife into the UD district at this hour of the morning? Mister, how do you expect me to believe that?"

I was about to say something rude, but Lisa intervened in her most dulcet tones. "Officer, it's an emergency. Someone who works in my husband's office is very sick and we have to take her to the hospital."

The officer obviously found that story hard to believe as well. "Do you have an ID, ma'am?" Lisa dived into her purse and produced the red card. The guard turned it around in his hands, shook his head, gave it back. "So you are Mrs. Grimal. A new one on me. You ought to know, ma'am, if your husband hasn't told you, that there's lots of criminal elements across the river. If I were you I'd go right back to my comfy quarters, and wait until morning. No UD is worth risking your life for."

"Shall I take you back to your 'comfy quarters,' Lisa?" I inquired sarcastically.

Lisa ignored me. "Thank you, Officer." Her eyes grew bigger and brighter and more luminous. "It's very thoughtful of you, but, you see, I feel a moral obligation."

Faced with such spiritual courage, the guard stepped back respectfully, but his opinion of me hadn't improved any. "O.K., Mister, go ahead; but if she were my wife, I sure wouldn't take her into that sewer."

We crossed the bridge and descended into Lower Canal Street, which had two lights dimly burning at either end, outlining figures which must have been men but could just as easily have been dogs on their hind legs or androids or alien spacefarers. They slouched against the dark buildings, sat on the rampway curb, curled up in fetal positions, walked in crazy circles, howling. Yes, someone was howling. Lisa checked to be sure her door was locked; she pulled her sweater tightly around her shoulders. The guard was right; should anything happen to the car, I'd hate to have to try to protect Lisa from these crazies. However, oddly enough, Lisa was calmer than Penny had been on her first trip. Lisa must have spent so many hours imagining the UD district to be just like this, only worse, that nothing shocked her.

I avoided the open hole in the middle of the street near the turn-off to Rockaway Pitts, not because I saw the hole, I couldn't, but because I had once plunged into it coming home from Christie's. There were no street lights on Rockaway Pitts, only an occasional kiosk with a candle and the moon illuminating faces that belonged to bundles of clothes parked on steps and alongside buildings. Somebody was singing a magic song, a wailing without melody. At the corner of St. Agatha's Square a man in a long coat threw a rock at us; it struck the hood, glanced off. I pushed the velocity button. We sped past. At the next corner I had to swerve up over the rampway curb to avoid running over a man with a smashed head spread-eagled in the middle of the street. He was probably dead already but running over bodies did nothing for the vehicle. Lisa made her first comment. "I don't believe this. Where are the police?"

"They don't come here often."

"Why not?"

"Police protection is a citizen service. UDs have no civil rights. The duty of the police is to protect the rest of us from the UDs, not protect UD from UD."

"Well, then, how do UDs like Christie survive?"

"They band together in clusters and try to protect themselves. The UD district is a gigantic prison, a self liquidating laboratory. We're protected from them, and they either control or destroy one another for free. Social costs minimal. To us anyway."

"All right, Mark," said Lisa. "Keep calm. I understand what you're saying."

When we arrived at the house Christie lived in, I told Lisa she'd better come inside with me—not that I wanted to take her in, but I was afraid to leave her alone in the car. Reluctantly she accepted that logic. Inside the house, I took Lisa's arm and guided her up the stairs, following the handrail; I'd forgotten to bring a flashlight. When we reached the landing, she tripped on the torn carpet, but I held her upright. On the second floor, a faint light from Christie's open door helped us to find the room.

Inside, the room was full of people. I felt Lisa's arm stiffen. Three veiled, mumbling magic sect attendants kneeled before one of Jacques Laye's carvings, which was set on the table between two candles. Jacques Laye was on his knees at the foot of Christie's bed. The old lady from downstairs was seated in one of the armchairs, an old man in the other. Ambrose had set up an IV beside Christie's bed. The foot of the mattress had been raised slightly with books. He had removed the pillow from beneath her head. I let go of Lisa's arm and approached the bed.

"I couldn't get you earlier," whispered Ambrose. "There wasn't a telephone within a fucking ten miles that worked." Sweat glistened on his forehead; he looked exhausted. When I touched Christie's hand, it was cold and damp. "Pulse is one hundred and five per minute," Ambrose said. "Not good."

"Shall we try to move her to the hospital?"

"You really want my opinion?" I nodded. He gestured me over to the wall so that the others couldn't hear us. "Look, I've worked in the hospital here. They don't have equipment. The intensive care unit is a joke. The operating room is without water. There are about maybe...ten doctors, huh?...not very good ones. A couple of them are drunk all the time. One of them humps the female patients. The director is on heroin, everybody knows it. They mix up what medicines they have. If you're a good MedUnit doctor you don't have to serve time in the UD district hospital...."

"In other words, forget it."

"In my opinion," said Ambrose, "these weird magic sect people will do her just as much good."

I glanced in their direction. One of the attendants had convinced Lisa to sit down in a straight chair, where, feet planted together, her hands in her lap, she held herself as rigid as a department store dummy. She hadn't looked at Christie; I didn't know if she'd even seen my photograph.

"What about trying to get Christie to a hospital in the City?"

"The City?" Ambrose raised his eyebrows. "Well, I never heard of that happening. If a UD is injured while in the City, the MedUnit emergency will take him for twelve to twenty-four hours, but nobody goes from here over to there."

"We could try."

"Well...sure, we could try. But moving her to try....I don't know." Ambrose shook his head. "It'll be rough."

"You know, Ambrose," I said, "I'm sure you're right, but I can't just stand here and watch her die, which seems to be the alternative, right?"

Ambrose bit his lip. "Okay, Mr. Grimal. I just hope you've got enough clout to pull it off."

Clout? Clout with MedUnit? No, I hadn't any clout with MedUnit; if I'd had I would have used it before now. The MedUnit officials wrote their own speeches. I once met the director, Dr. Fisher Schleka, at an official dinner. A tall, cold man with a yellow mustache, he expounded at length on the benevolent use of drugs to restructure dissident personalities; so much more civilized a method than in the old days when they used to lock them up, he said. Now dissidents could be returned to their families within six weeks, with new, socially approved values and stable character traits. True, the patients suffered a loss of creativity, but that, according to Dr. Schleka, was a minor problem compared to the immense benefits conferred on the family, the community, and the world at large. No, I wouldn't waste my time calling Dr. Schleka. What I was counting on was not clout but medical ethics. If I could get Christie to a hospital emergency unit, I figured the personnel might be too embarrassed to refuse her treatment.

But moving her wasn't going to be easy. Beginning with Lisa, everybody in the room thought I had lost my mind. Lisa had finally seen the photograph on the bedside table, and her mouth was pursed in disgust, but even Lisa couldn't be jealous of a dying woman. "They're not going to accept a UD patient, Mark. Let the poor girl die in peace." I ignored Lisa.

Jacques Laye was more difficult to cope with. While Ambrose

was dressing Christie in a blue uniform, which I found hard to believe was necessary but "They won't let her past the checkpoint otherwise," said Ambrose, Jacques Laye preached the wisdom of resignation to the will of God. I supposed that if one were a UD, being resigned to the will of some magician might be just as good as being resigned to the will of the People's TV Assembly, but since I'm not a UD—although indeed I might end up worse off someday, with my brain cells rearranged in neat, orderly, socially approved patterns—I couldn't grasp the concept of resignation.

The old couple were even harder on my resolve than Jacques because they wanted her to spend "her last hours on earth among her friends who love her." I could see their point; it was tough; but patiently I explained that after all Christie was now unconscious and couldn't be aware of who was around her. Unfortunately I suspected that if Christie were conscious, she'd opt to stay right here among her friends and in resignation, if not to the will of God, then to fate, to destiny, to the end of suffering. She'd say, "Don't worry, Mark. Don't worry. You've done everything you can, Mark. Don't worry."

While Ambrose borrowed a blue uniform for himself from Jacques Laye, I folded up the seats in the back of the vehicle so that Christie could be laid on blankets on the floor. Ambrose and Jacques carried her limp body out of the house; one of the magic sect attendants accompanied them with the IV; they placed her in the car. Every time she moaned, I felt as though I were hurting her more by insisting on doing something, but I'd gone too far now to turn back.

I drove as slowly and carefully as I could in order to minimize the jolts and swaying of the car. By the time we reached the bridge checkpoint it was 5:45 a.m. and the sky was beginning to lighten behind the towers and blocks of the City. The guard came forward. It was the same guard.

"Oh, it's you," he said. Then he looked into the back seat. "What's this?" Ambrose had both his own and Christie's IDs ready. The guard took the documents, but he just held them and stared at me. "Mister," he said, "what do you think you're doing? You can't cart these UDs into the City."

"Why not?" I asked. "Mr. Fitzhugh is a paramedic. Miss

Riccardi is the girl my wife mentioned earlier, the one who works for me. We're taking her to a hospital."

"Over here?" The man shook his head. "Sorry, Mister. Look, they've got their own hospital in the UD district. You want to take her to a hospital, you take her back there."

"It's full up. No beds."

"That's not my problem," said the guard.

"Who's problem is it then?"

Next to me Lisa murmured: "Easy, Mark, easy."

"I'm giving you the facts," said the guard. "The hospitals in the City don't take UDs. If you're such a big shot, Mister, you ought to know that. Now turn your vehicle around over there in the clearing and get these two out of here." He handed the IDs back to Ambrose through the window.

I killed the motor. "No. I want to discuss this further."

The guard jerked his arms up. "Oh, shit." Then he remembered my wife. "Excuse the language, ma'am. Mister, there's nothing to discuss."

"I think there is. You say that the hospitals won't accept a UD. Well, maybe you're right. But that's for the hospital to decide, not for you to decide." Lisa was giving me warning pats on my arm. "Maybe I'm such a 'big shot' that I can get her in."

The guard hesitated. "You, ah, got authorization in writing?"

"No."

"Then I have to assume the instructions hold. Sorry, Mister."

"The girl is dying."

"Hire another one."

"What did you say?"

The guard shouted: "I said Hire another one!" Three buses full of UDs had drawn up behind us and his patience was exhausted. "Mister, the district is full of these sleazy dames. They come cheap. Dump her into the ground and tomorrow you'll have three dozen of them on your doorstep applying for whatever it is she does. And if your wife weren't here," he finished with a bang, "I might give a few opinions about what she does."

My hand hit the door button. The door flew open. I was half way out of the car and the guard was backing away in surprise when

Lisa seized my arm and Ambrose grabbed me from behind.

"It won't help, Mr. Grimal," said Ambrose. "Take it easy."

He was right of course; it wouldn't help at all. In fact it would ruin us. Slowly I sank back down.

"Hold him, Ambrose," said Lisa. "I'll handle this."

She got out on her side and crossed in front of the vehicle to where the guard was standing. The sky was clearer now, but the arc lights were still on. Lisa approached the guard like a beautiful suppliant. Her blonde hair gleamed, her blue dress swirled slightly in the early morning breeze, her hands were clasped together, her features pleaded for understanding, kindness, charity. Not even Danzig was immune to Lisa's charms when Lisa chose to exert them; this clod was dazzled.

"Ma'am," he said, "I'm sorry, but what kind of a nut are you married to anyway?"

"Officer," she said, "he didn't mean it. He's just upset about this poor girl. And I am too. I know this is hard to explain, but we feel a great pity for her since she has nobody to care for her. Probably you're right, the hospital will refuse to accept her, but, please, do let us try. It means so much to us." The tears were actually rolling down her cheeks. I knew Lisa was capable of histrionics but that she would use them on behalf of Christie astounded me.

The guard protested, but he was weakening. He scratched his head, he pulled an ear. Lisa kept talking, tears kept flowing. At last he surrendered, "Okay, okay, ma'am," and made a curt gesture at me to move on. Drenching him in gratitude, Lisa scampered back to the car. To me, through clenched teeth, she muttered: "Tell him you're sorry." I wasn't sorry, but I took a deep breath, stuck my head out of the window, and said, "Sorry, Officer."

The guard rolled his eyes. "Go on. Get out of here."

We crossed the bridge. The sun was coming up now. I clutched the wheel. "Thanks, Lisa. Superb performance."

"So was yours," she snapped. Then in a low voice so that Ambrose wouldn't hear: "Get a grip on yourself, Mark."

We decided to take Christie to the MedUnit branch nearest the Monroe Institute because that's where Lisa's gynecologist operated; however, Dr. Lansing was not on the premises this Sunday morning, and the intern on duty in the emergency unit was baffled about what to do. Not hostile, just baffled. "I've never had this problem before, Mr. Grimal. This isn't an accident that happened right now?" I shook my head. "You brought her all the way from the UD district?" I nodded. "Whew!" The young man's stethoscope bounced on his chest. "Well, let me check with the head doctor. Hold on a minute." He disappeared.

The receptionist seated behind the white counter on the right said, "Sorry, folks. We can't take her. That's going to be your answer."

I ignored her.

After about fifteen minutes the intern came back with the head doctor, a middle aged, black woman with hair cut short around her head. She gave both Lisa and me a quick appraisal, evidently found us sufficiently bureaucratic-looking, and then sighed. "Mr. Grimal, I'm Dr. Pierce-Owen. You know what the policy is about our accepting UDs in the City hospitals?"

"Yes."

"And you brought this young woman here anyway?"

"I'd like you to make an exception to the policy."

"I see." It was impossible to judge from her expression what she was thinking. "Well, tell me what's wrong with her." I told her what I knew. Ambrose filled in the details. Dr. Pierce-Owen went over to the car and glanced in at Christie, who hadn't moved since we left the checkpoint. "You tried the UD hospital?"

"They threw her out of the UD hospital."

She nodded. "Yes, they have their problems there." Another sigh. "Well, Mr. Grimal, this is going to sound very hard-hearted to you, but I cannot accept this young woman, even for emergency treatment, at Federal government expense."

"But if it's at my expense?"

"At your expense?" Dr. Pierce-Owen gave me that speculative stare again. "Do you have any idea how expensive intensive care is, Mr. Grimal? It's about one thousand five hundred dolyens a day."

"I'll pay it."

Lisa turned and walked away to the driveway entrance,

where she turned her back to us and gazed out on the cool September street full of red and green and yellow leaves. But she didn't say anything, and for that I was grateful.

"Interesting," said Dr. Pierce-Owen. She looked at Lisa's back, and she looked at me.

"You work in the Admin, is that correct? May I ask what your position is?"

I handed her my ID card. "M-SAO grade.   Ninety-five thousand dolyens per year salary."

"I don't mean to question your credentials, Mr. Grimal." She returned the card, with a tired smile. "I just can't afford to pay the bill myself if you fail to do so."

"Don't worry. I'll pay."

"All right, I'll admit her. Fill out a form here—" She directed me to the receptionist. "Then please go to the waiting room inside. Don't get your hopes up. I'll let you know as soon as possible what her condition is."

"Thank you, Doctor."

The receptionist was caustic. "Live and learn, live and learn. I've never seen this before. Lucky girl. You're paying for it yourself? How do you want to do it? Payroll? Bank charge?" I gave her one of my bank account numbers. Tomorrow I'd add the money Christie returned to the account; that should cover about two days. One thing at a time, I told myself. One step at a time. On the admission form, for "Next of Kin," I wrote my name. "You don't want to do that," said the receptionist. Carefully she crossed out the "Next of kin" and replaced it with "contact."

"Thank you, Miss," said Lisa.

The attendants had removed Christie from the car and taken her inside on a stretcher; they permitted Ambrose to accompany them with the IV. I parked the vehicle in the underground garage, rejoined Lisa at the entrance, and we went into the waiting room where I sat down in a chair and wiped a handkerchief across my face. I felt shaky. I didn't know if it was relief at finally getting Christie admitted to a genuine hospital or dread that I'd waited too long. Without a word, Lisa got up and left; she returned in a few minutes with a cup of water and a tranquilizer.

"I don't need that."

"You need it. Assaulting a police officer..."next of kin" to an Undesirable...one thousand five hundred dolyens a day, easy, no problem, you'll pay it.... I'm trying to be sympathetic, Mark, but I can't understand what's going through your mind."

"Oh, odds and ends. Bits and pieces." I took the tranquilizer. It wouldn't hurt; it wouldn't help either. "You've been a help, Lisa. I appreciate that."

"Oh, yes," she said. "A wife confers respectability on these antics." To my surprise, she took my hand. "Well, I guess you loved her. That's hard to believe, but there can't be any other explanation for why you're so willing to bankrupt us. Maybe she's the only difficult thing that ever happened to you. The rest of us are just good lays, or bad ones."

"It's not like that, Lisa."

She twisted my wedding ring around my finger. "No? Well, tell me what it's like someday. Figure it out for both of us."

At a quarter after ten a nurse behind the glass partition called my name over the loudspeaker. She took Lisa and me into a private consulting room where Dr. Pierce-Owen was waiting, armed with a thick file of papers.

"We've done all possible tests, Mr. Grimal. I'm afraid the results are not encouraging. It appears that the young lady has had a negative reaction to one of the drugs she was taking for the infection—"

I closed my eyes. Harrison, I thought.

"—This is not an ordinary allergic reaction. The paramedic you hired to take care of her would have recognized that. Where did you purchase the medicine? In the UD district?"

I nodded.

"Unfortunately I suspect it was adulterated."

"Oh, shit!" I covered my eyes with one hand. Lisa slipped her arm through mine.

"Not your fault, Mr. Grimal," the doctor said quickly. "I'm sure the medicine looked fine, seal unbroken, everything proper. There is no way for you to have known that the UD district is not a good place to buy pharmaceuticals, although it's an easy place to buy them, no prescriptions necessary. Drug rings operate freely there. They steal the genuine medicines, which are in great demand, and either adulterate them or replace them with fakes. They're very clever, the way they concoct these things. Mr. Fitzhugh has promised to send me a sample of all the medications so that they can be tested; however, even that will not be definitive, because the same bottle can contain both real pills and phony ones."

"That's criminal!"

Dr. Pierce-Owen leaned across the table. "I think you've had enough contact with the UD district, Mr. Grimal, to know why something isn't done about it."

"Yes, Doctor," I replied. "If an Undesirable dies, so what? Hire another one!" The doctor blinked and drew back slightly.

"Mark, please!" Lisa whispered.

But an astringent smile formed on Dr. Pierce-Owen's mouth. "Your husband is correct, Mrs. Grimal. Those people have no one to complain to; that's exactly why it's allowed to go on. But what can you and I do about it, Mr. Grimal?"

"There ought to be something. It's genocide!"

She leaned back in her chair and eyed me appraisingly. "Isn't that the point of the entire federal government policy toward the UDs? They're meant to die out; that's why they're sterilized. A young girl like that thrown in with murderers, the mentally disturbed, rapists, thieves, the incurably ill, political terrorists, people with all sorts of contagious diseases—"

"Yes. It's genocidal."

"And then we come back to the question, what can you and I do about it? You're a Senior Admin official, Mr. Grimal. Why don't you do something about it?"

Lisa gasped. "Dr. Pierce-Owen, you shouldn't say things like that to my husband! He's the kind of person who might try."

"Really?" The doctor raised her eyebrows and smiled. "If true, Mr. Grimal, then you'll be the first Admin bureaucrat I've ever met who would." She tapped the bottom of the file folder against the table. "What I hear is 'Oh, I can't change anything because I don't work for Polyguide. I'm just digging wells in EcoDev or defending the Amazonian Indians in Legal or diffusing art in Programs or immunizing children in MedUnit.' Want to know what I say? I say, 'I'm just an overworked doctor who always gets the Saturday night after-midnight shift, and I'm too busy trying to keep people alive to have time to worry about policy,' What do you always say, Mr. Grimal?"

"I say, 'I just write speeches for other people to read.'"

She waved her arm at me. "So write a speech that'll change the policy toward the UDs. You can do it." I guess she must have seen a strange expression on my face because suddenly she slapped the file folder down on the desk. "No, it's not that easy, is it? Besides, there's always the risk you might end up a UD yourself, or...or worse—over there in the Billings Psychiatric Hospital being restructured to fit policy rather than vice versa. I wouldn't want to see that happen to you, Mr. Grimal, so forget what I've just been saying."

"No," I replied. "I won't forget it."

Lisa groaned. Dr. Pierce-Owen looked at me steadily for several moments. Then she stuck her hands in her deep coat pockets. "We're both exhausted, Mr. Grimal. Sorry. Your wife's right. I've overstepped myself. Let us deal with the problems we can solve and not worry about those we can't." She stood up. "I'll be going off duty at noon time. Dr. Karageorghis will take over. If you want to see Miss Riccardi, it can be arranged, but I doubt very much that she'll be regaining consciousness."

"Any chance that she'll live?"

"Like that? Let us hope not." She tucked the folder under her arm. "Senseless deaths are hard to come to terms with, Mr. Grimal, but senseless lives are even worse, aren't they?"

NINETEEN

I dropped Lisa off at home and then drove Ambrose, slumped in the seat beside me, back to the UD district. When I tried to pay him an additional hundred dolyens, he refused, saying that he considered what had happened his fault because he should have warned me not to gamble on buying medicine in the UD district; only in the City I couldn't have gotten it without a doctor's prescription. For fifteen minutes we sat in front of his house, talking about all the things we ought to have done differently, talking about Christie as though she were dead already, and maybe she was; but it was a relief to talk about it because while I was talking about it, I didn't have to think about it.

I returned Jacques Laye's blue uniform to him. I told everybody that Christie's condition was critical and that she was in intensive care, although I couldn't bring myself to confess that I unwittingly had purchased adulterated medicine for her. They were so impressed that I had gotten her admitted to a City hospital, the miraculous powers of which they undoubtedly overrated, that I was embarrassed. Already I was wondering what I should do with Christie's belongings if she died. I was her next of kin, whether my wife liked the idea or not, and I'd have to make the arrangements. I began by removing my own photograph from the frame on the bedside table. Should a miracle occur, I could always give the photo back to her.

I returned to the City. It was now one p.m. In the hospital, I asked to see Dr. Karageorghis. After about thirty minutes, he appeared, a short man with a limp and a sad expression, made sadder, it appeared, by Dr. Pierce-Owen's having foisted a UD patient off on him. "Yes, yes, I know about the case. We're going to get all kinds of flak from our admin people about this. It's very irregular, Mr. Grimal."

"In what way?"

"Oh, come! You know in what way. It just isn't done."

"But there's no regulation against it?"

"Oh, no. Because it's never been done. Now that it's been done—" He vigorously shook his head up and down. "—I'm sure there will be a regulation issued against it."

"Who issues these regulations?"

"They come from our admin office."

"Who in your admin office?" He was beginning to look at me as though he thought I were not quite normal. "I'm just wondering with whom I should discuss the issue if I were going to discuss the issue with anyone."

"Why, I have no idea, Mr. Grimal. You know how admin sections are. They send us pieces of paper saying 'Do this' or 'Do that.' I'm sure they must check with higher sources."

"Like who? Like the Director?"

"Oh, if it's a serious matter, undoubtedly with the Director."

"Then the Director, on his own, makes the final decision on what the admission policy will be?"

"I doubt that," said Dr. Karageorghis. "He probably brings it up with Polyguide, maybe Global Health...."

"But Polyguide is supposed to interpret the policy, not make it."

The doctor was scowling now. He tucked his hands deep into the pockets of his white coat. "Mr. Grimal," he said, "I really do not have time to stand around here discussing bureaucratic procedures. If there's something I can do for you in the medical line—"

"I'm just trying to figure out who makes the decisions to accept or refuse a dying patient for treatment."

"Well," said Dr. Karageorghis, "this morning it appears to have been Dr. Pierce-Owen."

Although I didn't really want to, I asked to see Christie, because I figured the staff would take better care of her if they knew I'd be checking. A nurse took me into the intensive care ward. Of the six patients in the room, more tubes and bottles and packs and trolleys were spread out around Christie's bed than around anyone else's. Her black, curly hair fanned across the pillow; her pale face was slack. During the hour I sat there, Christie never moved. I wished I could ask her forgiveness. What I touched, I ruined; it was as simple as that. But I knew she'd never think she had anything to forgive.

Christie died on Monday morning at 1:32 a.m. No mortician in the City would take charge of the remains, which the hospital insisted had to be removed as rapidly as possible. For a while it looked as though I might have to carry her dead body back to the UD district in my own vehicle; however, I finally located a UD district mortician with a telephone who agreed for one thousand dolyens, seven hundred payable at the hospital entrance, to cross the river and pick her up. The cremation would be an additional five hundred. The hospital bill, including all the tests, came to four thousand sixty-two dolyens; but the hospital agreed to give me thirty days before it debited my bank account. Lisa stayed grimly calm as these figures were being shuffled about. I guess she figured that if she objected, I might dig the hole even deeper, and besides it was such an ugly mess, the kind that only I could have gotten myself into, that until the day we'd be tottering around in a geriatrics ward, she'd be able to whack me over the head with it.

In public, however, Lisa was superb—the understanding, compassionate wife, the generous woman who brought a wreath of red roses to Christie's funeral, when it was held at three p.m. on Tuesday in the mortician's parlor. We closed down the Speakers Division at 2:30 p.m. so that the entire staff could attend the funeral. Jacques Laye had his magic sect leader speak; the attendants mumbled away; the candles burned; the mortician kept opening the windows. Ambrose and Harrison were there, the old couple from downstairs, an anemic young man who claimed to have attended third grade with Christie back in some remote epoch before her father had been declared an Undesirable, and—to my surprise—Steve Maine, but not Rita. Steve kept shaking his head. "The poor kid," he kept saying. "The poor kid."

After the ceremony, Lisa placed her roses on top of the disposable coffin; Jacques followed with a carving of a man on a cross. I had something too, but I knew they took things off the coffin when they did the cremation.

"Open it," I ordered the mortician.

"No, no, Mister," he protested. "You don't want to see her now. She wasn't embalmed, remember?"

"I'll try not to look," I replied sarcastically. I was not terribly happy with this character, who had charged me double what he would have charged Jacques Laye, if Laye had arranged the funeral. Lisa was tugging at my elbow. Maybe she thought I was going to throw myself on top of the corpse and create a scandal in front of everybody. "I have something to put inside."

"Should have given it to me before."

"Mr. Rollins," I said, "I'm paying for this show. If you want the rest of your money, you'd better open the fucking coffin."

Lisa covered her mouth with one hand and coughed delicately.

Rollins opened the coffin. I did look—just to be sure that he hadn't switched corpses on me—but he hadn't; and then I took a white envelope with her photograph of me in it, and placed it on top of her body and told Rollins to reseal the coffin.

Following the cremation, which lasted no more than ten minutes, Rollins handed me the urn with her ashes. I hadn't realized that I would end up with her ashes. I'd never had anybody cremated before and so somehow I had just assumed that the technique must now be so advanced that the corpse would turn into smoke, with maybe a handful of dust at the bottom of the incinerator. But now here I had a twelve-by-eighteen-by-twelve-inch urn with ashes to dispose of. Nothing seemed appropriate.

"What are you going to do with that?" asked Lisa, when we got into the car. No doubt she had visions of Christie resting forever on the bookcase between The Complete Shakespeare and the twelve volume Global Encyclopedia of the Humanities.

"Put it on Danzig's desk."

"No, Mark."

I pushed the starter button and the vehicle took off with a jerk. We still had to go back to the house where Christie lived because the old lady there had insisted on preparing food for the mourners at the funeral. Evidently funerals were a big social event in the UD district.

"Sprinkle her ashes over the Admin rooftop at the spot where she was raped."

Lisa took a deep breath. "Mark, I know you're under great stress. Just try to hold on until we get home, will you?"

The old lady's husband turned out to be a Professor Amos Zilke, who had once taught physics at the Federal Territory University and who had gotten into trouble at the same time Christie's father had and for more or less the same reason, only for bombs rather than guns. I told him that I wanted him and his wife and Jacques Laye to divide up Christie's things; if they found anything they thought I should have, fine; but going through her belongings myself was not something I felt capable of doing.

Then I asked Jacques Laye what he thought I should do with her ashes. "Leave them with me," said Jacques. "I'll see they're buried in sacred ground." Briefly I wondered what sacred ground looked like—Did it have trees, grass, flowers?—and where it might be located, but since I intended to remember her in my own way—not in marble or granite or eternal fiberglass or music or poems or statuary or sitting by her ashes and weeping, but rather in some action, I didn't know what yet, that would catch the attention of the world and change the way things operated, even if it meant the end of me, of Mark Grimal—I told Jacques to go ahead, the more sacred the better.

TWENTY

I made it through the next few weeks by accepting more work than I could comfortably manage. I'd leave the Atlas Towers West by seven each morning and return by eight p.m., sometimes ten, but Lisa knew where she could find me. When I kept my appointment with Wong on Thursday, I told Fairouz about Christie; however, after that, I didn't try to contact Fairouz again. It wasn't that I was being faithful to Christie dead when I hadn't been faithful to her living; it was that I didn't want to talk about Christie to anybody, and that included Fairouz. I didn't care—in Lisa's pop psycho phrase—"to come to terms with my grief," since that would have swept me back into the standard Admin mode of assuming I couldn't do anything about it. I was going to do something about it. I didn't know what though; I couldn't put the pieces together.

In the beginning, the nights were the worst because then I did too much thinking, of the undisciplined sort. The first two nights after Christie's death I hardly slept at all; then I slept, but found myself waking up with nightmare images of her disfigured face in the coffin. Since I didn't wake up quietly, but rather with violent, upward thrusts that propelled me out of the bed, Lisa always woke up too, until finally she convinced me to take tranquilizers before sleeping. That helped some, although I didn't like to do it because it confirmed Lisa's opinion that I was on the verge of a crack-up. She wanted me to stop working so much, relax, let's have friends in, go to a multimedia sound concert, play Word PRO, read murder mysteries. I kept working.

Work didn't prevent me from thinking about the UD policy. Up front, I dealt with human rights or nuclear energy or famine in Bangladesh, while overlaying these concerns like a cloud were the Undesirables. In this situation, Comrade Wong's "project" was exactly what I needed: he had been asked to do a three-part program on the cultural heritage of the Philippines for Manila television. I said yes without bothering to check with Eberhardt. I figured anything the other two chairmen asked me to do at the same time I could handle.

At work I stopped joking with people. Not that I was rude or short-tempered, I just didn't have time, didn't want to discuss anything but work. Not even with my own staff, particularly with my own staff, because they wanted to talk about Christie, and I didn't. Ten days after the funeral when Waldir told me that the staff had drafted a memo to Danzig about Christie's case and that they wanted me to sign off on it, I said: "Good idea, Waldir. Please sign for me," even though he had the memo right there in his hand ready to show it to me. "Mark," he said, "we're getting worried about you."

"I'm fine," I replied. "I've just got this deadline for Dick Schaeffer in Social Welfare."

I knew I couldn't try to change everything at once, that I had to choose a limited aspect of the UD policy, the area where I would most likely garner support. Even if I'd had the patience for the channels route of interdepartmental staff meetings and proposals, I wasn't in a key position to effect change that way. I'd just end up being regarded as this harmless kook who dropped into people's offices and took up their time with his pet mania. Well, if the channels didn't open readily, I was prepared to try something else, anything else, including insert the proposal, unauthorized by Polyguide, in a Voice of the People broadcast, and try to have it put before the People's TV Assembly for ratification. Of course if I failed, nobody—certainly not Kelly Hallihan—was going to give me a second chance.

Three days after my staff sent its memo to Security, Danzig buzzed me on the intercom and asked me to come to his office at my "convenience," like 10 a.m.... No? 10:30 then? Okay, 11:00 would be perfect. Whether I wanted to or not, I knew I was going to have to talk about Christie and to the person I least wanted to talk to about her; therefore, before leaving the office, I asked Penny to show me the memo. The staff was expressing its concern, which bordered on outrage, that to date nothing had been reported on the investigation into the assault on Christine Riccardi, even though the assault had taken place on Federal Territory Admin property. I swallowed. I was ashamed to admit I'd refused to read the memo. "You guys are great," I said, handing the copy back to Penny.

Jake Danzig's office on the tenth floor was an awesome sight. One wall was covered with nothing but medals—fifty-three of them, I had once counted—while mounted on the opposite wall was a collection of antique rifles, along with a few hand grenades and a defused bomb that had been planted under his car back in 2113 during an Associated Territories conference in Abidjan. Behind his chair hung an enormous photograph of the Director-General, Mr. James Francis Finley III, whom hardly anybody except Danzig and Kelly ever caught a glimpse of, surrounded by tiny shots of the current Chairmen; and the fourth wall, the one through which visitors entered, was decorated with bows and arrows, boomerangs, hunting knives and sticks, slings, Stone Age hatchets, poison blow darts, and other primitive weapons. Danzig liked to give his victims a lot to think about.

"Sit down, Mark," he said, oozing cordiality, which put me on guard right there. He waved to a wooden chair that looked as though it had served time during the sixteenth-century Spanish Inquisition. "You, ah, look all right, contrary to the reports I've been hearing."

"So do you," I replied pleasantly. Time enough later to wonder—as I was meant to do—what reports he'd been referring to.

"You're aware of this memo your staff sent me?" Danzig held the paper in the air.

"Yes."

"Doesn't look like your signature, that's why I wondered."

I ignored the comment. "Do you want to meet with them to discuss the problem?"

"Oh, no," he said. "That won't be necessary, Mark. You can pass on the good word, although I'll also be sending a written reply. You know the bureaucratic motto: 'Get it in writing, put it in writing.'"

"So what's the good word?"

"You should be happy about this, Mark," he said. "We've

arrested someone in the UD Riccardi rape case. In fact, you probably know him—a guy named Ike Dresmond in EcoDev."

Dresmond!

"The son-of-a-bitch!" I snapped involuntarily.

"Yeah," said Danzig, smiling. "A lot of people know Dresmond as a son-of-a-bitch. We just never realized he was such a perverted son-of-a-bitch."

But immediately questions began to pop into my mind. Without eyewitnesses, how had they discovered that it was Dresmond who had done it?

"You sure it was him?"

Surprised, Danzig hesitated, a split second only, but it was enough to confirm my doubts. "He's confessed."

I admitted that was tidy. "Did he confess how he knew Miss Riccardi ate lunch on the roof?"

"He says he used to see her after work and she told him." This was such a blatant lie that Danzig must know I couldn't be expected to believe it. He was watching me now from beneath lowered eyelids. No doubt he had wanted to nail Dresmond for something for a long time now, and so why not this? Somebody would suffer for Christie's rape, even if it were the wrong somebody. That was good enough for a UD, wasn't it?

I got to my feet. "In that case," I said, "I doubt very much it was Dresmond."

Danzig shook his head. "All this unexpected cynicism, Mark. Here I thought I had good news for you. Don't tell me you feel sorry for Dresmond."

I should have. If Danzig could get Dresmond to confess to a false charge, then, on another occasion, Danzig could equally well get me to confess to a false charge; that was basic human rights logic, Steve would tell me. Moreover the person who had raped Christie was still walking around free. But, as Danzig well knew, this got into lofty principles that few of us were up to. After all, Dresmond had forced Christie to have sex with him on several occasions, although probably not on the roof; and therefore, as far as I was concerned, they could do anything they wanted to with him.

"Not me. What will happen to him?"

"That'll be up to the Board. He's not exactly EcoDev's most valuable player, but having the People declare him an Undesirable in an on-camera trial is tricky, might raise questions."

I wondered what kind of questions. Battered-face questions? Recanting-on-world-wide-TV questions? Criticism-of-Security-procedure questions?

"I anticipate a complete, six-week restructuring under a medical ruling, after which, when he comes out, he'll piss in his pants if he so much as looks at a woman."

I didn't want to hear about it. I headed toward the blow darts and boomerangs.

"I'll tell my staff you're answering their memo, Danzig."

When I got back to Programs, I called a staff meeting in the cafeteria, which was marginally safer for all twenty-two of us than in my office, and told them, without comment, what Danzig had done in response to their memo. Tony and Kirsten knew who Dresmond was; Ramona and Waldir and Louis knew of him by reputation. But it was the transmitter operator, Beatrice, who put the matter most succinctly: "Sounds like they just nabbed the first sex maniac they could get their hands on."

Then for two hours, through lunchtime, we sat there discussing Christie, which was what they had wanted to do for two weeks and what I had been avoiding. The event was played over and over again; it was pure catharsis, and I knew it was good for me, because obviously my behavior had begun to attract attention, and I didn't want to attract attention. The image of Admin playboy was the best disguise I had going for me.

My staff suggested we conduct our own investigation. Louis volunteered to canvas other Programs personnel to find out who might have been around that day during the lunch period. Ramona said she'd find out which guard was on duty. We made a trip to the roof, the door to which we found open the way it always had been— no guard, no sign. As we were climbing the stairs, Penny took my hand as though I were a tottering invalid, and she continued to hold it all the time we were on the roof. Louis and Ramona, who seemed to have constituted themselves into Speakers Division detectives, recreated possible scenarios. I had trouble breathing. I focused my gaze beyond the roof; the trees in the mall were losing their leaves, a distant air shuttle shot into the sky like a firecracker, workmen were re-gilding the Government House dome. The pebbles on the roof crunched beneath our feet.

"Hey!" called a voice from the doorway. A guard in an olive uniform stepped onto the roof. "Nobody's supposed to be up here. What are you guys doing?"

"Why wasn't that door locked?" demanded Ramona, bearing down on him, in red-haired fury. "Where were you?"

"I had to go to the bathroom, ma'am."

"Bathroom!" Ramona shrieked. "Who gave you permission?" She berated the guard all the way back down the stairs. I could see that Ramona might be the appropriate person to deal with Jake Danzig when he learned about the Speakers Division investigation.

That evening I returned home at 6:00 p.m. and, after dinner, I suggested to Lisa that we go out and do whatever she wanted, a proposal that so astonished her that she spilled coffee grounds on the floor and I had to help her clean them up. But then she gave me such an enthusiastic kiss that I knew we were going to have a good time, and we did, the best we'd had in several years—dancing at the Moons of Jupiter, taking in Walt Hewitt's midnight gig at the Romany, finishing at 1:30 a.m. with Irish coffee at the Loch Loman. If I'd just taken Lisa out more, we'd have gotten along better; I knew that; and the reason I didn't do it was because I'd never figured out how, graciously, to handle her admirers. Whenever we were out, there was always one overweight, loud-mouthed drunk who couldn't resist Lisa's attractions; and here he came now, swaying away from the Loch Loman bar to our table, which I had temporarily left in order to get a package of cigarettes from the dispenser. I shoved my way back through the crowd in time to hear him say: "Honey, I hope you don't mind my telling you this, but you're just the prettiest, juiciest little morsel of a woman I've seen in all the northern territories...." I grabbed his shoulder and shoved him to the side, where amid shrieks and shattering glass he fell over somebody else's table. Lisa leapt up and clutched my arm. The waiters intervened. I paid our bill and that of the tipped over table. On the way to our vehicle Lisa berated me for behaving like a cave man. "Now don't you dare ruin this evening by telling me I asked for it!" she cried. Well, sometimes she asks for it, for instance when she's mad at me, or if she's trying to even the score by flirting, but I was sure that she had never even seen this slob before he accosted her; so I apologized for letting my adrenalin take over, and we went home and made love until four o'clock in the morning, and I remembered all the good reasons I had married Lisa.

Of course the next day I called Fairouz Moked.

TWENTY-ONE

Fairouz had not been sitting at home waiting for Mark Grimal to call her. She was going to an opera that evening, and tomorrow she was having some people in, but definitely I should join them. I'd like her friends; they were people I should know, from the Board of Government offices, working with all three Chairmen; and she would have invited me before except that she wasn't sure I was ready to resume living. I assured her that I was ready to resume living.

Lisa was not happy when she discovered the next day that I was going to a buffet dinner without her, even though all I said was that it was "work-related." I escaped from the apartment and reached Fairouz's by 8:00 p.m. to encounter fifteen people already in her small basement flat. Others kept coming until 9:30, when we finally ate an elegant moussaka. She had Algerian wine for conservatives like me and Carlos and Harvey Milliard, and fruit juice for the marijuana smokers. Fairouz was on fruit juice, as were Jean-Paul, Babatunde, Can Mabuza—Mallam Ahmed's South African media assistant—and, oddly enough, Mr. Brown's secretary, Evelyn Thompson, who looked as though she should be drinking hot chocolate, not smoking marijuana. The evening was definitely not in the Admin function tradition. Very few spouses were present; maybe they didn't exist. Working for a Chairman, having to travel continually, must be hard on doublestyle living. Ahmed's program coordinator, Tosca Pinelli, a dramatic, blonde Argentine in whom I might have been interested, given different circumstances, delivered a scathing attack on the Lifestyle Department's genetic testing as an infringement on human dignity, human dignity being better served, according to Tosca, by the hit-or-miss method. Half the room applauded her. The other half said, "Who wants to miss?"

I was the only Admin official there. Why I was there was

clear to everybody. Fairouz kissed me on both cheeks when I came in; she introduced me as "Mark"; she asked me to help her open the wine; when dinner was ready, while others lined up at the buffet table, she prepared me a plate of food. Although she was attentive to everyone, I felt as though I had been "announced," and it was not a completely comfortable feeling. I was, after all, a Senior Admin Official with a wife, and Danzig on my tail, and, in Security's books, for all I knew becoming an official lover might be a new record in moral degeneration. Eberhardt would certainly object, if only on the pragmatic grounds that the relationship allied me too closely with one of the Big Three. Besides I was not sure what the obligations might be as Fairouz's official lover. If we broke up, would people here hold it against me? They didn't seem to have the same snide ho-ho-you-lucky-dog-you attitude that I continually ran into at the Admin. But still there must be some ground rules I'd yet to encounter.

However, Fairouz was right: these were people I should know better. Amongst themselves they seemed to get along well. My staff determined my agenda, and I was sure these people did the same for their Chairmen. If they wanted to, they ought to be able to convince the Big Three to agree on issues rather than waste their energies bickering over trivialities. Imbued with these idealistic thoughts, I sat down beside Can Mabuza, whose aggressive beard and shaggy eyebrows screamed revolutionary ardor, and asked how he thought the refugee problem on the South African border would eventually be resolved.

"Never will," said Mabuza. "Resolving it is in the interest of no one except the refugees." The refugees were all descendants of coloreds who had been caught in the middle of the war between the blacks and Afrikaaners around the time of the Transition, or at least that was the story. "They're a symbol of the racial intolerance that we've abolished; they remind people about the bad old days."

That certainly was a different view from any I'd heard before. "You really believe that?"

"Sure," said Mabuza. "I believe any crap Polyguide sends us."

"Well, they can't have sent you that one," I replied. We then got into a confused discussion about the difference between official policy and real policy, which was clear to me because I dealt with it all the time in speeches, but evidently not so clear to Can Mabuza, nor to Harvey Milliard nor to Wong's staff director, Carlos Acevedo, who joined us. The official explanation for the failure to resolve the South African refugee problem was that those people wanted to return to South Africa and they couldn't until the war ended. Meanwhile the global community took care of them. But of course there was no war in South Africa.

"The country was bombed out of existence with nuclear weapons eighty years ago when one of the Chairmen tried to set up headquarters there," explained Harvey. "The reason nobody goes back to South Africa is that nobody wants to until the radiation level gets back to normal."

"Which will be in about another hundred years," said Carlos.

Before I could ask how in the hell they knew that, Babatunde Adedipe, who was dressed that evening in a two-piece outfit of lavender lace, tossed a news sheet clipping into Mabuza's lap. Mabuza glanced at the headline, "Wong Hails Abeokuta as Model for Eastern Regional Development." "Oh, shit!" said Mabuza. I was glad he didn't know I had edited the speech.

Babatunde chortled and winked at me. His round face was beaming. "Can, you go hire that kid Okigbo for wetin you want do. Im be fit man for im own house."

"How can I get him working for us when he's studying at the university in Australia?" asked Mabuza. "Why do you guys do this to me?"

Carlos tried to calm him. "Now, Can, Tunde just tried to smooth things over at the press table when they refused to seat Okigbo and he started yelling media imperialism."

"Well, did he have to make a friend out of him?"

"I be friendly type," said Babatunde. "I done give im chop, palm wine, speech. I no wan palaver."

Mabuza slapped the shiny page against the coffee table. "Seriously, you guys, what good does it do you to keep hitting the Southern regional publications? Nigerians don't vote for the Eastern chairman. Why can't you get Wong to stick to his own area rather than try to cover the world?"

"We work on it," said Carlos, "but he has—"

"Global vision." Babatunde waved his arms in a circle.

"And you two southerners working for him—"

"Not to mention the northerners," chimed in Harvey Milliard. "In fact, Nha's the only easterner on his staff."

The Vietnamese economist, who appeared to be one of the few people there with a wife, was perched on the top of a sideboard beneath a painting of beggars rolled up in blankets on the steps of a monument. He took a sip of wine. "Comrade Wong," he said, with an amiable smile, "believes that he himself is sufficiently knowledgeable in Eastern affairs; what he requires is expertise in other areas."

"Like Abeokuta in Nigeria," growled Mabuza. "Sorry, but I get tired of hearing Mallam Ahmed ask 'Why can't I get the same publicity as Comrade Wong?'" He stuffed the clipping into his pocket. Then suddenly he re-noticed me. "I've got it. Mark should help us out."

"Right," joined in Harvey Milliard. He sent me a knowing smirk. "Can and I have talked about that, Mark. Why, you could write us a North-South Trade speech, for example."

"You want a North-South Trade speech?" I asked.

"Not really."

"That's why Comrade Wong gets the publicity," I said. "Do ten speeches a week on a variety of topics and you're bound to hit with some of them."

"Hear! Hear!" Carlos pounded the coffee table. Babatunde did a high-life shuffle across the room. Nha raised his glass. Jean-Paul said: "Perpetual motion machine leaving now for Papua New Guineaeeeeeeeeeeeeeeeeeeeeeee," and flip-flopped backwards like one of the clowns in Fairouz's collage. Fairouz lit another reefer.

To my count, this was Fairouz's third joint since I had arrived, and I didn't like it. Not that I was stuffy about these things; one was fine, it got rid of the air hostess; but I wasn't sure what three or more were going to do to our lovemaking. Assuming we ever got around to lovemaking. Here it was, 11:30 p.m. on a work night, but nobody gave any indication of leaving. I doubted I could leave before they did: official lovers were probably expected to help with the dishes.

Although I was enough of a bureaucrat not to care for the loud music and the heavy, sweet smell of marijuana that hung over the room, in many ways these people seemed more my type than did those in the typical Admin gathering; however this was a work-and-play-together crowd, the elite high flyers of Government House with their current sexual partner "in-laws," so in-bred that outsiders like Mark Grimal couldn't always follow their conversation. I was making work, not social, contacts; but that was what I needed right then anyway.

Tosca put a tango record on the stereo. She was tired of all this serious talk. Coming toward us, she held out her hand to Carlos. "Let's dance, 'Che' Carlitos," she said. "For tomorrow we die." He jumped up with alacrity, and they flowed into a heavy cultural display of swoops and bends and swirls that made me feel they should be programmed. I wondered what Tosca's body felt like in those bends. But this was not private dancing; it could only be performed by two people who hadn't the slightest sexual interest in each other. Everyone stopped whatever he or she was doing and gathered around, except Jean-Paul, who pulled a pretty girl with bangs down on the floor beside the circus painting and started fondling her. Jean-Paul had had too much marijuana.

When Tosca and Carlos finished their performance, we applauded. To my surprise, this appeared to be the climax of the evening, and people started drifting toward the door. "I'll give you a call, man," said Mabuza, as he left with Tosca. "Equal time for Mallam Ahmed." Carlos hoisted Jean-Paul and his girlfriend to their feet and got them out the door. Evelyn Thompson left with the Nhas, Babatunde with a pink-cheeked Israeli, Harvey with a tawny Jamaican. The door finally closed on the last guest. Fairouz was singing to herself, picking up glasses and ash trays and taking them to the kitchen. Her hair looked disheveled. I helped empty the garbage. Being an official lover was a lot like being a husband.

"So did you enjoy the party, Mr. Grimal?" Fairouz asked.

Mr. Grimal? "Oh," I said, "are we back to 'Mr. Grimal' now? I thought we'd switched permanently to 'Mark.'"

Evidently something in my voice didn't sound right, because Fairouz stopped wiping water off the kitchen sink and turned around, sponge in hand, a startled expression on her face.

"I'm sorry. What was that you said?"

"Nothing important." I knew I should shut up, but there's something about this kind of routine that, once started, makes it impossible to stop without crashing. "It's just that it was 'Mark' all evening to your friends, and now suddenly when we're alone, I'm 'Mr. Grimal' again."

"Does that bother you?"

"Oh, I don't know that it bothers me. I just find it a little puzzling, that's all."

"Why?"

I closed the door to the dish ozonator and pushed the button. "It's not important, Fairouz. Let's forget it." She was staring at me with her big green eyes as though she'd never seen me before.

"It must be important if you thought it important enough to mention. Out of all the things that happened this evening, that is the one you think is important to mention."

Definitely I had made a mistake, but the marijuana wasn't helping things. "Fairouz, you're the one who wanted to call me 'Mr. Grimal' in public. I was just wondering why you changed your mind, that's all."

"Those were my friends," she said. "Not public."

I cleared my throat. "Fine. Now I understand."

"I don't believe this," she said, shaking her head. "How can we have our first quarrel over such a trivial issue?"

I didn't believe it either. "There's nothing to quarrel about. Come on. Let's forget it." I reached for her, but she backed away, put down the sponge, and wiped her hands on a towel. Then she stalked into the living room.

I followed.

She sat down in the center of the sofa, folded her hands in her lap, and said, "You didn't seem yourself tonight, that's true, but how natural, I thought, because of your recent tragedy. Now I see the problem was another thing: you objected to my introducing you as 'Mark.' What do you think this says about you, Mr. Grimal?"

"Fairouz, don't build this up out of all proportion."

"I think it does say something about you."

"Sure, it says something about me." I was beginning to get annoyed. "It says I shoot my mouth off at the wrong moment. And if you weren't so high on grass, you wouldn't be making an issue out of it."

Fairouz rose to her feet, a six-foot volcano, and, for a moment, I thought she was going to hit me. A fight with Fairouz would be a grim undertaking; she'd be harder to overpower than Lisa, and the scars might be permanent.

"I am high on grass?" she asked. "Just who are you to talk to me like that?"

"Your lover, darling. Your officially approved, formally announced lover."

She started to say something, changed her mind, and sat back down. There was a soft menace in her voice. "Now I understand. You don't want to be known publicly as my lover? Is that it? How interesting."

"Fairouz, I'm a married man."

"No one would ever guess it."

That was as good as a slap. I took a deep breath. "Well," I said, "it does look as though we're having a quarrel, doesn't it?"

"Yes, we're having a quarrel. Suddenly Mr. Mark Grimal is a married man, with a reputation to protect. But it's not his reputation as a married man that he's trying to protect, because he doesn't have a reputation as a married man; it's his reputation as a free, unattached Don Juan that he wants to protect. Isn't that right, Mr. Grimal?" Her eyes were wild, and she was shooting closer to the target than Danzig. I was appalled. How had this happened? "That's what was wrong tonight: you thought I was being too possessive. Correct, Mr. Grimal? That is it, isn't it? Possessive. You wouldn't want anybody to think that Fairouz Moked has any claims on you—"

"Fairouz, stop this! You don't know what you're saying."

"—Well, Fairouz Moked doesn't have any claims on you, and doesn't want any claims on you. I haven't time for a spoiled boy who thinks he has a right to all the candy in the store." She leapt up, hurled herself at the door, and flung it open. "Go home, Married

Man!"

I didn't move. "This is ridiculous."

"Oh, I agree," she said. "I haven't made such a fool of myself in a long time as introducing you to my friends."

Since I had drunk no more than one and a half glasses of wine over the entire evening, I knew that I had done nothing to deserve even a fraction of this abuse. Fairouz had taken a grenade to kill a mosquito.

"Fairouz, please, I'm asking you. Close the door. Sit down. Don't ruin everything we have going for us because you've misunderstood what I said—"

"Had going for us," she snapped, holding the door open at arm's length. "Good night, Mr. Grimal.

Nothing like this had ever happened to me before. Next time I'd confiscate her marijuana at the start of the evening. I moved toward the door. "I see there's no sense in trying to talk reason to you until you come back down from wherever you're circulating. I haven't hurt you, Fairouz. You're hurting me." I stepped out into the hallway. "Tomorrow you'll realize it."

"Good night, Mr. Grimal," she repeated, and slammed the door in my face. I stood there for several minutes, just looking at the door. Of all possible endings to the evening, this was the one that would not have occurred to me.

Finally when I realized that she was not going to open the door on her own in contrition, and I was not going to make a fool of myself by knocking on it, I left. It was one a.m. and Lisa was surprised to see me home so early. She was reading a space romance in bed. "What happened?" she asked. "Fight with your girlfriend?"

Since I wasn't supposed to have been with my "girlfriend," I should have been able to come up with a convincing retort; however, I said nothing, just hung my clothes in the closet.

Lisa closed her book and laid it on the bedside table. "Well, I see this is serious. You must be losing your touch, darling."

TWENTY-TWO

I told myself that the next day Fairouz would call, but she didn't. Or the day after that, but she didn't. I told myself that I'd see her in person on Saturday at the Global Television Studios, but Jean-Paul was there in her place, carrying Comrade Wong's briefcase. I sent her a handwritten, unsigned note that said only: "I missed you," accompanied by a drawing of a stick figure tumbling off a tightrope. No answer. I dreamed up a pretext to call in connection with Comrade Wong's Filipino cultural heritage series; before connecting me with the Chairman, she came close to asking me how to spell my name. No, Fairouz Moked had not awakened the next morning, wondering how she could have treated her lover so badly. Fairouz Moked had cut her losses.

And Mark Grimal was now an ex-lover.

The moment I realized this, I knew I had to get her back again, if not on her knees, at least on her back with her legs spread apart so that I could have the last fuck. Lisa's wish had come true: at last a woman had walked out on me. I was surprised at my anger. Fairouz, toward whom I had felt so close, had done it over nothing, just a few random intuitions laced with marijuana thought.

But how was I to get her back? If Fairouz wouldn't talk to me in person or by phone, I'd have to write, since tapes, whether video or audio, were even more dangerous and required acting skill besides. But a letter? Letters were evidence. I had never written a love letter to a woman, nor anything remotely resembling one; I wasn't even sure how to begin.

I wrote the letter. I wrote several letters. Over a week, in between all the other work I was doing, I wrote and re-wrote and re-wrote again. It wasn't easy to apologize without admitting guilt or lure back without promising anything. I tried humor. I tried pathos. Finally I settled on straightforward honesty as the best method. I imagined Fairouz reading the letter, tried, like a spider, to weave a web of words around her, as though she were a suspicious, recalcitrant fly that I intended to have for breakfast. And I did intend to have her for breakfast, and for lunch and for dinner and for snacks in between, for just as long as I wanted to have her, though no longer—provided I could only once more get my cock and tongue into her.

At last I produced a letter, which my professional ego told me wasn't too bad for a first try.

Dear Fairouz:

I have never written a letter to a woman before. A letter means a commitment, and, as you can tell, I am not good at commitments.

What happened between us the other night shocked me because I had felt that we understood each other. I was wrong. Merely because I consider you a remarkable woman doesn't mean I understand you. I should have been more careful.

I won't argue with anything you had to say about me that evening. My remark was stupid; however, I did nothing to justify your extraordinary anger.

It seems, my dear, that you are a woman who cuts her losses so fast that you don't even wait to see if they're losses. Please at least give me an opportunity to apologize. That's only fair, my dear. Not this numb silence.

On Thursday, October 10, I shall be at The Sub-Orbital Restaurant between 7:00 and 9:00 p.m. Please join me, or send word if you can't. I need you.

Mark

After I had finished editing the letter on the computer, I copied it by hand, added a few minor corrections to make it appear more personal, and then inserted it into an official Admin envelope to eliminate the risk that Fairouz might toss a too obviously personal note, unopened, into the shredder. When I gave it to the robot messenger to transmit to Government House, I programmed the robot to require Fairouz's signature before handing it over.

Meanwhile my work was piling higher and higher. I had to

call people, apologize, ask permission to give the job to another writer, postpone deadlines, take stimulant tablets, explain complaints to Eberhardt. My staff tried to bail me out; they were still sympathizing with me over Christie; they would have been less understanding had they known about the letter.

On Thursday at 6:30 p.m. I took my notepad computer and two speech files with me to the Sub-Orbital and asked Jerome to give me a private room. Although the cost—seventy dolyens cover charge—was exorbitant in my financial condition, I also couldn't affor to spend two hours sitting in the bar, drinking Scotch-and-sodas and waiting for Fairouz, when both of these speeches were due at 9:00 a.m. tomorrow. After ordering smoked oysters and a large bottle of spring water, I spread out my work on the table and opened the drapes so that I could glance from time to time to the city lights below me. Certainly I'd have enough to keep me busy if Fairouz failed to appear, although since she had signed for the letter, common courtesy would dictate at least a reply sent by messenger.

She did not appear by 7:00; however, I was then deep in a speech for Hans Benning of Social Welfare about stopping the use of psychotomimetic drugs by the street children of Indianapolis. At 8:30 when there was still no sign of Fairouz, I ordered dinner—a steak with rice pilaf, which was going to cost me another twenty-five dolyens.

Nine o'clock passed. At 9:15 Jerome brought my food and a half carafe of red wine. I ate slowly, reading the background notes for the second speech I had to finish that night, this one a comparison between ancient Greek democracy and the People's TV Assembly. The speech was for Telecom's Peter Neumann; he wasn't interested in the policy side of it, only in the mechanics—how many people reached, how easily, that sort of thing. Greek democracy excluded women, slaves, and foreigners; the People's TV Assembly included women and Associated Territories nationals, although not of course the Undesirables, who were genetically deformed and therefore not entitled to participate. Rereading the policy guidance on this annoyed me so much that I deliberately opened the speech with a statement comparing the federal government's view of the UDs to the Greek view of women and slaves. Writing the sentence made me feel better, although of course I'd have to erase it later.

It was now 10 p.m. and Fairouz had neither appeared nor sent word. I ordered another half carafe of wine from Jerome. I don't drink when I work, but then I don't usually work in a restaurant either. Many great writers, none of whose names I could at that moment remember, had written, seated in restaurants, with a bottle of wine at their elbows. Maybe even waiting for women. I was almost through the first draft of the speech; the best thing to do would be finish it, sleep, then get up at three o'clock to revise the text. And try not to think about Fairouz Moked.

But I did. After all, that's why I was there, rather than in some more suitable, less expensive setting. With each sip of wine I found my mind wandered more, my eyes moved from the computer to the lights below me, it became more difficult to cope with the People's TV Assembly. I remembered Fairouz in San Francisco...Fairouz floating down the escalator in Government House...Fairouz telling me about Artazio Colonna.... What had turned her into that ferocious virago who threw me out of her apartment when I hadn't done anything?

Or had I done something?

I tried desperately to recall the exact words of our conversation that evening. She had asked me, what?—how I had liked the party. And instead of replying to her question, which would have been easy enough to do—after all, I had had a good time and had made valuable work contacts as well—I had come up with a snide remark about her use of my first name with her friends. I had not cared to be flaunted before them as her lover; yet the other outsiders there were all, like me, current sexual partners, and I wouldn't have been at the party at all if I hadn't been her lover.

I loosened my tie, closed my eyes and leaned back against the cushions. Shit, what an asshole. Every time I found something I liked, I deliberately dropped and broke it. I was thirty-eight years old, my marriage was a mess, my work deteriorating; but I had my freedom. I was free to go out and find another woman who stole paintings, agreed with me on the Undesirables policy, made love superbly, and helped me in my work. I thought of all the dead-end relationships I was going to get into over the next few years laying women, all the fights with Lisa over women who weren't even as interesting as Lisa, all the thrusts and spurts followed by boredom. This was not rational behavior. Maybe I should see a Lifestyle Department psychiatrist.

I sat back up. My watch said 11 p.m. I had to finish the speech and get out of there. I would have said that this had been an expensive learning experience, except that, since I never learned anything, I'd probably repeat the same mistakes with the next woman.

At 11:15 p.m. Jerome opened the door. I glanced up.

Fairouz Moked stepped into the room.

She was dressed in a red brocade evening dress. Her hair was wound around her head in coils laced with red ribbon. Over her shoulders was a black stole; in her hand a velvet purse; on her feet shiny, black, high-heeled sandals. She was not smiling. In fact, as Jerome proudly escorted her to my table, she was staring at me in dismay. I scrambled to my feet before this apparition whose appearance downstairs must have made the space scientists think she'd teleported in from another planet.

"Fairouz."

"Good evening, Mr. Grimal."

I had shed my jacket over an hour ago; my shirt sleeves were rolled up; there was a pencil behind my ear, and, for all I knew, salad dressing stains on my shirt, although I hoped not. My notepad computer and papers were strewn over the table, which Jerome pulled out so that she couldj slip into the seat beside me. She glided in, keeping her distance. I sat back down. The brocade gown spread out to my leg. She ordered a glass of sherry. Her elegant head pivoted away from me.

"Would you like anything else, Mr. Grimal?"

"Some coffee, please, Jerome."

Jerome was smiling as though he personally had found her for me and had brought her here from where she had been holding court in a Government House chamber. That seemed as likely an explanation as any. At this hour, Fairouz should have had no reason to expect to find me here; but if so, then why had she come?

"I see you're working, Mr. Grimal. I should have guessed you would be working." That was good. At least I was working.

I shuffled the papers in front of me. "A couple of speeches with deadlines tomorrow morning."

"Is there anything I can do to help?"

"Oh, I don't want you to...to work...."

We weren't even looking at each other.

"Why not?" she asked. "I am here. I don't mind helping you do useful work. It is the most attractive thing about you."

No woman before Fairouz had ever considered work to be the most attractive thing about me. So much for my reputed charm, my legendary sexual prowess.

"Forgive me, Fairouz." I didn't say for what; I didn't know for what. Maybe everything.

Avoiding my eyes, she dropped the stole behind her. Small, thin, red straps crossed her bare shoulders. She reached for a pencil. "First, we finish the work. Afterward we can discuss other matters." She looked around her at the subdued, recessed lighting. "But how can you work in this light? You are paying too much for this room, I am sure. When the waiter comes back, ask him to find you a lamp. I'm sure he can locate one in an office somewhere."

The lamp helped. I gave her the narcotics speech to edit, and, fortified with caffeine, re-tackled the People's TV Assembly. We worked quietly, no personal comments. When she started on the second speech, she asked if I wanted to retain the sentence comparing the Greek attitude toward women and slaves with that of the federal government's attitude toward the Undesirables.

I had forgotten the comment was there. "No. Peter Neumann would never buy it."

"You are experimenting again, Mr. Grimal." She almost smiled, although she still wasn't looking at me.

It was one o'clock when we finished all that could be done that evening. Fairouz stacked the texts in neat bundles and straightened them on the table. "And now, Mr. Grimal, you invited me here. What is it you wish to talk about?"

"Do we have to do it here?"

"Yes," she said. "I would prefer to do it here. Besides, you shouldn't waste your money; you have paid for the room until two o'clock when the restaurant closes."

"You are a very practical woman."

"I am," she agreed. "That's why I cut my losses."

I winced. Her voice was cool and controlled, but apparently my letter had been another blunder. "As a writer, I guess I should stick to speeches."

"Oh, no," she said. "The letter was most clever. You eliminated everything awkward. After reading it, I too could not understand why we had had such a quarrel."

I rolled down my shirt sleeves. "Why did we have the quarrel, Fairouz? I know I made a stupid remark that hurt you. And I'm sorry. But that's all I did. You have a low tolerance level for stupidity."

"When it comes from intelligent men, yes."

I switched off the lamp, dimmed the other lights even further, and pushed the button that sent us revolving slowly around the room. As she had said, I was paying for it; I'd better use it.

"Intelligence has nothing to do with it. You announced to the world, 'Look at my wonderful lover.' And I thought, 'Oh, shit! Now I am going to have to be a wonderful lover.'"

"Grow up, Mark," said Fairouz. "Grow up."

She had used my first name. I had broken through.

"I know. I'm only trying to explain why I hurt you that evening without intending to."

"You intended to."

I took a deep breath. "Not consciously, Fairouz. To assert my independence, why would I want to hurt a woman who's everything I've ever wanted in a woman? That makes no sense."

She bit her lip, said nothing until the revolving platform reached the area where we could see yellow arc rays outlining the Transport Cabins in the distance.

"Don't exaggerate my value to you, Mark. You say that now, because we always think something is most desirable when we're about to lose it. Another woman will do just as well. You'll see. The candy may not all taste the same, but caramels and chocolates are both sweet and sticky."

The distant lights of an enormous airship climbed ponderously into the sky. My rage built, went up with the plane. What was it with this woman?

"Fairouz," I said softly, "I think you just insulted me."

She bowed her head. Her clasped hands were resting on the table. "I'm sorry, Mark, but it wasn't consciously intended."

I reached out, grasped her chin, and turned her face so that she was forced to look at me. "If you think I'm like that, then why are you here?"

Half of her face was in shadow, half reflected the glow from the City. "Because I'm in love with you, of course." Her cool voice was all air hostess.

Love? Quickly I pressed her head against my chest, in relief, yes, but also because I didn't want her to see dismay spread across my features. I hadn't asked for love, had I? The Federal Territory capital shimmered around us in black and gold and silver like a masquerade costume.

"I know it's not smart to love you," she said. "You're a talented man. And, in many ways, a good man. You're just not any good at loving a woman. So tonight at the Bangladeshi Embassy I told myself, 'I shall go the the restaurant long after he has given up and left, long after there is a chance that he will be there. But if by accident he is there, well, then we shall see....'" Raising her face from my chest, she placed her hands on her cheeks and gave a small laugh. "And so here you are. Working."

"'The most attractive thing about me.'"

"The most attractive thing about you." Now she did smile. "I lost my bet."

"No, you didn't. You won it." I kissed her. In my relief I was too hasty, too fierce; I bit her lips, I thrust my tongue far down her throat, I sucked her tongue into my mouth, with one hand I slid the thin straps off her right shoulder and popped one of her breasts out of her dress. "No, Mark," she murmured, as I pressed the nipple between my fingers. "We can't make love here."

"Nobody will come until I push the buzzer."

"The windows—"

"Oh." Still holding her, I reached over and pressed the control for the drapes. They closed, blocking out the City. Her right breast curved forward on top of the red brocade dress. I pulled down the straps on the other shoulder and carefully raised her second breast, like an egg, from beneath the cloth. With her firm breasts exposed above the tight bodice, she looked like a Minoan woman in an ancient painting.

We left the Sub-Orbital at 2:30 a.m. The restaurant had closed. Jerome waited patiently downstairs. The bartender was stacking glasses, a male Undesirable in a blue uniform vacuumed the floor, the cashier was counting the money. The bill was one hundred and forty-seven dolyens. I gave Jerome an additional fifty in cash, and handed out twenty dolyens each to the others who had been waiting. Fairouz ignored all these extravagant transactions. She stood at the glass door, looking out at the boulevard. Her hair was no longer as smoothly coiled, her cosmetics had smudged and melted, there was a broken shoulder strap hidden beneath the stole, tomorrow there would be bruises on her throat from my harsh kisses. My performance this evening had been all hard desire; there wasn't much else that could be said for it; but I had her back now, although at a psychological cost I'd never paid before, and I wasn't sure that all the charges had come in yet.

TWENTY-THREE

Since October was Comrade Wong's month to be Global Chairman, he stayed in the Federal Territory capital except for brief trips to Manila and Helsinki. Fairouz was in great demand at Government House functions; she spoke nine languages, including both East and West Arabic, Russian, and Catalan, and looked good besides. Sometimes I saw her before she went out, sometimes I saw her afterward. Thanks to her help, I managed to get my work back under control. Although Fairouz's attitude wasn't all that different from Lisa's, I didn't want to keep Fairouz working every night to bail me out after she'd already put in ten-twelve hours with Comrade Wong. The first time the Government House staff gathered for another party, this one at Harvey Milliard's residence, I overdid my public devotion a little.

Fond as I was of Fairouz, however, I still couldn't talk to her about Christie. Had I done so, perhaps my determination to change UD policy wouldn't have become an obsession. But I didn't tell, and Fairouz didn't ask. Like many people who control their feelings, she thought clamming up and swallowing grief was what a strong person did rather than lash out, seek vengeance, wallow in the past. Knowing that to be her view, I kept my mouth shut and pretended.

When I went to Records to ask Vimalachandra for the results of the latest opinion polls on the Undesirables policy, he expressed surprise that I should be covering that subject again so soon.

"I thought the unrest had subsided."

"Temporarily," I agreed. "But you know Polyguide. The topic is one of their favorites."

While Vim's transmitter operator was printing me a copy of the poll results, he poured thick espresso coffee from his machine into two hand-painted ceramic cups, and added an equal amount of liquid sugar. Enough of Vim's coffee might cause diabetes. Vim was watching me closely, the way people do when they suspect you have a hidden motive for whatever it is you're doing.

"I was sorry to hear about the girl who worked in your section. Barbarous."

"Worse than you think." Although I was sure Vim's office was bugged, on this one I didn't care if Security were listening. "The act was bad enough, but she didn't die of that. She died because the Federal Government refuses to provide adequate medical care to UDs or protect them from adulterated drugs."

"Bad," said Vim. "But—that's not policy. Flows from policy, maybe, yes, but not policy."

"All right," I agreed. "Maybe it just flows, but the result's the same." I could see I was beginning to pick up the Government House staff's attitude, that policy's the real reason behind the official reason. I'd have to watch myself.

"Easier to change though," said Vim. He placed his pipe carefully into an ashtray and then took a sip of the sweet coffee. "Changes in applications of policy don't have to be ratified by the People's TV Assembly."

"Who has to approve?"

"In this case MedUnit. Or maybe James Francis Finley III." Although there were people in the Admin who doubted it, I was sure that the Director-General, James Francis Finley III, did exist; I had seen him once at an official function for the visiting Head of Government of the Associated Territory of Ethiopia; but why it should be any easier for Mark Grimal, Chief, Speakers Division, to reach James Francis Finley III rather than to reach the People's TV Assembly wasn't clear to me.

"Interesting."

Vim smiled at me. "How about you and Lisa coming over for dinner this weekend? Pappadams and chicken curry."

"Talked me into it. Friday? Saturday?"

"Let me get back to you after checking with Jacintha."

Vim was playing big brother. Well, that was fine with me provided he didn't overdo it. Vim had a much better feel for the bureaucracy than I did; and if James Francis Finley III could be persuaded to do something about MedUnit admission policy and

adulterated drugs, so much the better. The important thing, however, was to change the policy, and although people talked about
"working within the system," I could identify nobody within the
current system who might do that. Not Polyguide, the keeper of the
flame. Not the joint Chairmen, who, as Kelly said, couldn't agree on
a breakfast menu. And not, according to the latest opinion polls,
which Vim's secretary had just handed me, the People, who agreed
that the Undesirables policy "protects the global community from
crime, disease, warmongering, and tendencies that destroy the
social fabric." Those tendencies varied from community to community as social fabrics varied, although there were defined limits,
based on universal global opinion and monitored by the Legal
Department's Human Rights section, such as protecting nine-year-
olds who stole candy from being declared Undesirables in some of
the more primitive areas.

"Popular policy we have here, isn't it?"

Vim re-lit his pipe. "Always has been, Mark. Human nature's
a great thing."

I glanced quickly down the subject ratings. As I suspected,
the most popular aspect of the UD policy was "protects community"; least popular was "effect on UD children."

Although Lisa considered the Vimalachandras stuffy, she
was delighted to be going to dinner at their flat on Saturday, because
taking her to the home of my friends restored her to the number one
position in my life, at least for public consumption.

The Vimalachandras lived in a flat with wood and leather
furniture, striped curtains, bronze plates with magico-religious
scenes on them adorning the walls, braziers and incense burners and
real flowers in pots that hung from the ceiling. Dressed in a sari,
Jacintha was so small and well formed that she would have reminded me of a ten-year-old if ten-year-olds had breasts like that
above their bare midriffs. After greeting us politely with bows, their
three teenaged children disappeared into bedrooms. We sat down on
the hard seats, with bright pillows at our backs. Vim lit the ceremo-
nial oil lamp—a bronze cock on a pedestal in the corner—while
Jacintha served us sweet, non-alcoholic fruit juice concoctions,
purple or red or yellow, all tasting the same, accompanied by

cashew nuts and roasted bits of coconut. Lisa printed a rapt expression on her face, the way she did when she couldn't think of anything to say to people. In fact, Jacintha was a bit beyond both of us: she had a doctoral degree in architecture, and worked as a consultant to Social Welfare's Urban Development section.

The dinner was delicious. After we left the table, Lisa asked Jacintha to give her the recipes for the chicken curry and pappadams and dahl and brinjal; and the two women withdrew to chairs on the opposite side of the room, which was the way they did it after dinner at the Vimalachandras—women on one side, men on the other—and got into an animated conversation about spices.

I lit a cigarette to accompany Vim with his pipe. "So tell me about James Francis Finley III." Finley had been Admin Director-General for eleven years now, a tribute to his soothing conflict management, since the D-G was appointed by the Chairmen and served for as long as they and their successors agreed to keep him on. "Is he reachable?"

"Yes, but." Vim plumped up a red batik-covered pillow and put it behind his back. "He likes filters, the more the better. The main ones are Kelly, Danzig, Rublev, and Dharmasena of Foreign Interests. They see him every Tuesday. Theoretically the rest of us Directors have access once a month—" He smiled wryly. "—however, at the staff meeting only what Finley considers to be vital topics of 'general interest' can be raised, and so in practice it all boils down to policy or security questions or inaugurations of economic projects by one of the Big Three, and occasionally a flap over the local political scene in some Associated Territory."

I tapped my ashes into the crimson caparison that decorated the saddle of a white marble elephant ashtray.

"Sounds like he's not much interested in what's going on among the Admin troops."

"As Director-General, he considers it his role to serve as political liaison with the Chairmen. We're the experts, we should solve our own problems in our own departments."

"Then why would he take an interest in MedUnit admission practices or drug adulteration in the UD district?"

"In general he wouldn't," Vim agreed. "First you'll have to

approach Schleka of MedUnit, who's the proper person to resolve the issue."

I didn't have much hope of Schleka. I told Vim what had happened to Christie after the rape from the time of her admission to the City MedUnit hospital to my conversation with Dr. Karageorghis. "Schleka's going to have a lot of imposing reasons in addition to policy as to why he can't change things. Higher incidence of disease among UDs, particularly incurable disease, mental illness, violence-induced injuries, drug abuse. Why waste resources on those people? That will be his reaction."

"Nevertheless," said Vim, "if you don't try Schleka first, Finley won't even look at the proposal. Once Schleka turns it down, then you can send a memo to Finley through Polyguide; Kelly'll give you the format."

It all sounded like a longshot to me, but I was anxious to prove that I was a responsible, proper-channels bureaucrat.

"Okay. Worth a try."

Vim tapped his pipe gently on top of the elephant. "The young woman's hospital bill must have been exorbitant. You...need any help? I could loan you a couple of thousand."

This was going beyond official big brotherliness. Even friends didn't usually offer to loan you large sums of money. Quickly I lit another cigarette.

"Thanks, Vim. But things are under control. I have a bank loan."

"Well, don't hesitate," he said, "if you need it later."

I could have talked to Vim, then, but I didn't, because I didn't want him involved if I stepped outside channels. I didn't want anybody involved except Mark Grimal. If Danzig had his way, win or lose, I'd likely end up in Billings Psychiatric Hospital being restructured. Why take Vim with me? Assuming of course that he didn't report me first to Polyguide when I declined to listen to reason, for, although I liked Vim, he was definitely a channels man, and they tend to do things "for your own good." Besides, I figured that he'd been informally assigned by the Club to keep me out of trouble, and if one is determined to get into trouble, the last person to talk to is someone bent on keeping one out of it.

In mid-November Can Mabuza invited me to Government House to discuss guidelines on a major speech about energy resources. The entire staff met with me in Mallam Ahmed's chamber. We drank mint tea. Tropical plants were scattered among the furniture, which was all blonde cane with bright tie-dye cushions. The room was like a hot house; here it was November and I was sweating.

"Brasilia would be delighted to host the event," said Tosca Pinelli. "I've informally discussed the speech with the Speaker of the Assembly."

"Wonderful, Tosca," murmured Mallam Ahmed.

"Africa's where we need the publicity," counter-attacked Can. "I suggest Lagos as the venue. Vibrant media, richest sub-Saharan country—"

"Mmmm...good idea," said Mallam Ahmed.

"A major policy speech delivered in an Associated Territory?" asked Tosca.

"They vote too."

"It's not a question of votes. The influential government officials are in Brazil."

"Government officials already know what we're going to say. We need to reach the academic community."

"In Nigeria?"

Clearing his throat, Rodrigo dos Santos, Ahmed's chief staff assistant and a Brazilian, turned to the Chilean econ assistant. "Isaías, what's your view?"

"Nigeria is foot-dragging on the solar energy issue."

"Then," said Rodrigo in relief, "we'll kill two birds with one stone. We'll go with government officials in Lagos."

"Splendid, splendid," murmured Mallam Ahmed.

During the remainder of the meeting Can and Tosca continued to snipe at each other; they agreed on nothing, as though someone might accuse them of collaborating because they were lovers rather than cooperating because they were colleagues. Accustomed as I was to dull, by-the-book Admin staff meetings, I felt as though I had wandered into a family quarrel and ought to excuse myself and come back later.

But then neither Can nor Tosca were bureaucrats, nor were most of the people who worked for the Chairmen. Although Security investigated all candidates for Federal Government employment, in practice the Chairmen could override the Board's recommendations. Mabuza had once served as chief information officer for a splinter guerrilla group in Sierra Leone. Carlos Acevedo Mejía had been a Colombian labor organizer; the labor included a group of Undesirables picking coffee beans. Jean-Paul Dornier's luggage was always sniffed out by the dogs at the airport. In this age of scientific birth control and medical backup termination procedures, Tosca had an illegitimate son living with her grandmother.

Even Mr. Brown's staff, the most conservative of the group, had its own peculiarities.

When Mr. Brown's secretary, Evelyn Thompson, hosted the Government House staff party, she invited us for 6:00 p.m., rather an early hour for this group, I thought.

"She likes to have the children there," Fairouz explained.

"Children? I didn't know Evelyn was married."

"She isn't. They're adopted children. It's a story you'll very much like. I'll tell you later."

Evelyn opened the door—a chubby, cheerful, middle-aged lady with greying hair and a wilting bouquet pinned to her pleated, white blouse. She took our coats and handed them to a young girl with curly blonde hair, who looked as though she were about twelve. "This is my daughter, Earledeen," she announced.

"Hi, Earledeen." I winked at her.

Earledeen ducked her head and fled with the coats. "And there's Vernon," said Evelyn, pointing across the room to a four-year-old boy dressed in pajamas, who was seated on Rodrigo's shoulders. "And in the chair there—" She wafted her hand to an overstuffed chair in which a boy of about seven was reading a book aloud to Jean-Paul's girlfriend. "—we have the intellectual, Alan. Welcome to the Thompson household."

For the next three hours I adapted myself to a sober, family atmosphere of pork chops, light beer, mashed potatoes and gravy, carrot sticks, apple pie, sentimental mood music. Earledeen was persuaded to play her guitar; she managed to hit most of the notes but it wasn't exactly what I would call a musical experience; the Government House people applauded wildly. Standing on a pouf, Alan told us everything he knew about global space stations; shaking Alan's hand, Babatunde solemnly assured him that he had a great future as a space scientist. Vernon spilled milk on the carpet, added a few mashed potatoes, and then fell asleep in Tosca's arms.

Mr. Brown popped in to join us.

Mr. Brown was dressed in denim trousers and a soft flannel shirt with full sleeves, gathered at the wrist. He picked up Vernon, who immediately woke up and said: "'Allo, Daddy," and then snuggled back down into Brown's shoulder. Nobody seemed surprised, and Brown only reacted when he caught a glimpse of me, standing by the piano with Carlos's girlfriend, a gorgeous Thai woman in orange silk and elaborate braids wound around her head. Brown called over his program assistant, Ole Grieg, and evidently asked him whose "in-law" I was, because Grieg nodded his head toward Fairouz, who was seated on a couch talking to Earledeen. Great. Now, after this, whenever a speech by Wong scored, Brown would have no doubt out of whose bed it had come.

When Brown carried Vernon into the hallway that led to the bedrooms, he passed me. "Hello, Mark," he said with his fake smile. "Where's your wife this evening?"

No question about it: I was on Mr. Brown's shit list; and that was too bad because the revelation that a man who was as self-consciously modish as Brown could permit a child to drool all over his expensive flannel shirt forced me to look at Brown a little differently.

When Fairouz and I returned to her apartment at ten o'clock, I said: "Well, that was a...an unusual evening."

"Poor Mark." She put her arms around my neck. "I could tell you were suffering."

I kissed her. "Pork chops and children aren't within my area of expertise." We dropped our coats on a chair and headed for the bedroom, my arm around her waist.

"For us sometimes it is a nice change to go there," said Fairouz. "When Mr. Brown travels, he allows Evelyn to stay at home. Most of us don't have the domestic life."

I started undoing the buttons on Fairouz's blue velvet dress. "So tell me about her children." I lifted her long hair to one shoulder and kissed the back of her neck.

"They were born to a woman in London who was declared an Undesirable for cheating the government out of welfare money. Evelyn was a social worker on the case. She felt sorry for the children."

"And Evelyn adopted them?" I was astonished enough to interrupt my kisses. "That's not supposed to be possible."

"Mr. Brown made it possible. When they tried to take the children away from her to sterilize them, she wrote directly to Mr. Brown and he tacked an exemption onto the budget bill—"

Mr. Brown was turning out to be quite a surprise.

"—and after that he hired her to work for him."

"And then he screwed her." I dropped Fairouz's dress down around her hips and cupped her breasts in my hands. Pulling her onto the bed, I slid my hand under the front of her dress, down her stomach and between her legs. She cried out, reached for the zipper on my pants. My penis disappeared into her mouth, emerged; I thrust it back down her throat. We pulled off the rest of our clothes, rolled over, and I entered her from behind.

"Evelyn likes him," murmured Fairouz. "He's good with the children."

Well, I could accept that. Why Brown, who, as a Chairman, presumably had his pick of women, preferred Evelyn was a bit more mysterious.

Mr. Brown and Evelyn Thompson and the three "innocent victim" children all came together in my mind with Christie, who had also been an "innocent victim." If any aspect of the Undesirables policy was vulnerable, this was it. Although the official rationale for treating UD children as UDs was that the children must be at least dormant carriers of their parents' undesirable genes, the real reason, I had always suspected, was that it served as an added deterrent to those considering anti-social activities. As a deterrent, it was probably effective; however it was the sort of deterrent that was abhorrent to people who had a soft spot in their hearts for children. And people particularly had a soft spot in their hearts for children during the December holidays when Mr. Brown would again be Global Chairman.

TWENTY-FOUR

When I called the MedUnit Director's office to make an appointment, his secretary told me that Dr. Fisher Schleka was in Geneva at a mental health conference, and from there he would go to Mombasa to inspect the new surgical facilities, and then to Tehran for a demonstration of crowd control through use of an experimental restructuring drug spray that was supposed to remove all memory of the reason for the protest from the minds of individuals participating in the mob.

"You people are getting too advanced over there," I said, appalled.

The secretary gave a throaty laugh. "Oh, they're not going to use it on real people, only on some UDs demanding food from the storage warehouses."

She gave me an appointment for December 1, the earliest I could get in after Schleka's return, and requested that I submit a written outline of the issues that I wished to discuss with him. I decided to write the outline as though it were the basis for the later memo to the Director-General. I knew I'd have plenty of time to draft it during my trip with Mallam Ahmed to Nigeria, because the speech on energy resources was finished and Ahmed's staff hadn't planned anything for me to do there.

"Something may come up," said Rodrigo.

Well, yes, something might, although if it did we'd be back home before Ahmed's staff could agree on what they wanted me to do about it. However, since I had accompanied Comrade Wong to San Francisco, Eberhardt okayed Ahmed's request on diplomatic grounds; and on a Tuesday morning we took off from the Transport Cabins an hour and a half late because Ahmed's secretary had forgotten to remind him that he had a dental appointment that morning.

I figured this was a forecast of what I could expect over the next three days, although I had already had a rehearsal in trying to get the speech on energy resources cleared by his staff. As Rodrigo wearily explained to me, Mallam Ahmed believed in consensus. Everyone made his "contribution," or, to my way of looking at it, his objection to the end result. We went through six versions of the speech before I finally hit one on which they could all agree. Even the venue changed, because somebody pointed out that during mid-week Nigerian government officials were gathered, not in vibrant Lagos, but in the dreary capital of Abuja; and therefore we were going to exchange the glittering night clubs, the pollution, the restaurants, the traffic jams, and the humid mangrove swamps of Lagos for Abuja's sterile government buildings dominated by gigantic mosque and cathedral museums. This had the beneficent effect of so depressing both Can and Tosca that they were civil to each other all the way to Abuja.

The hour trip was pleasant enough, since traveling on a Chairman's hypersonic air shuttle couldn't help but be pleasant once the rocket motor took over from the scramjet and we settled into near orbital velocity. The only trouble with such travel was that we got there too quickly to enjoy all the amenities.

Can had rounded up an impressive group of global journalists to take with us. Over the smoked oysters and cheese, an attractive woman named Ruthellen Janniger, whose economic articles I'd read in the English-language *Bonn Program World*, introduced herself to me; she thought I was a new member of Mallam Ahmed's staff. I confessed I was just a dull Admin speech writer. "Oh," she said, "then you wrote the speech Ahmed's giving in Abuja?" I demurred: "Let's call it a group effort." She laughed. "I know what you mean. Aren't they a crew?" Then she tried to get an advance copy of the speech. "Sorry, honey," I said, "but Mabuza probably shoots traitors." She took my refusal amicably. Her green corduroy jumpsuit bulged with pens, notebooks, micro-recorder, breasts pushing upward against the zipper. "You're a pleasant addition to this trip," she said, eyeing me up and down. "Come join us in the press cabin." In the sun, her curly red hair formed a wispy halo that made me want to put my hand in it.

We flew directly over rain forest and savannah to Abuja; but, as it turned out, some charter aircraft with faulty autopilot had crash-landed on the Abuja tarmac that morning and therefore we went on to nearby Kaduna instead and waited two hours in a stuffy V.I.P. lounge, drinking strong Nigerian beer in large bottles, until vehicles from Abuja could pick us up. While we were waiting, Mabuza arranged an impromptu press conference for some of the local news sheet journalists, but Mallam Ahmed was so busy being gracious, he didn't say anything.

Ruthellen Janniger and I had been drinking together and therefore, when the twenty Federal Government vehicles from Abuja finally pulled into the airport, I started to follow her into one of the press cars. A small fist closed around my wrist, and I discovered Tosca pulling me in the opposite direction. "You're with us," she snapped. When we got away from the press car, she muttered: "Keep away from that broad, Mark. You want to get the clap?"

I was shocked. Not even Danzig had ever physically pulled me away from a woman. "Hold on, honey. You are out of line."

"Maybe so," she agreed. "But you'll have to live with it." She nudged me toward a limousine in which Rodrigo and Mallam Ahmed's Senegalese secretary, Mety Diob, were already sitting. Furious, I got into the vehicle; but since I was not going to quarrel about my sex life with Tosca in front of Rodrigo and Mety, I spent the hour and a half trip to Abuja scrunched down in the back seat, pretending to sleep, and silently cursing Tosca Pinelli, who sat stiffly beside me, making notes on a clipboard.

Finally we reached Abuja. Mallam Ahmed was staying at the Nigerian Government Barracks. The rest of us checked into a splashy hotel with gold-plated reproductions of Nok, Ife, and Benin heads peering down from the lobby molding. It was now 7:30 p.m. I went to my room, took off my clothes, and lay down on the bed. Thanks to the long day, the time changes, and all the beer I had drunk in Kaduna, I fell asleep and didn't wake up until ten o'clock. The room was chilly, with a thin cover of dust on the furniture. Briefly I considered trying to locate Ruthellen, but by now she'd probably have made other arrangements. To hell with it. I asked room service to send me a steak with chips and a bottle of spring water.

It was harmattan in northern Nigeria. I opened the window and looked down on black trees lining the drive to the hotel. The city beyond seemed to be in semi-darkness. From the rooftop night club, high life music splattered past me into the cool silence below. I wished Fairouz were here. I wanted to travel with her around the world and stand like this in dark hotel rooms to look out at the smooth surface of strange cultures and unknown peoples; and then voyage once again into her almond-flavored body, which was as familiar to me as my own and yet as surprising as these unexplored places.

In the morning, after a 7:00 a.m. breakfast in my room, I called Rodrigo to ask what time we'd be leaving for the Assembly House where Mallam Ahmed was scheduled to deliver the speech at ten o'clock. Rodrigo told me that the event had been postponed until 12:30 to allow the Government Head of the Associated Territory of Nigeria to reach Abuja from Sokoto where he had been conducting some kind of national guard exercises. I found it hard to believe that national guard exercises would take precedence over the visit of a Global Chairman. "This is Nigeria," said Rodrigo.

Many decades ago, Nigeria had become eligible to join the Federation; however the Nigerians had figured out that there was no advantage in doing that. As an Associated Territory, they could run their own local government affairs, vote like regular members in the People's TV Assembly, keep a national guard, and receive heavy doses of economic aid under the guise of technology transfers. All they were prohibited from doing was implementing an independent foreign policy, like invading their neighbors, or running a candidate for Southern Regional Chairman. Even the latter was not beyond them, however. According to what I read in the Nigerian news sheets that I picked up in the hotel lobby, Nigerians considered Ahmed to be a Nigerian although his grandparents had left Kano and emigrated to Brazil in the last century, and he himself was born in Recife. They pointed to the detail that Ahmed had always chosen to be addressed as mallam, a Hausa word, rather than as senhor or mister. Although this was just Ahmed's subtle way of eliciting votes from the disparate cultures of the Southern Region, the Nigerian attitude explained why, in spite of his bumbling staff organization, Ahmed kept getting elected. Everybody claimed him.

I was sitting outside by the pool, reading the publications and drinking coffee, when Can Mabuza, wearing a yellow wool sweater, joined me. He looked wary, as though he thought I might shove him into the pool.

"Tosca tells me you're annoyed with her."

I smiled. "Nothing to worry about. You know women."

Can looked as though he wasn't sure he did, but he nodded vigorously. "Well...glad you're not angry. Sometimes these trips are a strain."

"I can believe it."

"Mind if I pick your brain for a few minutes?"

"Go ahead."

He stared unhappily into the green pool in which algae seemed to be thriving beneath a thin crust of harmattan dust. The weather was too cold for swimming anyway. "You've travelled with Wong. I guess Jean-Paul doesn't have the same trouble with Wong that I have with Ahmed in press conferences. Ahmed never says anything."

"That's not Wong's problem," I agreed. "But don't believe his off-the-cuff pose. Wong always has prepared remarks in his pocket."

Mabuza grunted. "So how would Jean-Paul have handled that scene in Kaduna yesterday? I didn't have time to prepare anything."

"I thought that was the reason I was here."

"Oh," said Can. He thought about that, then smiled wryly. "Yeah, I guess so, but wouldn't it have been rather short notice?"

"I'm fast. It's you guys who are slow in clearing things." We laughed. A smell of roasting meat and fried plantain wafted toward us from the thatched roof snack bar. "I have nothing to do this afternoon. Want me to write some airport departure remarks for tomorrow morning?"

"Well, sure, if you don't mind...."

"Mind? You'd better keep me busy," I said, "or I might get

into trouble again with Tosca over lady journalists."

When we arrived at 12:15 in front of the Assembly House, Ruthellen Janniger suddenly emerged from behind a welcoming banner and, to the consternation of the security officers, Mabuza, and the rest of the press corps, shoved a microphone into Mallam Ahmed's face as he stepped out of the limousine. She asked Ahmed why he had chosen Abuja as the site to deliver this major address on energy resources. Ever gracious, Ahmed murmured something obscure about iron smelting in the ancient Nok culture, and moved on. "Was that helpful?" I asked. She stuck the micro-recorder back into a pocket of her rust-colored jump suit. "Open to interpretation, but definitely exclusive." I admired her energy. She had already interviewed the Nigerian Finance Minister, the local head of the EcoDev operation, a solar energy plant manager, and six market women. "What happened to you last night?" she asked.

"Went to sleep," I admitted. "Must be getting old."

She laughed. "I thought maybe the Argentine bombshell had you reserved." My alarm must have showed. "No, I suppose only a former guerrilla fighter could handle her. But she did rather unceremoniously remove you from our midst yesterday."

These ladies did not like each other, I thought, and decided to bow out gracefully, given the limited breathing space on a Chairman's air shuttle.

"Miss Pinelli worries about my image as a grey-suited Admin bureaucrat." I handed Ruthellen my card. "Next time you're in the Federal Territory capital, give me a call."

"Coward," said Ruthellen.

"'Low profile' is how we describe it in the Admin."

"Do you remove your grey suit on home territory?"

"I've been known to," I admitted, "but only for beautiful, hard working women who one-up the competition."

She stuck my card into a pocket that curved over her breast. "Watch out, Mark Grimal," she said. "I may check your follow-through."

The energy speech went off well, although it was not delivered until 1:30 after the Nigerian Government Head and the Mayor of Abuja had both spoken. Afterward, while the media filed their stories by satellite, the rest of us went to Government Barracks for a large lunch of jollof rice, fried plantain, egusi soup, moyin-moyin, pounded yam, stockfish, suya, Portuguese wine, cold beer, and, for the adventuresome, pitchers of palm wine.

Ahmed's staff had its own table. As I feared, Mabuza brought up the proposed airport departure remarks in order to get everybody's "contribution." Rodrigo thought we should focus on thanking the host country, Nigeria; the econ assistant, Isaías Rojas Yanez, was all for summarizing the speech; Mabuza wanted a global perspective; Tosca sided with Rodrigo; Mety said the Abuja airport was still closed and we'd probably have to depart by road for Kaduna anyway. I tuned out. As soon as lunch was over, I returned to the hotel and tried to work on the memo to Dr. Fisher Schleka, but the heavy lunch had made me drowsy. The next thing I knew, it was five thirty.

If I lived in the tropics, I'd go to seed very quickly. As I splashed water on my face in the bathroom, I thought what a wasted three days this was turning out to be, unlike the trip to San Francisco during which I had been stretched to my limit. That trip would have been a good one even without Fairouz, the cream that made it memorable. I wiped my face on a towel. It was morning now in the Federal Territory; what was Fairouz doing?

Was she alone?

The idea that she might not be alone set my nerves to jangling. I asked the switchboard to try to reach her. The operator told me there was "something wrong with the satellite." Well, there couldn't be anything wrong with the satellite; the switchboard maybe, the ground receiver-transmitter maybe, but not the satellite. While we were arguing about this, Fairouz's voice suddenly came over the line. "Mark! Are you all right?"

I closed my eyes. "Yes, darling. I miss you."

"I miss you too," she said. "I've been so worried. Last night I heard on the evening news that a charter jet had crashed in Abuja. Of course that could not be you, because if a Chairman's shuttle crashes, there would be many details, special reports, twenty-four hour coverage. I knew that, but still...." Her voice trailed off. "How silly of me, no? Nevertheless I am glad that my worry traveled all those miles to you so that you would call me."

"I love you," I said, violating all my principles.

"You're lonely," she replied. "Now you know how I feel when I travel. There are always so many new things that I want to bring to your mind.... I'm sorry, I must tell you: we're going to Singapore on Friday."

Shit, I thought. "Then I have to see you tomorrow night."

"You'll be tired."

"Doesn't matter. I'll come straight from the Transport Cabins."

During dinner that evening, Can admitted that the staff had still not come to a consensus about the angle they wanted me to give the airport departure remarks. This was no way to run an operation. Under normal conditions I would have said to hell with it; however I knew that, whether it was reasonable or not, I'd be the one who'd be blamed if Mallam Ahmed didn't receive as much publicity for his major speech as Comrade Wong had received for his; and very soon I was going to need all the friends I could get at Government House. Therefore, after dinner, I decided to draft some remarks, using a bit of what everybody had said he or she wanted; and the next morning, as we were getting into the vehicles to head for Kaduna, I handed the text to Mabuza.

"If you think it's okay, take my advice and don't consult, just give it to Ahmed. Tell him I did it on my own. He can revise en route."

"You must think we're daft, the way we work," said Can, holding the paper between two fingers as though it were a time bomb.

Actually I did, but I replied: "I'm just trying to justify all the free food and booze I've consumed this trip."

As I had anticipated, Mallam Ahmed was delighted with the text, added a few flourishes about the glorious Nigerian contribution to global culture, had Mety print out fifty copies in the back of the limousine, and delivered the speech with style, standing in front of the air shuttle on the Kaduna tarmac, in the dusty air with cameras around us relaying the event via solar-powered transmitter to the satellite, and on to the world. I watched Ruthellen. When Ahmed reached the sentence about the ancient Nigerian Nok culture that prefigured, in its iron-smelting technique, modern energy technology, her head whirled around until she found me. She glared. I nodded and smiled. She gave me the finger. I was sure now I'd see her in the Federal Territory capital; she'd come around, if only to kick me in the balls. We were two of a kind; we were not straightforward people.

TWENTY-FIVE

At the sight of me coming out of the Admin cafeteria, Danzig bounded over the ascending escalator's handrail and cornered me next to the map office.

"Mark," said Danzig, "what the shit is your staff doing?"

I was impressed at this athletic display; he must be in his fifties. "Great form, Danzig."

He ignored the compliment. "That red-haired dame. And the Malian. They say they're conducting an investigation into the Riccardi rape. What kind of shit is this? Don't they read memos?"

"Your memo? Sure, they each got a copy." The candy bar that I had bought to take away the taste of the cheese sandwich had raisins instead of peanuts; I should have read the fine print. "I don't know what to tell you, Danzig. It's their idea, not mine. You know me: I go with the flow."

Danzig dropped his hand to my shoulder. I could feel his grip clear through my wool jacket; he had a thumb to put out eyeballs. "Well, tell them to drop it." He grinned without humor, like an Aztec god. "My officers are getting annoyed."

I cleared my throat. "We certainly wouldn't want to annoy your officers." Danzig's hand relaxed. "However—just for curiosity's sake, why are they annoyed? What's wrong with asking questions?"

The hand tightened again like a clamping screw. "It's bad for morale to raise questions about security procedures."

"Whose morale?"

"Everybody's."

"Not mine." Pain surged through my shoulder; I almost dropped the candy bar. I felt as though I'd been caught in an automatic stamping machine. This was Monday at two p.m. in the main Admin building. The corridors were full of people.

"Danzig," I said, "if you want to break my shoulder, you'd better do it in your own office. Out here there are too many witnesses. You'll get a red slip from Human Rights."

He laughed aloud, lifted his hand, and patted me as though he were brushing lint off my jacket. "Sorry, Mark. I just don't know my own strength sometimes." Buddy-buddy again, he winked. "Now get your staff straightened out, okay? I don't want to have to kick ass all the way to China."

I took a bite of candy. "Sure. I'll explain that I'd rather not visit them in the hospital." My shoulder was still throbbing.

When I got back to my office, I told Ramona and Louis that I wanted to buy them a drink after work; then I asked Waldir to join us.

We went to the Bom Retiro bar behind the Monroe Institute. Classic bossa nova music was beating away in the background. The walls were plastered with posters of two centuries of Brazilian popular musicians, most of whom, both male and female, seemed to have their shirts open to their waists and their hair sprayed either stiff and spiky or long and coiled in oily ringlets. I should have chosen some place less *alegre*.

After I told them about my conversation with Danzig, Ramona hooted with delight.

"That's confirmation we're on the right track, Mark!"

"Can't stop now," said Louis, smacking his hands together. "We've got them scared."

I cleared my throat. "Look, you guys are dealing with people who maim and kill when they get scared. Suppose you discover the truth. What are we going to do about it?"

Louis started tapping his fingers on his wine glass in tune to the bar's Brazilian music. "Hey, man, I thought you were big on truth."

"This isn't the twentieth century, Mark," said Ramona. She scooped a handful of peanuts from the wooden bowl and put one in her mouth. "Nobody's going to kidnap us or run us down on the street or detain us for asking questions." Her vibrant red hair was much too bright for her thirty-six-year-old face. "We're Admin employees. We know our rights."

"I admire your spirit," I said, "but I've never seen Danzig as irate as he was this afternoon. Sure, he's trying to protect someone—"

"Maybe himself," said Louis.

"Yeah," added Ramona. "Betsy Wickeldorf in Performing Arts saw him on our floor at lunchtime that Friday. What do you say to that?"

What do I say to that? I stared at her, momentarily stunned.

Waldir glanced at me with apprehension. "Not proof of anything," then went on talking about proof. I barely heard him. I was picturing Danzig straddling Christie, muffling her screams, methodically cutting her, leaving her to bleed to death on the rooftop.

Waldir shook my arm. "It didn't happen, Mark. Stop it."

I swallowed most of my Scotch-and-soda.

Ramona was looking at me with frightened eyes. "Sorry." I'd never seen Ramona contrite before. I decided to seize the opportunity.

"Seriously, you guys, drop it. Tell me what you've found out so far and I'll follow up. I'm already on Danzig's shit list. No need for you to join me."

Louis and Ramona handed me their notes. They'd interviewed everybody in the Programs Department. They had lists of people seen, times noted, suspicions voiced. They'd talked to the guard on duty; the guard was furious with them; but none of it added up to anything. Nobody saw anyone climbing the stairs to the roof. Nobody guessed a rape was going on on the roof. Nobody heard or saw anything.

Although the remark about Danzig stuck in my memory, made me sick at odd moments, and I was even paranoid enough to believe that he might have set up Christie's rape to trap me, I didn't believe that he, personally, had done it. No, I couldn't believe that. Danzig had enough genuine security problems to keep him busy.

World-wide, UD unrest was again growing.

The housing riots in Stockholm had spread to other cities in the northern region. UD organizations had been formed to demand public services, jobs, and police protection. Tehran UDs were marching daily on the government storage warehouses demanding food. In Tokyo the entire mass transit system had been taken over for two hours by UDs asking the government to provide public buses for the UD district. Security forces were putting down these demonstrations with brutality; but the scenes were filmed and carried on the satellites, to the repugnance of many people. The experimental drug demonstration in Tehran scheduled for Dr. Fisher Schleka was an attempt to substitute "humane" mob control methods for the unpopular strong-arm ones.

On the Monday before the last Saturday in November, Polyguide requested that I write another speech about the Undesirables policy for this week's "Voice of the People" program.

According to Kelly's memo, the Admin needed to clarify why UDs had no claim on the living standards taken for granted by most individuals in the Federation. Genetically diseased, inferior stock, UDs possessed no civil rights and were allowed to live only because of the magnanimity of the People. If certain communities chose, in charity, to provide services for the UDs, then that was fine; however there could be no question of those nonpeople demanding services.

The topic had come too soon. I wanted to wait until December, when Mr. Brown would be Global Chairman.

After I read Polyguide's directive, I buzzed Kelly Hallihan on the intercom and asked when I could talk to her about the Saturday TV program guidelines.

"Give me until eleven," she said. "I've got a briefing."

At eleven I was waiting outside her office. Her new secretary, Billie Sue Burns, a dimpled brunette with a page boy hair style, was dressed the way Kelly dressed, in slacks, shirt, and vest.

"How do you like working for the world's most powerful woman?"

"Zowie good. She's teaching me karate."

I wondered what else Kelly was teaching her.

At that moment Kelly flew in the front door, beige vest in the wind, ponytail wagging. "Hey, Grimal!" she cried, yanking open the door to her office. "Move your ass over here. Stop trying to make my new bodyguard."

Bodyguard? Billie Sue collapsed in giggles over her keyboard.

"You need one?" I asked.

"None of your fucking compliments," said Kelly. She banged the door behind us. "Sit down, Mark. What's your problem?"

I sat down. She perched on the edge of her desk, as though I were a delegation and she still briefing. Her leather-moccasined foot swung back and forth. The clocks were beeping, the computers humming. I wondered if she cleaned up her act when she represented Finley.

"I've got a moral problem with the Saturday program guidelines."

"Moral?" The foot stopped swinging. Kelly stared at me as though I were a lizard. "What kind of crap is moral? This is the Global Administration Organization, son, not the Spiritual Values Meditation Gallery."

"I knew you'd never guess my problem."

"You're fucking right there," she said. "Well, go on. Tell mother where it hurts and she'll put a boo-boo strip on it."

"I don't agree with our policy of denying UDs basic public services and adequate living standards."

"Shit," said Kelly. "What have I done to deserve this on a Monday morning? First off, Tiger, it's not our policy; it's the People's policy. Repeat after me: People's policy."

"All right. Sorry. The People's policy—"

"Your mind's beginning to shred, Mark. Secondly, it is not policy to deny basic public services, etc."

"I remember. That flows from policy."

"You got it. Whew! Whatever you did this weekend, lay off it. Now—where were we?"

"I was not agreeing with the policy on the UDs."

"Me either," said Kelly. "Tough shit for both of us. Comes with the territory. You know that."

"Yes, I know that," I said. "But this week I'm writing an outline for a December 1st meeting with Dr. Fisher Schleka on changing MedUnit admissions policy for Undesirables, and I'd like to get that out of the way first. Can't you switch the topic to next Saturday?"

Kelly shook her head. "Where're you coming from? Don't tell me we should time policy statements based on whether or not you've got your fucking head together. If you want to stay squeaky clean, give the speech to some other program hot dog in your office."

"You know something, Kelly?" I said. "You don't remind me a bit of my mother."

She laughed, and bounced off the edge of the desk. "No, I'll bet you had the doting kind of mother who sang you to sleep every night, made sure you had your warm sweater on, wept over your skinned knees, interceded with daddy-o when he wanted to whack you. Right?" I didn't like her grin. I decided to ignore it.

"There's another reason you might consider postponing the topic until December."

"I can hardly wait."

"Mr. Brown's always complaining that you don't give him relevant topics. Most of these recent UD demonstrations are in his territory, and he'll be Global Chairman next month. This would be relevant."

"A marginally better reason than your head. But keep going. What's the third reason?"

"That shoots it."

"Bullshit," she said. "You've got a third reason. You're not going to come all the way up here to ask me to change a topic, when you've never done it before in the six years you've been working on the program, unless you have a fucking good reason to want the topic changed. So let's have it. What kind of hot grease are you trying to get your ass into?"

I saw this meeting might have been a tactical error.

"Kelly," I said, "maybe I just can't deal with it."

"You've got to deal with it, Mark," she replied. "No options. The world's a shithouse and you've got to swim around in the crap just like the rest of us."

I got to my feet. "Okay, if you say so."

Kelly's eyes were pools of blue acid. "Not going to tell me

the fucking real reason, huh? Not going to tell anybody, are you?"
She went behind her desk and started tossing red classified papers
into a basket on the floor. "Congratulations, Mark. You've got me
worried."

"About what?"

"Your fucking handsome head, dearie. What goes on in it.
You're a loner. You don't seem to realize the universe is an
interrelated galaxy."

"You're seeing depths in my character I don't have, Kelly."

"Am I?" She leaned back in her chair and put one foot up on
an open drawer. "All that fuck-like-a-bunny routine you put on is
for real, huh? Not," she added, with a grin, "that I doubt you could
bring me testimonials about your pecker power, but if that's all you
add up to, then how come you've got these frigging moral imperatives spewing out of you like piss in the wind? Take this Undesirables issue. Concern for abstract justice is one thing. But you really
feel—" She made a fist and punched it through the air. "—personally involved. And I don't think this is just because of recent events,
bad as they were. A childhood trauma maybe?"

"Keep out of my childhood, Kelly."

She laughed. "Okay, okay. We've all got our problems." She
slammed her foot down to the floor and changed the subject. "So
you've got an appointment with Schleka, have you? He won't be
sympathetic."

"I know. But Vim tells me I've got to do it that way before
I can approach you to approach Finley."

"Clear to the top, huh?" She buzzed her secretary. "Billie
Sue, bring me a P2099 form, please." She stood up and stuck her
hands deep in her vest pockets. "If I can live with what you write,
I'll add a memo."

"Thanks, Kelly."

"Anything you want to do via channels, Mark, no problem.
Just keep away from dipsy-doodle end runs that'll send us both up
like flaming rockets."

"I wouldn't do that to you, Kelly."

"You wouldn't mean to maybe," she replied. "You just
wouldn't see the connections."

By going to Kelly I had wrecked my plan to use the UD topic speech. Now she'd not only have her beavers going over every word of the speech, she'd have them hanging from the catwalks during the program.

Moreover meetings with Kelly always ruined my composure. How had she come up with that bit about my childhood "trauma"? Was it in Security's files? It might be, I supposed, although if it were, I doubted that Danzig could have resisted the temptation to taunt me. No, Kelly had just accidentally hit a bullseye.

While I was growing up, we lived in a small town called Austin Hills. My father taught at a nearby community college; my mother baked cupcakes and bread, knitted us all sweaters, and sang in a chorale group once a week as her artistic outlet. I was an only child, both precocious and spoiled—in a nice way, no tantrums, just carried along on a wave of unmitigated parental approval, never expecting problems because none had ever occurred. My parents read all the proper books and practiced all the proper child psychology. This was fine so long as I was doing childish things. The trouble erupted when I discovered sex at the age of fourteen, a little later than most of my classmates.

Not that my parents hadn't carefully explained about sex to me before, even showed me the pictures in a medical book; but the pictures didn't mean anything. From the age of four, little girls had pursued me—carried my books, my backpack, my lunch bag, my comb, gave me their chewing gum, invited me to their birthday parties, held my jacket at ball games. I couldn't stand them. The other boys teased me about the girls, particularly when, as we all got older, they knew more about what was in the little girls' panties than I did. There was one girl in our class who followed me everywhere—a dim-witted redhead, who smelled of menstrual blood every month and let most of the boys screw her. One day when I was with three of my friends, they decided to visit her; I tagged along, a mistake, and they goaded me into doing it. In no way was it a pleasant experience. When I got home that evening, I couldn't eat supper.

Shortly thereafter the girl's parents discovered she was pregnant. The girl said it was me. This was highly unlikely, but my father didn't ask me to explain what had happened. He just told the girl's father he'd pay for an abortion, and then he beat the hell out of me.

The beating was the worst shock I've ever received; not the physical beating itself, although that was bad enough because I wasn't used to it, but that my just, kind, rational, indulgent father would have assumed I was guilty just because the sleazy father of some sleazy girl had said so.

Of course I was mad at my mother too, because she didn't stop him; but I forgave her because not only didn't she believe I'd impregnated the girl, she didn't even believe I'd laid her. My mother had taken one look at Maggie, and that was enough to establish my innocence. I could hear them arguing until late that night, neither one of them giving an inch. The house finally quieted down by two a.m.

At four o'clock, I got up, dressed, put my allowance money for the month in my pocket, filled my backpack with a change of clothes and a couple of books, and slipped out of the house. I walked to the transport center, where I caught the six a.m. limited train to Fawkesburg, a slightly larger town than where we lived. In Fawkesburg I sat in the central park until 11:30 a.m. trying to decide what to do.

In the park where I was sitting a man, dressed in a baggy, blue UD uniform, was picking up waste papers and stuffing them into a bag. There were a lot of candy wrappers around my bench; I gathered them up and put them in his sack. He thanked me politely, and we started talking. I had no opinions about UDs one way or the other. We didn't have many in our town and those we had were mainly alcoholics or welfare cheats, nothing very dangerous. He asked me why I wasn't at school and I said I was from another town and he said, Don't they have school in that town? and I said, Oh, sure, but I'm dropping out. I'm going to get a job and make money. And he said, What kind of money can you make without an education? Look at me. You don't want to be picking up garbage in a park, do you? No, I agreed, but that's because you're a UD. I'll bet you can read and write like anyone. You're right, he said, I can. Used to be a salesman at Jabbers Mart. Men's wear. Good commissions. What happened? I asked. Made a bad mistake, he said. Got into a brawl in a bar after work one night and killed a guy. I had never met anybody before who had killed a man. Wow! I said in awe. I wished I could send him to beat up my father. Not kill, just beat up. Let him know what it felt like. We talked some more and then I went to buy tacos and beans for lunch from a fast food place.

After lunch I walked around Fawkesburg, carrying my bag and wondering what in hell I was going to do. The most sensible thing would have been to go home, but I didn't want to do that, at least not for another twenty-four hours; my parents would hardly have gotten into the swing of worrying properly. But where was I going to sleep? My money would run out in a couple of days. I didn't have any hope of getting a real job. My ID stated clearly that I had been born fourteen years before, and child labor laws prohibited the hiring of anybody under eighteen.

At four o'clock, after buying the Fawkesburg *Minute Man* news sheet, I wandered on back to the park. The bag was cutting into my shoulders, which were already pretty bruised from my father's belt. The UD was still in the park, sitting down, resting now, smoking a cigarette. I shared the publication with him, and we chatted a bit about the football scores. The sun went down and a chill swept through the park like a wind. He got up to leave. Look, son, he said, what in hell are you doing in Fawkesburg? You get mad at your old man or something? Yeah, I admitted. I buttoned my jacket. Well, you can't sleep in the park, said the man. In the first place you'll freeze and in the second place you'll get mugged. Don't you know anybody here? I shook my head. You have enough money for a hotel? You look young, he said, but some hotels don't care about anything but your money. I've got enough for a night, I said, but then I won't have enough to buy a train ticket back home if I decide to go back there. I see your dilemma, he said. He stood there looking at me for a few minutes, while I bit my fingernails. At last he said, Well, if you don't mind going to the UD district, you can come with me. I've got five boys of my own and they'd probably enjoy the company. You'll have to sleep on the floor, though; we don't have enough beds. As my father told me later, I was taking a terrible chance; after all this was a man who had killed somebody.

Doesn't matter, I said. That would be great.

So I went with Mathias Beck to the UD district and I spent five days there. This was a small town UD district, not so different from the rest of the town, really; and since Beck had had a good job before he had gotten into trouble, his family owned furniture, bedding, pots and pans, just like real people. The house was small, that's all, and the food boring—mainly rice and black-eyed peas and boiled carrots. His wife sighed a lot; she worked part-time in a pharmaceutical company. The five boys, aged eight to fifteen, were all sterilized of course, although that didn't mean anything to me at the time. They didn't go to school because there was no school in the UD district. They just hung around. The oldest one stole things from the stores; he joked that if they caught him, all they could do to him was make him an Undesirable. We got along fine. I showed the younger boys some simple science experiments and helped them sound out words in the Fawkesburg *Minute Man*.

On the third day Beck convinced me to call my parents from the telecommunications office, just to let them know that I was all right. They'll be worrying, he said. My mother sobbed all the way through the conversation. My father traced the call to Fawkesburg and notified the police, but the police never found me because they never thought to go to the UD district. On the fifth day Mathias Beck and I had a long talk about fathers and how they make mistakes too, sometimes even bad mistakes, like he had done, and I agreed that since my own father had done pretty well as a father for the previous fourteen years, maybe I ought to give him a second chance. On the morning of the sixth day Beck took me to the transport center. That's when they got him. The police had been watching the trains and buses; they recognized me from my father's description, and they arrested Mathias Beck for "corrupting" me. The next few hours were a nightmare. I tried to explain what had happened; nobody would believe me. One of the policemen hit Beck with a truncheon. I slugged the policeman. I didn't really hurt him, just surprised him; but policemen, I discovered, don't like to be surprised, particularly by fourteen-year-old boys whom they think they're protecting from evil UDs, and so I wound up in a cell of my own.

Fortunately as soon as the police notified my father, he

drove to Fawkesburg. My father has such a ponderous, self-righteous air about him that he inevitably impresses authorities. They kept calling him "Doctor." When he told them to release Beck, they released Beck; and when he told them to erase the charges against me, a minor, from the computer, they erased them from the computer; and when he said he'd prefer them to remove his report that I had been missing, they obligingly wiped out that data as well. It was my father in his most impressive authoritarian posture, and I had to admire him even as I hated his guts. After all if he hadn't reported me missing, the police would never have arrested Beck at all; and therefore it was my father's fault that we were in jail, if one wanted to look at it that way, which is the way I looked at it. Then he drove Beck home and tried to give him money for taking care of me. Beck wouldn't take it. We drank hot tea in the Becks' living room, which was about the size of our attic at home, and my father and Mathias Beck exchanged views on inflation and solar energy and the Fawkesburg football team. That was the father I liked, my father at his most egalitarian. Then my father and I drove back to Austin Hills, in silence because, although I was grateful that he'd gotten Beck off, I was still mad at him. And he was mad at me too, because I'd caused all that trouble, although, as a just man, he recognized that he'd had a part in it.

TWENTY-SIX

When I went to the December 1st appointment with Dr. Fisher Schleka, he kept me waiting for forty-six minutes in a reception room that was all aluminum and clear plastic, with mobiles dangling from the ceiling. The mobiles did tend to keep your mind engaged. His secretary, who had straight brown hair that reached her waist and eyes like a calculating panther, brought me a cup of herb tea ("The doctor disapproves of coffee.") and told me she'd seen me before, in TV shots broadcast from the Kaduna airport. "I wondered who that handsome man was," she purred. The eyes and the silky voice didn't go together.

When at last I was allowed into the doctor's private office, he apologized perfunctorily for the delay. "Satellite phone call from Tehran."

"How did the demonstration go?" I asked.

He looked annoyed, as though I'd stumbled onto classified information. "Still a few bugs to work out. Sit down." He gestured to a clear plastic couch covered with floppy pillows. The pillows slid around behind my back. It was probably a psychiatric test of some kind; I noticed that the cushions on his chair were wedged in tightly. "I've read your memo," he said. "So you're the man in the Pierce-Owen case."

"Is that a case?"

"One of its kind," said Dr. Schleka. "Didn't do much good to bring the girl here, did it? She died anyway."

"If she'd been allowed to stay in the City MedUnit hospital to which she was originally admitted, she wouldn't have," I replied.

"Perhaps not." Schleka looked at me with the same cold, appraising eyes his secretary had. "I assume you must have had some personal relationship to the girl to feel so strongly about what reasonable men consider a natural law of social justice."

"I don't follow you."

"You ought to," said Schleka. "I've been told that you're the person responsible for last Saturday's public service program on Undesirables policy. As you clearly pointed out in the program, UDs have no right to social benefits. If we had sufficient resources to be able to waste them on such people, we could do it. But we don't. Excellent program. I suggest you go back to your office and re-read your script."

If I had been anticipating support from Schleka, I'd have been angered at this point; but since I hadn't, it didn't matter.

"Oh, I know the policy reasons," I said. "And I know the economic reasons. And I know the political reasons behind it all. What I was hoping you could tell me are the ethical, medical reasons for denying sick and dying people proper care." One of Dr. Schleka's eyebrows arched upward like a boomerang. I knew I had to talk fast now because he was going to throw me out.

"You're a genuine doctor, I assume, not a politician or an economist. You should be concerned with medical needs. Let the politicians worry about how to pay for it. Let them decide whether it would be cheaper to spend money on developing UD mob control drugs or put the same money into providing medical services for them."

"Mr. Grimal," said Dr. Schleka, "you have confirmed the conclusions I drew about you from the Pierce-Owen case. You strike me as a seriously disturbed individual. Although I have not looked at your medical and security records, I imagine they will corroborate my speculations when I request them following this meeting." This was more than throwing me out; this was a threat.

"I can see you're not a believer in dialogue, Dr. Schleka."

"At the very least," he continued, as though I hadn't spoken, "I intend to recommend psychiatric counseling. You will find it greatly beneficial. Any officer in a high position in the Admin needs to exhibit emotional stability, Mr. Grimal, not try to turn personal tragedies into international policy, costing millions and millions of dolyens and subverting the social order. We have a responsibility to the world, Mr. Grimal, not to our egos, with their trivial loves and hatreds."

"I gather your answer is 'no change.'"

He smiled frostily. "That is correct."

I stood up. "For a man in your position to talk the way you talk scares the shit out of me."

"Excellent. I was hoping to do exactly that." He too got to his feet. He looked at me as though I were already strapped to a bed in the Billings Psychiatric Hospital and he were wondering where to stick the electric prod. "Perhaps you'll be interested to know that Dr. Pierce-Owen has been transferred to the hospital in the UD district." My face must have registered shock, because he smiled again. "Yes, Mr. Grimal, certain types of initiative must be discouraged."

When I got back to my office, I called the UD hospital and asked for Dr. Pierce-Owen. They told me she was on the midnight shift. That meant every night she had to drive alone through the UD district to go to work in a place where the facilities were so inadequate there wasn't much she could do once she got there. I felt angry and depressed about my role in this, although I knew that if I had it to do over again, I'd behave the same way, and I hoped she would too. Nevertheless, once the consequences are spelled out, acting on principle wavers. I knew, because Dr. Fisher Schleka had, indeed, scared the shit out of me.

He had raised the stakes. I now knew that if I continued with my plans to try to change the UD policy, I'd definitely be condemned to a six-week mental restructuring program, because Dr. Schleka, personally and with great joy, would certify that I needed "medical treatment."

From the Admin library I obtained some books on restructuring personalities through the use of drugs. The popular idea made it sound humane, as though the person checked into the hospital, received daily drug injections to the sound of soft music playing in the background, and emerged six weeks later with a new, stable personality, and grateful for the kind medical treatment he'd received.

The real thing was a different matter—"behavioral modification" training of a most unpleasant sort, facilitated by the use of drugs to make the individual passive and obedient, no matter how illogical or repugnant the command. When committed to Billings, the person was stripped, shaved, and strapped to a hospital bed like a laboratory animal, under the eye of a constantly monitored TV camera. From then on he or she was never alone, never allowed to perform any activity without the express approval of an attendant. The first two days no drugs were used, only electric shock and brute force, so that the doctors would be able to determine the strength and combination of drugs needed to destroy the aggressive drive. On the third day, they began to administer the drugs and, by the end of the first week, the person's resistance had disappeared so completely that the straps could be removed, and only occasional electric shock was needed to compel obedience when he accidentally forgot a command, which was easy to do because all of the commands for the first three weeks were illogical and designed to create the ideal "blank tablet" on which to engrave the new personality. Obey, obey, obey. Don't question. Your judgment is worthless. Others know what's best for you. Shave with your left hand if you're right handed. Hate sauerkraut? Eat it for breakfast, lunch, and dinner. Beg, bow, jump, cringe, kneel, prostrate yourself, eat shit if you're told to. And you will be told to; that was one of the tests they administered to determine how ready you were to take on your new personality.

Beginning in the fourth week, they allowed the individual, if he could manage it, to return to his harmless old habits while they educated him for his new, socially acceptable role. During this period educational discs expressing the "good values" were played twenty-four hours a day; the person had to learn formulas, participate in role-playing games with counselors, answer test questions on the computer, condemn his old, evil ideas with sufficient force to avoid electric shocks. By the sixth week, if he'd learned his lessons well, he could start wearing clothes again and regain some dignity, provided he continued to be prompt, obedient, and grateful to his torturers. Because, whatever they might call it, that was what it was: six weeks of torture. How could the Human Rights Legal Division let this kind of thing go on?

On Friday afternoon I cornered Steve in his office and demanded answers. Steve took one look at me and suggested we dash over to the Alt-4 Tech Museum on Quincy Street to see a special exhibit on ancient computers. "Closes tomorrow. I've been meaning all week to get there."

At the museum three groups of school children were milling around the exhibit; they kept us from seeing anything and their shrill voices made conversation difficult; however, from the security angle, they were far more effective than running water in the bathroom. We found a pillar to lean against.

"So what's going on?" asked Steve.

I told him about Dr. Fisher Schleka.

Steve whistled. "You've scared him."

"Schleka doesn't look like a man who scares easily."

"He doesn't."

I thought about that for a moment. "In that case—"

"I think you're on to something more than just questioning his authority. Although he does hate to have his authority questioned." Steve grimaced. "Damn it, Mark! I wish your file were cleaner. You leave yourself wide open on these things."

"You mean he could have me committed?"

"Not easily, but with Danzig's help, yes, he could do that."

I cursed the entire repressive Security apparatus—its intrusion into personal lives, its immoral hijinks abroad, its sleazy underworld. Steve blinked away during this diatribe; he'd heard variations on it before. "How can you people put up with it?" I demanded.

"Funny thing," said Steve, "but I'm no more interested than you are in going to Billings Psychiatric Hospital."

The Billings Psychiatric Hospital was a monument to a mid-21st century scientist, Dr. Elmer Billings, who had molded the thought of the post-Transition period on dealing with mental illness and deviant behavior. Faced with limited resources in a chaotic world, the newly formed People's TV Assembly had refused to continue to vote funds for prisons, mental hospitals, juvenile delinquent homes, medical care for destitutes and terminally ill patients, and a large array of welfare services for non-productive members of society; however, after decades of Human Rights rhetoric, the People also refused to authorize capital punishment, except in extreme cases. Caught in this dilemma, the Admin developed the Undesirables policy, which, as an out-of-sight-out-of-mind-and-anyway-they-deserved-it approach to social problems, worked very well for almost a century.

That it worked so well was mainly due to Dr. Elmer Billings, whose opposition to the policy had been based, as he phrased it, "on the loss of human resources for scientific experimentation." Sterilization, he said, was a "negative" approach to solving social problems; instead he advocated that the "most interesting cases" among those condemned to become UDs, should be selected as a gene pool for experimental study and treatment. Although liberals argued for sterilization as being less destructive of the human personality, Dr. Billings won a partial victory when his "scientific" argument was taken up by a Chairman from the Eastern Region, who pointed out that if dynamic, high-status dissidents were made UDs, they might become the leaders of rebellions, pressure organizations, and cooperatives within the UD districts. Elites should be treated more "humanely" by restructuring them. The People's TV Assembly overwhelmingly ratified his proposal, and Dr. Billings got his gene pool.

"Of course it's an abuse," said Steve. "But it's going to take a lot more clout than you or I have to change the law. Meanwhile let's work on keeping you out of there. Drop your crusade for awhile—"

"No."

"Mark—" Steve stopped, shook his head wearily, then said nothing more for a few minutes while we watched a harassed female teacher in a rumpled purple dress try to line up twenty six-year-olds in front of the entrance to the mixed media show. "So what's your next move?"

"Finley."

"Finley! You're going over Schleka's head to Finley? That's an official way to get clobbered."

I looked at Steve with amazement. "You mean you don't think I should go the approved route?"

Steve shrugged. "Well, if you're going to do it at all, you have to, but, believe me, Mark, if you think Schleka was upset now, you wait until he learns about Finley."

    My talk with Steve increased my paranoia. The Admin was a minefield where the world might blow up in my face at any moment, whether I followed the proper procedure or not; and, as Steve had been quick to remind me, some of those mines had been planted by myself. I started taking tranquilizers again to help me sleep. Dr. Schleka would have been delighted.

    Nevertheless, I went ahead and wrote the memo to Finley, adding that I had already discussed the matter with Dr. Fisher Schleka, who did not feel that he had "the authority to make any changes."

    Kelly chortled when she read that part. "You've got balls, Mark. You're lining up some high level enemies."

    "Dumb of me, right?"

    "Probably. But what the shit." She tossed the P2099 form into her "Action" basket. "That's the way you want it, that's the way we'll do it. You won't get everything, but Finley may toss you a bone or two. He likes a well reasoned argument."

TWENTY-SEVEN

On the third of December, Fairouz was in Guatemala and I was at home with Lisa, who, after having prepared lasagna for dinner, had refused to eat any of it. She was watching television and I was seated at the table, eating and reading a book on techniques for surviving torture, which had been written by a 21st century Chinese political prisoner. The basic idea seemed to be that you should make your torturers so angry that they'd knock you unconscious, thereby granting you a respite from torture. I doubted that this was going to work in the Billings Psychiatric Hospital, but it might work with Danzig, assuming Danzig also managed to get his hands on me. Anyway I couldn't afford to overlook any useful information.

In the background, "Jingle Bells" was playing for a TV commercial on educational toys. Lisa had put up an artificial silver tree with blue lights in one corner of the living room, hung mistletoe and wreaths everywhere, left candy canes in little baskets on the coffee table for her friends when they visited during the daytime. She had wanted to have a party this year, but I had too much on my mind to think about a party.

"Really, Mark," said Lisa. "How can you read that disgusting book while you're eating? Read something cheerful. This is the Children's Holiday Season."

"We don't have any children."

"We shall soon."

I read another paragraph before what she had said registered. I jerked my head up.

"We shall soon what?"

"Have a child," said Lisa. She was looking at a TV commercial for baby's talcum powder. "Well, not too soon. About seven months."

"This is a joke."

"You can believe that if you want to," she said. "Just be sure you have enough money available next July to pay the hospital bill."

I put the book down and stared at her, but she wasn't looking at me. Did she appear chubbier? No, actually she looked thinner, but then she hadn't been eating much lately, and maybe I hadn't been around at throw-up time. My shock was giving way to anger.

"What the shit are you trying to tell me? That you went off the injections without letting me know?"

"Tit for tat," said Lisa. "Biter bit. Since when have you been telling me things?"

"This is fucking different!"

"Oh, stop swearing," she said. "It's not your style. Sure this is different. It's respectable to have children. What you do isn't respectable."

"We can't afford children, you know that."

"Oh, but for your girlfriends we can afford hospital bills of four thousand sixty-two dolyens and funerals for one thousand five hundred dolyens and dinner for two at the Sub-Orbital for one hundred and forty-seven dolyens, can't we?"

"Lisa," I said, "I don't want children. You told me you didn't want children. That's the one thing we've consistently agreed on is that we don't want children." I shoved my plate halfway across the table.

"I changed my mind."

"This is a lousy trick! Have an abortion!"

She looked at me now. Her eyes were like marbles. "Shut up, you selfish bastard! I don't care what you want. For a change, instead of taking care of your other bedtime playmates, you can do something for me. No abortion! Whether you meant to do it or not, you stuck it in me. And don't tell me what a terrible father you'll make. I know what a terrible father you'll make. Fortunately, you won't be around much, will you? So just pay the bills, darling, that's all we'll ask you to do. Pay the bills."

She turned back to the television wall screen, which was now advertising a teddy bear that sang a lullaby. A picture of Santa Claus, dandling a child on his knee, flashed on the screen. Afterward came a teledrama in which a cold-hearted bank manager fell in love with a young widow with two children. An hour passed. I was still at the table, my head in my hands. Lisa stared at the monitor. Neither of us said anything else. I could have told her what I was planning; that might have stopped her. But Lisa was the last person I'd tell; she'd go straight to Danzig.

To make sure I stayed in the box into which she had stuffed me, Lisa immediately burbled the news to my parents and then told my staff and before the week was out, half the Admin knew I was going to become a father. People who I had thought were my friends enthusiastically hailed the forthcoming blessed event. Vim clapped me on the back. Steve took credit for recommending the idea, which I guess maybe he had at some point, although not to me. Julio called out: "Hey, *macho!*" Penny was planning a baby shower for Lisa. People congratulated me in the same spirit in which my mother had told me that she just knew I'd found the perfect woman in Lisa. As Lisa had anticipated, I was not going to shock these good-hearted friends by telling them that I didn't want the kid. When they congratulated me, I made the best of the situation, and changed the subject quickly.

At home I got even with Lisa by moving permanently to the couch in the living room, on the theory better late than never. I answered her questions in monosyllables. I left untouched the food she prepared for me. I refused to pay any attention to her "symptoms," or read the articles about "the birthing experience" that she left on the table for me. When Fairouz was not in town, I stayed at the office until midnight. I realized my behavior was childish, but I was too angry to pretend to act like the "adult" Lisa was forcing me to become.

I wondered what, if anything, I should tell Fairouz. I didn't discuss my marriage with other women, never had, but I knew that in love affairs women made distinctions. A man living with a, presumably, unloved wife was one thing; a man whose wife was carrying his newly conceived child had a different image—more con man. If I didn't tell Fairouz, then one of those nameless gossips who adored meddling would tell her.

I waited one night until we'd finished making love on the royal blue sheets under the brass headboard, and were lying naked, drying off in the cold air from the window, which she kept open six inches even when, like now, there was snow on the window sill. An antique clock struck eleven. Her hair was spilling over my chest. Directly facing us was a large mirror with a gilded frame in which, if we raised our heads, we could see our reflections. I liked everything about the room except for a small picture in a corner of a nude girl who resembled an adolescent Fairouz; the girl was stretching backward, her genitals exposed, her breasts tiny knobs, her hair hanging behind her. Once while Fairouz was in the bathroom, I had read the signature on the drawing: "Art. Colonna." As a teenager, she must have been his mistress; the idea revolted me. I tried never to look at the drawing.

"There's something I should tell you," I began.

She raised her head. "Is it a bad news?"

"My wife thinks it's great. She's pregnant."

"Ah," murmured Fairouz. She lowered her head again to my shoulder. After a moment she asked: "And what do you think?"

"Big mistake."

"Why?"

"I've never wanted children. Too selfish, I guess. I wouldn't want me for a father."

"But your wife wants a child?"

"She does now. She didn't when we married."

"People change," said Fairouz. "Don't begrudge her."

The comment surprised me. "I suppose women feel differently about these things than men do."

"I suppose." She rolled on top of my body, her thighs spread on either side, and laid her cheek against my chest. I brushed her hair out of my face. Putting my hands on her hips, I gently moved them down until her pubic hair was against my penis. The room was beginning to seem chilly. I pulled the sheet up over us.

"Haven't you ever wanted a woman to have your child?" she asked.

Well, I knew the correct answer to that one. The answer was: Yes, Fairouz, I'd like you to have my child. But giving Fairouz a child had never crossed my mind.

"Frankly, no."

"Ummm," she murmured. "I don't mean rear the child. I mean sow the seed."

"That wouldn't be responsible, would it?"

She gave a low laugh against my chest. "I thought all men wanted to prove their potency; I thought it was a law of the male hormone system."

"Only in primitive cultures."

"No, no. Some very advanced cultures—Spanish, Italian."

"Ethnic diversity, then."

She began to lick at my throat with her tongue. "Think of going deep, deep, deep inside me. Think of part of you and part of me uniting forever...."

She was making me nervous; she was also giving me another erection.

"Fairouz...."

"Don't worry," she said. "You know I am a practical woman."

I rolled her over underneath me, placed my penis between her legs, and my mouth over hers. Her thighs contracted around my cock. When I thought of our uniting, I never thought of a third person growing out of us; I just thought of our flesh melting together like that of two plastic dolls left outside in the sun. I'll bet Artazio Colonna thought of sowing the seed. I wondered if he had. I wondered if somewhere there was a little Fairouz growing up, making circus collages.

Fairouz was rubbing her thighs back and forth. I now definitely had a hard-on. She moaned into my mouth as I slipped back inside her. "Don't move," I whispered, then covered her mouth again with my own. We lay, unmoving, joined together, until the clock struck twelve.

While I dressed, she sat among the pillows, robed in purple silk now, watching me in the mirror.

"I envy your wife," she said. "Your child will be beautiful."

I didn't know what to reply to that. I decided to ask what I'd been wondering.

"Have you ever wanted a child, Fairouz?"

"I had one once," she said calmly. "A girl. She died at birth. I was too young. I almost died too."

That answered that question. "I'm sorry."

"It was sad. Still I suppose it was best in the end. A fifteen-year-old girl alone is not going to make much of a mother. Now...well, the life does not allow it, flying around all the time. Besides, there's my husband. Legally he's still my husband; I never went to court to abandon him. If I were to have a child, he'd be considered the father. They could take the child away, sterilize it, leave it with him."

I stuck my necktie in my pocket. "What a shitty system we have." I felt personally outraged, as though the policy affected me somehow, which it didn't. Fairouz wasn't going to have my child, let it be sterilized and dumped on the incurable husband. The more I thought about it, the angrier I got. "I suppose Comrade Wong could get you an exemption, like Mr. Brown did for Evelyn Thompson."

"Yes, he'd do that," she said. "He'd also hire a more efficient secretary. Comrade Wong does not care to have his staff's personal problems intrude on their work."

That made me angry too. Everything about this conversation was making me angry. "Something's got to be done to change things."

She looked lovingly amused, as though I were a precocious child who'd just discovered that all was not right in the universe. "It's not easy, darling." She got off the bed and walked, barefoot, to the door with me, her arm around my waist. "You see how moral we are because of this system, how careful we are, how responsible, how socially well adjusted." I kissed her, wishing I had time to slip the robe off her and start caressing her again.

At home in the bedroom, the lamp was still on and Lisa, as usual, was sleeping. She looked blotchy. Her hair was glued to the pillow in wads. Her lips were cracked. On the bedside table stood a bottle of vitamin tablets, three dry crackers, a can of apricot juice, a box of tissues, and half a cup of cold herb tea. I stood looking at her for five, ten minutes. My ploughed earth, my sown seed. She wasn't enjoying it. Good. Don't begrudge her, said Fairouz. Well, I was definitely a begrudger, and it wasn't a charming characteristic. It was mean, small, not appropriate to a man of my "moral imperatives." Artazio Colonna would have been calling Lisa *mamacita* and stuffing her with chocolates.

I undressed, hung up my clothes, and turned out the light. I didn't leave the room though; I kept standing there. After a few minutes, I went over to the opposite side of the bed and lay down cautiously, so as not to awaken her. No doubt the child would be beautiful. That was the one thing everybody always said about Lisa and me: we were beautiful people.

TWENTY-EIGHT

December was sliding right along on snow and ice and blasts of cold air from the Arctic Circle. Lisa holed up like a rabbit in her burrow. I left my car in the garage and took the underground to work. The Federal Territory capital looked like a stack of children's blocks half buried in the snow. The election for Chairmen would be held on December 27.

For one reason or another, Mr. Brown complained about all the public service programs in December, even the Democratic Ideal and the Brotherhood of Man. "He gets that way sometimes," said Harvey.

At 9:30 Kelly buzzed me on the intercom and told me Finley wanted to see me at 10.

"In person? That's awesome."

"Come to my office. I'll take you over."

Although this ought to mean at least partially good news, you never could tell about men like James Francis Finley III. Sometimes they believed that giving the deferential underling an intimate glimpse of power, accompanied by a high level show of sympathy, understanding, but, alas, regret, would flatter him into silence. It was the same principle around which the Club had been organized. I determined not to be flattered. Quickly I got together my notes and, leafing through them, headed for Kelly's office.

According to BioFacts, James Francis Finley III was the son of a previous Chairman from the northern region, James Francis Finley II, who in turn was the son of a solar power industry magnate, James Francis Finley I. The business, which still formed the basis for number III's wealth, was kept in a trust while he served as Director-General of the Global Administration, a position he had held for eleven years. Other than being D-G, he had never performed any function in the Admin, although he had written a book entitled The Bureaucratic Dilemma: Advise and Consent.

When we entered his office, Finley graciously got to his feet and came forward to greet us, hand outstretched, a smiling, white-haired, grey-suited politician. The image didn't jibe with what Vim had told me about Finley's staff meetings. We sat down on a sectional couch, upholstered in a turquoise fabric that glowed in the sunny room. The walls were covered in abstract art works, computer-designed in shades of blue, green, purple, lavender, magenta. An ornate, silver cage, holding a canary, hung from the ceiling in front of the large picture window that overlooked the snowy mall leading to the Board of Government House. The bird sang throughout our meeting, little twittering warbles that I found distracting. I suspected that Finley was well aware of the effect the bird had on his timid bureaucrats, and enjoyed it, although if one were to ask him he would have claimed to be "humanizing" the atmosphere—a touch of life in a dull, diskette-shuffling world.

"A well written memo, Mr. Grimal," he said. "But of course one expects everything coming out of your division to be well written. I particularly enjoyed the recent energy resources speech you did for Mallam Ahmed. Your analysis of the need for further solar energy development was right on target."

He was "humanizing" with a vengeance.

"Thank you, sir."

"Now, about your concern for the provision of adequate medical care for Undesirables—a concern I want to state right away does you a great deal of credit, Mr. Grimal, a great deal of credit—and particularly for that nasty aspect you mentioned about the prevalence of adulterated drugs in the UD district.... This is obviously an area where action is needed and I appreciate your bringing it to my attention. I have talked to Dr. Fisher Schleka. One question, Mr. Grimal: was the memo that you sent to me basically the same as the one you forwarded to him?"

"Yes, sir." I pulled out a copy of my memo to Schleka and handed it to him. "The only changes were to conform to the P2099 format, plus the additional paragraph mentioning that I had previously discussed the matter with Dr. Schleka."

He looked it over. "Good, good. Excellent. Well, in cases

like this, Mr. Grimal, where there is a disagreement between Admin officers, I usually invite both of them to be present at the meeting with me. However—" He smiled ambiguously. "—in this instance, I decided against the idea. Would it be fair to state that you and Dr. Schleka did not...ah, hit it off very well?"

"It would."

"A basic lack of empathy between the scientific and the literary minds? What do you think, Kelly?"

"I'd guess they hated each other's guts," said Kelly.

Finley laughed. I saw why Kelly scored at the upper levels.

"Anyway I decided nothing would be gained by your continuing the unfortunate exchange in my presence. One thing I've discovered in the Admin, Mr. Grimal, is that frequently experts become too specialized in their fields. They lose the large picture. Up here we try to keep the large picture—"

The bird was trilling away like a Paraguayan flute.

"—and so we are going to do what we can to meet those of your concerns that are within our authority...."

The concerns that were within his authority were 1.) to allow those UDs originally admitted in an emergency to a City MedUnit hospital to remain in that hospital until discharge; 2.) to restore the "loophole" whereby a UD could be admitted to a City MedUnit hospital provided the medical charges were paid for by either the UD or someone else who agreed to do so; 3.) an immediate investigation by Security into the adulterated drug traffic, with a commitment to stopping it; and 4.) an upgrading of the facilities and personnel at UD district hospitals around the world.

"On the negative side," said Finley, "there is no way in which we could possibly provide free medical care for all Undesirables at all MedUnit hospitals until we estimate the economic costs and propose funding for it in the annual budget. However—" He smiled that tight, knowing smile again. "—I have asked Dr. Schleka to set up a task force to do just that. We shall see if it's feasible, Mr. Grimal. In the meantime, I want to thank you for your initiative in this matter."

Finley stood up. The meeting was over. A curtain had come down before his eyes; he was already thinking about the next

project, the next memo, the next "vital concern of general interest."
I thanked him. We shook hands.

When we got outside in the reception rooms, Kelly whacked
me on the back. "Congratulations, Mark. You did it."

"Well, not quite."

"On, come on," she said. "What did you expect? A fucking
supernova in the shithouse?"

"I mean, I didn't do it. I'm sure it was your memo that did it."
That wasn't entirely what I had meant, but I figured it was a
diplomatic response.

"Hardly," she said. "All I scribbled was: 'Recommended
reading from a Club member.'"

The system worked. That was the message I knew I was
supposed to pick up from Finley's magisterial review of my memo.
When I told Vim, he treated me to an espresso with double liquid
sugar. My staff was jubilant. You'd think we'd won some famous
victory. Well, we hadn't. On analyzing the actions taken, I could see
they were minimal. True, the new regulation allowing UDs to
remain in a City MedUnit hospital if originally admitted there,
would have saved Christie's life. But how many UDs would be able
to take advantage of the restored "loophole"? And for the rest of it,
we had one investigation, one task force, and "an upgrading,"
whatever that meant, of UD district MedUnit hospitals. I realized I
should be grateful for any change, and so I was; however this wasn't
exactly revising the policy. Appoint a new D-G, and Dr. Schleka
could go back to his old system.

Moreover Dr. Schleka was not taking my going over his head
quietly. He was as good as his threat. When I sat down at my desk
the following Thursday, I discovered an envelope from Security in
my in-basket; the memo inside informed me that beginning next
Monday at three p.m., I was to report for the first in a series of
counseling sessions at the Billings Psychiatric Hospital, upon the
completion of which my continued security clearance depended.
The order was signed "J. Danzig."

Did I have to submit to that? I damn well didn't, or at least
I thought I damn well didn't. It was obvious retaliation for my
"working within the system."

"Isn't that right?" I asked Steve when we got together in the underground garage after work.

"Well, sure, you can file a grievance alleging reprisal disciplinary action under Section 12753 of the Manual of Personnel Policies. Trouble is, you have to file the grievance with Danzig first—"

"Shit!" A cream-colored minivan swung by our corner, followed by a black limousine with curtained windows.

"Of course if Danzig turns it down, then you can appeal to the Security Board."

"And if the Security Board turns it down?"

"You can appeal to the general Admin Grievance Board."

"All this can't take place before Monday."

"So long as it's in process, you don't have to comply."

"Good." I wanted to stay away from the Billings Psychiatric Hospital as long as possible.

"On the other hand...," Steve began.

"Oh. There's another hand?" The limousine honked at the minivan, which had stalled on the exit rampway.

"If Danzig sticks to the order, and the Board backs Danzig, and they pass your security records to the Admin Grievance Board with the insistence that this is a security question, the AGB will accept the argument, irrespective of Schleka's role."

"So I'm screwed sooner or later."

Steve jangled his keys in his pocket. "By appealing, you make more waves."

"Maybe I want to make waves."

Steve looked at me warily. "That's an option of course. Sometimes it works. No more nice guy, huh?"

"Not if they're going to screw me anyway."

"You've got a point. Okay," said Steve. "Write up something for Danzig. I'll review it, but keep me in the background until you really need me. Danzig will consider your appeal confrontational enough without involving the Human Rights legal section. We're not one of his favorites."

Danzig made a special trip to my office the day after he

received my memo asking him to rescind the counseling order on the grounds that it was retaliatory action by Dr. Fisher Schleka.

"Now, Mark," said Danzig, placing my memo down on top of the speech that I was preparing for the Saturday "Voice of the People" TV program. "Be a good boy. Take your medicine."

"That's a condescending thing to say, Danzig."

Danzig smiled. "If you think Dr. Schleka's involved, Mark, you'll have to prove it. It's my decision you need counseling. That's my signature on the order, and I'll stand by it."

It occurred to me, suddenly, that perhaps he was telling the truth, maybe it was his idea rather than Schleka's.

"Of course!" I snapped my fingers. "You're pissed off by Finley's order to investigate the adulterated drug racket in the UD district."

Danzig's chest swelled, his eyes bulged, his face was more than ruddy; it had turned a blackish-red. His arm began to mount above my head.

Quickly shoving against the edge of my desk, I propelled my swivel chair backward. "Easy there, Danzig! Why, I'm sure that investigating the adulterated drug racket is something you always intended to do, right? It's been on the agenda. It's just that, well, a man in your position has so many important things to take care of...."

Danzig pulled himself together. The hand went down. The breath grew steady, controlled. The eyelids lowered. I keep forgetting: these police types don't like to be surprised by small boys; it makes them madder.

"Mark," he said, "you live on the edge. You don't want me as an enemy. I'm doing you a favor; if you weren't a Club member, I'd tell the Board to kick you out. You've got all the symptoms of someone ready to crack. Well, not on my shift, Mark. Not on my shift. Now on Monday, like I told you, haul your ass over to Billings."

"I'm going to appeal to the Board."

"Go ahead," he said. "Appeal to anybody you want. But either you go to Billings on Monday or I take interim action. You know what that is? That means I collect your ID and your passes and make sure you don't have access to any classified information and bar you from all Admin premises until your appeals clear. In effect, Mark, that means you'll be suspended indefinitely as a security risk. Am I making myself clear?"

"Oh, yes," I said. "You've never had too much trouble along that line, Danzig."

Steve sighed when I told him. "Do what Danzig says. You can't win this one."

"I'll bet the son-of-a-bitch is up to his neck in drugs of all kinds—adulterated, narcotics, psycho-active...."

"Probably," Steve agreed. "But, at the moment, irrelevant. He's got a thick file on you for other indiscretions. Why don't you stop screwing around, Mark? Stop playing into his hands."

I protested: "What's screwing around got to do with security? You know, I've never understood that. My wife knows I sleep with other women; she doesn't like it but she knows. I'm not blackmailable by anyone. I sure don't talk about classified material in bed. So what's the big deal? Danzig probably wishes he could get it up so frequently."

"Mark," Steve warned, "along those lines, be very careful what you say to Danzig."

Saturday evening I called the UD hospital and asked for Dr. Pierce-Owen. Yes, she was there, they told me, but she was in surgery. She'd be off duty at eight a.m.

The next morning by a quarter to eight I had arrived at the dirty reception area of the UD hospital. I tried not to think about the last time I'd been there. If an "upgrading" had started, I could see no signs of it. I preferred to stand rather than sit down on one of the broken, plastic chairs, most of which were already occupied by apathetic relatives who looked as though they'd been stuck to them for months. A boy with a runny nose asked if he could shine my shoes. "You have shoe polish?" I asked. He showed me a coin-sized, cracked, black wad in a can. I handed him five dolyens. "Go buy some more." He darted away. Behind a smeared glass window, a nurse studiously ignored all of us. At eight o'clock I knocked on the glass until, with an exasperated shake of her head, she pulled it open.

"I want to see Dr. Pierce-Owen."

"You and everybody else," she snapped. "Well, you'll just have to wait." The window slammed shut, almost catching my cuff in the frame.

At 8:30, Dr. Pierce-Owen came into the room. A good three-quarters of the people there converged on her. She raised her hand. "Sit down. One by one. Mrs. Bunzel!" A woman in an old tweed coat burrowed through the mob. The others fell back, but hardly anybody sat down. I watched this scene for thirty minutes. Finally Dr. Pierce-Owen noticed me leaning against one of the pillars. She made a wry face. "Are you waiting for me, Mr. Grimal? It will be some time."

"No problem."

When she finally finished with the last relative, it was 9:30. I ambled over. "May I buy you breakfast in the City?"

"What a civilized offer." Her ironic eyes glowed in her haggard face. She looked twenty years older than when I had last seen her.

"If they were going to transfer you to this dump," I said, "I wish they'd done it before Miss Riccardi was admitted."

She tapped my forearm. "No regrets. Waste of time for both of us. Do you have your car here?"

I nodded. "And you?"

"Oh, I come by bus," she said. "The first week I tried driving, but there's no secure place to park, and someone smashed my headlights."

During the drive back to the City, I told her about my meetings with both Schleka and Finley. "It doesn't look as though anything's been done so far at the hospital."

"Don't expect miracles. Give them a couple of months." She leaned back wearily against the headrest. "The Director was changed, but so far the new man just hides in his office. Not that I blame him. I wish I had an office to hide in."

We went to the Parkside Hotel for its buffet brunch—a long table laid with plates of meat and fish, baked beans, crepes, eggs, cheese, ten different kinds of rolls, six tropical fruits, four types of cereal, tea, coffee, chocolate.

Dr. Pierce-Owen draped her coat on the back of her chair.

"This is obscene." We both ate heartily, as though it were our last meal. Over a second cup of coffee, I disclosed that Security had ordered me to Billings for psychiatric counseling. "The timing is pure coincidence, of course."

She made a wry face. "Of course. Wait until you start receiving death threats."

"You've had those?"

"Indeed. I no longer answer the phone at home. If anything happens, they'll blame it on some UD. For all I know, it might even be a UD, someone making money on the drug trade. You realize, of course, that we're both paranoid."

"Precisely." I poured cream into my coffee, which turned a light walnut, beaded with oily bubbles. "However this is just the first round. I figure that since they're persecuting me anyway, I might as well charge ahead."

"I had a feeling you would." She nodded. "Well, don't become a terrorist, the kind who plow their cars, loaded with bombs, into steel gates to blow up the place and themselves in the process." My hand jerked and I slopped coffee over the rim of the cup into the saucer. "Exactly what you had in mind of course."

Carefully I spread a napkin in the saucer to sop up the spill. "Drastic action sometimes seems the only way to go about it."

"Perhaps," she agreed. "But behind every terrorist there are a dozen other terrorists waiting to replace him. Who's behind you?"

I decided I'd better change the subject. "You know, Security is supposed to be investigating the adulterated drug racket...."

"Easy for them," she said. "They won't have far to go."

"I doubt they'll take any action."

"Oh, they'll do something. They'll clear the shelves in a few pharmacies, close down one or two chemists, who will then reopen elsewhere."

"I know a journalist who might write a story about it if I could come up with information, or at least sources to check—the money involved, who it goes to, the industry—"

"Do you?" She brushed the bread crumbs on the table into a neat pile near her empty orange juice glass. Her jaw was clenched in small, muscle-y knots. She had more to be angry at than I had; all she'd done was try to save a life. "That's an unorthodox approach."

"Not really. People leak stories all the time around here."

"Um, yes, but not this kind of story. Well," she said, "I could find out some names for you, but don't you do the investigating. Make sure the journalist does it. Give him leads but keep out of it. Discretion, Mr. Grimal. Discretion."

"I'm not too good at discretion."

Her clenched jaw muscles relaxed in a smile. "I can see that. But try anyway."

TWENTY-NINE

On Monday at 2:30 I headed for my first counseling session at Billings. Every day for six weeks I'd have to leave the main Admin building in order to get to the hospital by 3:00; spend an hour there and then come back, in time to learn, before 5:30 closing time, about all the crises that had occurred in my absence. My staff wanted me to complain to Finley, but I knew that, to Finley, personnel matters were neither of "vital concern" nor of "general interest." I took my coat and caught the underground subway.

When I emerged from the South City mall station, the Billings Psychiatric Hospital loomed in front of me, an immense phallic symbol, whose projecting stem was broken with round glass inserts behind which medical personnel scurried from one section to the other. I felt like an animal being herded into a trap. Although the temperature around me was four degrees below zero, I delayed going into the artificial warmth of this building, where brains were recycled into trash. Surely there must be an out-patient entrance. I asked a guard. He pointed to a block down the street, but "You can go in this entrance and take the tunnel if you want." "I'd rather freeze," I replied. He laughed into his muffler. "Good luck, fellow."

It was two minutes of three when I entered the lobby of the out-patient clinic. The lobby was decorated, like a gifted children's waiting room, with bright furniture and framed statements by famous psychiatrists. The receptionist gave me a three-part form to fill out. "This could take me the entire hour," I said.

"Oh, you'll be here much longer than an hour today. We have tests to do."

"Tests?"

"Lots of them. This is scientific counseling, Mr. Grimal. Not that birdbrain stuff they do at Lifestyle."

Seething with rage, I telephoned my office. Over the next

two and a half hours I was poked and prodded, had monitors attached to my penis, machines scan my brain, my blood, urine, and semen analyzed, graphs made of my heart, bones, teeth, and lungs, my reflexes checked, my blood pressure raised and lowered artificially, instruments screwed into my anus, my hearing bombarded with shrill noises that would kill a bird, pressure applied to my eyeballs, my balance shattered as I was strapped into a revolving chair and flipped at eighty miles an hour around a room until I was ready to vomit from nausea. It was systematic degradation under the guise of a medical exam, and it culminated, when my heightened blood pressure alarmed the doctor and his two male nurses, with an injection to make me relax, which was administered in spite of my protests. "Now, Mr. Grimal," said Dr. North with a jovial laugh, "we don't want you to die on us. This is emergency, discretionary medical treatment." He patted me on the buttocks as though I were a two-year-old.

After the "physical exam," I spent another hour in front of a computer identifying colors and shapes and sizes and answering "logic" questions and "what if" emotional involvement "thought questions." The injection had relaxed me so much that I sailed through this exercise in one quarter of the time that anyone else had done it in the past three years.

At last, tests completed, I was led into a counseling office, a small, claustrophobic room, equipped with video and audio recording equipment, an emotion barometer machine, a shelf of books, and recessed lights. Dr. North told me to lie down on the contoured couch and take off my shoes. By now I knew it was a waste of time to question the "requirements." I should conserve my will power for the coming psychological onslaught.

The door opened, and a man with a red beard entered. He was dressed in a plaid shirt, denim slacks, and sneakers. "I'm Dr. Bernstein," he said, extending his hand. I ignored it. He dropped the hand and, settling into a chair across from me, put his feet up on the coffee table. North handed him the test results; they mumbled together in medical lingo. North left, and Bernstein smiled like Big Brother. Maybe I was supposed to be relieved to get out of the hands of North and into his.

"Well, Mr. Grimal," he said, "you're probably mad as hell at us about now. Can't say I blame you, but the tests are necessary, you see, in order to eliminate any possible physiological basis for your marginal behavior. I'm happy to tell you that you're perfectly normal. Physiologically speaking, that is."

Only Kelly Hallihan's vocabulary would have been adequate to respond to that one.

"Therefore," Dr. Bernstein continued, "over the next few weeks we're going to zero in on your psychological problems —" He was pawing through the test results and filing them, one by one, into a folder. "—your feelings of insecurity—" Plop! "—your adolescent rejection of authority figures—" Plop! "—your failure to maintain relationships—" Plop! "—your, um, yes, tendency toward sado-masochism." Plop! "And when we locate the root causes of those neuroses, we're going to drag them into the light of day, examine them coldly, and replace them with positive feelings that will improve your stability and enhance the socialization process."

I turned my head to face him. "What in shit are you talking about?"

Dr. Bernstein chuckled. "I know, I know." He waved the papers at me. "The computer can do wondrous things nowadays with just a little data. Imagine! Your problems diagnosed from a few tests! This saves us a lot of time."

"Why don't we just move on to the positive feelings stage?" I said. "That'll save us even more."

"I would not presume to offer advice without getting to the root causes. There could be seventy quadrillion causes...."

"Back to the computer."

Dr. Bernstein laughed as though I'd made a joke. "Fortunately, Mr. Grimal, you are your own computer and I'm sure you can process the data faster than anyone. Now—let's set up the framework. You have a choice. To facilitate our dialogue, we can use drugs or emotion barometer. Which do you prefer?"

"Neither."

"Oh, come now, Mr. Grimal. This is just to make things easier for you. I can assure you that everything you tell me will remain in strict confidence, within these four walls, except of course for the videodiscs, which will be used by members of the evaluation panel to make their recommendations."

"Isn't it going to inconvenience a lot of people, to make them come over here to read and listen within these four walls?"

Silence. Dr. Bernstein cleared his throat. "Mr. Grimal, it's normal, especially for high strung, creative people like yourself, to exhibit a certain amount of hostility—"

"High strung? Thanks to that illegally administered drug, whatever it was, I'm so relaxed I'm about to sink through the couch into the basement."

Dr. Bernstein took his feet off the table. He confronted me sternly. "Mr. Grimal," he said, "there are a few things you'd better get through your head right now. We don't need your permission to administer drugs or to do anything else when medical necessity requires it. We're trying to help you. We have a lot of experience with cases like yours. What we do is for your own good. We expect you to cooperate. If you don't cooperate, you're in the soup, fellow."

"Ah, now we're getting somewhere. Clarity, Dr. Bernstein, is the essence of good communication."

"Then which is it? Drugs or emotion barometer? You can choose or I'll choose for you."

"Emotion barometer."

"Whew!" He wiped his forehead with a handkerchief and tried to regain his friendly manner. "I hope we don't have to do this confrontational routine on every question, Mr. Grimal. I think the best course would be for you to go home now and come back tomorrow with a more positive attitude."

"Oh, thank you, Doctor," I replied with heavy sarcasm. "May I sit up? May I put my shoes on? Right or left foot first?"

Dr. Bernstein closed the file folder with a slap. "Occasionally the chemistry isn't there. It's possible that I'm the wrong person for your case."

I sat up and stuck my feet, both of them at the same time, into my shoes. "Oh, I should think you'd do just as well as any other Billings shrink." He looked at me with distaste, although he was trying to hide it with a half smile that left a pink hole in the middle of the red beard. I tied my shoe laces. "Don't get me wrong, Dr. Bernstein. I'm sure you think you're contributing to the greater good of mankind by turning out regulation-size zombies from this splendid institution." I stood up. "However as far as those of us who value our 'marginal' behavior are concerned, your so-called 'help' is nothing but a voyeuristic invasion of privacy, which you can shove up your ass."

"Mr. Grimal," said Dr. Bernstein, "I think perhaps we'll try a different counselor tomorrow."

It was almost seven o'clock when I escaped into the cold air of the mall. I knew I had made a tactical error in letting my rage boil over. Who was Bernstein? Nobody. I should have played along since, as a tool of Security, he had the advantage of being as transparent as a piece of plastic wrap. The next day, however, I was reassured when Dr. Auberge, a worried-looking woman in her late twenties, entered the room. She wanted to talk about my sexual problems.

"Honey," I said, "I haven't got any."

"Kindly do not refer to me as 'honey,'" she snapped. Then she told me about her degrees in psychiatry, three different branches of it, and the patients she'd cured of sexual disfunction or malfunction, some kind of function anyway, and how men like me should get over our primitive attitude toward women and start treating them as equals. I winked at her. Dr. Auberge stomped out of the room.

On Wednesday they tried Dr. Velasco, a burly, bearded, six-foot-four heavy; I clammed up for the entire session. On Thursday a Dr. Skurdenis ("Call me 'Dave.'") attempted the intellectual gambit: did I like movies? books? music? art exhibits? I told him what turned me on was horse-racing.

He leaned forward. His earnest eyes blinked behind modish tinted glasses. "Mr. Grimal, why are you refusing to relate to us?"

"Relate? To you? Well, frankly," I said, "I'm not used to relating to people who link me up to emotion barometer machines."

On Friday morning I took Lisa to the airport. She had decided to spend the holiday with my parents. I promised to join her in Ottawa on December 23 for four days, after which I'd return to the Federal Territory capital and she'd remain with my parents until New Year's. I was delighted to have a respite from Lisa's symptoms, which were trying my already limited patience, and eating in restaurants was a minor price to pay.

In the afternoon when I went to the counseling session at Billings, a woman with a pleasant, although not beautiful, face stepped into the room. She was dressed in a trim, navy blue suit and was carrying a beige coat over one arm. Her hair was clipped short around her head. She looked about my age. Oh oh, I thought. They'd finally hit it.

"I'm Madeleine Picard," she said, with a winning smile. "You're the talk of the corridors, Mr. Grimal." She placed her purse on the desk and, picking up the emotion barometer in one hand, stuck it onto a bookcase shelf. "In your case this toy is worthless. All it's telling us is that you're angry, and we already know that, don't we?" She gestured toward the door. "Let's take a walk outside on the mall."

I got to my feet. "I see you're trying to 'establish trust.'"

She laughed. "Oh, you shouldn't trust anybody at Billings. We're all out to improve your attitude."

The afternoon was crisp and clear. No wind. We walked under the bare trees down the long mall in the direction of the main Admin building. When we came to a bench, we brushed the sprinkling of snow off it and sat down. Dr. Picard's cheeks were flushed from the cold. Her hands were covered with long, black leather gloves; she clasped her fingers together, and smiled at me.

"This is better, isn't it? Fresh air, fresh minds, fresh ways of looking at things."

"They must trust you a lot to let you get away with it."

She ignored my implication. "Oh, they only give me the difficult cases. After everybody else has thrown up his or her hands and said: 'This person is impossible!', then they call in Madeleine. 'Oh, Madeleine, be a darling, see what you can do with him...her...it....' I have counselled a couple of its. They were the most interesting of all. Nothing you could tell me would be anywhere near as interesting."

In spite of myself, I smiled. She beamed with delight, and,

reaching over, squeezed my arm. "There, that's better! Please don't give yourself a heart attack over this foolish business, Mr. Grimal."

"Foolish business?"

"Counseling only works if the person wants to be counseled. With individuals like you, it's a waste of time. You don't think you need help, or, if you do, certainly not help from us. Correct, Mr. Grimal?" She smiled pleasantly, her hand still on my arm. Farther down the mall children were playing on the banks of a frozen pond. A squirrel ran up the tree and out onto a branch, dusting snow down upon us.

This was an unfair, calculated assault on my glandular system. I opted for charm. "I need help in getting out of this."

She squeezed my arm again. "I'm glad you know that. I'm your last chance, Mr. Grimal. I assume you like your job. I'm sure you don't want the panel to recommend your dismissal for 'valid psychological causes,' but unless we can develop a working relationship, that's what they're going to do; they've already discussed it."

I felt as though a snowball had been thrown into my face by one of the children. Dr. Picard removed her hand, said nothing else. Taking a package of cigarettes out of my breast pocket, I lit one and smoked it in silence. My anger was blinding, but controlled. Box after box after box after box. Marriage, fatherhood, my accumulating debts, now this—it was like one of those computer games in which you could never move fast enough through the tunnels to keep from being zapped by the alien's disintegrator gun.

Madeleine Picard was wrong about one thing though: I would never have come here just to keep the job I liked. I was here because, before losing that job, I wanted to use it as a vehicle to change UD policy; and therefore she was correct: at the moment I didn't want to be dismissed for "valid psychological causes."

I finished the cigarette and flicked it across the sidewalk into a snow drift. "So. How do we establish 'a working relationship,' Dr. Picard?"

"Oh, we've already done that. From the moment we met. Don't you agree?"

"It's hormones. I respond to attractive women."

She laughed. "How nice of you to say that! Well, whatever the reason, Mr. Grimal, what you have to do now is get through this program as quickly as possible and back into the real world. First of all, I want you to re-take the psychological test. The results of last Monday's are pure garbage...."

"How can you say that when all of my problems were diagnosed so efficiently, so acutely, so scientifically—?"

She was back to squeezing my arm again. "Dr. North gave you an injection during the physical, didn't he?"

"He certainly did."

"That explains why you finished the psychological test in record time. Ordinary people take an hour, geniuses take about forty minutes. Nobody completes the test in twenty minutes, Mr. Grimal, not unless they're hitting the keys at random or high on something. You were quite right to be annoyed at the diagnosis."

I was astonished that she had checked into it.

"We'll do that on Monday. Then afterward...." She put her gloved hands together and placed them under her chin. "I'll ask you searching questions, and you'll figure out candid, sincere ways to avoid the answers."

"Games for bright children."

"Exactly."

I stretched out my arms on the back of the bench so that one of them was behind the nape of her neck. In the dimming sun, the shadow of the Billings Psychiatric Hospital slanted across the mall. A mother in slacks, coat, and a long muffler was rounding up the children.

"Dr. Picard, has this been set up so that I'd fall into your hands?"

She burst into a peal of laughter. "What a lovely idea! No, Mr. Grimal. If you fell into my hands, it's because you held out for them."

Arriving home that evening after work, I discovered Jacques Laye seated in the twenty-second floor reception area, dressed in his blue UD uniform, holding a large envelope, and under surveillance by one of the building guards, who had, remarkably, let him get this far into the building. "I figured if he asked for you, it would be okay to bring him here," the guard said. "He causes any trouble, he's your baby."

"Sorry, Jacques." I opened the door to my apartment and switched on a light. "You should have called me at work to let me know you'd be coming; that way I could have headed off the security apparatus."

"I tried," said Jacques, "but there was no answer."

"Where did you get the phone number?"

He looked around my messy apartment at all the things a Senior Admin officer took for granted. "My wife's gone," I explained, rather lamely, as I pulled the beige drapes across the picture window.

"From the *Federal Program News*."

I gave him my card. "Never trust an official publication. You found the apartment though."

"In Christie's address book." He peered at the card the way he had gazed at the room. "Look," he said, "I don't mean to bother you at home. I brought you some things, Christie's things, we thought maybe you should have." He handed me the envelope. It was brown and thick and through the crude paper I could feel different-sized, flat objects, photos maybe. Quickly I dropped the envelope onto the coffee table.

"Thanks, Jacques. I appreciate it. Please sit down. What can I offer you to drink?"

"Nothing, thanks, Mr. Grimal. I've got to be going." He headed toward the door. He wasn't being exactly friendly, but then he never had been. "The buses don't run after seven."

I reached the door ahead of him and opened it. "I'll drive you."

"No need."

"Maybe not," I said, "but I have a question I want to ask. If you don't know the answer, I'll try the Zilkes."

In the garage Jacques got into my vehicle and sat stiffly as though he expected it to start flying. I had to show him how the buckles work. There was a taste, like petrol, in my mouth. When we left the garage, the City streets were already lit. I waited until we had turned off Transition Avenue and headed for the bridge checkpoint.

"They've charged somebody with Christie's rape," I said. "But I doubt he's the right person." Jacques was silent. "When I asked her if she had recognized the man, she said he had been wearing a mask. Do you know...if she told anybody anything else?"

He was looking out the window. "Forgive your enemies," he said. "Do good to them who hate you."

"Christie would have," I agreed. "But I don't feel that way about it."

"They weren't her enemies," said Jacques. "They were yours."

My hands clenched around the steering wheel. I'd always known that if I asked that question, I'd get that answer.

The guard at the checkpoint waved us past. We sloshed over the bridge behind an old pick-up truck that stalled near the exit. I managed to swerve around it, down to Lower Canal Street. The snow hadn't been cleared off the streets in the UD district. Rockaway Pitts was icy. It took us fifteen minutes to get around St. Agatha's Square.

"How do you know they were my enemies, Jacques?"

"She said the man told her...." His voice stopped. Then: "'Let's see if Grimal wants you after this, honey.'"

We said nothing more until we got to the house. I helped him undo the seat buckles. He got out of the car, then turned and looked back in the window.

"You meant well, Mr. Grimal," he said. "But why did you have to come after Christie? You've got a wife, you've got a home, you've got a job. Sure, Christie loved you. She said you loved her. Well, sorry, but whether you loved her or not, you didn't do her any favors."

When I arrived home it was 8:30 p.m. I didn't feel like eating anything. I opened the envelope. There was a notebook some documents, and photos—of her as a baby...as a chubby five-year-old...at ten, the year of her father's arrest...an awkward thirteen...in the backyard holding a kitten.... Photos of her father, a man with a puffy, alcoholic's face...of her mother, dressed in a fashionable suit, smiling at the camera. Their marriage photo, taken in some garden. Christie's birth certificate. Her report card from the Manhattan New School—all A's. The Primary Four teacher had written at the bottom: "Hard working student. It's a pleasure to have her in the class."

I opened the notebook. *Be careful of kindness, said my mother*....

At six o'clock the next morning, I was still sitting in the living room, piles of cigarette butts in the ashtrays and a large burn on the back of my left hand, where, at two o'clock in the morning, I had deliberately stuck a burning cigarette. The pain brought me back to reality, but it was a good thing that Lisa hadn't been there; she would have called a psychiatrist.

THIRTY

During the last two weeks of the year many people in Alternative Four returned to their home countries for the holidays; Waldir was in Belo Horizonte, Tony in Budapest, Penny in Atlanta. Around the world activity shut down, except for gift buying and the election campaign. The election was always held on the last Friday of the year. Voting for a candidate was like making any other purchase. So long as you had your voting registration card, you could insert it into any television set in the world and have your vote properly counted in your own region.

Although I never had before, this year I intended to vote for Mr. Brown. I wanted him around for tactical reasons.

On Tuesday the week before Christmas I was seated in a viewing chair at home, watching an international newscast anchored by my good friend Ingrid Armfeldt. Ingrid looked a little peaked that night; too many holiday parties, maybe.

Earlier that morning a group of UDs invading a Chicago department store had dismantled the towering, decorated Holiday tree before startled guards could stop them. The camera showed police smashing heads above blue uniforms, glass shattering, salespeople ducking behind counters. The Mayor of Chicago recommended execution of "these criminals." A social worker blamed it on "rising expectations." The police chief said Chicago UDs, even workers, would be restricted to their district until New Year's.

From UD unrest, Ingrid glided, to the tune of the World Federation anthem and a montage of patriotic photos, into a report on the upcoming December 27th election. All three of the incumbents were ahead. There stood Comrade Wong shaking hands with a fisherman beside the Ganges River; behind him Fairouz stared fixedly at nothing. Comrade Wong was forty percentage points ahead of his nearest rival. All smiles, Mallam Ahmed kissed a

Togolese baby; he was reported to be twenty-seven points ahead, if Associated Territory polls meant anything. In Berlin, Mr. Brown, clothed in layered artificial furs, addressed a rally; his main rival, Mr. Klitgaard, lassoed a cow in Albuquerque. A close race, said Ingrid, but Brown was marginally ahead by two points.

I sipped my Scotch-and-soda.

As this month's Chairman, whether he won again or not, Mr. Brown would deliver the post-election "Voice of the People" address.

Traditionally the end-of-year broadcast was a summation of election results, with hints of future action on the part of the Chairmen, and of course laudatory remarks about the wisdom of the People. All the Chairmen, both incumbents and, if there are any, new ones, would be physically present in the global studios.

There it was: the grab-bag program in which to insert my "innocent victims" proposal.

I jumped up, switched off the television set, sat down at my computer terminal, and started to work on a fill-in-the-blanks draft speech. Better to do this at home than to risk it in the office, at least until the final stages.

Mr. Brown and I would make history together. This was one speech guaranteed not to bore him.

Once into serious planning for the program, I realized that there were a lot of things I didn't know.

The ideal would be to have all the voters punch in replies immediately after Brown had finished his presentation. But how could I, Mark Grimal, turn on the People's TV Assembly? I knew where the levers to activate the Assembly were located, in a steel cabinet, locked by a computer, in the main production control room of the Global TV studios; however access was Top Secret, to my knowledge only in the hands of Polyguide, and I was about as far removed from the hands that pulled the levers as was anybody in the Admin. And even if by some fluke I did manage to turn it on, I wouldn't know how to open only those buttons in the areas of the world where the polls indicated a chance of success. I'd have to gamble on the wisdom of the People, all of them, and, for my project, that was carrying democracy a bit too far.

I made a lunchtime trip to GTV on the pretext of researching a speech on the use of satellite broadcasting to teach African villagers how to read. After checking out the educational programs, I hung around in the main production control room, chatting with the production crews. The steel box glowed like marble. The computer was locked. A bored guard kept curiosity seekers at a distance. Nobody knew, or really seemed to care, how the People's TV Assembly operated; that was Polyguide's business, George told me. Even the technicians who serviced it belonged to Polyguide; they doubled as transmitter operators.

At night, using my home computer terminal, I paged through the entire legislative data bank file on the People's TV Assembly, searching for clues to its operation.

The legislative data bank was no help.

The only person I could think of who might know how it operated was Telecom's Julio Meza. If he did know, I doubted he'd tell me; but since it was worth a try, I invited him to a holiday lunch at the Sub-Orbital—private dining room, the works. Once there he went through his check-the-sound-system routine and had us change dining rooms twice. "Why would Security bug this place?" I asked, as we finally settled into one of the more modest rooms—no turntable, view only of the EcoDev building, its roof vegetation covered partly with snow, partly with opaque, plastic bubbles.

"The Club members come here. They drop juicy tidbits. They think they're safe with one another."

Since, after all, this was the holiday season, we asked Jerome for a couple of gin-and-tonics to start, then proceeded to paella for Julio and lobster for me, accompanied by a bottle of white wine. Julio chose the wine. It was superb; I'd never heard of it.

"Private winery in the Canary Islands. I keep a case stashed in my office refrigerator in case of an emergency."

"What kind of an emergency would require a case of white wine? Or shouldn't I ask?"

Julio laughed. His handlebar mustache bobbed up and down above the wine glass. "A meltdown, man. That's when I lock the system, destroy the access routes, and wait for somebody to dig me out in two weeks."

"In that event one case doesn't sound sufficient."

Julio agreed. "I've also got a case of red and two cases of fifty-year-old brandy." He squeezed lemon over the paella and wiped his hands on his napkin. "Tell me what you want, man. I know I'm great company, but I've never yet been invited to the Sub-Orbital by somebody who didn't want something."

"Information."

"Right. That's what everybody wants."

"Unclassified information."

Julio nodded his head up and down and rolled his eyes. "You've tried all the data banks?" I nodded. "Then it's classified. Don't ask. If you ask, I might figure out what you want it for."

"I'm just writing a speech!"

He tore a hard roll apart and buttered it. "Mark," he said, "in my books, you're a good guy, see, but I wouldn't last twenty seconds in this job if I made exceptions for good guys. So forget it. Let's just have a pleasant luncheon. Sorry, hate to disappoint a friend. I'll split the tab with you."

I refilled his glass. "No way. The wine alone is worth it."

When I got home, I checked "meltdown" in the security data bank. It was part of a low-level classified contingency plan to keep global telecommunications out of the hands of radical revolutionary groups, like the rebels in the New York subway system. I doubted Julio would ever find an occasion to use his office wine supply.

Convinced that Madeleine Picard was one of the maze players on Danzig's payroll, I changed my strategy at Billings. The important thing was to hold out for a few weeks until after the End-of-Year program, when it wouldn't matter one way or the other. I decided to pretend I was being converted. I wasn't crude about it; I'd argue a bit, then pretend to give in. Had I resented my authoritarian father? Of course not...well, maybe sometimes...now that I came to think about it, sure.... I figured she would credit my transformation to her own talent for bringing out the best in difficult cases rather than to my expertise in playing games for bright children. After each session, when we were clear of the building, I laid on the charm so that, if she were suspicious, she'd connect my miraculous change with a desire to get her into bed with me. Of course I made no move in that direction; I wasn't sure how it would read in the computer, and, besides, knowing that she was a feminine Danzig dulled my interest in her. The last counseling session before Christmas I brought her a large candy cane.

"Compliments of the Season, Dr. Picard."

She smiled. "As a little boy did you give apples to your teachers, Mr. Grimal?"

"Not to all of them," I replied. "Some got frogs."

Following the Saturday program I caught the plane to Ottawa and arrived before midnight. Lisa and my parents met me at the airport. Lisa looked more robust, cheerier: Mother had been taking care of her. Mother's soft grey hair framed her face in a stylish cut. My father's eyes were failing; he needed my help in getting the right key into the vehicle. I volunteered to drive us home on the icy roads. They accepted. A son should be useful for something. Like giving them a grandchild. Well, yes, I'd done better this time. They were both so pleased about the prospect of a grandchild that I had to brighten my mumbles with a few positive comments. After all I wanted this to be a good holiday since it might be the last weekend we ever spent together with me in my original, unrestructured state. I tried hard to be thoughtful, helpful, all the warm, family virtues that they valued so highly, and that I should but didn't. I replaced the light bulb in the hallway, made the eggnog, shoveled the snow off the path to the backyard gazebo. On the evening before the holiday, I tended the music on the media unit and mixed drinks when my parents' friends dropped in. I kept away from heart-to-heart conversations, which was where we always tripped and ended up quarrelling. Lisa was sleepy, placid, shot full of hormones. When I made love to her, I pretended she was Madeleine Picard.

On Wednesday evening I flew back to Alternative Four. From the airport I went directly to the office. There on my desk was a memo from Polyguide: the Saturday program topic was The Election and the Future—just what I needed.

THIRTY-ONE

Thursday after work I made a brief appearance at the Program Department's annual New Year's office party for those of us left in the capital. Eberhardt presided—a massive, organized man, who ran the party the way he ran his department—smoothly, everyone knowing and doing his job, all the wheels revolving inside the wheels. It was an achievement, this management, and I wondered how he would react if he knew that he would soon be looking for a new head of the Speakers Division. However, the effect of routine was so strong, I still couldn't believe that next year I wouldn't be here. Where would I be? Data Flow maybe—something that wouldn't tax what little remained of my mind.

Boris Baratynski, who produced video disks for the Media Net division, came up to me. "Hey, Mark. Someone was looking for you downstairs. Ruthellen Janniger of the *Bonn Program World*. I told her I thought you were on leave."

"Just as well." I had the post-election speech to complete that evening.

"Where did you meet her?"

"Abuja."

"Watch out. They tell me she sleeps with Vasili Rublev. Gets all her good econ development scoops straight from him."

"Out of my league," I agreed mildly. Next to James Francis Finley III, Rublev was the most powerful man in the Admin—a hard-driving over-achiever who attacked underdevelopment as though it were a personal insult and treated his staff like disposable razors.

"I told her if I saw you I'd let you know she'd be at the City Condos through Wednesday."

"Thanks. Where's Rublev?"

Boris laughed. "Good old Mark! Rublev's visiting his mother

in Kiev. If she won't tell, I won't, buddy."

On the morning of election day, I cast my ballot for Mr. Brown by inserting my voter registration card into my TV set at home. When I got to the office everything was quiet, the last main working day before the New Year. Based on the assumption that all the present Chairmen would be re-elected, I finished the Saturday speech and sent the text, minus the final page, to Polyguide for clearance. The last page had the "innocent victims" proposal in it. Inserting it there made it easier to get around not only Polyguide but also Mr. Brown, who was not likely to stop on the last paragraph, but might —just might—do so if he came upon it earlier and had time to think about it for another ten minutes. Once the speech was over, whatever he or any of the other Chairmen might feel about my ploy, I couldn't see him admitting to the world that he had delivered the speech without knowing what was in it.

About ten o'clock I told Ramona she was in charge; I was going over to the Global TV studios to watch the election process.

In the principal TV studio the lights on the tally board were turning too fast to follow. Every five minutes a new subtotal replaced the old one at the bottom. All the incumbent Chairmen were comfortably ahead, but this would go on for twenty-four hours in some parts of the world, so it was much too early to make any predictions, although I was sure Polyguide already had, based on other data.

I looked into the production control room. Kelly wasn't there; someone else from Polyguide, Jeff Rogers, was guarding the open steel box, with its levers and blinking lights. The program coordinators for each of the Chairmen were present as observers— Tosca Pinelli, Ole Grieg, Babatunde Adedipe, other people for the opposition candidates. They had returned early from the campaign tour in order to monitor the voting. Later in the day the Chairmen would fly in with the rest of their staffs and the other candidates who could afford to come to the Federal Territory capital. I wondered if the Government House people really knew what to look for in the operation of the People's TV Assembly. If Polyguide decided to rig the election in favor of rival candidates, would Ole, Tosca, and

Babatunde suspect? I was sure they'd been told the minimum Polyguide could get away with, namely the codes for their own areas.

Tosca waved to me. I ambled into the production control room and sat down beside her where she was perched, legs crossed, on the top of a desk. Jeff Rogers looked as though he felt he ought to tell me to get out, but he didn't because Tosca and I were chatting. Babatunde joined us. I asked him if Fairouz would be working later; he said, No, just Jean-Paul, Carlos, and Nha. I was relieved since I wanted to spend this last evening with Fairouz. While we talked, I glanced casually from time to time to the control box for the People's TV Assembly, but since I hadn't been there when they activated it, none of the buttons and lights meant anything.

When Kelly arrived, she shoved me toward the door while chewing Jeff out because he'd let me into the production control room. "Don't be a fucking patsy, Jeff. Grimal's not cleared for Top Secret shit. These program hot dogs'll snow you."

Babatunde laughed. "Una forgive im dat one. Mark 'e be friend Gov'ment House."

"Speak English, Tunde!" ordered Kelly. "You can do it."

"So can you," said Babatunde. "If you want to."

Since there wasn't much sense in my hanging around outside with the waiting journalists, I took the underground back to the main Admin building. In a sense, I felt relief: since I couldn't figure out how to activate the People's TV Assembly, at least now I wouldn't be accused of tampering with it. With only the doctored speech, perhaps Steve could get me off with demotion, suspension without pay, and, if they obtained Lisa's signature, no more than one or two weeks of restructuring—torture enough but over before my brain could be completely riddled with chemicals. Whatever the punishment, it would be informal and "administrative." A TV trial would make Mr. Brown look like an idiot.

Before the end of the day the diskette came back from Polyguide, with Kelly's initials tagged at the end of each page. Now only if there were an upset victory would I have to go back to her for a revision. I scanned the clearance symbol, fed it back into the computer, and onto the final page of the script. Then I printed it out.

At a quick glance, the clearance looked okay, although, if you examined it carefully and in a bright light, the initials were too rounded, the shading too sharp for it to be an original; but would Harvey Milliard notice, reading it quickly in the studio on Saturday? To be on the safe side, I'd omit the last page in the advance copy I gave to producer George Abish.

Of course if Mr. Brown got stuck in a snowdrift and never made it to the studio on Saturday, I'd scrap my plan and hand out only the approved copies, since either Wong or Ahmed might question the entire UD policy change; they should have heard about it before it reached that stage. However, Mr. Brown, as I knew from experience, never checked anything.

When I got home that evening, I tried to reach Fairouz by phone. At 8:45 she finally answered. She was watching the returns on television. "I'm too tired to go to the studio," she said. "Poor Jean-Paul and Carlos. They must stay there all night with Comrade Wong."

"I hope you're not too tired to see me."

"Oh, darling," she said, "I'm never too tired to see you. But, please, don't expect much. I may fall asleep in your arms."

"I'd like that. A whole night with you asleep in my arms."

She laughed, but I meant it. I picked up some cheese, French bread, and wine at the Atlas Towers West all-night gourmet shop, then drove to Fairouz's apartment. When I got there, she was already in her silk robe. Her hair was loose. Deep black smudges beneath her eyes showed through her eye shadow. I set the food and wine on the bedside table and placed the television monitor on top of the chest of drawers. When we got into bed, we left one light burning to keep me from knocking over the wine in the darkness. Quickly, efficiently, I made her come. "But you, darling...," she murmured, half asleep already. "Can you stand it?" "Yes, of course." By the time I finished, all she could manage was a soft kiss before her head went limp against my shoulder.

I spent the rest of the night holding her and watching the election returns, with the sound turned off on the television set. I nibbled at the bread and cheese, drank the entire bottle of wine. By two a.m. it was clear all the Chairmen had won re-election. I turned off the set and tried to sleep, but it wasn't easy.

In the morning I let Fairouz sleep until nine o'clock when I could restrain myself no longer and started stroking her body. Without opening her eyes, she pulled my head down to her breast. My mouth closed around her left nipple. We made love until noontime. I put on my best performance; it was essential to leave her good memories since, unlike Artazio Colonna, I couldn't give her paintings.

While I showered, she fixed us a brunch of fresh melon, cold ham and the rest of the cheese, accompanied by toast and foamy espresso coffee. We ate it seated on the window bench beneath the painting of the three drunks in a bar. She told me about the grueling campaign tour throughout the Eastern region. "It seemed the only time we could sleep was when we were on the plane, and poor Jean-Paul couldn't even do that, because of the journalists accompanying us."

"Comrade Wong should hire more people. You'll all be burned out in a couple of years."

"It's true he doesn't think of that." She slowly buttered a piece of toast. She had put on fresh makeup, but her face still looked too pale, like a sick person recovering. "He sleeps no more than two hours a night himself. He's like a little motor. Never seems to tire. He was astonished when Carlos told him Jean-Paul had to sleep. 'Sleep?' he said. 'Why sleep?'" She covered her eyes with her hands and gave a laugh. "It would be funny, but it isn't. Carlos is the only one who can stand up to him. You see, darling, it really is not all the time fun like it was in San Francisco."

She wanted to know what had happened here. I told her about my meeting with Finley.

"But that is wonderful news, Mark!" She squeezed my hand. "You have made changes in this horrid system—real changes...."

"I'm not sure how real they are.... More like bandages. The policy's untouched."

"You've done what you could. That's the important thing."

"It's strange," I said, "but that's the way Christie used to talk. You women seem to think everything is all right so long as a person has done what he can. But I have to do more than what I can before I'll be satisfied."

"Oh, Mark," she said, "I don't think you'll ever be satisfied. Who's higher than Finley?"

"The Chairmen, when it comes to changing policy."

"That's the way it's supposed to be, but I don't see how it can be true when the People's TV Assembly is under the control of Polyguide."

"You people do it backwards," I said. "You should get together, agree among yourselves on legislation, sell it to your own Chairmen and then—only then—ask Polyguide about the feasibility of ratification. If the Chairmen all spoke together Kelly'd listen."

"I wish you'd tell that to Carlos."

I wondered when I'd see Carlos again. "You tell him if I'm not able to."

"But you'll see him Tuesday: our New Year Eve's party is at his place. Or will your wife be back?"

"No, she's flying in Wednesday afternoon." I had asked Steve to meet Lisa at the Transport Cabins since I would "be in a meeting."

"Then it's all right."

Not after the broadcast this afternoon, I thought, but I said nothing. The silence went on a little too long. With a puzzled frown, Fairouz swiveled on the bench to face me.

"It is all right, isn't it, Mark?"

"Of course," I replied, avoiding her glance. "I was just thinking how we always make plans as though we expect to live forever. A philosophical New Year's reflection." Quickly I leaned over and kissed her on the lips. "I love you very much. What time Tuesday?"

"About eight-thirty. Mark—is everything all right?"

"Of course. Sorry. I should keep out of philosophy."

It was now after two o'clock and by four-thirty I must be in the studio. When I kissed her goodbye at the door, I opened her robe and ran my hands down her naked body, reached between her legs and pressed her gently until she quivered against me.

"I'll see you Tuesday, my love."

"Oh," she said, "I'll be at the studio this afternoon. Everybody else is resting."

THIRTY-TWO

The news disconcerted me. In recent months Jean-Paul had been the person accompanying Comrade Wong to the studio; but now it was clear why Fairouz had been allowed to stay home last night—so that she could take the duty today while Jean-Paul collapsed from exhaustion. This was going to make it harder for me to concentrate.

I drove directly to the main Admin building, entered with my pass, and ran off on the printer both the approved and the unauthorized copies of the speech.

I'd thought hard about whether or not to give Harvey the same version that I intended to hand to Mr. Brown. It was a risk, but in the past Harvey had never questioned details. Moreover he'd be tired from last night, wouldn't arrive at the studio as early as usual, and therefore might not find out that the text contained an unusual proposal until Mr. Brown was actually delivering the speech. In that case I doubted Harvey would interrupt the broadcast; he'd just wonder what was going on. However, if I didn't give him the same version I gave Mr. Brown, when Brown started reading that final page, Harvey would know he'd been tricked and might try to stop the broadcast. I'd have to take my chance on Harvey.

At the TV studios I was relaxed, cheerful, greeted the production crew, joked with Magda, discussed football with Muamar, kidded the propman Billy about his new orange cardigan. When Harvey arrived, I complimented him on Mr. Brown's election victory. Harvey's eyes were bloodshot. He said Mr. Brown's staff had stayed up until 6 a.m. celebrating. We exchanged hangover stories, although, in fact, I hadn't had a hangover in fifteen years. Finally Harvey settled into a chair to read the speech; he'd never reach the last page in time.

When Comrade Wong arrived with Fairouz, I congratulated

him on his re-election. "Tough fight, Mark, but we made it." Tough fight was 76.3 percent of the total vote in the Eastern region. Fairouz, clothed in a red wool tunic gown, was carrying the briefcase. She gave me an uncertain glance; I smiled reassuringly.

Mallam Ahmed, dressed for this occasion in Brazilian international style, glided in, followed by Rodrigo. Again I offered my congratulations. Mallam Ahmed gave me credit for helping him. "The energy resources speech was a real contribution, Mark."

It was now 5:25. Still no Mr. Brown. "That man," muttered Magda. "One of these days I'm going to put a pin in his chair." I resisted telling her I was about to do exactly that.

Sure enough, at 5:28 he flew through the door and zoomed into his chair like a hungry pigeon. He was wearing a denim suit stitched with gold braid, a red silk scarf at his neck, leather cowboy boots, a loose string tie. Darting to the desk, I handed him the unauthorized speech, loose, not in the red Admin binder. "Congratulations, Mr. Brown." "Why, thank you, Mark," he said. He took the speech without a glance, smiling beyond me at the cameras. I dashed back out of camera range. Here we go, I thought. Off the parapet.

The speech began the way all these speeches begin, with the Triumph, Once Again, of Democracy. The People had spoken. All over the world they had exercised their sovereign right to elect their leaders.... Of course Mr. Brown, Mallam Ahmed, and Comrade Wong weren't leading the People, whoever they might be, anywhere. The real leaders were tucked away in the Global Administration Organization pulling the levers and letting these three puppets receive the applause. There the Chairmen sat, actually thinking they'd won a victory, instead of realizing that they'd been allowed to win because they were harmless, irrelevant, of varying personal competence but masters only of empty symbols—a trendy suit, a cry for ethnic diversity, a switch from Hausa gown to Brazilian trousers. Finley could count on their petty rivalry to keep the Admin in control forever. Well, next year somebody else would be writing the crap for them.

Out of the corner of my eye, I noticed Fairouz get up and move over to the chair next to Harvey. I turned and looked. Shit, what was this? She was reading part of the speech. I jerked my head back to Mr. Brown, who was now pausing for Mallam Ahmed and Comrade Wong to express their thanks to their electorates. The cameras were on Ahmed. Harvey Milliard strode across the studio floor. He took the speech from Brown's hands, extracted the last page before the Chairman's startled eyes, returned the rest to him, and backed away. Involuntarily I took a step forward. Fairouz grabbed my arm from behind. "No, Mark, no!" Her nails dug into my hand. Harvey crossed the floor directly toward me. He took my other arm, prodded me backward. "Come on. Sit down, Mark. You can't do it this way." I let myself be propelled backward and into a chair. The words sprayed out of Harvey like muffled bullets. "I like my job, friend. I want to keep it. From here on out, you don't hand anything directly to Brown, only to me, got it? Every scrap goes through me...."

I closed my eyes. I said nothing. I'd blown it. After her first words, Fairouz also had said nothing; she just clutched my arm, which was resting in her lap on top of Comrade Wong's briefcase. I didn't pull away; I didn't acknowledge it. I did nothing at all. A sort of paralysis kept me calm, listening to Harvey's whispered words without grasping them. Mr. Brown cheerfully delivered the balance of the speech. What a long speech it was! Why had I been so wordy? I allowed Fairouz to take all of the speech copies, both authorized and unauthorized, out of my other hand and stuff them into her purse. She left me with the empty, red Admin binder. Maybe that was what had alerted her: I hadn't used the binder. When Brown finished speaking and the program was over, Harvey picked up the text from him. I heard him say to Brown: "Oh, nothing, just a duplicate page that got in by mistake." My friends. My dear friends. Harvey handed the speech to Fairouz, not to me.

Now the Chairmen were leaving. Harvey drifted toward Mr. Brown. Fairouz stood up with Comrade Wong's briefcase. "Mark, I'll call you in an hour. Will you be home?" I didn't look at her. "Mark—" Comrade Wong was getting impatient. "I'll call you," she repeated, moving off, glancing back at me. I stayed seated. Fairouz disappeared out the door behind Comrade Wong. The technicians were stacking away the equipment. Magda came over.

"Another triumph of democracy, Mark."

I pulled myself together; stretched, yawned elaborately. "Yeah, I'm getting tired of writing this crap. Maybe I should consider a career change. Do something useful, like dig ditches. May I buy you a drink for the New Year's, Magda?"

"Sure." She tucked her long salt and pepper hair under her wool knit cap. "I didn't like this year much. What about you?"

"The pits." I stood up and put on my overcoat. "Where shall we go?"

"How about the 'Black Warden'? It matches our mood."

I laughed. The sound reverberated oddly in the now empty studio. "I remember. Black drapes. Good double martinis."

"Too good. Remember the time we apologized to our reflections in the mirror, thinking we'd run into other people?"

I grimaced. "Maybe we'd better not go there."

"Oh, that was three years ago. The waiters will all be different."

We spent the next hour and a half seated in a bar decorated to resemble old war-time blackouts, with drapes, candles, mixed drinks in flasks, peanuts in containers marked "Emergency Food Supply." We reminisced about past programs at the Global TV Studios, people we'd worked with who had gone on to different jobs, the changes of Chairmen. I drank two double martinis. When we left the bar, it was snowing outside. I remembered that my vehicle was parked in the main Admin building garage. Shit. I gave Magda a big hug and kiss. "Why haven't we ever slept together?"

"An oversight," she agreed. "Next year. That's a promise." She headed in the direction of the Carlyle Heights station, I returned to the Admin.

When I got to the building, I decided that driving home in the snow, even on autopilot, after drinking two double martinis would be suicide, and while I had nothing against suicide, I preferred to bequeath the car unscathed to Lisa. In the cafeteria there was only one serving line open. I grabbed a coffee and a bowl of overcooked spaghetti. Three other people were seated in the cafeteria, scattered at different ends of the enormous room. I stayed there until 10 p.m., drinking mug after mug of acid-y coffee. I wouldn't say I was thinking. I wasn't thinking. I was like a man who had been geared up for a space flight, having Mission Control call it off thirty seconds before blastoff. I'd said my goodbyes; I'd resigned myself to an infinite number of hazards, including detention, torture and a blasted mind, and now the worst I had to look forward to was driving home in a snowstorm after drinking two double martinis. Pop went the balloon. Sorry, Christie. You shouldn't have loved such a loser.

When at last I felt sober enough to attempt the trip home, I tossed all the plastic garbage into the maxi-disposal, and, carrying my coat over one arm, descended to the garage. About twenty cars remained parked on that floor. The guard waved me goodbye. "Happy New Year!" I drove home and into my own garage. When I reached the twenty-second floor, my phone was ringing. I ignored it. The phone stopped on the twelfth ring. I took off my clothes, hung them in the closet. The phone started again. This time, when it stopped, I pushed the phone's disconnect button. I turned off the light and flopped onto the bed.

I didn't sleep. I just lay there. The skylobby lights glowed through the curtains. Somewhere from another apartment I heard music, laughter, glasses clinking, a New Year's party. The acuteness of each sound seemed unnatural. Entire conversations began, ended, resumed, floated through the window, jabbed my consciousness, flowed into music, out of music, sloshed through bottles, clinked with ice, exploded into dots of light beneath my eyelids.

I sat up and turned on the light. All the coffee on top of the martinis had my stomach churning in canned spaghetti sauce. Getting out of bed, I put on a robe and returned to the living room where I plopped into a viewing chair and turned on the TV.

On my wall monitor the world flickered into full-color view.

Some ponderous journalists in Colombo, seated before rotating slides on an enormous screen, disagreed about the meaning of the election results. I switched channels. There was Vasili Rublev in St. Petersburg, fur hat down around his ears, predicting formidable changes in agricultural yields, satellite education, intercountry cooperation over environmental issues, desalinization of sea water; the producer had thoughtfully added English subtitles. I punched another button. To Los Angeles where a Brazilian jazz trumpeter swayed before a dancing crowd. Next, to Nairobi, for a talk on war game preserves—places where human beings, on costly package tours, could pretend in the daytime to kill one another and, in the evening, discuss strategy over cocktails. Sounded like they needed restructuring.

I began to laugh.

It wasn't a real laugh; it was a laugh-at-myself laugh.

I went into the kitchen and prepared some hot lemonade. The spaghetti sauce gave a final gurgle.

By two o'clock in the morning, while a woman on the monitor was describing the invention of stained-glass windows in the eleventh century, I leaned back in my chair, cold sober, and considered what an ass I'd made of myself. Not only had I failed, but I'd ruined my good relations, not just with Harvey, but with all the Government House staff members except of course Fairouz, who'd find excuses for me. Although Harvey would cover up the details for Fairouz's sake, he'd spread a general look-twice-at-anything-Grimal-writes-for-you warning to his colleagues. Well, I'd asked for it.

Lisa's mistletoe had dried out. The artificial tree needed dusting.

THIRTY-THREE

At 8:30 Sunday morning I was awakened from a nightmarish sleep by the sound of the doorbell chiming its little melody again and again like a broken music disk. Turning over, I stuck my head under the pillow. Tee-too-tee-tee-tee-too, it kept on. Finally I staggered into the living room and flicked open the entrance video monitor. Mr. Wong's staff director, Carlos Acevedo, appeared on the screen—slick black hair, olive skin, straight nose, thin mouth, not looking at all friendly.

Shit. Who needed Carlos Acevedo at 8:30 in the morning? I was tempted to ignore him and go back to bed, but if Carlos thought I was in there—and he obviously thought I was in there—then Carlos would keep pushing that little buzzer, or, worse, get the downstairs guard to break down the door, until he could get in. Carlos hadn't been a labor organizer for nothing.

"Hold on, Carlos!" I groaned into the microphone. "I'm coming."

I pulled on some slacks and a sweatshirt, washed my face, and ran a comb through my hair. Whoever that stranger in the bathroom mirror was, he looked as though he had barely survived a plane crash in the Andes.

I opened the door. "Come in, come in."

"Sorry for the unexpected visit," said Carlos. "Turn your phone back on."

Phone? "Oh." I lied: "Must have accidentally hit the switch last night." I picked up the phone and pushed the "on" button, then flopped into a nearby chair. I hoped Fairouz wouldn't call while Carlos was there. "Sit down. Want some coffee?"

"No thanks," said Carlos. "But go ahead. You look like you need it."

He seated himself on the edge of the sofa near the window

and picked up an art catalogue from an exhibit on the Traditional Primitive Movement that Lisa had once attended in her artistic phase. I went into the kitchen. I could see this wasn't going to be a friendly visit. A reserved man, Carlos had always been pleasant enough, but even in the best of times he lacked warmth, except on the speaker's platform, where he exploded into oratorical pyrotechnics, which I, personally, found alarming. As a labor organizer, he must have driven the police crazy. I hoped he'd just tell me what an asshole I'd been and leave quietly.

I returned to the living room, bearing the coffee pot and a mug and set them down at the other end of the coffee table. I poured a cup. "So what can I do for you?"

"Get out of Fairouz's life," he said. "That's what you can do for me."

I said nothing. I sipped the coffee. Glasses and crumpled papers and books and shoes and empty nut cans and computer printouts and full ashtrays were strewn around the room as though I'd dropped them at random. I ought at least to try to pick up a few things before Lisa returned on Wednesday. I'd do that. Tonight I'd do that. The silence grew longer.

Seeing that I didn't intend to answer this direct assault, Carlos cleared his throat and tried a new tactic. He gestured around the room.

"How's your sound system?"

"I have it swept once a month," I replied. "The detector company's never found anything. I'm not important enough to wire at home."

"That's what they think," said Carlos.

He was beginning to get on my nerves. People like that— cold and hard and full of pent-up emotion—just aren't my type. I guess Carlos was okay to work with, particularly on the trips during which he was always either organizing support and setting up spectaculars for Comrade Wong, or else picking up the pieces for the other staff members; but I wouldn't have wanted to deal with him on a regular basis.

"You blew your credibility last night," said Carlos.

That wasn't all I'd blown. "No argument."

I guess my passivity was beginning to get on his nerves too; he wanted a fight; he wanted a good reason to slug me.

"I don't know where Fairouz finds you savior guys," said Carlos. His voice grew more heated. "She must turn over all the rocks, look down the drains, scratch the bark off the tree trunks."

"Thanks," I replied. He was edging into it. You savior guys implied a whole succession of us, a division maybe, out there climbing up the cross; but who else besides Artazio Colonna would qualify?

"Funny thing is, none of you appears to have a thing in common. You faked me out. Grimal's okay, I thought; she's got a normal one for a change. But no; I should have known. Only Fairouz can peer through the layers and find, hidden beneath the scarlet plumage, the idiot who intends to save the world for us."

He was really climbing now into his pyrotechnics. I burst into a smile. "Damn it, Carlos," I said. "I never knew you were in love with her."

I said it; and even while I was saying it, I didn't know it; but the moment I had said it, I knew it. Truer than true. The skin on Carlos's hands rose in goose bumps; his eyes darkened; had he moved an inch I would have expected a knife to come hurtling at me. But he didn't move; and after a moment he said in a voice to match the temperature outside: "That's the way men like you always think. I have to consider the operation. I'm fond of Fairouz; we all are. She's hard working, bright, and loyal. She doesn't give me any trouble by herself; it's the in-laws she loads onto us who cause disaster. We don't need another Balthazar De Jonge around here."

Balthazar De Jonge!

The knife had zapped me after all, right through, and nailed me to the back of the chair. I took a deep breath. I picked up a crumpled pack of cigarettes, found it empty, dropped it, fumbled for another pack lying on the floor, took out the last one, tried to light it, discovered the igniter was out of fluid. Carlos tossed me his. I could tell from the smug look on his face that he knew he'd ripped me open.

"Remember him? The Assistant EcoDev Director who was funding the rebels?"

"Sure," I muttered. All I could picture was De Jonge's insane face on the People's TV Court. "So he was an in-law...." The idea of Balthazar De Jonge screwing Fairouz appalled me, as though she had been gnawed by an animal.

"One of our most valued. Fairouz doesn't talk about him; he was a bad trip. When De Jonge blew, he took a lot of innocent people with him, including her. She was held incommunicado for two days. Danzig kept insisting he didn't know her whereabouts, but when Comrade Wong went above him to Finley, Danzig found her. I picked Fairouz up at the Billings Psychiatric Hospital. I don't want to have to do that again, ever. She didn't say one word for forty-eight hours. Then she asked to see Wong; wanted him to save De Jonge. Wong told her she was lucky he'd been able to save her. Then she asked for Rublev. Rublev roared that the scandal had disrupted EcoDev operations and at that point he didn't give a damn what happened to De Jonge. Fairouz went back into zombie land for a week. We kept her away from the TV during the trial. That would have finished her."

I couldn't say anything. I kept trying to connect the dots, to build a new reality in my hungover brain. Steve Maine was over there...Fairouz Moked over here...Balthazar De Jonge flailed away in the middle, slipping, slipping through the tube...then Mark Grimal took his place.... I felt as though my balls had dried up and were about to fall off.

"The only thing Fairouz learned from the experience," said Carlos, "was to watch you guys for the signs. Lucky for all of us, because if she hadn't, life this Sunday morning would be very different, wouldn't it?"

I crushed my cigarette butt in the ash tray. The cold morning light turned the dust in the room to frost. I had just learned that beneath every pit there's a deeper one.

"Okay, Carlos," I said. "You've gronked me. You can get out now."

He hesitated. He wasn't sure I understood. "Now I can't order Fairouz not to see you...."

I could have told him that. Carlos was far too correct, righteous, nothing personal, all for the greater glory of Comrade

Wong and the organization. Fairouz wouldn't buy it.

But I would.

I stood up. "Don't worry. We all have our limits, Carlos." I walked to the door and opened it for him, giving the subtle nudge there. "Your odds are better at ordering me."

Frowning, he got to his feet. "I wouldn't think of ordering you. You're not on my staff."

"Poor reason, Carlos." I kicked an empty beer can under a potted palm. "Order away. You remind me of my father."

After Carlos had left, I made myself another pot of coffee and tried to decide what I could do to keep myself sane for the next couple of hours. Thinking about Fairouz and Balthazar De Jonge wouldn't do it. I had the wrong images. Although from his photos, he had appeared big, awkward, balding, and paunchy, perhaps before his crackup De Jonge had had charisma. He must have had something to appeal to a woman. I'd never met him—personally, that is; I'd talked to him once on the phone about a speech I was writing for him and he'd seemed sensible enough then, if a bit free form.

At that time I wasn't Chief of the section, just one of the writers. The Chief was a nervous man named Carroll McHenry, an ultra-channels type, who, rather than let the rest of us contact the high officials we were writing for, insisted upon filtering their comments to us via his notepad computer; it was like feeling cloth through plastic wrap.

After my draft had come back three times from De Jonge, the Assistant Director telephoned me. "I hear you're the one writing the speech for me," he said. I didn't know how he'd managed to get even that much information out of McHenry. "I can tell you can write, but you're not writing for me. What I want is..." and he told me. "If I like what you draft, I'll send a note directly to your personnel file. The next time, just call me, and we'll work around the obstacles." A glowing note did indeed go to my personnel file, but there never was a next time because McHenry's secretary told him De Jonge had called me, and so I was on McHenry's shit list, researching garbage, until he was transferred out of Speakers to Program Formation. The new Chief, Ben Allen Bozeman, spent all his time trying to get a transfer to some "important" department. As De Jonge had advised, I started going straight to the source, and discovered that it worked. When Bozeman finally wrangled his job as flack for Global Health, I was appointed Chief of the Speakers Division. Maybe I owed it all to Balthazar. Maybe somehow, even back then, I had become the intellectual heir of Balthazar De Jonge, who eventually also bequeathed me his mistress.

I couldn't deal with it.

Up until that moment I'd been viewing my misfired project as a bird-brained script involving only myself. Now, thanks to Carlos, I saw it as a potential horror story. Like De Jonge, I had tried to protect my friends by not telling them my plans; yet they might have been arrested anyway, just for knowing me, just for being in the studio at the wrong time or sharing my bed or not noticing the tiny forgery that changed everything.

Knowing that, how could I take Fairouz to Carlos's party, how could I ever take her anywhere again, when I knew that if she hadn't sabotaged my speech yesterday, I might have dragged her back with me to the Billings Psychiatric Hospital?

I dialed Fairouz's apartment, hoping she wouldn't be there; but she answered on the second ring. Her voice had a little catch in it. "Oh, Mark! I've been so worried. Are you all right?"

"Sure." I cleared my throat. I figured it was best to put what I had to say in such a way that she wouldn't try to contact me again. "You were superb last night, Fairouz. You saved my neck, Harvey's neck, who knows how many other people's necks. You're a heroine and I stand in awe."

"What?" she said. Then: "Oh, don't be angry, Mark. I had to do it. I love you."

"I'm not angry," I replied. "How could I be angry at you? I just feel like a shit-ass and unworthy of your devotion."

There was a moment's silence. "Mark, let's meet somewhere. Don't talk this way on the phone. We're going to hurt each other."

"Better now than later," I answered. "Look Fairouz, sorry, my love, but I can't pick you up on Thursday. If I set a foot inside Carlos's apartment, he'll amputate it."

"Oh," she cried in alarm. "Carlos.... Has he been to see you?"

"'See' is not quite the word."

"You mustn't pay attention to Carlos. He never gets things straight. Harvey shouldn't have told him what happened yesterday. We won't go to Carlos's home, darling. We'll go some place else."

"Fairouz, my dear, my dear," I said. "Carlos told me about Balthazar De Jonge."

Now there was a longer silence at the other end. I swept cigarette ashes off the end table onto the carpet. I straightened the lamp shade. I closed my eyes and thought of fucking Ruthellen Janniger as a penance.

"Mark," Fairouz said. Her voice was unsteady now, almost pleading. "That's something I should talk to you about."

"I know about it."

"No, you don't," she said. "Not if you heard about it from Carlos, you don't. Carlos hated Balthazar."

So Carlos hated Balthazar.... That figured, I thought, just as now he hated me, but I couldn't see how Carlos's hatred changed anything.

"Listen, darling," I said. "I've already killed one woman I loved. I don't want to kill another. Forgive me for what I almost did yesterday. Goodbye, Mrs. Moked."

I hung up the receiver and disconnected the phone again. I sat there for an hour, loathing myself and wishing I had the courage to do something about it.

But I couldn't. I wasn't a hero.

At 11:30 a.m. I stopped by the City Condos where the out-of-town media houses kept leased flats for their correspondents. The reception desk clerk buzzed the *Bonn Program World*, then handed me the receiver. "Hello," said a sleepy feminine voice.

"Ms. Janniger? Mark Grimal."

"Mark Grimal," she drawled. "Well, Mark Grimal, you do keep weird hours."

"Sorry, but it's eleven-thirty. A.M."

"Already?" A pause. "Shit, you're right. Come on up. I'm in

my pajamas, but don't let that stop you."

"Take them off."

She laughed. "Not until you get here. You might be abducted en route again by the Argentine."

I got into the elevator and pushed the button for the eleventh floor. Ruthellen Janniger no longer appealed to me, but that was a problem I'd just have to overcome because I'd better be up to Vasili Rublev standards.

She opened the door, dressed in faded blue, flannel pajamas that made her look like a twelve-year-old boy. She'd combed her hair, but hadn't had time to put on makeup, which was just as well because she smelled like she needed a shower. I figured we could start right there. I dropped my overcoat on a chair and began to unbutton my shirt.

"Would you look at this!" she cried, hands on hips. "The man doesn't even say 'Happy New Year'! Who invited you?"

"You're supposed to be monitoring my follow-through, remember?"

"Well, yeah, but. What about small talk? What about a cup of coffee?"

"After, after. First things first. Off with the pajamas."

"You'll have to catch me first." She darted toward the bedroom. I charged after her before she could get the door closed, wrestled her down onto a torn-up bed sprinkled with cracker crumbs, stripped the pajamas off her, and dragged her struggling into the shower.

I had had a hunch this would be an athletic occasion.

Once in the shower, Ruthellen started laughing and it was all I could do to get my trousers off before she pulled me in with her. I rubbed soap all over her. I decided I'd rather screw her there than on the bed, where the sheets looked as though they hadn't been changed for three weeks and several men. Tosca might have been right about the clap. "Got any condoms?" I asked. "Plenty," she said. "Medicine cabinet."

Afterward we sat naked at the kitchenette table, drinking bloody Marys, while my underclothes dried in front of the living room heating panel.

"You're okay," she said. "Pleasant, unexpected Sunday morning romp. Although I suspect I'm not your type. A certain amount of forced labor there. I'll bet you go in for the romantic ladies, don't you?"

"Sorry." She was more aware than I had thought. "You're too damn smart, Ruthellen."

She laughed. "That just means you want something, and I'm always interested in what people in Alternative Four want. So you've done for me, now what can I do for you?"

I guess I wanted something all right, maybe a couple of somethings.

"Do you know if this place is bugged?"

"Don't think so now. Rublev pulled some cables out of the bedroom one night, said he was going to strangle Danzig with them."

"Ah, Rublev.... I'd rather you not mention me to Rublev. I don't want to be strangled."

She tossed half a lemon at me. I caught it. "I know. You're a grey suit. Not to worry. You're cuter than Rublev; I'd like you to stay that way. Go on."

"I've got a story someone ought to cover. It's not really your sort of thing—"

"Stop right there!" she cried. "How do you know what my sort of thing is? It it's a good story, I want it."

"Well, it has an econ angle, but it's also criminal. Goes high up in the Admin. If you're not interested, maybe somebody else would—"

"Come on," she said. "You're just trying to intrigue me."

I told her about the adulterated drug operation in the UD district. "Someone's getting me the names of people who might be willing to talk to a journalist about it."

She swished the semi-melted ice cubes around in the tomato juice. "So what's your interest in this? How come you want someone to investigate the story?"

"I had a UD girlfriend who died from taking an adulterated drug that I bought for her in the district."

She poured more vodka into glass, sloshed in some tomato

juice. "That's a bitch. You do get around, don't you?"

"Here and there."

"How high up does this go?"

"I've no proof. All I know is that when I mentioned it to Jake Danzig, he almost slugged me."

She chortled. "Well, well.... Tell you what, I have to head back to Bonn on Thursday...cover a currency meeting in Geneva on Friday, then to London for a week.... I'll be back here about February third, fourth. See what leads you can get together for me, and I'll check them out."

"It might be dangerous."

"Won't be any fun if it isn't." She grinned at me, swallowed the rest of her drink, laid her legs on top of my thighs, and pressed her heels into me. "So. I imagine you're screwing some other broad on New Year's Eve, right?"

I put my hands around her ankles and lifted her legs into the air. "I was, but I changed my mind." I moved forward until my prick was rubbing against her cunt.

"Then join us at the Inter-Order Media Club. You know the place?"

"I know the place."

"I'll change the sheets for you this time," she said. "I can tell you're one of those health addicts."

New Year's Eve was a binge; too much booze, too much smoke, too much talk, too much cunt. That was the way the journalists wanted it, and I played along—had to, being with Ruthellen, but also because I felt like it—no class, rock bottom. The reporters, however, considered this having a good time; through all the bedlam most of them kept working. They faxed pages stained with the seventh Scotch, broke out of a dance to do a satellite feed, talked to their computers while searching for a lost shoe underneath the table. They joshed Ruthellen about her Admin contacts, speculated on which unnamed source I was. Some dropped into the Inter-Order Media Club, had half a dozen drinks, and then returned to work. I couldn't figure out how they did it. Their profession required strong kidneys, steady heads, the ability to keep four or five things rolling around at once while focussing on the right comma. Within this group I was definitely "establishment," forced into defending every outrageous Federal Government action of the past twenty years, while Ruthellen twisted and curved on the dance floor beyond our dirty table. Considering my Admin reputation, that was damn funny.

After the Technocrats Band departed at two a.m., we covered the city in mini-glidercopters, searching for "action," landing on the roofs of nightclubs, grazing the snow off building cornices. One journalist brought his blonde, doll-like robo-reporter, who kept saying, "Just give me the facts, man," her computer whirling, her eyes blinking. He kissed her; he danced with her. He brought her back to the City Condos and did it with her while I fucked Ruthellen. Then he wanted to change partners. That was going too far, even for Mark Grimal on a binge, so I cut out and left Ruthellen in bed with him and the robot. I was sure the three of them would have a great time together.

THIRTY-FOUR

My "meeting" having been cancelled, I headed for the Transport Cabins on Wednesday to pick up Lisa. That was fortunate because when Lisa got off the air shuttle, she was followed by my mother.

"We tried to call you," said Lisa, "but nobody answered the telephone."

Mother had come to help Lisa turn our guest room into a nursery. "We thought you might be too busy," she said reproachfully. Now every time I sat down at the computer, I was faced with a humming baby catalogue. Our home was full of alphabet cutouts and a crib that converted into The First Bed, and baby albums and mobiles to make the kid cross-eyed. We didn't even have this alien invader yet and he was costing us a fortune.

Although I liked my mother, having her with us meant that I had to be nicer to Lisa than I was accustomed to or I got into trouble with both of them. Our quarrels now took place only in bed, muffled beneath blankets. If I couldn't make it home for dinner, I called. Our sex life suffered. We watched a lot of television. Lisa had stopped throwing up all the time; however, she warned me that I had to be careful when we made love; but anyway I knew I had to be careful because if Mother had heard any thumps or crashes, she would have dashed right in to rescue Lisa. One good thing about having broken with Fairouz was that when my mother insisted on a little heart-to-heart chat with me about why expectant fathers should clean up their lives, I could say truthfully: "Don't worry, Mom. That's all over."

It was all over. Throughout January I kept away from the Global TV Studios on Saturday afternoon. That was easy because Mallam Ahmed was Chairman that month, and Waldir, as a fellow Brazilian, could better discuss Brazilian soccer teams with him. Comrade Wong went off to Peking for two weeks. During that time his senior staff took their vacations. Fairouz sent me a faxcard from Tunis; no message—just her name in Arabic.

With two weeks to go on the counseling sessions, Madeleine Picard suddenly told me that "they" had decided to pull her off my case. She hadn't been getting her usual results, she said.

The conversation took place on a Friday evening in the lobby of the outpatient clinic. I was astonished. "Why? I thought we were relating splendidly."

"We are, Mr. Grimal. But they've noticed you aren't saying anything, although you do say nothing most pleasantly. Therefore they think another analyst might have more luck. Dr. Skurdenis will be here on Monday."

I shook my head. "Be nasty to people, they don't like it; be nice, they don't like it. Now that I'm no longer a patient, how about having an after-work drink with me?"

She tapped her fingers against her forehead. "Poor Dr. Skurdenis!"

I didn't feel sorry for Skurdenis but I did for Dr. Picard. Danzig couldn't have been happy that she hadn't come up with more dirt on me.

And Skurdenis? Well, did I really want to talk about the movies to the beat of an emotion barometer? Why in hell should I put up with this crap? My reasons for fearing to risk my job had vanished. I no longer had a project.

On Monday I didn't go to the session. On Tuesday I didn't go to the session. On Wednesday somebody from Billings called to ask where I was. I said she could tell where I was. She asked if I'd be coming to counseling that afternoon and I said no, that I wasn't coming any more because after having established a good working relationship with a fine psychiatrist, they had torn her away from me. The woman at the other end of the line said she would consult. The next day somebody, not Danzig, called from Security and asked if I intended to go to counseling that afternoon. I said no. He said I had to. I said well, no, I didn't think so. He said if I didn't, they'd suspend me and confiscate my passes. I laughed and said come get them. After that I never heard anything more from Security about counseling. This confirmed one maxim I'd already learned from life: if you don't care about it, you'll achieve it easily.

The only useful thing I did during this period was see Dr. Pierce-Owen. Early one Saturday morning at the end of January I drove over to the UD district and waited for her to get off duty at the hospital. Nothing had changed in the waiting room, nothing had changed in the facilities, nothing had changed in the staff. They couldn't even keep in bandages, said Dr. Pierce-Owen. The lines on her face had hardened into an angry mask that didn't lighten over brunch at the Parkside Hotel, where she handed me a computer printout with the names of fringe people involved in the UD district adulterated drug operation. She wanted them dead. I wasn't sure what frightened me the most—the list or the change in Dr. Pierce-Owen; however, by the time she had finished explaining to me what each of these deviants did, I wanted them dead too. I doubted that Ruthellen Janniger would be able to arrange it.

Ruthellen called on February fourth. She was back in town; so was Rublev. No matter. She wanted me to meet her at the Press Club that night after dinner—10 p.m.

This created the first mini-crisis of my mother's visit. Lisa knew I must be meeting a woman. "Here we go again," she cried. Mother wanted to know what kind of work I did at 10 p.m.

"Leak stories to reporters."

"Oh, Mark," said my mother, "don't joke with us."

After a few sharp words with Lisa, I escaped and made my way to the Press Club where I found Ruthellen in the bar drinking Black Russians with three French TV reporters and Jean-Paul Dornier. Jean-Paul jumped up, all friendly puppy, and embraced me. "Hey, Mark! How you doing? Where you been?"

"Oh, here and there." I was surprised at his warm welcome. We sat around for an hour drinking at a wooden table, which had been marinated in a century of alcohol. The French TV crew had returned from filming a UD riot in Seoul. "'Riot.' That's what they call it," said the director, a dapper man with hair falling over his forehead. "But, you ask me, it's a damn insurrection. Every city I've been to it's the same thing. These people know what they want. They've got leaders. But the Government keeps calling it a 'riot.'"

"What do you grey suits say to that?" asked Ruthellen. She

was wearing a velvet shift with a necklace made of tiger teeth; she looked a lot better than the last time I'd seen her.

"Nobody tells me anything," I replied.

Jean-Paul couldn't get off that easily. He started talking about a task force Comrade Wong had set up to collect hard data. Although I would never have considered Jean-Paul a "grey suit," I could see that he was, here in this setting. I wondered how I was going to get Ruthellen away long enough to explain the list to her.

She resolved the problem by suddenly calling out: "Hey, Mark, they're playing our song!" and dragged me off to dance to piped-in zaranga music on the glass-enclosed terrace. Her tiger teeth pricked through my shirt. "What do you have for me?"

"Names."

"Great. Let's go to the john."

We went into one of the unisex rest rooms, where she locked the door and turned all the water taps on full blast while I deciphered Dr. Pierce-Owen's computer notes. Afterward Ruthellen asked me if I were up to doing it in a public rest room. "I can't take you home," she said. "Rublev drops in when he gets an urge and expects me to pop his cookies for him."

Since I had been afraid that Ruthellen might come up with something like this, I'd brought a condom.

Afterward I tried to slip unobserved past the bar and out of the building, but Jean-Paul saw me and waved. He came into the lobby. "Do you have your vehicle here?"

I nodded. "Need a lift?"

"Dilanthi lives somewhere near you, I think. McAllister Close?"

Dilanthi, I assumed, must be Jean-Paul's current girlfriend. He burned through them faster than Mark Grimal.

Outside the winter sky was clear, the slush on the sidewalk frozen into treacherous bumps. Despite the Black Russians, we made it safely to the car, which I had parked in an underground garage near the subway entrance.

"It's good to get away from Government House occasionally," said Jean-Paul. "Vacations aren't long enough nowadays."

"Where did you go this year?"

"Sri Lanka with Dilanthi. Not bad. Some good marahoochie. Nice beaches. Bombs in the papayas."

"Bombs?"

"You ought to travel more, Mark." Jean-Paul sank down in the seat and braced his feet on my dashboard. He closed his eyes. "The world's falling apart. Blowing up in little pieces—bing, bing, bing—all over the place. Sometimes I ask myself, How long has this been going on? Maybe for centuries. Stay in Alternative Four and you get the idea everything's stable, but we should be so lucky. The UD thing those guys were talking about, that's part of it, maybe most of it at the moment. I don't know. Nobody's doing anything but Danzig, and he's clubbing people. Is that the best idea we can come up with? I mean, shit, nobody's doing anything."

I thought of Dr. Pierce-Owen telling me to write a speech. "Try to do something and you discover how useless you are, maybe positively dangerous to everyone's health and sanity." I set the car on auto-pilot.

"I suppose," said Jean-Paul, who didn't appear to think the remark referred to me. "Well, Carlos says we've got to get organized, plan what to do, convince the Chairmen to cooperate, push legislation through Polyguide...."

I could smell my idea floating past. "Oh, well," I said, "if Carlos is organizing it, I'm sure it will get organized."

Jean-Paul laughed. He opened one eye. "You and Carlos have a fight? That why you haven't been around?"

"I wouldn't call it a fight...."

"No," said Jean-Paul. "More like an ultimatum, right?"

"What a tight-assed son-of-a-bitch...." I knew I shouldn't say that, but I felt better immediately.

Jean-Paul jackknifed into a spasm of laughter, feet kicking in the air. "You're telling me? You ought to work with the Christian! If he weren't all the time saving me from instant death, I'd hate his guts. I should have guessed. Fairouz has barely spoken to him since New Year's."

I felt a surge of pleasure.

"Of course," said Jean-Paul, "that's made him twice as hard to work with, because Fairouz is the one who defuses him before he gets to the rest of us...."

The pleasure departed.

We had come to the block where the shaded windows of the Atlas Towers West rose above us. Taking over the controls, I turned the car into Westminster Street, which flowed into McAllister Close, an empty fountain glistening with ice, flanked by townhouses. Jean-Paul pointed to a house on the corner. "That's it."

"Well...regards to all."

Jean-Paul grinned. "Even Carlos?"

I grunted. "Especially Carlos."

My meeting with Jean-Paul spawned a rash of odd phone· calls. In the past Government House people had never invited me personally to anything; I just came with Fairouz. Now suddenly Ole Grieg wanted me to go skiing; Tosca Pinelli and Can Mabuza invited me for Sunday brunch; Babatunde Adedipe suggested dinner at a West African restaurant; Evelyn Thompson held a wiener roast on her snowy terrace. I begged off. If they were trying to get Fairouz and me back together again, I knew the initiative hadn't come from Fairouz; she was too proud for that. My showing up would only have embarrassed both of us.

Then Carlos called. I decided I had misread the signals.

"Mark," said Carlos in his controlled voice, as though nothing had happened between us, "I've been discussing your idea about the Chairmen coordinating legislation. However—I know this sounds ridiculous, but we don't know that much about how the Admin works. We're having a meeting on Sunday afternoon at Can Mabuza's house. If you could drop by and give us a few hints about procedure, you would make a real contribution."

"Real contribution...." Now wasn't that nice. Here was Carlos giving me a chance to redeem myself. I put my feet up on my office desk. Across the room Penny was trying to extricate a jammed paper sheet from my printer.

"Glad to hear you're doing something along those lines, Carlos, but my mother is visiting, and on Sundays she wants to do touristy things. You know how mothers are." Actually I figured he probably didn't know; may indeed never have had one.

"Sure," said Carlos, without missing a beat. "Pick an evening next week, any evening, and we'll do it then."

I took a deep breath. Trust Carlos. If I could find an excuse for every night next week, then he'd fast forward to the following week and then the following and then the one after that, until I looked like a sulky idiot. Besides, after all, it was my idea they were discussing.

"Okay, let's see—how about Tuesday?"

"Great," he said. "I'll have Can call you to confirm the time. Thanks, Mark." Then, having trapped me, he turned generous. "Also please accept my apologies for that scene at your home New Year's Eve. I overreacted. History never repeats itself; we just like to think that it does, because then we're absolved of past errors."

I didn't know what he meant by that; however I figured that if Carlos could be generous, then I could too. "No problem, Carlos. You had your reasons."

THIRTY-FIVE

When I reached Can's house on Tuesday evening, Tosca opened the door. She was dressed in tight black slacks and a bulky red sweater, her blonde hair pulled back in a chignon.

"Mark! How nice!" She kissed me on both cheeks, as though we'd always been the best of buddies. Behind her I could see most of the Government House senior staff, even Mr. Brown's staff director, Alice Greenbriar, a severe-looking woman who rarely attended the parties. "We hadn't seen you for so long we were beginning to worry."

"You know, the family scene. T.V. every night. Early to bed. Up with the chickens."

"Tell me more stories," said Tosca.

I moved warily toward the living room, only to be greeted with a warm chorus of greetings. Was it possible that Harvey had told no one but Carlos about my freaking out at the studio? Anything was possible. From across the room Harvey himself gave me a curt wave. Can Mabuza came forward, with Carlos Acevedo behind him, like a co-host. "Welcome, Mark. Glad you could come." Carlos and I shook hands. I felt as though everybody should applaud us.

Mety Diob, Mallam Ahmed's secretary, nudged me toward the sofa where she had been sitting. "Sit here."

I started to protest, but then saw Fairouz on the sofa. Stuck. I sat down beside her and said in a very low voice: "Sorry about this, dear."

"We are doing work, no?" replied Fairouz. "There is no need to be sorry." On her lap she held a notepad computer. She looked away from me in the direction of a black and red African mask hanging above the electric fireplace. Her dark hair fell loose around the shoulders of her beige caftan, which had thin, green stripes that matched her eye shadow. How could I ever have given up this woman? Nobody in the room except Carlos seemed to realize that I had.

Carlos led the discussion in a relaxed, collegial way, deferring frequently to Rodrigo dos Santos and Alice Greenbriar. I wondered where I was going to fit into all this, but it didn't me take long to find out.

All of the Chairmen had set up task forces to determine the causes of UD unrest in their areas. Although the Admin spent millions of dolyens every year on electronic polling, the UDs didn't participate since they had no access to the voting channels. Having realized this, the task forces were sending volunteers—real people—into the UD districts to try to find out what was wrong; this wasn't working very well because the volunteers were getting mugged. Getting mugged reinforced everybody's idea about UDs being dangerous. Lots of UDs were, of course, but I couldn't understand why anybody needed a poll to find out why UDs were unhappy with their living conditions.

As though reading my mind, Carlos asked: "What do you think about the problems we're encountering on this, Mark?"

I cleared my throat. "Guess I'm kind of slow, but I can't figure out why you need polls." At first nobody seemed to understand the question.

Alice frowned. "If we're going to formulate policy proposals, we have to have hard data."

I replied: "Sure, but what could be harder data than a mob marching on a government food storage warehouse? Or taking over a subway system to protest the lack of transport?... If you have any doubt about why the UDs are rebelling, talk to Fairouz and Evelyn; they can tell you."

A few throats were cleared, a few legs crossed. Everybody looked uncomfortable, including Fairouz and Evelyn. I could see that these people weren't any better at talking about unpleasant matters than were those in the Admin.

Oh, what the hell.

"Look," I said, "I'll give you a tour of the UD district some time, but if polls make you feel better, take them." Then I turned to Carlos, who was lounging in front of a display shelf that held a talking drum, a whistle flute, a raft zither, and three calabash rattles. "Is it all right if we move right along to the main point here, Carlos?"

Carlos looked at me as though I were an African mask that had jumped off the wall and started talking. He didn't ask what the main point was. He just said: "Go ahead, Mark. Moving us along is what you're here for."

"Okay, for the moment, let's forget causes. We have a problem. In dealing with the problem, there are three alternatives. You can batter the UDs: that's the Danzig solution. You can put bandaids on them: that's the Finley solution. Or you can change the damn policy that's created the mess...."

Harvey drawled: "And that's the Grimal solution."

Fairouz crumpled her dress between her fingers.

I forced a smile. "Lots of people within the Admin besides me don't agree with the policy, but their excuse is that only the People can change the policy, and the People aren't going to change it because they love the policy. It's a great policy: protects the community. No doubt there are groups within the People who disagree and would like to change things; those are the ones you should be working with. However, they can't initiate change; that has to come from the Chairmen, and the Chairmen aren't going to do anything unless you convince them to do something, because that's your job."

I paused and leaned back on the sofa, perspiring.

Carlos smiled then. "In other words, Mark, it's our fault nothing's been done."

"No. The system makes sure you waste your energy. You spend at least four months each year trying to get your Chairmen re-elected. And then what do they do? Nothing. They're just figure-heads, some prettier than others." I heard a few muffled laughs. Even Alice Greenbriar's mouth twitched. "It's the divide and rule theory." Then I caught myself; next I'd be violating Club rules by telling them about the Transition, which would do them no good and me a lot of harm. "I'm sure you've been told many a time that It'll-never-pass-the-People's-Assembly;-the-polls-are-against-it...."

"Well, isn't that true?" asked Rodrigo.

"Maybe yes, maybe no. Polyguide has good reasons not to want to put legislation before the People if they think it'll fail. But what happens is that everything we do reinforces the present policy. We're always explaining why the People should support it, rather than giving them reasons why they shouldn't. Then they run a poll and—surprise!—the People say it's a great policy...."

"Mark," said Can Mabuza, "I think you need a job change."

I laughed with the others. "Well, all it would take will be one more conversation with Kelly Hallihan about how writing crap comes with the territory."

Evelyn Thompson leaned forward. "Mark, I know you mean what you're saying, but Kelly's the one who controls the People's TV Assembly. If Kelly knows something's extremely important to Mr. Brown, the furthest she'll go is suggest he tuck it away in some recurring appropriations bill, something like that."

I nodded. "Sure. Okay. So Kelly gets a request from Mr. Brown. Let's say it's about Central Bank exchange rates. She looks at it and she says to herself, 'Ahmed will never buy this one,' and so she sends it back to you with fictitious arguments about why it won't pass, not mentioning that it's because she thinks it won't pass in Ahmed's region. If she goes ahead and puts it on a ballot in spite of her reservations, then she might be accused of favoring Mr. Brown over Mallam Ahmed...."

"Wait a minute," said Rodrigo.

"She doesn't think it's her job—and it's not her job—to call Ahmed's office and ask, 'Can you live with this?'"

"We aren't going to accuse her of any such thing," protested Rodrigo.

"Oh, she's not worried about you."

I looked at Jean-Paul. Jean-Paul raised his eyebrows. "The Man," intoned Jean-Paul.

"Precisely. The Man."

There was silence while we all thought about The Man.

"Jake's got the guns but Kelly's got the policy, and she's damn well going to keep it pure because that's all the leverage she's got. However, according to policy, the Chairmen are the highest ruling body; therefore if the Chairmen presented a united front, she'd do what they asked her to do, because then she'd be covered by policy. Do you see what I'm saying?"

"Yes," said Carlos. He was ahead of most of them. "Mark, this is more than I think we bargained for." He moved forward. The discussion erupted into frank comments, which Carlos sifted and rearranged. For the next few minutes I tuned out, wasn't listening, thought, well, at least I've said it; let them do whatever they want to with it. Suddenly I felt Fairouz's soft fingers grope their way into my left hand, which lay on the sofa between us. I pressed my thumb into her palm until her fingers tightened around mine. I didn't let go of her hand for the rest of the meeting. Afterward we went to her home and made love until midnight. Plenty of time later to discuss Balthazar De Jonge.

Of course when I arrived home at 12:30 a.m. I found that Lisa had gone to bed, but Mother was waiting up for me, robed in flannel, and drinking hot chocolate in front of the TV set. "You could at least have called," said Mother. "Mark, how can you be so inconsiderate?" She went on like this for thirty minutes until I finally escaped to our bedroom; but that wasn't much of an escape because Lisa wasn't asleep.

"My, my," said Lisa. "I recognize the perfume."

Over the next two weeks I frequently saw the Government House people, as they drew up a draft proposal on the UD question for their Chairmen to consider. They wanted my input, and I was happy to give it. In the Global Admin building, my name was dropped in so many different departments that I was acquiring the reputation of being the Government House contact man in Admin. Eberhardt didn't like that. Following one of his Monday morning staff meetings, he invited me into his inner office, the walls of which were decorated with miniature engravings of mountains and small ceramic house models among all the framed awards for twenty years of Admin service.

"Mark," he said, "tell me what you're doing at Government House these days."

I told him, as honestly as possible: the staffs of all three Chairmen had asked me to give them advice on things the Admin organization charts didn't tell you, like obtaining polls from Records rather than Polyguide.

Said Eberhardt: "That's not your job, Mark. Finley's staff people are the ones to take care of their queries."

"Well, sure," I agreed, although actually I had forgotten that Finley's staff might do anything but feed the canary. "It's just that they find it easier to ask a friend, and I'm friendly with a lot of people up there."

"So I'm told," said Eberhardt. His jowls moved slowly; his fingers tapped one-and-a-two-and-a-three on the arm of his swivel chair. "Wong's secretary being one of them."

I didn't want to confirm or deny, so I said nothing.

"Use more discretion, Mark. I don't like things like that coming at me in Finley's staff meetings."

Ouch. Then I got mad. Why the shit should my sex life be on the agenda of a staff meeting? "I thought Finley's staff meetings only dealt with 'vital topics of general interest.'"

Eberhardt smiled faintly. "You fell under the heading, 'Admin/Chairmen Relations.'"

"I have friends on all three staffs, Helmut. Ask them."

"I believe you," said Eberhardt. "But that doesn't help the image any. Maybe some people feel threatened. Maybe they're afraid that Finley might think they're not doing their job right if Government House bypasses them. People think all kinds of weird things. You're not an Admin liaison man, Mark. Tell them the channels people are on your back. Make me the heavy if you want. Keep your friends. But get out."

That was certainly an order. "Okay. Sorry I embarrassed you."

Although I was annoyed, I decided I could treat Eberhardt's order creatively by referring people to Guggenheim or Chaudhuri or Kimball, but always with the proviso that if they didn't like the answer they got, they could check back with me. "Just don't mention my name." People like Can Mabuza shook their heads and asked how I could stand working for such a bureaucratic organization, but of course the same thing happened at Government House, only in a different manner.

According to Fairouz, bureaucratic infighting had been at

the root of the problem between Carlos and Balthazar De Jonge, although maybe that wasn't the whole story.

She didn't want to talk about De Jonge, but I decided I had to hold her to her promise.

We went to Iroko Park on a Saturday morning when the sun, having stayed around for a few days, had sent a breath of false spring into the Federal Territory capital. The bare trees looked as though they were struggling to blossom. The ground had little mounds of sooty snow heaped near rocks, around tree trunks. We sat down on a bench near the arboretum. She hugged her arms across her chest and gazed away from me.

She said the trouble began in those days because whenever Balthazar telephoned Government House, he would insist on talking only to Wong, never to Carlos. "Of course many people think they are too important to talk to a staff director," said Fairouz. In cases like that, Comrade Wong's practice was to ask after their health and then switch the call to Carlos. But when Comrade Wong tried doing that with Balthazar, Balthazar would ask Carlos to make an appointment with Wong. Since making appointments was not Carlos's job, he'd switch the call back to Fairouz....

"Sounds worse than the Admin."

Fairouz gave a small laugh. "I tried to convince Balthazar to be flexible, but no: he said he didn't like gatekeepers. So he and Carlos kept getting more and more angry at each other."

One day they were in Wong's office for one of those appointments. Balthazar wanted the Eastern region to participate in a trade fair.

She paused. "I don't recall why—a competing fair or wrong time of year—something, but Carlos objected. Balthazar saw that he was getting the worst of the argument, so he did an unforgivable thing: he started to make fun of Carlos. 'Don Quixote,' Balthazar called him, 'tilting at windmills.' It is true, you know, that Carlos is somewhat rigid, and has all these notions about honor and *machismo*. Oh, Balthazar could be very amusing. Even I, even Comrade Wong smiled. Of course in the end Carlos won, because Comrade Wong could see that Balthazar was not answering the objections...."

A squirrel scrambled over the path and stopped in front of us, sniffing. I cleared my throat. I could see that making fun of Carlos might cause problems.

"...Carlos never forgave Balthazar for ridiculing him. And so...when...when what happened, happened and I told Carlos that Balthazar was innocent, he didn't believe me. Comrade Wong believed me, but Carlos said I was hysterical."

Balthazar De Jonge had once made Fairouz laugh at Carlos, and therefore Balthazar could not be just crazy; he had to be guilty as well. That made perfect sense to a jealous man like me, but why should I tell her that Carlos loved her?

Still, forty-eight hours is a long time in the hands of Danzig's goons. Maybe Carlos had been right; maybe Fairouz had been hysterical.

Very cautiously, I said: "I watched the trial on the People's TV Court. De Jonge seemed...well, disturbed."

"Insane," she said bluntly. "Yes, by then he was insane. That is what they did to him."

Her remark put a different perspective on the trial. I considered the idea, maybe because I knew more about the Billings Psychiatric Hospital than did Carlos.

"How do you know?"

"Oh, Mark," she cried. "I saw him! It was terrible." She thrust her gloved hands before her face. Tentatively I put my arm around her shoulder. "They were injecting him with all sorts of drugs; three times they did it while I was in the room. What he said—all that about the Liberation struggle—it was on a recording that they were making him repeat over and over again, and if he got a word wrong, they...."

She was shaking. I tightened my arms around her. "I know, Fairouz."

"You see," she said, "they took me there to make him suffer, but it didn't work because he didn't recognize me...."

I felt a sickening jolt. I didn't want to think what they might have done to her; I didn't want her to tell me.

"...Balthazar had discovered something. He didn't tell me what. Something involving Security. He should have let Rublev deal with it, because Rublev terrifies everybody; but Rublev was out of town and so Balthazar decided to handle it himself. The day before he was arrested, he told me he had an appointment with Danzig. 'Watch the fur fly!' he said. 'He's got some explaining to do on this one....'"

"Poor De Jonge. He probably didn't even take another officer with him."

Fairouz was silent. Then she drew back and looked at me, solemn and incredulous. "Do you believe what I say is true?"

"Of course."

To my alarm, large tears brimmed in her eyes and started dripping down her cheeks, carrying streaks of green eye shadow with them. I wiped them away, and she kissed me passionately, right there on the olive park bench, in the daylight, in front of the squirrels and a group of children playing tag and a woman with a baby buggy.

I thought how lucky for me that, way back when Fairouz had needed him, Carlos hadn't believed her.

Ruthellen Janniger visited Alternative Four several times during the early part of the year. She always called me at work, but I managed to avoid meeting her because I knew what she wanted, and now that I was back with Fairouz, well, I didn't have the taste for it. I could see that Ruthellen might well be Rublev's kind of woman, but she wasn't mine. Maybe I owed her more than I had delivered, but at the time I just didn't have the stomach.

In early April her series on adulterated drugs in the districts hit the *Bonn Program World*. The first article was low key: a scene setter. She hadn't limited herself to Alternative Four; she'd moved around—Los Angeles, Rome, Cairo, Calcutta, Kiev, Santiago. Wherever she'd been covering another story, she'd also popped into the UD pharmacies, come up with gruesome anecdotes, colorful quotes, shady characters with phony names who spilled details of a far-reaching operation, tied in, not so much to hard drugs, as to respectable manufacturing companies, government monitoring agencies, and internal security forces.

"Did you see Ruthellen's nuclear warhead in the *Bonn Program World*?" asked Jean-Paul. "I hope she's got proof for all that." "I'd put my money on it," I answered.

The second article went into greater detail about Calcutta. Things couldn't get much worse than Calcutta. This time the insinuations were clearer, the individuals more identifiable. The Chief Executive Officer of Mallow Winks Pharmaceuticals called a press conference to denounce the irresponsible reporting in the *Bonn Program World*. The newspaper stood by the story. Number three in the series moved to Rome, where she focussed on the mafia/security connection in the adulterated drug racket. Not much new about that; nevertheless the Chief of Police in Rome called a press conference to denounce her "unproved allegations." The newspaper stood by the story.

Article number four came home to the Global Federal Territory. Another scene-setter, only this time she was talking about coordinated operations, protected by global security forces. Pursued by journalists who finally trapped him as he was getting into a small, solar-powered aircraft on the roof of MedUnit, Dr. Fisher Schleka said that Ms. Janniger was obviously a disturbed young woman who needed psychiatric counseling.

Nobody in Alternative Four discussed much else the entire week. We were all waiting for the dirt that was sure to spew forth in the final article, which was scheduled to run on Friday.

But before Friday Ruthellen's luck ran out, and mine nearly went with hers.

THIRTY-SIX

On Wednesday it snowed, one of those spring surprises that tie up traffic in the Federal Territory capital, disrupt dinner parties, and send people groping in their closets for winter coats they hadn't thought they'd need again until October. It started about two p.m. From my window I could watch the flurries swirl around the flags at the visitors's entrance, then grow thicker and heavier until the air was white with only occasional splashes of red or green or blue flickering through the snow. Penny groaned. "It's going to take hours to get home tonight." At four p.m. the Director-General's office sent word that everybody could leave for the day. I should have left then, but I had a speech due the next morning for Harry Dharmasena, the Director of the Foreign Interests Department, and working at home was difficult nowadays, since Mother and Lisa chattered incessantly—nice for them, but hell on the concentration.

I finished the speech about 6:30, then called Lisa to tell her I was leaving the office, but not to hold dinner because I might be hours on the road getting there. Although my vehicle was parked in the Admin garage, I knew the sensible thing would be to take the maglev train; however when I reached the basement underground station I discovered a horde of Admin employees who had been waiting there for over an hour because snow had shorted out some connection at Prendergast Station. Rather than wait, I figured I might as well drive, or try to.

Oddly enough when I drove up the ramp into the street, I discovered the tie-up wasn't as bad as I had anticipated; people either had left their offices much earlier or had decided not to drive home. Traffic was slow but moving. I set the car on auto-pilot and turned on a soft music station. Even on auto-pilot one had to stay alert when it snowed. The car in front of me was barely visible.

Seven o'clock. A news bulletin. The usual disasters were

occurring: a small plane had crashed near Calcutta, killing two mid-level officials from Global Health; an earthquake had hit Tehran; seven bodies had been discovered in the Los Angeles sewage system; in Santiago four men had been hauled off a city bus and stabbed to death, then—flash! a bulletin.

Bonn Program World journalist Ruthellen Janniger had been shot dead in a pub in London.

It was a good thing I had the car on auto-pilot.

The announcer said that Ruthellen had been sitting at the bar with friends when somebody called her name. Turning around on the bar stool, she had taken the bullet right between her eyes. In the pandemonium that broke out, the gunman had, of course, escaped. The radio went back to music.

I turned it off.

I was now at the end of Transition Avenue. I pulled out a pack of cigarettes and lit one with a shaky hand. Ruthellen Janniger! I thought of her fluffy red hair, now blood red, her breasts pointing upward into the air. There was no question why she had been killed. What would happen now to the fifth article in the series? I turned the radio back on and found a news channel. The reporters had already called the *Bonn Program World* for a reaction. The editor was not available. The publisher said that unfortunately Ruthellen's fifth article, the one that would have pointed the finger, had accidentally been erased from the computer. The reporter asked who had erased it. The publisher reiterated that it had been an accident. No, there hadn't been a backup. No, the newspaper wouldn't be able to reconstruct the story from her notes; they couldn't find her notes. Yes, people at the newspaper had read the article but without the notes, without the tapes, there was nothing that could be done; the paper was not going to leave itself open to a lawsuit by publishing unverified material. Wasn't it already open to lawsuits because it had published the first four articles? The publisher hung up. I felt sorry for him. I wondered what had happened to the editor.

By now I was approaching the Atlas Towers West. There was a big snowdrift right across the street, straight across, like a covered hedge. Cars were turning around. I couldn't turn around; I lived there, damn it. I'd have to leave the car and hope it didn't get plowed under in the morning when the machines came by.

The annoyance was enough to erase momentarily the thought of Ruthellen from my mind. I got out of the car, locked it, and headed for the buried sidewalk, which I knew was over there somewhere to the right. I wondered what had created this large snowdrift. All I could think of was that a snow removal machine must have come by in the late afternoon and then, seeing the uselessness of it all, abandoned the job. But I wasn't really thinking. I just wanted to get over this pile of snow and into the warm lobby of the Atlas Towers West. The snow was still falling, enough to keep me from seeing clearly. Ducking my head against the wind, I scrambled up the mound, my shoes sinking into the snow with each step. Then I started down the other side.

I slipped.

That was what saved me, because as I slipped I fell backward and the bullet grazed my temple. The next two bullets plowed into my body. I couldn't see anything for the snow; after the first searing impact, I couldn't feel anything either, which was probably fortunate when the snow shovel hit me.

I woke up twenty-four hours later, with my father standing at the foot of the bed. I closed my eyes. That couldn't be right. I opened them and he was still there, white hair, peering intensely, his jaw working back and forth. Then I realized that I had just thought I was opening the left eye. It didn't move. Neither did the rest of me. I didn't feel any pain because I was so full of drugs I couldn't feel anything at all.

"Why aren't you in the classroom?" I asked my father.

Suddenly both my mother's lined face and Lisa's pink cheeks lowered into view, one from each side. Lisa was biting her lip. Mother was crying. I decided that this family trinity was too much for my one eye to take in; I closed it.

I was in the MedUnit hospital nearest the Atlas Towers West, my survival due to the action of an aerospace engineer named Conrad Kuhler, who had decided to walk home Wednesday evening, clambered up the same snowdrift about an hour after I had, slipped just as I had done, and landed on top of my body, which my would-be killer or killers had buried in the snow. As he fell, he dislodged enough snow to uncover one of my hands, with which he came in contact when he tried to get up. A grave shock, he told me solemnly when he visited me two weeks later in the hospital. But being the sort of organized, always-prepared person who carries Swiss knife, flashlight, and water purification tablets, Kuhler quickly verified that it was indeed a hand, belonging to a still live body, and dug me out with the help of the Atlas Towers West doorman, who recognized me.

Eight other people in Alternative Four were attacked that night; I was the only survivor. One of the dead was Dr. Pierce-Owen, who had been shot at a bus stop near the UD hospital.

I didn't learn all this for several days and then only bit by bit, principally from Steve Maine, whose constant visits could not be explained entirely by our friendship.

The first evening all Steve said to me was: "I'd like to move you out of here, but the hospital says no, your wife says no, your parents say no, and you aren't in any condition to decide. So we'll gamble. I've got some Human Rights boys stationed in the corridor."

That sounded ominous. "Sure. Whatever you say."

Steve looked at me and wagged his head. "You were out of your league this time, Mark. Definitely out of your league."

On the third day I remembered Ruthellen.

"Steve—"

He came over to the bed and sat down, displacing Lisa. "Don't disturb him!" cried Lisa.

"Yes, Mark?"

"Ruthellen Janniger...."

"Right." Steve cleared his throat. "Well, it's like this: a lot of people were killed Wednesday throughout the Federation. Mostly medical personnel, low level pharmaceutical employees, a journalist here and there—you get the picture?"

I groaned.

"In your case there was no connection—"

"What?"

"You heard me. No connection." Steve pronounced each

word slowly and deliberately as though he thought I had brain damage. "Case of mistaken identity. The media have asked. I've issued a bulletin in the name of the family—Mistaken identity."

"Must have been," I agreed. Who was I to contradict a bulletin?

Yet clearly I had made a selective hit list drawn up by the adulterated drug industry. That meant that either the City Condos apartment had been bugged again after Rublev had earlier debugged it, or the unisex john at the Press Center hid a video camera—in which case Danzig had some great footage—or my name had appeared in Ruthellen's missing notes, assuming of course that they were really missing. In any case Danzig plainly had concrete data implicating me.

However, through a fluke, I hadn't died, and what good was I without Dr. Pierce-Owen and Ruthellen Janniger? I couldn't get as worried as Steve did about my health; getting killed rather than restructured had to be a step in the right direction.

Danzig arrived late on Monday afternoon, accompanied by one of his flunkies, a bright-eyed, insolent man named Akbar Gillette, who slouched against the closet door and eyed Lisa's six-month-pregnant stomach, which was draped now under tucks and flounces like a pillow. The Human Rights lookout must have beeped Steve, because he hurried in two minutes later while Danzig was still shaking hands with my father.

"Good afternoon, Mr. Danzig," said Steve, stiffly formal. "Hello there, Akbar." He sat down in a corner chair beneath the "Get Well" balloon from my staff.

"Fancy meeting you here, Maine," Danzig drawled. "Sometimes I think they clone you."

I was sitting up now, more or less, and could see out of both eyes because they'd changed the bandage on the left side of my head to something more discreet. Danzig turned toward me with his buddy-buddy smile.

"Well, Mark, you've got the luck of the Irish."

"Are they lucky?"

"Figure of speech, Mark, figure of speech. Wednesday night—Bloody Wednesday, we're calling it now—we lost eight—

eight, Mark—Alternative Four Federal Government officials. But we didn't lose you."

"That's something to think about, all right," I agreed, thinking about it.

"You're the odd man out in this one," Danzig went on. "I can't figure what connection a speech writer might have with doctors and nurses and pharmaceutical company employees and that dippy journalist—what's her name?—Ruthellen Janniger, who was shot in London."

"If you can't figure it out, Danzig," I said, "I'll tell you." I felt rather than saw Steve freeze in his chair. "I've been thinking about that myself. Maybe I resemble a teledrama doctor—you know, like that good looking one on—Lisa, what's the name of the show?" Lisa gazed at me as though I were hallucinating. "You know—'Hospital Heaven' or something."

"You don't look a bit like Dr. Ritchie," said Lisa. "He has a blond mustache."

"That's the one," I said. "Somebody mistook me for a hero."

Danzig smiled. "Mistaking you for a hero is quite a feat, Mark. Careless of them, wasn't it?"

"Careless of me too," I said. "Why, I usually get in about midnight, right, Lisa? If I hadn't tried to go home early Wednesday night, it would never have happened."

Danzig moved closer to the foot of the bed. "But you did know Ruthellen Janniger, didn't you, Mark?"

"I met her on a trip with Mallam Ahmed."

Danzig nodded slowly and with a peculiar satisfaction. Then he looked sideways at my parents and he looked sideways at Lisa, and I guess he decided to skip the True-or-False sex question, at least for the moment, while across the room Akbar Gillette shrugged and, straightening up, stuck his hands in his pockets. They were ready to leave.

Danzig winked at me. "Well, Mark, I'm glad Eberhardt won't have to look for a new division head." He took my mother's hand, "A pleasure, Mrs. Grimal," my father's hand, "A pleasure, Dr. Grimal," my wife's fingers: "When's the happy event, Lisa?"

She blushed. "Mid-July, Mr. Danzig."

"Be sure to invite me to the name-giving ceremony," said Danzig. How jolly, I thought; Lisa will.

I tried not to think about Dr. Pierce-Owen's death, because, although she had provided the names willingly, I felt responsible for having involved her. Moreover the UD hospital was now without a good doctor.

Ruthellen Janniger, however, had pursued the story enthusiastically, and her dramatic death turned her into a media heroine. No one was going to pick up the report from her and run with it, not soon anyway; however the Inter-Order Media Club was renamed the Janniger Media Center. The Global Media Journalists Association set up in her name an annual one-hundred-thousand-dolyen award for investigative reporting. A posthumous collection of her articles appeared in an electronic book edition. A film, loosely based on her life, drew rave reviews. Given that we all have to die some day, Ruthellen had done it with style.

On top of that, her death annoyed Vasili Rublev so much that he refused to sit next to Jake Danzig in Finley's staff meeting.

To an outsider, a gesture like that might seem inadequate, Ruthellen being, after all, dead; however, within the bureaucracy gestures count, they portend, they unnerve, they signify. In certain circumstances they can even effectively demote, as Rublev proved with this one.

I don't know how many people in the Admin knew that Ruthellen Janniger had been Vasili Rublev's mistress, probably not many, because no one ever thought of Rublev in terms of human relationships. Certainly the media people knew and so did Danzig. One might have thought, therefore, that Danzig would have been a little more circumspect about letting someone kill her; however Rublev had permitted Balthazar De Jonge to go down the tube, why not Ruthellen? Perhaps Danzig thought Rublev wouldn't notice, just get himself another broad to fuck when he felt like fucking.

But Rublev noticed. Ruthellen evidently had been his type of woman—bright, energetic, aggressive, unsentimental, tough, and dirty. Moreover she had undoubtedly kept him informed of all the Admin gossip leaked to her from other sources. A combination like that is hard to come by, and so Rublev was annoyed.

On the Friday after Bloody Wednesday, Finley held his regular staff meeting for all department heads. At these meetings a certain hierarchy reigned. Rublev sat on Finley's right hand; Dharmasena on his left; then below Rublev, Danzig, and below Dharmasena, Kelly Hallihan. The Global Health Director sat below Danzig, the Management Counselor below Kelly. After those officers all the other department heads fought it out on a first-come-first-served basis, with any accompanying staff members perched in chairs against the wall.

According to what Vimalachandra told me, that Friday Finley, Kelly, Dharmasena, and Danzig were already in their seats when Rublev arrived. Instead of sitting down, as he always had, in the seat of honor at Finley's right hand, Rublev paused by the chair, looked at Jake Danzig, then, without a word, walked around behind Finley's seat and took a chair below Kelly.

Nobody knew what to do. Finley opened his mouth, said "Ummm..." and closed it. Kelly scrambled to her feet and offered Rublev her chair, which was at least a slot higher; again without a word, Rublev put his hand on her shoulder and popped her back down. There they sat. Danzig's face turned purple, but he didn't say anything. Horace Methuen, the Management Counselor, arrived, found Rublev in Methuen's proper chair, looked around bewildered, knew he couldn't sit at the right hand of Finley in Rublev's empty seat, and so made everybody else move down one chair. Finally, after a few more "Ummm's," Finley began the meeting. The chair on his right hand stayed empty throughout the session.

Next day the Global Admin corridors were buzzing with whispers about musical chairs and fighting elephants. Finley had a major personnel crisis on his hands. The smart money was on Rublev, and, sure enough, by the time of the next general staff meeting, Rublev was back in his proper chair at the right hand of Finley, but with Kelly below him and Danzig across the table next to Dharmasena. That meant Kelly had moved up a slot in the pecking order and Danzig down one, and although she'd had nothing to do with it, Danzig was mad as hell at Kelly.

During my third and final week in the hospital, a delegation from Government House brought me a bottle of 12-year-old Scotch, a "Get Well" card designed by Evelyn Thompson's son, Alan, some enormous Nigerian smoked snails, the mere look of which made Lisa queasy, and a golden Hand-of-Fatima amulet guaranteed to ward off future bullets. I was feeling pretty good by then; all the tubes were out and I could walk up and down the corridors with the ever vigilant Lisa pattering beside me.

Fairouz was not in the group. She had called me beforehand and explained that she wouldn't be with them, because I might find her presence embarrassing. Carlos didn't come either; Steve's bulletin probably hadn't convinced him of my innocence any more than it had Danzig. The group consisted of Rodrigo dos Santos, Can Mabuza, Evelyn Thompson, Jean-Paul Dornier, Babatunde Adedipe, and Ole Grieg. By that time my father had gone back to the university in Ottawa, but they charmed my mother and, after meeting my beautiful wife, viewed me with wonder. "You're a funny guy, Mark," said Can. Lisa put on an elaborate show of affection— patting me, dropping kisses on my forehead, holding my hand, massaging my neck, not missing an opportunity to flaunt her swollen belly. I was thankful Fairouz had had the good sense not to come with them.

The group brought me a copy of the UD draft legislation. "If you need some reading material, Mark, try this," said Rodrigo. "We're presenting it to the Chairmen on Monday."

I spent the weekend reading the document.

THIRTY-SEVEN

Given the traditional popularity of the Undesirables policy, the Chairmen's staff personnel had drafted a far more extensive piece of legislation than I would have thought likely to pass the People's TV Assembly. They hadn't tried to overturn the entire policy, but they did attack the most unjust parts of it. Thanks to Evelyn Thompson, the draft bill eliminated the sterilization of Undesirables' children, and, thanks to Fairouz, that of people with infectious diseases. It abolished the sterilization penalty for crimes such as treason, which could only be genetically based by stretching the definition, and for practicing unpopular magico-religious customs so long as they weren't illegal. The most drastic clause scrapped the death penalty for "corrupting" right-minded citizens.

In addition to the actual policy changes, the bill dramatically increased funding for UD police protection, medical services, and public utilities, redistributing money already allocated elsewhere in the budget. Imagining the screams that would soon be spewing forth from every Admin department ranging from Security to Local Government, I argued by videophone against combining money and policy in a single bill.

It took the Government House staffs an entire month of lobbying with their Chairmen before they could reach agreement. Mallam Ahmed signed off on it first; in drafting the bill, his staff had reached consensus; therefore he had no objections. Mr. Brown came next, thanks to Evelyn Thompson's influence. The main obstacle turned out to be Comrade Wong, who had no objection to the policy changes but agreed with my argument that policy and money should be kept separate for tactical reasons. Surprisingly, Carlos couldn't see this, I guess because, to Carlos, words without money meant rhetoric without substance. Comrade Wong and Carlos finally compromised on two different bills, to be submitted on the same ballot. Back again the staff assistants went to get the other two Chairmen's approval. The process was as bad as obtaining Admin clearances.

Then they approached Kelly Hallihan and asked her to put the two bills on the agenda for the People's TV Assembly.

"What the fuck's going on?" asked Kelly.

I suppose I had made Kelly's flexibility sound greater than it was. For one thing, Kelly believed that nobody could take her by surprise; and here the Chairmen were, doing the one thing she'd never expected them to do, namely agree on something. And what a something! Changing a sacrosanct policy! Worse, playing around with funds already allocated, particularly those in Jake Danzig's budget! "We're up shit creek on this one," said Kelly. She handed them Polyguide polls that proved how popular the UD policy was; they showed her Records polls indicating some things were less popular than other things. Although she skewed information all the time, Kelly didn't like to be caught skewing information; therefore she was furious. "Why are you guys fucking around with raw garbage?"

"Are you trying to tell us we have to filter it through you?" asked Carlos.

"Shit, no, Acevedo," said Kelly, realizing her error just in time. "But here in Polyguide, we take other things into account: letters, articles, independent research. We put all the hot poo into one bucket."

"Reads like it too," commented Alice Greenbriar tartly.

Rodrigo intervened with soothing Brazilian charm. "Kelly, we'd like to ask you to study these two bills and consult with Finley if you find any serious problems."

"Not 'serious,'" said Kelly. "Nuclear. We're talking fucking nuclear."

She carted the two bills off to Finley and came back with a more conciliatory stance, focussing on the money bill—a sort of hold-on-and-let-me-try-to-clear-this-with-the-affected-departments approach. Although the Government House staff found it annoying that their bill would have to be cleared with Admin departments, they said okay, but that in the meantime the Chairmen would start explaining to the People the rationale behind the upcoming UD policy change proposal in a series of television talks. By this time, nothing surprised Kelly. She couldn't stop them since that was Eberhardt's department; but she could sure give the speech writer scheduled to write the talks a major headache.

When I arrived that first Monday morning back at work, it was fairly late, about 9:30. I was still wobbly on my feet and sporting a jagged scar on the left side of my face that would require a second round of laser plastic surgery. Amid my staff's warm greetings, Penny whispered: "Better look at your desk, Mr. Grimal. Kelly Hallihan came down earlier."

On my too clean desk was a copy of the draft UD legislation attached to a large piece of paper across which Kelly had scrawled in red: "Welcome back, you s.o.b. Let's discuss your latest moral imperative ASAP."

"I haven't been here fifteen minutes, and I'm in trouble already," I complained to Penny. I buzzed Kelly on the intercom. "Come, like now," said Kelly.

I went, like now, though rather slowly like now, not only because I was moving slowly these days but also because people kept stopping me in the corridors to ask how I was. When I finally reached Kelly's office, she was springing around like an annoyed chimpanzee. "You didn't tell me you needed a fucking wheelchair. I would have sent one. Anything for our favorite Government leaker."

"What?" I asked, not expecting an attack from that angle.

She calmed a bit and plopped into her swivel chair. "Sit down, sit down. I don't want you to black out on my fucking carpet." I sat down. "How do you get yourself into these ballups? You're not even good looking fly bait any more."

"Damn it, Kelly," I said. "Stop building my ego."

She laughed, but not with much humor. Her scrubbed face looked flaky. A string of hair had come loose from the clasp at the back of her neck. "So you're going to write some speeches on UD policy for the Big Three...."

"I am?" I asked.

"You don't know?"

"How could I know? I just got here."

"Come off it," she said. "You've seen that draft legislation before."

"Well, yes...."

"In fact you fucking well helped draw it up."

"Not me," I said. "I've been in MedUnit."

"I don't mean wrote the fucking mush, Grimal. I mean spark-plugged it. Told them to get their polls from Records—"

"That's where I get mine."

"You're Admin. That's different."

"I don't get it."

"I know you don't get it," she said. "You think we're all one government or something."

"Aren't we?"

She leaned across her desk and snapped her fingers in my face. "Wake up, sweetie. Stop futzing around. You'll get the Doomsday machine operating."

I frowned. "What are you talking about?"

"I'm talking our mutual friend. I'm talking the Man."

I've always figured that if there were one office in the Global Administration building with a clean sound system, that would be Kelly's—clean, of course, of all bugs but Kelly's bugs. This confirmed it.

"Why should he care? Except of course about the money...."

"Oh, the money's a big thing, son. He's already said over his dead body."

Kelly's frankness took me by surprise and sounded suspiciously as though, threats having failed, she were about to pull a feminine ploy on me. That would be startling. My mind found the idea of Kelly as a woman hard to accommodate. I could see her as a 12-year-old tomboy swinging through the trees, but a first dance? a kiss in the back of a car? lipstick? screwing the boss? The secretary maybe, but not the boss.

She switched on the intercom and asked Billie Sue to bring us coffee.

"It's more than just the money though. Danzig's in one of his paranoid phases: the whole fucking universe is out to get him. That includes the Chairmen."

"Why the Chairmen?"

"They're a bunch of wimps. The Man's spent his life clamping down on the UDs and now the Chairmen are saying that's not the way to do it. They're backing down, changing the policy, saying we were wrong all the time, criticizing him. Now they even want him to protect the UDs. History! Danzig is pissing history at me. Any time an Empire tries to loosen the clamps, he says, the whole structure comes tumbling down. Now he's got a point there, Mark. Think about it."

I thought about it. "First off, do we have an Empire? And second, the system's going to come down anyway if we don't change some things in it."

"Talking to you," said Kelly, "is like going back to grammar school."

The door opened and Billie Sue came in with a tray that held two mugs of coffee, a tin of cream, a dispenser of liquid sugar and a large plastic plate filled with chocolate chip cookies.

"You trying to ruin my fighting trim?" asked Kelly. She pushed the plate at me. "There, Grimal, you need these more than I do. Thanks, Billie Sue. Try making pickles next weekend."

Billie Sue giggled her way out of the office. I wondered if I could convince Penny to start making cookies for me.

"So what is it that you're trying to tell me?" I asked. "That we should all run scared of Jake Danzig?"

Kelly swished her black coffee around once with a spoon handle. "Look in the mirror, Tiger."

"I'm a slow learner," I said. I picked up a cookie and bit into a soft mound of chocolate. "Not bad."

"Yeah, Billie Sue's a natural." Kelly took a sip of coffee and gazed out the window as though she could see Empires falling beyond it. "Look, Mark, I need your help on this one." Here it came. Kelly needed help about as much as I needed chastity. "I can't talk to Acevedo and company about this; it wouldn't be appropriate...."

"You mean it's appropriate for me?"

"Anyway you do it. Tell them something useful for a change. Tell them their bill's a no-go. If they push it, we'll end up finger food for monkeys."

I swallowed some bitter coffee. "I've got a better suggestion. Cart the Man off to Billings and restructure him."

She grinned, again without humor. "You first, Tiger."

"Don't tell me you're scared of him, Kelly."

"Sure, I'm scared of him. I've got more sense than you, Grimal. Half the time he's off his hinges."

I considered that. Not a good thought.

"What does Finley say?"

"Finley would like to handle it at a lower level."

"Meaning?"

"Meaning he wishes it would melt into the sunset."

"That's where I come in?"

"That's where you come in."

I picked up another cookie. The coffee was lousy but the cookies compensated. "And you think this is a reasonable idea?"

"Shit, no!" said Kelly. "But it's no more off the wall than any other fucking game plan I've come up with."

It didn't make sense. Kelly was in a bind, and Finley was waffling, hoping, after Rublev's power play, to avoid another confrontation with Danzig; but why should Mark Grimal help Kelly Hallihan play war games at the top? If she couldn't get a simple bill put before the People's TV Assembly for fear of Danzig, what good was she to us? I knew that if Kelly were in my place, that's how she'd think; and so I didn't feel much sympathy for Kelly.

"You know, Kelly, I'd like to help you, but I believe in this legislation...."

"He believes," said Kelly, nodding away to herself. She addressed the shredder. "Would you listen to that? We're all going down the tubes because Grimal believes...."

"...I'll tell the staff directors what you said, but I won't try to talk them out of it. That's a job for Finley's office, not mine." Kelly raised an eyebrow. I grimaced. "I quote Eberhardt." Eberhardt had given me the kind of excuse she could live with.

"So Big Daddy kicked ass, huh? None of us thought he would do it to his fair-haired boy." She crossed her legs, pursed her mouth, and stared gloomily at an electronic wall map flashing with red dots. "Okay, Mark, forget what I said. It wouldn't have worked anyway. This thing's too far down the fucking pipeline. We'll play it straight. I'll put the bills on the agenda."

"That's...that's great, Kelly."

She sprang to her feet and stretched—a wiry, boyish body, arms shooting straight upward, blouse pulling out of her slacks—to reveal a white line of hard flesh. I expected her to start doing calisthenics. Instead she suddenly smashed one fist down on the desk. My mug of un-drunk coffee splashed over the rim.

"Great? You fucking idiot! Get off your head trip and polish the amulets. We're going to need them to break even."

I left Kelly's office convinced that everybody at the top was crazy—Finley, Danzig, Kelly, Rublev. They were an experiment in small group dynamics that had gone awry and now threatened the universe. Maybe Dharmasena was okay, but only because he refused to play their game, kept traveling, meditated during staff meetings. The other four, or even any one of them, could smash him easily should they ever consider it necessary.

This discovery was too much for my first day back at work. By three p.m., I had a crashing headache. I decided to go home early on the underground, taking the UD lecture series file with me to work on later if I felt better. When the maglev train reached the Government House station, however, I thought of Fairouz and how I hadn't seen her for over a month now, and just as the subway doors were about to close, I stood up and squeezed through them.

I had been surprised that, although she called daily, Fairouz had not made more of an effort to see me in the hospital. Had she asked, I could have suggested a time when Lisa wouldn't be there. But Fairouz didn't ask. It was one of those details that you file away in your mind and later dredge up to help you pinpoint the moment when your great love affair starts to fray at the edges.

Fairouz had read the news sheets; she'd made the connections: she didn't doubt that I had been involved, deeply and without telling her, in providing Ruthellen Janniger information about the adulterated drug racket in the UD district. And she was hurt. I hadn't trusted her enough to tell her what I'd been doing. If I had seen her immediately, we could have talked about it; but I was undergoing a life crisis, wife in attendance; and it wasn't the sort of thing you could discuss on the telephone. When Carlos played it smart and said nothing, she didn't even have to defend me.

However, that afternoon when I entered Wong's office suite, her face broke into a radiant smile and she jumped up, all warm and loving, and embraced me, something she'd never done before in the office, while the rest of the staff crowded around. Even Comrade Wong stepped out of his office to shake my hand. Even Carlos.

Carlos asked if I'd seen the plan for the lecture series. I waved the file at him. "Looks good," I said. "But why not include a couple of panel discussions? Get some participants who object to the legislation and then demolish them?"

His face came alive. He invited me into his office. Panel discussions were really Program Formation's job to set up, not mine, but although my head was throbbing, I managed to sound coherent. We talked until 4:15 when Fairouz informed him that the Foreign Interests Desk Officer for Nepal had arrived. As I got up to leave, I decided that in spite of Kelly's having told me to forget our conversation, I ought to warn Carlos about Danzig.

"I saw Kelly today. Wait for her to advise you, but she says she's putting the bills on the agenda for the next People's TV Assembly."

Carlos looked at me with respect, as though somehow I'd done it. "That's good news."

"Kelly seems to think we have some bumpy times ahead of us with Danzig. Better pass the word to Rodrigo and Alice."

Back in the reception area, Fairouz said, no, I couldn't visit her that night; I should go home and go to bed; if I exerted myself too much I might have a relapse.

"Tomorrow?" I asked.

"We'll see how you feel." She accompanied me to the top of the escalator and kissed me goodbye, but chastely, like a sister. I knew we had trouble here, but I didn't know what; and I figured I'd straighten it out tomorrow. By the next day, however, Fairouz, having decided that she was being overly sensitive, made up for it with a passion that reassured me, and so we continued to act as though we were two halves of the same orange. But we weren't any longer.

Although each one of the Chairmen delivered a speech about different aspects of the UD policy aimed specifically at the concerns in his area, what turned public opinion in our favor were the TV panel discussions held with participants at a lower level. Tom Ugaki deserved the credit for that. In addition to the Chairmen's three media assistants, Tom found some articulate geneticists and sociologists who considered the UD policy a perversion of science, then lined up opponents of the legislation whom he could trust to be coherent but play by the panel rules. Rodrigo dos Santos chaired the three sessions; he'd had a lot of practice under Mallam Ahmed. After each program when Vimalachandra conducted an electronic poll on the subject, the percentage of those supporting the targeted reforms increased.

We were beginning to congratulate ourselves, when a man named Dr. Joe Kuron, editor of a small publication called *Military Strategy in the Post Nuclear World*, demanded to participate in one of the panels in order to rebut the "Federal Government's misguided attempt to brainwash the world into psychological disarmament." Sorry, said Tom Ugaki, the schedule's already set. Kuron then wrote to the Director of the Global TV Studios, asking for a special program slot. The Director said, Sorry, we don't grant air time to individuals; use your own forum. That should have been the end of Dr. Joe Kuron, but it wasn't. Two days later Everhardt received a memo from Danzig, demanding to know why this respectable academic had not been included in one of the UD programs.

Kuron was respectable, I guess; at least he had a genuine Ph.D. from Stanford University, and *Military Strategy in the Post Nuclear World* was one of those specialized publications that libraries stock in order to reflect ideological "balance." His most impressive credential, however, was that he was a friend of Jake Danzig's. When Danzig didn't receive a reply from Eberhardt in twenty-fours, he followed it up with a trip to Eberhardt's office. Later in the day, Tom got the word: See if you can include Kuron in something.

Tom was furious; however, Eberhardt so seldom made requests that when he came up with one you felt you had to comply. Said Tom: "Helmut's got problems with the hardware floor, but I'll be damned if I know what to do about it. Kuron will try to take over any program he's on."

"Put him on with me," said Carlos. "I'll debate him."

Like me, Tom considered Carlos primarily a mass rally rabble-rouser. "You're too 'hot' a speaker for the media."

"I'll cool," said Carlos. "Watch me."

I don't know if Carlos restrained himself or just looked like it alongside Kuron. The hour-long duel was intellectual entertainment at its best, and if I hadn't been committed to one side of the argument I would have cheered them both on. In the end, Carlos pulled it off because to him rhetoric was a technique, whereas to Kuron it was truth; he began to chew up words and wander off into side issues from which Rodrigo had to rescue him. An electronic poll taken immediately after the debate awarded the victory to Carlos by nine points. To our surprise Kuron shook Carlos's hand and told him he hoped they'd have an opportunity to tangle again some day on another podium. "Now I know your style, watch out! Next time I'll be better prepared," said Kuron.

We were elated. Danzig had had his say, and at the highest level. Now how could he complain? That evening we met at Fairouz's to celebrate. A great party, one of the last we had before the People's TV Assembly, marred only, for me, by a small incident. Carlos was being kissed by all the women—Tosca Pinelli, Mety Diob, Evelyn Thompson, Alice Greenbriar.... Okay, so he was a hero. Fairouz kissed him twice. Once when he came in—that was normal; but then again when she brought him a plate of couscous. He was sitting at the end of the sofa where she and I had so often made love. In handing him the food, she bent over and kissed his forehead. Carlos looked up with a surprised smile, warmer than any smile I'd ever seen before on Carlos's face—vulnerable almost, if one could apply that term to Carlos. Neither of them said a word, but I didn't like it, no, not in the slightest.

"He won! What a fucking half-assed thing for Acevedo to do."

As usual, Kelly Hallihan threw me off balance before I could even sit down in her chunky visitor's chair. Because I was the only Club member in the group pushing the UD legislation, she had taken to calling me up to her office for what she described as "a status report."

"Come again?"

"If I hadn't thought Acevedo'd lose by, oh, say, two, three points, I would have suggested he throw it."

"Throw it?" I was almost as outraged as Carlos would have been. "You don't know who you're talking about."

"I know, Hot Dog," she said. "I know. Acevedo is a frigging white hat, still organizing coffee pickers in the Andes, but Danzig's got more in his hands than a whip and a pistol. What Carlos should have done was lose by just enough so that Danzig might have thought he had a chance to win fairly on the ballot."

This was Thursday and the People's TV Assembly was scheduled for next Tuesday. I had completed the short introductory speeches by the three Chairmen; that would take thirty minutes. After they spoke, at precisely eight p.m. Kelly would activate the mechanism for the People's TV Assembly and voting would go on somewhere in the world for the next twelve hours.

On Monday morning Kelly Hallihan called me again to her office. "Grimal," she said, "I've finally gotten Finley to agree to support the legislation."

Monday mornings aren't my best time. Did she mean to say that up until the day before the voting Finley hadn't been supporting us? I couldn't believe it. "Wait a minute...."

"Now," said Kelly, "I want to avoid all possible distractions. I've taken a nice little cottage down at Cape Winnemucca. I'm sending my dog there this afternoon...."

"Your dog," I repeated.

"...Vim's wife is going to dog-sit. Her children are on vacation in Sri Lanka. She'll be lonely. I think Blondie should join her...."

"Wait a minute...."

"...Tom Ugaki's wife will also be there. They'll have a great time hunting sea shells, eating crabs, holding a wiener roast on the beach at midnight.... They won't even have to cook. Billie Sue will do it for them...."

"Billie Sue," I repeated. "Kelly, what the crap is going on?"

She smiled. "Nothing's going on, Hot Dog, and I want to be fucking sure nothing does. A vacation at the beach. Blondie will love it."

"My mother's staying with us."

"Mother?" She shook her ponytail. "You've got a mother? Shit. Okay, Mother gets to dog-sit too. No more dear ones tucked away, I hope?"

"Not here."

"Good," she said. "The house is getting a bit crowded.... Tell Blondie and Mama to pack their bags. Billie Sue will pick them up at 4:30."

"Today? Kelly, look, I can't ask Lisa to—"

"Shit, Pussycat, tell her. It's an order."

The coffee was cold. The clocks ticked away. Kelly's grin was as macabre as a lab skull. She wore a long gold chain that had snagged on a vest button and straggled across her breasts, which resembled golf balls caught in a sand trap. I was going to confide my wife and mother into her hands? But then I remembered: Jacintha.

"What's Vim got to do with this?"

Her grin broadened. "Vim can take care of himself. You and Tom Ugaki are spending the night at my house. Just in case. And no fucking sexist remarks, Lover-Boy, or I'll feed you wine and toffee."

Tom and I met after work in the basement parking garage. We went through a pantomime of raised hands, shrugged shoulders, grimaces, whirling fingers pointed to the head. Leaving his car parked, we departed in mine, heading, first, to his flat to pick up a change of clothing, then to mine.

"I thought you'd know what this was all about," said Tom. "You're Kelly's buddy, always in her office nowadays. I won't repeat the rumors...."

I groaned. "Please don't."

Tom half-smiled. "Never believed a word of them: you're

normal. Compared to Kelly anyway. The weird witch of the Gospel according to James Francis Finley III. My wife is spooked, I can tell you. You don't think Kelly's going to sacrifice them on a barbecue grill, do you? Toasted Becky, smoked Lisa, grilled Jacintha...."

"And my mother."

"Special sauce for mothers...." Tom settled his thin, wiry frame into a corner of the front seat. "My theory is that we're being held hostage in a floating crap game."

"You and I aren't important enough, Tom."

"Speak for yourself," said Tom. "Something's fishy, though maybe it's just Kelly."

When we reached Kelly's building at 6:30, the place was ringed with what appeared to be street gangs wearing plastic jackets with the initials KH on them. They were lounging about, nothing casual though, on edge, looking around, tight pants, swinging key chains; they could have come from the UD district.

Tom said: "You know, my father told me to become a computer programmer."

One of their leaders demanded our IDs. We showed them to him "You here every night or is this something special?" I asked. Ignoring the question, he waved us on. "Park in the basement. J-25." The guard at the escalator ran our IDs through a machine. The guard on the second floor ran our IDs through a machine. The guard on the third floor pointed to a door at the end of the hall. "Down there." Kelly's maid, a dour woman named Isabel, ran our IDs through a machine before admitting us. Kelly Hallihan was decidedly para- noid.

At 7:30, without comment, Isabel fed us a reconstituted dinner of creamed tuna on toast accompanied by hard, wrinkled peas, mushy carrots, and something that might have been squash, although Tom thought it more likely a sponge had fallen into the pot. "No wonder Kelly's the way she is," I said, yearning for the wine and toffee.

After dinner, we opened every cabinet in the living room until we finally found a bottle of third-rate brandy stashed next to some dried flowers and an Asante fertility doll. The whole flat smelled of dog. I could tell that this was going to be one of those evenings that you remember for the rest of your life, although you wished you didn't. By now everything seemed hilarious to us. We split the bottle, using plastic cups with alligators on them that Isabel gave us from the kitchen. When Kelly arrived at 10 o'clock, we were both drunk. Tom was practicing martial art manoeuvers while I, stretched out on the couch with my shoes off, was loudly humming a pop song and thinking of Fairouz.

"What the shit have I let into my life?" asked Kelly. She undraped her rope bag and dropped it to the floor. Tom, who had been balanced on one foot, toppled over.

"Hi, Kelly!" I called out. "We'll replace the aged brandy tomorrow."

"Shit," said Kelly. She picked up the bottle and turned it upside down. Nothing came out. "What makes you think there's going to be a tomorrow? Don't you dumdums know enough to stay alert when the shit hits the fan?"

Tom nodded wisely at me from the floor. "Wisdom of Orient say: Much better be drunk when shit hits fan."

We doubled up with laughter. Kelly raised her eyes to the ceiling. At that moment the videophone near the bookcase buzzed. Kelly darted toward it. "With any luck," she said, "this will take the hilarity out of your evening."

Vimalachandra's face swam into view, looking a bit under water. Shaking my head, I sat up. Tom twisted around on the carpet.

"Hi, Vim," said Kelly. "Just got in. What's happening?"

"Bomb found in the Global TV Studios at twenty-one hours seventeen minutes. It's been dismantled. Production control room is secure."

"That asshole can't even set bombs," said Kelly. I swung my stockinged feet to the floor. Tom scrambled up. The hilarity had indeed dissipated. "Anything else?"

"Do you have Grimal and Ugaki with you?"

"Do I ever."

"Good. Their apartments were both broken into, computer and telecommunication systems destroyed. Personal effects tossed around a bit but otherwise okay. Sorry, fellows."

Tom let out a low whistle. I leaned backward against the

couch. We were both now totally sober.

"Anything against Finley or Government House staff?"

I sat up again with a jerk. I could think of somebody else I wished were in Cape Winnemucca.

"Nothing to report so far. They're fairly well protected."

"Okay, Vim, thanks. Keep me informed."

He faded from view. Kelly turned around, grinning evilly. "Sober now, you goofballs?"

We were both silent, thinking about what might have happened if our families had been at home.

"Well, Kelly," I said at last. "I guess thanks doesn't quite cover it, does it?"

"It does," she said. "You guys take some aspirin and go to bed. It's going to be a long thirty-six hours."

THIRTY-EIGHT

In spite of the aspirin, neither Tom nor I slept very well that night, and Kelly hardly at all if the buzzing videophone in the living room meant anything.

"I can't understand it," Tom muttered in the twin bed to my right. "A thirty-thousand-dolyen computer system.... What's the point? We're just doing our jobs, right?"

"Right." Tom, who led a squeaky-clean life, had never had any run-ins with Danzig, but even for Danzig this seemed peculiar. Trashing our apartments couldn't have the effect of frightening us into stopping our work; we'd already completed our work. Injuring or perhaps killing us or our families would have done nothing but shock people—in Kelly's words, provide a distraction. The bomb in the Global TV Studios could have delayed the People's TV Assembly for a week or so until the equipment was repaired; but a delay isn't a cancellation.

Nevertheless the random, spiteful attacks were more unnerving than if some conscious plan to sabotage the bills had unfolded before us.

By six a.m. both Tom and I were up, had showered and dressed and converged on the dining room because we didn't want Kelly to slip off without us. She was sitting at the table, up to her elbows in news sheets, drinking black coffee and eating a brownish sweet roll out of a package. "Help yourself in the kitchen," she said. "Isabel won't be here until eight." Tom found some stale cold cereal and I a piece of moldy cheese to go with our bitter coffee. I didn't think Isabel could be a real maid; a bodyguard maybe.

"Any other bad news last night?" I asked.

Kelly tossed us some of the news sheets. "One of Tom's speakers was killed in a motor accident. What's his name? That geneticist from Wisconsin."

"Armstrong?!" Tom grabbed a paper. His mouth twisted. "What's going on, Kelly?"

"Battle of nerves, son. Time to go on the offensive." She stood up and jerked her head toward the living room. "Let's hit 'em at breakfast. You guys stay quiet and keep out of camera range."

In the living room, Tom and I, clutching our coffee, moved over to the bookcase, from which we could observe the videoscreen without being seen. Kelly seated herself cross-legged on the couch and punched in a few buttons on the laptop terminal. After three tries, Jake Danzig's glowering face darkened the room. "Yes, Kelly?"

"Good morning, Jake," said Kelly. "Where the shit were your boys last night? Out on Acapulco gold or something?"

"Any problems, Kelly?"

"Nothing my people couldn't handle. But it looks fucking bad, Jake, to find a bomb all the way inside GTV next to the switch box. That's a court martial offense. Better find out what happened before Finley asks questions."

"Well, I'll be damned," said Jake Danzig. "You should have called me, Kelly."

"Called you?" asked Kelly. "Who had the fucking time to make a fucking phone call? But no sweat. You know my boys are super competent in the technical line. What we didn't know we'd have to get into was the security line."

Danzig scowled. "I'll send troops to protect the building."

"No, thanks, Jake. We've already secured the area. Nobody in, nobody out."

Now Danzig was really scowling. "That's overreacting, Kelly."

"You can bet your sweet ass it is," said Kelly. "By the way, there were a few other little diversions around town last night."

"Is that a fact?" asked Danzig. "Like what?"

"If you don't know," said Kelly, "then you'd better x-out Akbar. Got to run now, Jake. See you at staff meeting." She pushed the off button. Danzig vanished.

"He knows nothing from nothing," I commented.

She grinned at us. "Fucking beautiful, isn't it?"

There was no sense in our going home to survey the damage even if Kelly would have let us. "Stick in crowds today. I know you guys got balls. Don't lose them." We followed her car out of the underground garage through a new rat pack of plastic-jackets ("My soccer club," said Kelly) and straight on to the Global Admin building. Tom now considered Kelly the greatest thing since frozen hydrogen fuel. Me, I didn't want to be ungrateful, but I figured I'd keep an open mind about it. Kelly had her own agenda, which if it coincided with ours, great; but if it didn't, tough shit, kids.

What really bothered me, though, was Vimalachandra. A spook. I was glad he was on the job, defusing bombs and protecting the People's TV Assembly of the World Federation of Democratic States, but I didn't think our friendship would survive my discovery that he was Kelly's spook. Spooks may be no worse than other people, but the one thing you can be sure of is that they're always working.

At ten-thirty I took the underground over to Government House to check on Fairouz and to fill in the Chairmen's three staff directors about what had happened. I figured nobody else would. Nobody else had. Maybe Kelly thought that the fewer the people who knew, the better; but more likely she simply forgot them: they were Government House, not Admin; let them fend for themselves. Since the Chairmen had their own special detail, physical protection, except in the case of a massive onslaught, would be no problem.

Alice Greenbriar said: "This sounds...well, kinky."

I agreed that "kinky" was a good word for losing my computer and telecommunications system and, but for Kelly's foresight, my wife, mother, and maybe even myself had I gone home early that evening.

"Somebody's mad at us," I suggested.

But trying to blow up the switch box for the People's TV Assembly was more than kinky. While we were sitting there, Carlos called Finley on the secure line. Although Finley was in the staff meeting, he took the call. Yes, terrible indeed; he couldn't agree more; he was just finding out about it himself. Danzig would investigate. No cause to worry about this evening; Kelly had secured the area. By the way, how had Carlos learned about the incident? "Human intelligence," said Carlos. I decided I'd better get back to Admin.

When I left Carlos's office, I stopped to talk to Fairouz, who had spent a quiet evening at home and was horrified to discover that my apartment had been trashed. Fortunately, I said, my wife and mother had been out of town, but even as I told her, I felt a sudden disquiet, as though I were watching Fairouz swing out into an orbit farther and farther away from me, as though somehow I had let go of her hand. True, it was Kelly, not me, who had taken the precautions to protect my wife and mother, but although last night in my drunken reverie I had thought about Fairouz, I hadn't thought to call to warn her to be careful, not even after I had learned about the break-in.

Fairouz said she'd be at the studio that evening, along with much of the rest of the senior Government House staff. The Chairmen's first piece of joint legislation was a big event. I didn't know if being at the Global TV Studios would be good or bad, but, showing belated concern for her welfare, I didn't want Fairouz sitting at home alone in her apartment either.

I arrived at the studio by five-thirty. Not that it was easy to get into the building. In fact for one frenzied moment I thought Kelly had pulled a coup on us and locked everybody out, effectively cancelling the People's TV Assembly. But then the guard found my name on the restricted list and, after running my ID card and me through several detector machines, let me in. Nobody else had arrived. Once in the building I didn't try to go near the production control room, which had four Polyguide technicians, if that's what they were, lounging around it, but instead I immediately called Carlos, Alice, and Rodrigo from a prop room and told them to forward to Kelly the names of the Government House people who planned to attend that evening so that we could avoid any embarrassing incidents at the entrance. After I left the prop room, a technician went in to check for packages I might have left there. Theoretically, considering what had happened the previous evening, I could sympathize with his concern; nevertheless I felt irritated.

Fortunately by six o'clock Polyguide's Rick Cotterman arrived, and, unlike the technicians, he could at least recognize people. I asked him how they had found the bomb last night.

He looked at me as though I had broken every code in the directory. "How do you know about that?"

"I was with Kelly when Vim told her."

"Well, keep it quiet, huh. Kelly doesn't want us to talk about it."

"Come on, Rick," I protested. "Everybody can tell this isn't normal security here tonight."

"Nevertheless," he said. "Let them think it's a visiting Head of State or something else relatively benign. Bombs make people nervous."

I couldn't disagree with that. Bombs certainly made me nervous.

At 6:45 p.m. Kelly arrived, and, with her appearance, George and Uche and Muamar were finally allowed into the production control room. I sat down beside George at the console. Out of the corner of his mouth, he asked: "What the shit is going on around here? Do you know?"

"They're protecting us from loud noises."

"Physics box?"

"More modest backpack."

"Headless is headless," said George. "What I won't do for a living."

Kelly must have been on uppers. She was bouncing around, white-faced and jerky, checking out the equipment herself, while from her mouth flowed a soft stream of obscenities that didn't seem to be directed at anything in particular. Once I heard Cotterman tell her to get some rest. "You first, SuperHero." "After the voting starts." "Right...."

So there would be voting. That ought to have reassured me, but Kelly's appearance beamed warning signals. Something else must have happened.

Finally at 7:00 Kelly came by my chair and, dropping her hand to my shoulder, nodded toward the main waiting room. We went outside. Mallam Ahmed and Comrade Wong were already seated behind the desk. Most of the Government House people, including Fairouz, had arrived and taken chairs in the audience.

"Look," said Kelly, "I may need help on liaison with your Gov House friends this evening. Stay nearby."

"Sure. Anything new?"

"Julio found a bomb in Telecom. He's so mad he's shitting bricks. That's the good news."

I cleared my throat. Evelyn Thompson's three children waved to me; I waved back. "And the bad news?"

"Finley's wavering."

"Too late now."

"That's what I said. We go ahead as planned. Maybe earlier."

"Earlier? But Brown never gets here early—"

"Your problem, Hot Dog," snapped Kelly. "Solve it." She bounced away. It was now 7:10. Quickly I asked George what we could do about the vacant chair if we had to start the program early.

George glowered up at me. "We never start early."

"Contingency plan."

"Bush league amateur night. We'll get a flood of complaints from people about cutting off the sitcom ending."

"George," I said, "this isn't my idea. Look, how about an opening shot of last Saturday's program without the credits?"

"Ahmed was in nightshirt. Today he's in pinstripe."

"The Saturday before...."

George was flipping through old programs. "Here's one...but Brown will never wear that outfit twice." A black leather suit with white stitching and a gold collar.

I groaned. "What the hell. At least it's dark. Go with it."

Dashing out, I gestured to the three staff directors.

"Sorry, Alice, we may have to start early."

"Early? What for? He'll be livid..."

"I know. Let's hope it's a false alarm. Wong goes first anyway. It won't affect the order of the speeches. We'll work around the opening."

"What's going on, Mark?" asked Carlos.

"When I know, I'll fill you in. Alert the Chairmen."

After briefing Magda, I hurried back into the production control room, where I found Kelly talking on the videophone to Finley. "Come on, Jim," she was saying. "It's 7:22. We can't back out now. Two of the Big Three are already on the floor...."

Finley didn't look well. There was sweat on his forehead and a weak smile on his lips. "I know it's awkward, Kelly. I'll be happy to talk to them on the videophone, try to explain things...."

"But what the fuck can you explain?" asked Kelly.

"Well, it's obvious we have this problem with some group that's trying to disrupt the voting...."

"So what?" asked Kelly. "You going to let them disrupt it?"

"But these bombs...."

"Bomb away. It's a splinter group, Jim. Stop worrying."

"Maybe not a splinter group. Maybe a...big group."

"The vote will tell us whether it's big or little."

Rick Cotterman was standing against a wall out of camera range. He motioned with his head for me to join him. It was 7:25 and still no sign of Mr. Brown.

"We just can't take the risk, Kelly...."

"Risk of what?" asked Kelly.

"The Chairmen will look bad if the legislation loses...."

"They'll look a lot worse if we cancel."

"Postpone, Kelly. That's what we should call it...."

Without changing expression and still looking at the monitor, Kelly reached behind, grabbed her ponytail in one hand, and yanked it over her shoulder. "Jim, be reasonable...."

"That's the signal. Start it, Mark," muttered Cotterman.

I moved to George. "Cut and start!"

"Seven twenty-six!..."

"Kelly's orders."

I left him grumbling, then, once out of the production control room, broke into a sprint. Mr. Brown still hadn't arrived; Alice stood by the entrance, waiting. I waved to Magda. Ahmed and Wong straightened themselves at the desk. The program started.

"Trouble with Finley," I explained to Rodrigo and Carlos. "He wants to postpone the vote. He's acting sort of spacey...."

7:29. Comrade Wong was beginning his speech when Mr.

Brown slid into the chair between Wong and Mallam Ahmed. I groaned: Brown was wearing a white summer suit with wide lapels. Stepping behind Brown's chair, Harvey handed him his speech, then backed off, shrugging before Brown's irate mutters.

Although Rick Cotterman looked unhappy when the Government House staff directors appeared behind me, he didn't try to stop them from entering the production control room. It was now 7:32 but Kelly was still arguing with Finley, who apparently hadn't noticed the time. Carlos tapped her on the shoulder. She jerked around.

"Let me talk to him," said Carlos. Kelly started to say something, thought better of it, stepped back and sent both Rick and me glares that could have fried us. "Mr. Finley," said Carlos, "excuse me, but what seems to be the problem? Why are you trying to stop this program?"

Finley cleared his throat. "It's like this, Carlos, as you know, there have been some ominous signs of trouble in the last day or so...."

"With all due respect, sir," said Carlos, "that's no reason to abandon legislation all three of our Chairmen want put before the People."

"Abandon, no, no! Of course not. Postpone is all. I'll be happy to explain to them...."

"I'm sure they'll want to hear you, sir," said Carlos, "after the voting starts. We're now on the air."

"On the air?" Finley's voice sank to a whisper. "Kelly!??"

Kelly elbowed Carlos out of the way, and not too gently either. "That's right, Jim." Her voice was level. "Not your fault, okay? I tricked you: started early."

"But, Kelly...." Finley shook his head. "I can't vouch for what will happen now. This is insupportable."

"Insupportable?" she asked briskly. "Did you say 'insupportable,' Jim?"

"That is correct."

"Okay. Anything else?"

"Close the barn door even if the horse is out." That certainly didn't sound like Finley.

"We'll do our best. Hang in there."

Finley smiled weakly and disappeared from the screen.

Alice Greenbriar was clamoring for an explanation to this mystifying exchange, but Kelly ignored her, punching in other numbers on the videophone. "Grimal," she snapped, "if you're going to let your buddies fuck around in here, get them out of camera range and give me room to piss in." That was clear enough. I nudged the staff directors back against the far wall. Julio Meza's face came into view. He was standing in the front room of Telecom.

"Yes, Kelly?"

"Six-twenty-seven."

"From whom?"

"Finley."

"Code?"

"Shit. You've got your own?"

He smiled grimly. "Sorry, *amiga*. I'll try Finley on the other line." For three agonizing moments, the screen showed nothing but equipment blinking in the background, then Julio reappeared. "Finley is—and I quote—'not available.'"

"Who you quoting?"

"Who you think."

"In Finley's office?"

"Right. Different instructions, which I am equally ignoring unless Finley gives the code. Now, for you—"

"The motherfucker!" yelled Kelly. Her whole body seemed to curl up into a fist, then string out, like a rubber band snapping. Cotterman took a step toward her; stopped.

"*Cálmate, amiga*," said Julio, making soothing motions in the air with one hand. "Don't waste time. Finley's not available. Get the Chairmen."

"They're on the air."

"I've noticed."

Pushing past me, Carlos was back in front of the camera. "*Hola*, Julio. What's going on? What do you need?"

Julio beamed at him. "*Ay, Carlos. Como estás, hombre? Qué te pasa? Qué has hecho?*"

They rattled away in Spanish while Kelly slumped against

the console, arms crossed, eyes closed. Finally Carlos turned and, gesturing to the other two staff directors to follow him, headed out of the production control room.

Kelly whirled back to the camera. "What the fuck did you tell Acevedo, Julio?"

Julio grinned beneath his handlebar mustache. "What do I know to tell him? Nothing. Only that you want a meltdown and The Man wants a crash. That's a serious difference of opinion, Kelly. What's a poor boy to do? Let the staff directors help you. They're big children."

She smiled faintly. "Okay. Muchus grasus, or whatever you guys say." Julio chortled.

Meltdown—the contingency plan to keep terrorists from taking over Telecom.... Maybe Julio would get a chance to use his wine supply after all.

It was now 7:46. On the video Mr. Brown was winding up the last few paragraphs of his speech. I sat down between George and Muamar. Uche shoved a cup of coffee into my hand.

"White suit," said George, pointing to Mr. Brown.

"Oh, yeah, right. Can't win them all, George."

"Meltdown," said George.

"If we're lucky."

"Posthumous superior service award," said George.

"Pessimist."

"No, optimist," said Muamar. "Who'll be around to award it?"

Rodrigo returned first. "Julio, it's ninety-two or ninety-three, he can't quite remember."

"Close enough," said Julio.

Then Carlos. "Five sixteen."

"Two out of three," said Julio.

Mallam Ahmed was delivering his speech now. Alice reappeared, out of breath and flushed. "We wish to table a reservation on the grounds that we do not understand the scenario—" Kelly clutched her forehead and played dead, back against a cabinet. "—However, given that Mallam Ahmed and Comrade Wong have agreed to implement, pending further information we join in. Fourteen point zero twenty-five."

"Beautiful, *señora!*" called Julio. He picked up a microphone and announced: "Six-twenty-seven. Clear area. Ten seconds to meltdown...." Reaching above his head, he pulled a lever. "...One and a-two and a-three...." Behind him Telecom staff members dashed for the exit. One woman dropped her purse, tried to run back. Still counting, Julio picked it up and tossed it to her; she scraped through the door just as it closed with a shudder. All the equipment seemed to be shuddering, the screen was shuddering. Then silence. Julio smiled at us.

"System locked. Watch your rooftop transmitters. *Buena suerte, amigos.*" The screen went blank.

The phone was already buzzing.

"Rick," Kelly shouted, "pull the switch at 8 dot if I'm up to my ass in horse manure." It was now 7:55. She opened the videophone. Jake Danzig materialized, looking worse than he had that morning—huge pockets beneath his eyes, stubble on his chin, perspiration rolling down the sides of his face as though he'd been jogging.

"Kelly," he said, "this is a crisis."

"Where?" she asked.

"Finley has had a heart attack."

Not a muscle moved in Kelly's face. "Poor Jim." Evidently she had blown all her fury in the call to Julio.

"I'm in charge now," said Danzig. "We must move quickly to put a lid on the upheavals of the last twenty-four hours."

"You're in what?"

"I'm in charge of the Global Administration Organization."

"How do you figure that?" asked Kelly.

"It's obvious."

"Not to me, Jake. Rublev's number two."

"He's in Port-au-Prince."

"Then Dharmasena."

"He's in Guam."

"Then me."

"Sorry, sweetheart," said Danzig. "You don't count. Finley gave me his death-bed blessing to restore the old pecking order."

"'Death bed,' is it?" she said.

"Manner of speaking, Kelly. Now, first order of business: cancel the People's TV Assembly immediately."

At that moment the clock hand moved to eight. Cotterman pulled the lever in the metal box, punched three buttons, adjusted a dial; red and green lights blinked on. The People's TV Assembly was in operation. In the main studio Legislative Bills No. 1 and No. 2 began accumulating Yes and No tallies. Kelly laughed—a brittle laugh but definitely a laugh.

"Tell you what, Jake. Go take a cold shower. It's this sticky June weather that's gotten to you."

"Look, girl, this is an order."

"Right," she said, rolling the "r," drawing out the syllables. "Yeah, well, order noted, Jake, but, assuming I wanted to, there's not a fucking thing I could do about it. The Assembly's operating and we're on meltdown. All channels open, all actions irreversible until normal termination."

"Meltdown!" yelled Danzig. "Who authorized meltdown?"

"The Chairmen."

Danzig jarred to a stop, like a wind-up toy with one leg in the air. The Chairmen weren't Admin; I guess he'd forgotten they existed. "Who suggested they do a stupid thing like that?"

"Finley. Before his untimely demise." She pronounced the words, "untimely demise," as though Danzig were hard of hearing. The remark put him on the defensive.

"Now, Kelly, I never said Finley was dead. Only inoperative."

She smiled. "Yeah, well, start the CPR, Jake. Then you take a couple of sleeping pills. Get a good night's rest. Everything will look better in the morning."

"Kelly," said Danzig. "You forgot one thing...."

"Only one?"

"One important thing, Kelly. If somebody takes out the receiver/transmitters on the roof, then you'll have channels open but nothing coming in or going out."

Out of the corner of my eye, I saw Carlos start forward. I jumped up and held him back. "Let Kelly handle it."

"The man's a lunatic!" he muttered.

Kelly was nodding at the monitor. "Yeah, well, I didn't forget, Jake. But who'd do a dumb-ass thing like that? Even a fucking fanatic would know it's better to take the building intact and so have access to a global communication network to explain his game plan."

Danzig considered that. "Not bad thinking, lady, but scenario-dependent. I'll send some men over to help you protect the building."

"Fine. Set them up a block away to make sure nobody approaches GTV."

"Sure, we'll post some on Transition, Lubbock, Vandermere, in the back of Duchesne Alley. But we'll need others on the roof and some inside the building."

"No, thanks," said Kelly.

"Don't be an asshole, girl. You need all the help you can get to fend off these crazies."

"I've got all the help I can get," replied Kelly. "We're doing just fine, Jake. Don't worry."

Danzig's eyes narrowed. "Kelly, I'll be there in ten minutes and if you don't open the fucking front door, I'll blast it into Duchesne Alley."

"Dear me," said Kelly. Coming from Kelly, this mild remark caused nervous giggles all over the production control room.

"What's that?" Danzig demanded.

"Canned laughter," replied Kelly. "Look, Jake, tell you what I'll do. The Chairmen are in the studio—remember them? They're those three guys at the top of the pyramid—"

"Okay, okay."

"—I'll consult with them. How about that? You know me, Jake: strictly channels. If they say open the door, I'll open the door. Then you can walk in, take over the satellites, and explain to the world the untimely demise of James Francis Finley III, and why you're in charge here."

"He's not dead, I told you."

"Glad to hear that."

"You've got ten minutes."

"Oh, come on, Jake, there's three of them. Give me thirty."

"Twenty."

Kelly sighed dramatically. "I'll do my best. You still in Finley's office?"

"Yes."

"Okay. Relax, put your feet up on the desk, have a cool lemonade, I'll be back to you in twenty."

She snapped the connection, looked at her watch. "Rick, get on the other phone and find Rublev. Tell him The Man's sprung a major leak in the upper story." Then she turned briskly to the Chairmen's staff directors, who were staring at her, horrified.

"Oh, come on, kids," she said. "Look like that, you're going to depress me. Let's talk to your Chairmen."

THIRTY-NINE

While Kelly was talking to the Chairmen, I went out into the main studio and sat down beside Fairouz, who was wearing a soft yellow dress with a black belt. She looked worried.

"I can tell from the way Carlos is acting that something's the matter, Mark. What is it?"

Carlos was sending off enough sparks to ignite the building. Spinning on his heel, gesturing wildly, an occasional booming "Maniac!" broke through Kelly's presentation, while Kelly, seated on the edge of the triangular program desk, would pause and look at him as though she hadn't figured out yet whether he were an asset or a drawback. I clasped Fairouz's hand, wishing now that she were back at home in her apartment.

"Danzig's freaked out and is threatening to blow us all up."

She gasped. "You are not making a joke? This is true?"

"Would I joke about Danzig? What gets me," I said, trying to zero in on what most disturbed me about the likelihood of being blown to bits in twenty minutes, "is that I'm sure he's been crazy for years. He's wrecked lives, destroyed people, run shady operations, but nobody at the top has ever connected his behavior with mental derangement. So Finley left him in charge of the guns. Rest in peace, Finley."

"Mark, he isn't—"

"Either dead or near it." Fairouz's head drooped against my shoulder. Placing my arm on the back of her seat, I pulled her closer to me and stroked her hair. "I wish I could get you out of this place, darling."

"No, Mark. Even if you could. I'm staying with you."

But Carlos had his own idea about that. Kelly suddenly clapped her hands to get everybody's attention. She stepped closer to the TV crew and onlookers.

"For those of you who don't know, Jake Danzig has flipped his lid and thinks he's in charge of the Admin. He wants to send troops into the building...." She waved down protests. "Sorry, no time for questions. The Chairmen have unanimously agreed that he is not to be allowed in. This means that if we can't talk Danzig out of it, he will probably launch some kind of attack against GTV. If necessary, we intend to wreck the system ourselves rather than give him access to it. As you can see, we have a highly volatile situation here. I would like to be able to tell you all to get out of the building; but we don't want to open the door. There is, however, a glidercopter on the roof. It has five passenger seats. Those seats will be taken by Mrs. Thompson and her three children and by Mrs. Moked. Please proceed immediately with Tadeusz here—" She pointed to a grey-faced technician. "—who will take you to the roof. For everybody else, sorry. We'll keep you informed." Kelly darted off to the production control room.

"How sexist!" Fairouz muttered beside me. "I'm not going."

I wanted to tell her that, after all, Kelly was a woman, sort of, and Alice and Magda and Uche were women, but they all had work to do here, and Fairouz didn't; however I decided my telling her that wouldn't help matters any.

Evelyn Thompson stood up and took Vernon in her arms. Earledeen grabbed Alan's hand. "Fairouz—"

"No, Evelyn. You must go because of the children, but I'm staying. Somebody else can take my place."

"Oh, Fairouz," scolded Evelyn, "don't make problems. Come along." She left without a backward glance. Fairouz didn't move. Carlos had been watching. From across the room he headed toward us, obviously angry. Quickly I turned to Fairouz: "Look dear, the other staff members don't know what's going on. Somebody has to keep them informed. You and Evelyn should set up headquarters at Government House and keep in contact with us...."

She was listening, albeit suspiciously. "Mark, I know you are just trying to get me on the glidercopter...."

Gently I drew her to her feet. "It's true I want you safe, but it's also true you can be a greater help to us there than here."

The technician was waving wildly at her from the stairway.

Carlos reached us. "Fairouz, get—!"

"Whoa!" I gestured and winked at the same time. Carlos drew back with a jerk. "Fairouz is going to set up a headquarters staff for us at Government House." I nudged her forward toward the stairs. "Take care, darling."

Taking a heavy breath, Carlos snapped: "Good. Excellent. Advise us where you'll be, Fairouz."

She looked at him, then turned and kissed me on the mouth, and ran toward the stairs, hair streaming behind her.

"Thanks, Mark," said Carlos, as though I'd done it for him.

I shrugged. "Frontal attacks don't work with Fairouz. You have to sneak up from behind and trip her."

He smiled wryly.

Giving Carlos advice about Fairouz was one of my dumber actions.

When I entered the production control room, Kelly was talking to Rublev in Haiti, but I couldn't make much out of it except that Rublev intended to smash Danzig into a nutshell within an hour, should we last that long. Good luck, Rublev. My theory about why Rublev terrifies everybody is that he comes on heavy and almost completely incomprehensible so that although he might be telling you about his pet orchid, he sounds as though he's describing a malign tumor. Kelly seemed to understand him, though; I guess at those levels you either learned fast or you cowered. Rublev told her he'd fax her some ammunition.

The production control room was crowded now. Tom Ugaki became the contact point with those outside, while I was asked to start drafting a script for the Chairmen to explain to the world what was going on just before everything exploded. Those weren't precise guidelines, but nobody could give me anything better. I sat down at the computer, which was near the fax machine, and started writing whatever came into my mind, but slanting it toward Wong's style, since he was head Chairman that month and would have to read it.

In the background I could hear Kelly talking to Danzig, fighting for time, trying to convince him that there was a problem

with the front door, that it couldn't open because when her technicians had closed it, somehow the hinges had jammed. I guess Danzig
thought she was just ding-a-ling enough to know how to defuse
bombs but not to close doors. He ranted about how this proved she
needed his men there to do things right, etc., etc., until finally it
occurred to him that GTV had several doors; another one would do
just as well. Unfortunately they were all jammed, said Kelly. Then
he got suspicious.

In the meantime the fax from Rublev was coming in. Nobody
paid any attention to it but me, and I wasn't paying much; I just
snapped the pages off the machine and scanned each one back into
the computer in case we needed to make copies. There were twenty
pages. At the end I clipped them together, and then for the first time
looked at the front page: Ruthellen Janniger's fifth article.

I let out a shrill whistle that disconcerted Kelly and brought
everybody else to my side. "Hey, Jake," I heard her say. "Hold on
there. Something's happened. I'll be right back."

She dashed over, ripped the manuscript out of my hands,
speed-read it, planted a kiss on the back page, and muttered: "Vasili,
you doll baby!" Doll baby? "Mark, you have this on the computer?"
I nodded. Then she dashed away, back to the videophone, while the
rest of us read the text on the computer.

Jake Danzig had made several million dolyens in kickbacks
from the adulterated drug industry. Ruthellen listed sources, bank
account numbers, laundry tickets. She had a few other names too,
fairly high up in Security, but she didn't waste time with them. She
said that Danzig ran Security like a Chief of Police in one of the
more backward Associated Territories. He sent the boys out on the
street every day to shake down people and deliver ninety percent of
the proceeds up the chain of command until thirty percent of that
reached him. Personally.

He'd been caught once, said Ruthellen. The EcoDev Assistant Director, Balthazar De Jonge, had discovered the involvement
of Security forces in the adulterated drug racket and had tried to stop
it. We all know what happened to Balthazar De Jonge, she said; but
in case we'd forgotten, she reminded us.

At this point I stopped and looked up at Carlos. His face had tightened into an olive mask. When I caught his eye, he turned abruptly and walked out of the production control room toward Comrade Wong. He didn't even wait to finish the article.

Although I couldn't figure out why Ruthellen had ever believed she'd be allowed to publish this article, I understood very well why Rublev had pocketed it. Ruthellen had probably received a lot of the material from him; however, reading between the lines, the article, far from turning Rublev into a hero, made him look like the kind of man to whom a budget item was more important than a body. That he was now willing to use the article against Danzig was a sign that he was playing his last card. I just hoped that Danzig didn't realize it.

And now that there was no longer any danger of my having to do so, I regretted that I hadn't slept more frequently with Ruthellen. She was a gutsy woman.

Trying to write a speech to cover a changing scenario is a challenge, yes, but not much else. Comrade Wong would probably end up winging it; nevertheless, I also knew that he liked to have those little notes in his breast pocket, so I kept redrafting. In the middle of my work, however, Cotterman brought me Kelly's notepad computer and asked me to use that while he set the main computer on global dissemination for the Janniger article.

"You mean we're sending the article out?"

Cotterman grunted. "We're going to threaten to send it out. I guess we shall if we have to; but it sure makes the Federal Government look bad."

Typical Polyguide thinking.

That kind of thinking was at work in Kelly too, as she tried to wheedle Danzig back to the barracks, or wherever he usually lurked, without bloodshed. I knew we'd all be better off if she succeeded, but her buddy-buddy tone annoyed me.

"Look, Jake, it's been a tough couple of days here—" Tough on whom? I wondered. "—We're all as nervous as dogs shitting razor blades. Perfectly natural things might get a bit out of perspective. I think we all understand that...." The hell we do, I thought.

Uche brought me another cup of coffee. She had a blunt face

with hair in cornrows that flowed back into a pigtail. "Good thing The Man can't read time," said Uche. "It's now thirty-five minutes since he threatened to invade us." The television was running a documentary on the life cycle of rodents. At every program break GTV would announce that the People's TV Assembly was now in operation and list short summaries of the two legislative bills on UD policy that were under consideration.

"We've got a pool going," said Uche. "Will the Assembly make it to eight a.m. or not? Ten dolyens each. Want to join?

"Sure. I say we'll make it."

"If we do, you'll get rich. You're the only optimist."

I wasn't really an optimist, but I hoped the Janniger article might divert Danzig's attention, if Kelly ever got around to bringing it up, which at last she did, reluctantly, and only after Danzig had told her that he'd sent a detachment of special unit forces to GTV.

"You're stalling, girl," he said. "What's the matter? Can't you explain things properly to the Chairmen?"

"Well, you're right on the button there, Jake," she admitted. "I have been stalling. You see, the Chairmen are peaceable types. They want us to resolve this amicably."

"I'll buy that," said Danzig. "Just open the door."

"Sorry. They say no troops in the building. They don't consider that friendly."

"Kelly," said Danzig. "There will be troops in the building. They can walk in civil-like or they can scramble in over the ruins, but there will be troops in the building. And if the Chairmen don't understand that, I'll explain it to them when I get there."

I was surprised that Carlos didn't leap forward on that one, but he remained stoically against the wall with the other two staff directors. Ever since he'd found out about Balthazar De Jonge, he'd been acting subdued. De Jonge, whom he had disliked so much, had been a genuine hero rather than a traitor. I was still irate enough at Carlos to be glad that he'd received this kick in the ass, but, give him credit, he had immediately faxed a copy of the Janniger article to Government House, attention Fairouz Moked.

"Shit, Jake," said Kelly. "You're putting me in a box here. I wish you hadn't done that."

"That's the way the cookie crumbles, girl."

"Guess you're right, Jake. Well, I hate to do this, but now I'll have to transmit the Janniger article to the media."

Danzig's eyes widened like grapefruit. "The what?"

"Remember that series on adulterated drugs in the UD districts? After the untimely demise of Ruthellen Janniger, the fifth article disappeared—"

"Kelly," said Danzig, "that entire series was nothing but trash, a shit-ass piece of gossip and innuendo—"

"Makes great reading though, Jake. Well, as I was saying, somebody gave me the fifth article. I'd fax you a copy, but, shit, why not read it in the news sheets tomorrow morning? Your name will be on every tongue—"

"Kelly!" bellowed Danzig. His voice must have been heard clear out in the main studio. "You send that dirt and I'll stuff your boobs up your exhaust pipe!"

Kelly didn't blanch. "Tell you what, Jake," she said. "Look at your watch. Ten minutes. You've got ten minutes to call off your goons or I'll push the fucking button."

She broke the connection. Whistling a flat tune, she dashed over to the other phone and punched in some numbers. Vim appeared on the screen. He seemed to be bouncing up and down and weaving sideways; then I realized he was in a glidercopter. 'Yes, Kelly?"

"Any action against GTV?"

"There's a detachment of troops at the end of Transition Avenue, but so far they haven't gone anywhere."

"How's the airport? Rublev should be arriving in thirty minutes or so."

"I'll alert him to land at Benning. Akbar's taken over the airport."

"Shit."

"We're negotiating."

"You are?" Kelly brightened. "What does Akbar want? Danzig's job, of course."

Vim smiled. "He wouldn't mind. Of course he claims he's just obeying orders and if he's not to obey orders, then we have to protect him—"

Carlos came to life with a slam. He shoved his way next to Kelly. "Wait a minute, wait a minute. Who's negotiating what here on behalf of whom?"

"Relax, Acevedo," said Kelly, patting his arm. "Nobody's going to cut a deal behind your Chairman's back."

Vim smiled benignly. "Hi, Carlos. Kelly's right. This is just low-level scrimmaging among the substitute players. Our plan is to split Akbar Gillette off from Danzig. Akbar's sleazy, but smart enough to know Danzig's gone around the bend. Any agreements reached will be tentative until approved by the Chairmen."

Carlos nodded, although when he stepped back, he was still frowning.

"There's one complicating factor, Vim," said Kelly. "Rublev sent me Janniger's fifth article on adulterated drugs. I've told Danzig we'll transmit it if he doesn't withdraw his troops. Akbar's name is mentioned in the article."

"Too bad," said Vim. "Can't you edit it out?"

Now it was my turn to be outraged; however, unlike Carlos, I didn't leap to Kelly's side. I figured I'd better stick close to the computer. "That's censorship, Vim," I shouted. "No government flack is going to edit Ruthellen's article!"

George gave me a right-on signal. Muamar clasped his hands above his head and shook them. Uche blew me a kiss. Everybody else looked as though he thought I'd floated in from the landfill at Fort Howard. "We're talking survival here, Mark," muttered Cotterman. "What world do you live in?"

Kelly cleared her throat. "Vim, you, ah, hear your boy's gentle voice? We have our own fucking in-house protector of journalistic values."

Vim smiled broadly, although he couldn't see me. "Hi, Mark. Point made. Akbar stays in. Maybe it will work better that way. Maybe it will scare him."

I cooled off a bit. I suppose that's what happens when you're a spook: you start editing reality. In the long run covering Akbar's ass for him would just lead down the road to another scenario like this one, with a different—and more deadly—starring player. But of course we were now thinking short run, and in the short run people like Cotterman and Kelly, who are against censorship in the abstract, think it can be good for you in the concrete. Realists they aren't; opportunists, maybe.

The main phone was now buzzing. "Got to run, Vim," said Kelly. "I think Heavy Leather is back on the line." Vim faded out, chuckling.

Heavy Leather? Although I could never be sure whether Kelly was using an epithet as a put-down or as a descriptive phrase, or both at once, the way she used to call me "Lover-Boy," for the first time I wondered about Danzig's sex life. Did he screw women? Or did he prefer young cadets and, maybe, good-looking speech writers?... The thought made me finish off the dregs of Uche's coffee in one gritty swallow. That would explain a lot of things. When Danzig came on the screen, I looked at him a little differently.

"Kelly," said Danzig, "we appear to be at an impasse."

"Are we?" asked Kelly.

"As far as I'm concerned," said Danzig, with a grand swoop of his hand, "you can send the article to Alpha Centauri or beyond. Means nothing to me. I can live with flack, have all my life, nothing to it. But—I've got to think of my people. The article may contain slanderous libel against some of them."

Kelly nodded. "It's possible."

"Therefore," said Danzig, "since the Chairmen don't want troops inside the building, no sweat. We'll send one unarmed man."

"Nobody in, nobody out," repeated Kelly.

"Oh, come on, girl," said Danzig, "I'm not talking about a human grenade. I'm talking about Akbar."

"That sleazeball!"

Danzig chuckled. "That's why you can be sure of him, Kelly. Akbar's not going to risk his skin for anything...."

No question about it: Danzig had freaked out.

"...He just wants to talk some sense into you turkeys—"

'He has a telephone, doesn't he?" said Kelly. "He wants to talk to us, let him call us."

"Eyeball to eyeball is better."

"Akbar's got eyeballs?" asked Kelly. "I never noticed."

"Now, Kelly," said Danzig, "don't be prejudiced. Akbar is a fine young man. He has my complete confidence."

"Oh, in that case," said Kelly, "send him around. Anyone with your complete confidence we want to talk to. He can eyeball us from the corner of Transition Avenue, and then if he's slimy enough, who knows? maybe he can slither in through the keyhole."

"Now you're talking sense, girl," said Danzig. "He'll be there in fifteen minutes." He hung up.

We were all silent for a moment, in awe at the thought of Danzig trusting Akbar.

"The pool odds have changed," announced Uche.

"I can't believe this," said Cotterman. "Danzig's frying himself."

"Don't we all frigging hope so," said Kelly. "Anyway it looks as though he told Akbar about the article and Akbar convinced him to deal, in Akbar's interest if not in his own. Good face-saver. Mark, what does the article say Akbar does?"

"He's the one who puts the screws on the erring pharmaceutical companies."

"Nice man," commented Rodrigo. The three staff directors left to brief their Chairmen.

By the time Akbar arrived from the airport at 9:30, Vasili Rublev had safely landed on the GTV roof in his Benning Field glidercopter, thanks to Vim's intervention with the Polyguide technicians, who otherwise would have shot the plane down at approach. Such was Rublev's image as a heavy hitter that the pool odds for our survival went up dramatically even though he wasn't carrying even a water pistol. He started off by terrorizing everybody inside the building, except the Government House people, whose relationship to him was different from ours, and Kelly, who kept calling him "Doll." And me. The reason he didn't frighten me was because my mind was elsewhere. Like everybody else I accepted it as definite that Rublev would save us. Even though Kelly and Vim had been the ones who had bought us time and set the strategy, Rublev would clinch the deal and, like his type does throughout the world, get the credit for it. He had, of course, provided the Janniger article. It was the Janniger article that was really saving us, and that's why I found

myself thinking about something quite different from what everybody else was thinking. I had jumped a few hours ahead. I was
thinking about that moment when Akbar would seize the hardware
from Danzig in exchange for amnesty and our guarantee not to
transmit Ruthellen's article to the media. I was wondering what
would happen to the article.

I stayed next to the computer, pretending to work, although
it was now unlikely that Comrade Wong would need a speech.
Nobody paid any attention to me. They were too busy rushing
around trying to do whatever they thought Rublev wanted them to
do, and hoping they'd guessed correctly, which, with a little trans-
lation help from Kelly, they mostly did. The first thing he decided
to do was open the front door. "Who the fuck's afraid of Akbar?" he
shouted. "Yes, Doll," said Kelly. Akbar walked in, took one look at
Rublev—six feet tall, four feet wide, and grimacing like a baboon—
and flinched. As a coup, it had been strictly a bounce-off-the-wall-
of-Danzig's-mind one, and I guess Akbar had been too busy trying
to keep Danzig from running stark naked into the street to have time
to track Rublev's movements.

"Don't blame me," said Akbar. "I just work here."

That was the wrong sort of smart-ass approach to take with
Rublev, who bellowed something containing the words "bullshit"
and "no longer." Akbar cringed. After a beginning like that, they
shouldn't have had to give Akbar anything, but I knew they were
going to anyway. Although I didn't want to get too far away from the
computer, I watched the "negotiations," such as they were, from the
production control room doorway along with George, Muamar, and
Uche. It was no contest. With the Chairmen sitting serenely in the
background, Rublev—Kelly grinning by his side—ordered Akbar to
march back to the main Global Admin building, put Danzig in a
straight-jacket, dump him at Billings Psychiatric Hospital, and then
return and formally hand over control of Security to Vimalachandra
who would forthwith put Akbar under detention, pending further
investigation.

Akbar complained, not too unreasonably, that that didn't
seem like much of a deal to him. There was Danzig, sitting in
Finley's office, blowing up classified files and pumping drugs into

a comatose Director-General, while aiming a revolver at anybody who entered the room. He'd shot the bird because he got tired of its singing. Danzig was dangerous, and the only way Akbar would be able to disarm him would be to play on their long-standing friendship and then slug him when his back was turned.

"Excellent," said Rublev.

"For that," said Akbar, "I should get something."

"You will," said Kelly. "Danger pay. Seventy-six dolyens per hour."

Rublev barked something that sounded like "mitigating circumstances to be determined" and "contribution to global stability."

Akbar looked front and back and around, jiggling his shoulders and his arms and shifting his weight from hip to hip. Like me, he probably didn't understand much that Rublev was saying.

"What about the Janniger article?"

"What about it?" asked Rublev.

"I want a guarantee you won't distribute it to the media."

"Why?" asked Rublev. "What's it to you?"

"Danzig says my name's mentioned in it."

"How does Danzig know?"

Things were now getting interesting.

Akbar shrugged. "Got me. But that's what he says. And I'm sure it's a bunch of lies because all the others were."

Said Kelly: "Ruthellen Janniger did not work for the Global Administration Organization. It is not our job to distribute her article. Nevertheless—"

Interjected Rublev: "We'll distribute it unless you follow orders. And I mean NOW, you motherfucker!"

Akbar flinched backward. "Okay if you promise to destroy the article."

"No," said Rublev. "We'll keep copies of the article."

"Well, all right, copies," said Akbar. "But—"

"It's set up on the computer," said Kelly, "ready for global dissemination. If you do your part of the job, we'll erase it from the computer when you get back here and turn yourself in to Vim." Rublev nodded curtly in agreement.

That was what I had been listening for. I went back and sat down beside the computer.

The next few hours were like a pre-election party. The TV crew dragged out all the soft drinks and snacks from the building's cafeteria and dispenser machines. The "yes" votes for the two UD policy changes kept mounting on the board; "yes's" were ahead of "no's" by about twenty-five percent, although most of the remote areas had not been heard from. Kelly called Julio at Telecom to fill him in on what was happening with Danzig, only to discover that Julio knew more about it than we did. When Danzig shot the bird, a bullet ricocheting off the bird cage had accidentally flipped on the camera switch in Finley's office. "Great late-night movie here," said Julio. Julio was sitting at his desk, drinking a bottle of red wine and eating reconstituted steak, which may not have tasted great but definitely had to have been better than our snacks. He was one well-prepared man, a good thing since it would take over a week to tunnel him out of Telecom.

I hovered near the computer. I tried not to be too obvious about it because I was afraid Kelly might notice, but fortunately her stimulant pills wore off and Cotterman convinced her to lie down in one of the offices while Akbar was out doing his dirty work. Cotterman didn't have Kelly's imagination; he didn't think it strange that I wanted to hang around the production control room, watching the first page of Ruthellen's story flicker on the screen, chatting with George and Muamar and Uche, while everybody else excitedly discussed the coup attempt in the main studio. Jean-Paul and Can Mabuza thought it a little strange; they came in once and we talked for twenty minutes, mainly about Ruthellen's article. They said it was a great story and just too bad not a news sheet in the world would touch it if the Federal Government didn't distribute it, thereby tacitly confirming the allegations, because without Ruthellen's notes they'd be open to libel charges. If there had been such a foolhardy news sheet, they said, they—Jean-Paul and Can— would have leaked a copy. I suppose maybe they would have, because the article made the Admin look bad, not the Chairmen.

At 10:30 p.m. I called Fairouz on the regular, secure phone

that we were using for "headquarters." Carlos had been keeping in touch with Fairouz throughout the evening, playing the game, once it had been set up, better than I would have remembered to play it. There was no need to talk about the coup; I wanted to talk about the Janniger article. We both agreed that it ought to be published if for no other reason than that it would clear Balthazar De Jonge's name.

"But now, of course, they won't send it to the media," she said. "And that's sad, although I guess it is the price we have to pay to keep that awful man from taking over everything and hurting more people."

This was the kind of thinking that Rublev and Kelly were relying on to excuse their action.

"That's a red herring, dear," I said. "They didn't need to promise to kill the article. They want to kill the article. Rublev knew what Danzig was doing and didn't stop him. Finley probably knew. I'll bet Kelly knew. If the article is published, people will ask how it was possible that nobody in the Federal Government knew. And if they knew, why didn't somebody stop him?"

There was silence for a moment and then Fairouz said: "You were one of Miss Janniger's sources, weren't you, Mark? Because of Christie."

I realized that I'd never explained my involvement in Bloody Wednesday.

"I was just a conduit, Fairouz. The doctor who gave me the information was killed...."

"I worry about you," she said. "You do one thing and, if that doesn't work, then you do something else; and you pop up here and you dive down there, and if I weren't in love with you, I would just sit and admire your performance on the tightrope and when you're almost killed, I would say: 'Ah, lucky again! Isn't he fabulous?' But I love you, and so I am sometimes exhausted by all these manoeuvers."

She was delicious. She was the best thing that had ever happened to me. What I did that evening I would have done anyway, but now that Fairouz had said what she'd said, my decision became irrevocable. I wanted her to see me bob down and up once again, to hear her scream of terror and her loving warmth on my mouth when

I made it.

At 11:15 Vimalachandra appeared. He had gone home, had a shower, dressed up in a white dhoti, and was now ready to receive the surrender of Akbar, who had phoned in from Billings after dropping off an unconscious Danzig. Vim was being thanked by everybody. Rublev actually managed a smile. Kelly came out from the office, bleary-eyed, and kissed him. I waved from the doorway of the production control room. I guess he thought that was peculiar, because he walked over and said: "How's everything, Mark? Other than the apartment, that is." We shook hands.

"Great," I said. "Congratulations. I didn't know you had all these talents."

At 11:30 Akbar Gillette returned. He had a black eye and two broken ribs, because—and you had to hand it to Danzig—although Akbar had managed to get the gun away from him, Danzig had slammed in a few good punches before going under. Kelly told Akbar he'd earned one hundred and fifty-two dolyens in danger pay. Vim gave him an orange soft drink and a package of peanuts, and then, as the new interim Head of Security, arrested him. At which point Akbar asked to see the Janniger article erased.

I left the production control room doorway and sat back down beside the computer.

I could hear them marching across the floor, glimpsed their heads outside along the glass panel, up to the door—Rublev first, naturally, then Kelly, then Vim and Akbar.

As they entered the room, I raised one hand. "Hold every-thing, folks! Let's discuss, as we say in the memos."

"Oh oh," said Kelly.

Rublev stopped. George looked up from the control board. Muamar turned around in his chair. Uche scrambled to her feet.

"Who are you?" thundered Rublev.

I ignored him. "Evening, Akbar," I said. "Thanks for taking out your friend. That leaves you, right?" Akbar recognized me and blanched.

Kelly moved a step beyond Rublev. "Come on, Mark. We've had enough crazies operating around this town tonight."

Rublev had finally figured out who I was. "Oh, yes, Grimal, Speakers. What is your problem, Grimal, Speakers?"

"It's like this," I said, "I know a few people who were killed over this article. I was almost killed over this article. I'm attached to it."

"Yes, yes," said Rublev. "And?"

"So now you say you're going to erase the story and let Akbar and his friends get away with it."

"Nobody is getting away with anything," said Rublev. "All points of law will be covered."

"Sure they will," I said. "A few demotions here and there, a suspension or two, nothing big, nothing for the cameras, because we wouldn't want to give the Admin a black eye, would we? And this article sure does that. If it didn't, you would have handed it out a long time ago, wouldn't you have, Mr. Rublev?"

"Watch your fucking mouth, Mark!" snapped Kelly.

"Oh, I'm grateful to him for all the heavy action here tonight," I said. "I just want to make a few points. For instance. Do we intend to put out a press release explaining what really happened to Balthazar De Jonge? Or shall we let the world go on thinking he was a traitor?"

Rublev's eyes narrowed. "I do not understand what Grimal, Speakers, has to do with Balthazar De Jonge. You will explain, please."

"It'd take too long," I said. "Just call me a concerned citizen." I noticed that Vim was moving around beside Kelly.

"Mark," he said genially, "You're quite correct. A grave injustice was done to Balthazar De Jonge. He was a hero. I personally assure you that we will clear De Jonge's name." Vim was a lot more deadly than Kelly.

"Thanks, Vim." I was watching him. "Glad to hear that. I'm sure with you running things, the payoffs will be stopped. But that doesn't change the past. This is what was going on; this is what happened. I don't see why we should hide it."

"Shit, Mark!" snapped Kelly. "There you go with your fucking moral imperatives. We're not hiding anything. This isn't the Press Center, son. This is the Global Administration Organization. We've no business sending out stories written by independent journalists."

"But we would have, if necessary."

"Different scenario, Hot Dog...."

"OK," I said. "If you'd rather the Press Center distribute the article, I'll buy that. Let's give it to the Press Center."

Rublev turned to Kelly. "This man is crazy. How did he get in here?"

"Oh, he's not really crazy," Kelly demurred. "Just kind of high strung. You know these creative types...."

"I do not know them," said Rublev. "Get him out of here!"

Kelly looked at Vim. "Your boy, Vim."

"Ah, yes," said Vim. He smiled wryly and shook his head at me. "Mark, you are making things difficult for us. We have an agreement with Akbar to erase this story. I know that offends your idealistic view of things, but it's the way the world operates. An agreement is an agreement."

"True," I said. "But you're lucky: I'm here to save you from it. I didn't have any agreement with Akbar. I had an agreement with Ruthellen Janniger, yes, but not with Akbar."

I pressed the transmitter key. The story zipped up to the satellites, then down to other computers in media houses throughout the world. Nobody moved. It wouldn't have made any difference if they had: they couldn't cancel it.

We were on meltdown.

FORTY

After what Vim described as my "clerical insubordination," Rublev wanted to arrest me as well as Akbar, but Vim said you didn't arrest people for doing what I'd done; you could suspend them, you held hearings, you demoted, you might even fire after following all the proper procedures, but you didn't arrest. Vim was going to be a big improvement over the previous Head of Security.

Therefore at 12:07 a.m. on Wednesday morning, Acting Director-General Vasili Rublev suspended me without pay for two months, and told me to get my ass out of the building. I started to leave, at which point, the Government House people learned from George what had happened. Although Harvey just smirked from a corner, Can slapped me on the back; Jean-Paul embraced me; Rodrigo chuckled; Alice said I'd gone too long without sleep; and Carlos asked Rublev to let me stay until the People's TV Assembly terminated at eight a.m. because I had been one of the main contributors to the UD legislation. Since Rublev didn't want to offend Government House, he conceded. Vim left with Akbar. Kelly and Rublev stayed around for another hour; then they departed as well.

By two a.m., the "yes" votes for the UD legislation were still a comfortable twenty-five percent ahead of the "no" votes. After the Chairmen went home, Jean-Paul, Harvey, and Can disappeared for thirty minutes and returned with Scotch, beer, and marijuana. Being in a minority, Cotterman didn't interfere with our party; he just kept his eye on the Assembly levers. At 6:30 a.m. Fairouz and some of the other Government House staff came in, bringing breakfast from a pancake restaurant. When she learned what I'd done, Fairouz poured a bottle of spring water over my head. I got even by luring her into a prop room and partially disrobing her before Cotterman started pounding on the door. "This isn't the Last Days of Pompeii, Mark!" he shouted.

At eight a.m. the People's TV Assembly ended on schedule, with the "yes" votes a good half a billion over the "no" votes. At that point we were all too tired to do anything but go home to bed. I went to Fairouz's. On top of being suspended, I knew I couldn't cope with my trashed apartment that morning.

Although officially I was in disgrace, I could tell that this wasn't going to be as bad as some of my previous scrapes, because when I called Steve Maine, instead of lecturing me, he chuckled. He had just finished reading the Janniger article in one of the numerous news sheets that had carried it, front page news, the morning after the attempted coup, and he felt that, after all these years, he'd been vindicated in trying to save Balthazar De Jonge. "Of course technically you're in the wrong, Mark," he said, "but I don't think anybody is going to push it."

Certainly not Vasili Rublev. Like most bullies, Rublev only admired people who stood up to him, and so, as Acting D-G, even though he'd suspended me, he started calling me at home to draft speeches for him. That annoyed me, but I couldn't refuse when I wasn't even sure what he was saying; therefore I dodged and feinted; I developed a strong working relationship with Guggenheim in his office.

As usual, when Steve got onto a case, people started looking at the fine print. Polyguide, not I, had programmed the article for global transmission; all I'd done was transmit it contrary to orders. On our first appeal, my suspension without pay was cut back to two weeks. Kelly testified in my favor, if that's what you'd call it. She said she'd always known what a fucking ding-a-ling I was and yet she'd given me the run of the production control room, so she accepted responsibility for my action. I protested, and to the Appeal Board's amusement, she chewed me out in English, French, and Swahili. Her grasp of grammar wasn't good, but her specialized vocabulary more than made up for it.

By the time of our second appeal, a large number of news sheets had published editorials praising the Federal Government for releasing the Janniger article, an action they said indicated a forthright resolve to correct former abuses. Steve brought copies of the editorials to the Board hearing. The Board maintained the suspension but reinstated my pay. By that time the two weeks were almost up anyway. Steve then filed claims for both Tom Ugaki and me, asking for reimbursement of our computer and telecom equipment, which had been illegally destroyed by the Federal Government. Nobody asked for proof that Security had actually done it; Management paid us both without question.

At the upper levels James Francis Finley III survived, but never fully recovered; and although he briefly resumed his Director-General duties two months later, that was mainly so that the Chairmen could pry Rublev out of the job. As soon as the Big Three agreed on a new D-G—a former soccer star who'd made a fortune in reconstituted food packaging—Finley retired for reasons of health. Just in time, too, since Kelly was delivering all his speeches and signing off on his memos.

At the TV trial, Danzig pleaded insanity and, after six weeks of restructuring, took early retirement. That was fine with everybody. Rublev, Kelly, and Vim protected Akbar, but demoted him. Although nobody could prove anything against Dr. Fisher Schleka, he resigned when the new D-G was sworn in.

All of this should have made me happy, but I was too busy worrying about money. In July, three days before her due date, Lisa gave birth to our son. When she left the hospital I owed an extra eleven thousand dolyens. I decided I deserved a promotion.

Eberhardt agreed. He said there'd been a little trouble in the past with my file, but he thought that it had been straightened out now that Vim had been confirmed Director of Security. Within a week the Program Department's Assistant Director, Carolyn Olivella, was made head of Records and, after the usual bureaucratic flim-flam about advertising position openings, I was named Assistant to Eberhardt, while Waldir became Head of the Speakers Division.

I suppose you could say that all ended well, and most of the time that's what I said, because Eberhardt kept me too busy to think about alternatives. He told me that I could try out any crazy program idea I wanted to—within budgetary constraints, of course—and so I did, and some of them worked and some of them didn't; but most of them worked well enough to keep me in the Global Admin building every night until ten p.m. and all day Saturday and Sunday.

Lisa didn't care. Now that she had a child, she hardly noticed whether I came home or not in the evening. In fact, my presence was an unwanted distraction. I was either being shushed, or berated for not being a modern husband who changed diapers, or told to leave her alone, she was fixing the formula.

However my schedule didn't allow me much time for Fairouz either, and that was a real loss, because you can't just pop in for an hour on Saturday night and expect to be loved forever. I arrived late at parties; I dragged her away early; I tended to fall asleep while she still wanted to talk; my creativity was flowing elsewhere, not into my lovemaking. She was gentle and understanding, but I had only myself to blame for what happened; and it was bound to happen, because in November her husband died. That should have flashed red signals at me, but it didn't. For the first time we talked about him. He had once been a violinist with the Rome Symphony Orchestra, not even a first-rank violinist; she had loved him, but she also felt that, being tied to him, she had wasted her life, and it was time now, before it was too late, to get on with living. It didn't occur to me that she hadn't been living; what had we been doing if not living? Although I realized, vaguely, that Fairouz was asking me to declare my intentions, there didn't seem to be much I could declare except that I loved her. Now that I'd fathered a child by Lisa, I didn't need Steve to tell me that my chances of obtaining a mismating decree were zero.

So I did nothing. And Carlos moved in.

Maybe he never would have if Fairouz's husband hadn't died, because Carlos was such a tight-assed guy that, although he'd been in love with Fairouz for years, he'd never made a move, no doubt having decided that an affair with her would be bad for staff morale. Marriage was different though; that meant stability and a lot of other things that I guess Carlos had never had but wanted. He didn't let on right away that he was interested; instead my busy schedule made it easy for him to infiltrate her life. He started calling to ask her if she needed a ride places with him and his girlfriend. It was always he and his girlfriend, some girlfriend. The girls were interchangeable—an exotic Thai or Bengali or Eurasian or Laplander, some woman whose looks made your mouth water but whose conversation seemed to come out of a very tiny brain. Like a lot of ambitious men, Carlos didn't waste time cultivating women; he chose them for decorative purposes. Fairouz was different though, always had been. Getting her was worth spending some time on the preliminaries. So Mark Grimal couldn't make it? No problem. There was Carlos.

I don't know how long this would have gone on, although Wong's frequent trips gave Carlos additional opportunities to cut Fairouz away from me; but in Goa one evening he showed the world—and Fairouz—that he was the true savior she'd been looking for, a twenty-four karat gold hero, light years ahead of the fumbling Artazio Colonnas and Balthazar De Jonges and Mark Grimals who had pursued her. We watched it on the evening news, over and over again: Comrade Wong speaking on the flood-lit platform; a gun shot, too low, that hit the podium; then Carlos flinging himself in front of Wong and taking the second bullet; followed by a close-up of Carlos lying on the carpet, blood seeping off the platform, and a distraught Fairouz kneeling beside him, her long hair hiding his face.

I watched it on the television in my office. When I arrived home that night, Lisa said: "Better turn on the eleven o'clock news, sweetie. I think you just lost your girlfriend."

The remark infuriated me, because of course Fairouz was upset; who wouldn't have been? But Lisa was right. When Carlos woke up in the hospital in Goa to discover Fairouz clinging to his hand, he quickly realized that the deranged gunman had done him a favor.

Carlos remained in Goa recuperating, while Comrade Wong continued his tour, with Nha temporarily in charge of the staff assistant functions. When the Chairman returned to Alternative Four, I called Fairouz at home. After a few remarks about the horrors of the assassination attempt, she said she had something important she needed to discuss with me. I didn't like the sound of that. I offered to come over, but she said, no, it would be better to meet for dinner the following evening. I liked the sound of that even less; however, I knew that bad news didn't get any better by waiting.

We met at the Sub-Orbital, which I'd insisted on, hoping

nostalgia might work in my favor. A slim hope. Fairouz wouldn't sit next to me but chose the seat across the table, her back to the shimmering view. She looked thinner, her body sheathed in a violet silk batik that turned her into a budding flower. After Jerome had taken our order and brought me a Scotch-and-soda and her a Campari, she didn't waste time. She said: "I'm sorry, Mark, but there is no kind or simple way of saying this: I have decided to marry Carlos."

It might not have been kind, but it was certainly simple. I said nothing for a few minutes because, although I'd expected something like this, I still felt an unpleasant shock, like touching an exposed wire that I'd known already existed.

"Marry?" I asked. "You mean you're going to do an Evelyn Thompson and stay home to raise babies while he air shuttles around the world and brings you pretty baubles from Bangkok?" That came out more bitterly than I had intended. Her fingers tightened around her glass. Quickly I added: "Sorry. I'm sure the best man won. A real hero." I raised my glass. "To Carlos."

She met my gaze steadily. "Do you think I'm marrying him because he's a hero?"

I shrugged. "I don't know what you're marrying him for, Fairouz. You could do worse. Carlos will certainly take care of you—so well you'll probably have trouble breathing."

She smiled faintly. I'd hit home with that one.

"He's a good man," she said. "Very kind. Very intelligent. I admire the way he has trained himself to be so...consistent. He never asks himself is it best to do this? is it best to do that? He just does what he thinks right without agonizing. In most cases he is correct, but when he isn't, then it is terrible. When he found out the truth about Balthazar, he wrote me a three-page letter. It was very touching, that letter. I had trouble making sense of it, because he wrote it to me, yes, but also to himself, trying to determine the point at which he had begun to act in error, wondering why he had let his feelings overrule his judgment. And yet all he had done was behave the way ninety-nine percent of the people in the world would have reacted."

I could see that Carlos knew more about letter writing than I did, but what a holy Joe, worse than I had believed he was. "And so," I said, "you think you can be happy living with somebody who has to be right or he falls to pieces?"

That annoyed her. "I'm sorry I told you the story. I thought you would understand more now why I am marrying him. Carlos thinks any decent man would have leapt in front of Comrade Wong to save him. Protecting people is what decent men do, thinks Carlos."

Worse than a hero: a saint. But my criticizing Carlos was having the same effect that in the past Carlos's criticizing me had had. Fortunately at that moment Jerome brought in the food. I suppose it was all in my mind, but the steak tasted terrible.

I decided to try a different tack. "You do know that I love you, don't you?"

Her face relaxed. "Yes, of course, Mark."

"I haven't been very good at expressing it recently. Getting old, I guess."

She laughed. "No. Just successful."

"If I hadn't taken this new job...."

"Work is your life, Mark. Women are just a hobby."

"Not all women."

"Well...everything in its season," she said. "I have no role in your life now—"

I protested. "That's not true!"

"—Carlos needs me. He wants a family. If I don't have children soon, it won't be possible...."

So that was why she was marrying Carlos. Suddenly I remembered our conversation following the death of her husband. I had gotten it wrong: she hadn't been asking me to marry her; she had just wanted a baby.

"Oh, lord," I muttered, "I blew it."

She was looking at me, puzzled.

But unlike Tosca, Fairouz had no grandmother. She would have had to carry the baby with her, papoose style, Wong's brief-case in one hand, a bag of bottles and diapers in the other; Wong never would have put up with it.

I decided it was better not to resurrect the past, which was, after all, past, and the noble Carlos was waiting. "Okay, sure, I

understand now," I said. "I understand why you're marrying Carlos."
Then I went into the usual routine that I always go into at moments
like this, although up until now I had been the one who had left, not
the woman.... We'd always be friends. If she ever needed anything,
call. In my heart there would be a special spot labelled "Fairouz."
She had transformed my life in mysterious ways....

"Oh, Mark!" she snapped. "Stop it! Don't ruin everything."

As soon as Carlos left the hospital, he and Fairouz took the
Lifestyle tests and then were married in an ostentatiously modest
wedding in Bombay, attended by Comrade Wong and five hundred
and sixty-nine journalists. The news sheets kept juxtaposing the
assassination photo of Fairouz and Carlos next to one of the happy
couple emerging from the Government House headquarters garden
where they had been married. "How romantic!" sighed Lisa. She
made clippings. I found them all over the apartment, stuck in
strategic locations: the bathroom mirror, the diskette file, the coffee
table ashtray, the clothes closet. I burned the one in the ashtray; that
delighted Lisa.

Although I'd lost Fairouz, I didn't lack women. Like Jerry
Hiraoka, I now kept a downtown flat where I went if I had to work
late, because, after our second child, we moved into a house an
hour's drive away from the Global Admin building. The flat served
multi-purposes. The only trouble with the women was that they
were now the wrong kind of women. They were pretty, bright,
young junior Admin officers on the make. At first I was flattered,
but after serving as a lover/mentor a couple of times and then
discovering that, their goals once attained, the girls suddenly fell in
love with younger, single men or—worse—older, more powerful,
married ones, I began to distrust the motives of anybody under
thirty.

I often ran into Jean-Paul Dornier at the Ruthellen Janniger
Press Center, and he kept me informed about Fairouz's life. To my
secret satisfaction, the honeymoon hadn't lasted long. Carlos was a
jealous man; after putting up with it for a while, Fairouz would
suddenly fly into a rage and walk out on him—go to a hotel, or if
already in a hotel, move to another room. The rest of the staff would
then have to coax them back together again. Nevertheless, while it

was still an option, neither one of them filed a mismating petition; and in time they had the maximum allowable number of children— two: a boy and a girl. Airport arrival scenes always showed Fairouz getting off the plane, holding one child, and Carlos another, except during election time when Comrade Wong carried the baby.

Then one day, as Assistant Director of Programs, I was invited to a retrospective of the art of Artazio Colonna, who, along with other dissident artists and intellectuals of the past generation, had been officially rehabilitated—too late to do him much good since he had died in Bolivia five years before, still carving llamas. Naturally Fairouz was there. Since most of Colonna's work had disappeared, the retrospective was a small one and consisted mainly of pen-and-ink sketches, a few engravings, and thirteen collages and paintings from private collections. Fairouz's circus collage dominated the gallery. I was happy to see it again. When the Global TV reporter covering the opening asked me to say a few words, I paid a glowing tribute to Colonna on behalf of the Admin that had restructured him.

Afterward Fairouz came up to me and said: "Mr. Grimal, I am surprised to discover that you are now such an expert on artistic matters." She wasn't smiling.

"It surprises me too," I replied. We started walking away from the collage toward the section with the drawings. "But if reporters ask me questions, I have to give answers. After all, nobody wants to know what Mark Grimal thinks of Artazio Colonna. They want to know what the Assistant Director of Programs thinks about him."

"What a model bureaucrat you have become," she replied tartly.

That wasn't friendly. She seemed determined to quarrel. Quickly I stepped up to a row of drawings, and encountered Number 26, "Nude Girl Bending Backward," on loan from Mrs. Fairouz Acevedo. The shock snapped my self control.

"Why do you have that here?" I demanded.

She hesitated, looked at me, and then said softly: "It is a work of art, Mr. Grimal."

"Well, I'll tell you a secret," I said. "It's a work of art I've always hated."

Her smile was chilly. "How odd. So does Carlos. Neither of you knows anything about art, how it functions, the way it transforms reality.... That's not me. That's...."

"I know, I know. Essence of young, nude girl."

She set her mouth. "You surprise me, Mark. Carlos I'm not surprised at, but you surprise me."

That pleased me. Compared to Carlos, I could still surprise her.

"Why? I loved you too."

Color rose in her cheeks. She glanced away.

Emboldened, I added: "Still do, I guess, or I wouldn't be so upset, would I?"

By now the reception was almost over. People came up to tell her goodbye. I hung around. When they left, I asked her if, in her busy life, she ever had time for lunch nowadays.

"Would that be wise, Mark?" She pushed a chair back against the wall, not looking at me.

"No. Terribly unwise I should think."

We made a date for Friday at an obscure restaurant near the art gallery.

At work I was, as Fairouz had said, successful, and there is nothing like success within an organization to give a person a stake in its smooth functioning. When a group of junior officers formed a "Young Turk" movement, they asked Steve Maine and me to join. We both did. Steve, who had been named Head of the Human Rights Legal Division, counseled reform from within and prudent guerrilla tactics; he at least was consistent. Much to everybody's dissatisfaction, I advised more or less the same thing. The idealistic young fools kept asking me why I hadn't practiced what I now preached. I always fell back on the argument that my work with Government House on the UD legislation had instituted further-reaching reforms than had any of my extra-channel activities.

Of course the passage of that first UD legislation created all the pressures that Danzig had feared. Before the next year was over the Chairmen had to place additional bills before the People's TV

Assembly to abolish the blue uniforms, lift travel restrictions on UDs, educate the UD children already living there, and, worst of all, build prisons within the UD districts to hold the most serious criminal offenders. We were also in a terrible tangle over what to do with the children of newly condemned Undesirables. Since the children were no longer sterilized, was it more humane to take them away from their parents (No, said psychologists.) or allow their parents to remove them to the UD districts (No, said sociologists.)? Or should an exception be made for UDs with children to allow them to remain living where they had been living before their condemnation? But if so, then what about all the UDs with sterilized children now living in the UD districts, whose children would undoubtedly be able to live more productive lives if they grew up in a better environment?

"Look what you started, Mark," Vim would needle every time a new problem hit us.

Well, to remake the world, you have to start somewhere. I often wondered what Christie would have said if she had been around to advise us.

Mary C. Smith is a retired U.S. Foreign Service officer. Her career included editing a magazine in Lagos, Nigeria; acting as Congressional Correspondent on Capitol Hill; producing radio programs for the State Department; running a cultural center in Medellin, Colombia; observing a police shoot-out with guerrillas in Guatemala; serving as Acting Consul-General in Kaduna during a Nigerian coup; reporting on the meeting of the Non-Aligned Heads of State in Colombo, Sri Lanka; and identifying a dead American in a morgue in Rio de Janeiro during Carnival. She once composed a speech that made its way up the bureaucratic ladder to President Nixon's desk. He didn't like it.

Ms. Smith's writing has appeared in *Americas*; *The Foreign Service Journal*; *Poetry, Narrative and Other Genres*; and *Seventeen Magazine*. Her first novel, *All the Gods Are Dying Gods*, was published in Medellin, Colombia.